EVEN AFTER ALWAYS

A Novel

STEVEN IVES

RIVER GROVE
BOOKS

This book is a work of fiction. Names, characters, businesses, organizations, places, events, and incidents are either a product of the author's imagination or are used fictitiously. Any resemblance to actual persons, living or dead, events, or locales is entirely coincidental.

Published by River Grove Books
Austin, TX
www.rivergrovebooks.com

Distributed by River Grove Books

Design and composition by Greenleaf Book Group and Sheila Parr
Cover design by Greenleaf Book Group and Sheila Parr
Cover image © Shutterstock/Designer things

Publisher's Cataloging-in-Publication data is available.

Print ISBN: 978-1-63299-872-9

eBook ISBN: 978-1-63299-873-6

First Edition

Dedicated to my family—Joel, Sheryl, Brian, and Maria Ives—for believing in me even when I found it nearly impossible to believe in myself.

In the loving memory of Susan "SASI" Ives, for teaching me true beauty and art can be found everywhere, if we only know where to look.

CONTENTS

PART THREE

PART FOUR

28   Too Close to the Sun 262

29   The Presence of Absence 276

30   Gone for Good. 284

31   No Time Left 293

32   Into Darkness 300

33   The Burning Down 307

34   A Sound Awake 313

     Epilogue 323

     Acknowledgments 327

     About the Author 329

Chapter 0

THE MATTER OF TIME

CARINA WAS GOING STIR CRAZY. She'd go mad if she didn't get the hell out of that bed. I had to do something. I swiped a wheelchair from the hall—certainly the hospital had several to spare. We raced to the elevator. Instead of going down, I took us up. She asked where, but I insisted on keeping it a surprise.

A beautiful day revealed itself as I wheeled my sister onto the roof of the building. Sunlight fractured through the scattered clouds and onto the flaming, autumnal tree canopy below. Carina called the view *postcard majestic*. Her smile was a supernova. I helped her from the wheelchair to her feet. She spread her arms outright, a messianic pose, the warm rays of our wayward star hitting her for the first time in weeks.

She had just turned eighteen, and I was a little more than three years younger.

Carina pushed the forest-green winter hat back on her head, allowing the sunlight to touch her face. Even in her bed, she'd wear it to hide the effects of the chemo. Her sandy-brown hair had thinned but not fallen out completely like the doctors said it might. My hair was the exact same color, falling in longish waves over an angular face and dusky, almond-colored eyes—another pair of features I was told I shared with my sister. I thought about what else we shared, standing together in the coastal Maine breeze on that sunny rooftop.

We talked. About Mom and Dad. Her and me. She recalled when I was a baby, always crying. I would only stop wailing when she scooped me up in her little four-year-old arms. She grew tired from talking. So we sat awhile in silence, together, her fingers entwined in my own.

"Craig?" she said. "I never really asked you, but . . . do you . . . believe in the afterlife?"

For months, whenever Carina would speak of death, I'd shrug it off. It was almost a reflex: I'd tell her she'd be fine. She would beat this leukemia. But now, the doctors had given us a terminal diagnosis. It was nothing more than a matter of time.

"I don't know," I said. "Maybe."

Her laughter startled me. "What do you think I'll come back as? Like, do I have to come back as a person again? I feel I've already done that and it sucks. I want to come back as something magical, like a dolphin. Soaring through the wild, blue seas with the sun on my back. Something that feels infinite, even in that moment. You know what I mean?"

"Dolphins eat raw fish, Carina. I'm not sure you'd like that."

"I like sushi," she said.

"You always get the veggie rolls," I replied. "They're just, like, rice wrapped around more rice."

"I think I'm going to miss rice," Carina said.

—

In the ensuing months, my family crumbled. Cancer is a ravenous beast. It just kept on destroying and destroying, as if uncertain what to consume once its initial victim was gone.

My mother was inconsolable after Carina died. She couldn't stop crying. Could barely get out of bed. Then she bought a bottle. The next couple of months, she was so drunk the world scarcely registered around her. And the next few months she was high, and finally she was just gone. My father and I woke up one day to find two suitcases missing and her bank account drained. A note pinned to the refrigerator by a smiling banana magnet: She just needed time. Weeks later, we received a phone call. She'd moved to Boston to clear her head, whatever that meant. She had an apartment in Allston–Brighton, wherever that was. She had a job at a bar but wouldn't say which one. Maybe, in time. She needed time.

I wondered how anyone could need time.

Time is all we get. We are all born in time and live in time and struggle to subsist through time. Time is what binds us all to the inherent pain of the existence we are trapped in. Time is the predator to which we all, inevitably, fall prey. How could anyone need it? As for me, I was desperate to escape it.

The idea of circumventing time became the central idea of a paper I was writing for my physics class. My thesis was intended to focus on the pure mathematical possibility of time travel, but each new conundrum fractured my analysis from its initial theme. Time travel is, more than anything, a Pandora's box of paradoxes.

Say you have a huge scar from being bitten by a shark. Then, you build a time machine and go back in time to meet your past self. You show your past self the scar and convince this past self not to go swimming in the ocean that day. Would the older you who traveled back in time still retain the scar? Or would the scar simply disappear, with the attack never having happened? Are the two events now separate points on the same time line, or do they fracture into two time lines the instant you enter the time stream to change an aspect of anything?

So let's say your scar did, in fact, disappear. Would that mean the shark bite never happened? How could something that never occurred act as the impetus to travel back through time? My thesis had somehow changed itself: Nothing that ever actually occurred could ever be completely erased. Everything had to exist somewhere.

Needless to say, my paper wasn't making much sense. If anything, an appropriate reflection of its author.

—

Where was Carina? Where was she now?

Decomposing underground? A skeleton? Or maybe somewhere in the sky, an angel, watching over me.

Maybe her wish had come true. I prayed it did. I prayed Carina got her heart's desire, despite having no idea what I could possibly be praying to.

I imagined her, a dolphin. Swimming through the seas, cutting dizzying patterns through the sparkling water. A vision of grace, streamlined and magical. The sun glistening off her back as she sliced through the blue, breaking waves.

Infinite in that moment, and forever free.

PART ONE

Chapter 1

INVISIBILITY

MY SCHOOL DAY PRESENTED A rockslide of present concerns to pile atop the past ones.

I had an algebra exam fifth period, and a history quiz sixth. In gym they were testing our forty-yard dash times, which could give me a leg up on making the baseball team for the spring 1993 season. And of course, there was my physics paper on time travel, which I still needed to complete; like time itself, my paper seemed infinite, with no end in sight.

As my father drove me to school, the physics paper was the specific distraction I fought to maintain my focus on. Classic rock blasted from the CD player loud enough to drown out any possible conversation concerning the significance of the calendar date.

One year to the day Carina died. One year without my sister.

My father parked. His eyes were tired, as if watching something impossibly far away. He was a slim man with impeccable neatness and a widow's peak hairline beginning to recede, who wore wire-rimmed glasses. He was the director at the town hall Department of Records. His job bored him but afforded us the ability to live in a decent-sized house in a respectable town in Midcoast Maine. It provided us the health insurance that had prevented us from losing everything material during Carina's prolonged illness.

He lowered the radio. "Craig," he said. He only called me "Craig" when it was something serious. Usually he'd just call me "CJ," like I preferred to be called and what everyone else called me. Usually, he'd tell me to have a good day. Even though he'd grown both overprotective and distant in the past year, he'd make a point of telling me that. But we both knew that on this particular day, no good was to be found. I felt like a mosquito battling back a meteor shower. For several weighted moments, my father struggled over what to say. Finally, he settled upon, "We'll talk later, I guess."

"I guess," I answered, well aware that when it came to discussing our shared pain, later meant never. I gnawed a nail as our car turned a corner, revealing my high school in the distance: a centuries-old building, originally a small Victorian schoolhouse, then expanded and re-expanded several times over to accommodate nearly five hundred students; refurbished with enough red brick to fortify every architectural schoolhouse trope in existence. Teenagers filed in from all available directions on the large, quasi-kept lawn that surrounded it.

At school, my entire social strategy amounted to invisibility. Not *invisibility* in the H.G. Wells or Fantastic Four senses of the word. More like shrinking into the shadows whenever possible. The less anyone noticed me, the less anyone saw me, the better. If I kept to myself, I was a threat to no one. I wouldn't have adults asking me questions that threatened to unearth what I fought to keep buried. I wouldn't have other kids hassle me or bully me.

I minded my own business. A few sort of friends here and there, mostly at arm's length. A weekend job at CD World that didn't ask much of me. I wasn't cool or charismatic enough to warrant positive attention, nor controversial or dorky enough to warrant negative attention. If people were so prone to judging books by covers, well, I'd paint my cover completely blank.

Of course, in a small town you're never completely invisible. Everyone either knows everyone or knows someone who knows that person. Even so, people find neat little ways to define each other. Before Carina got sick, I was *CJ Slater—quiet, brainy kid, pretty good at baseball*. In one year, it had completely changed to *CJ Slater—the poor, sad kid whose sister died of cancer*.

This label reinforced the walls I'd built around myself. No one really knew how to talk to me anymore, and when they did, their words were heavy footsteps traversing a minefield. As if Death of a Loved One was contagious.

Obviously, I was not truly invisible. It would be better described as camouflage against a wall of nothingness. The color of numb. But any camouflage is fleeting in a world of swiftly changing backgrounds.

After all, everything in my whole life was about to completely turn upside down.

—

Homeroom seats were alphabetical, so Jillian Sillinger was assigned the desk beside me. She'd always had what people called "issues." Jillian took a regimen of special education classes, only spending time with the so-called normal kids in art class, where she particularly excelled. Many kids made fun of her. She had a slight stutter and walked awkwardly, with a limp. Her hair grew straight over her eyes so that you could never really see what she was looking at.

Drawing furiously in her sketchbook, Jillian dropped her pencil. It rolled off the desk, skittering across the floor like an insect trying to escape. The pencil's journey was thwarted by the stomp of Paul Thurmond's size-thirteen work boot.

Paul was the biggest and oldest kid in the tenth grade. His father started his schooling late so that Paul would have a leg up in sports, then had him left back again in the ninth grade so he'd be more dominant in those sports. The plan worked: Paul was a three-sport star in football, basketball, and wrestling and a fixture in the in-crowd despite having the basic demeanor of a rabid gorilla. His hobbies included giving kids wedgies, smacking kids' lunch trays into the air when they were full of food, and shoving kids into lockers.

A couple weeks earlier, Paul had almost been suspended when a janitor walked into the bathroom to find him shoving Roger Loomis's head into a toilet. Then the school hierarchy remembered the magnitude of the football game that upcoming weekend and let him off with a stern warning and a week of detention.

Paul picked up the renegade pencil and smelled blood in the water. He offered it to Jillian before quickly pulling it back as her fingers closed on air. He laughed loudly, making sure everyone within eyeshot could bear witness to his dominance. He offered the pencil again, only to pull it back again.

Jillian stammered, her eyes welling behind a barrier of hair. Other kids laughed along, sacrificing empathy in lieu of the far safer alternative of staying on Paul's good side.

"Wh-what's the matter, J-Jillian?" Paul mocked. "You want your p-p-pencil?"

His laughter warped in my ears. Hideous, almost demonic. My connection with Jillian was simply familiarity. I'd never hung out with her in or out of school, but we'd been in the same grade forever. She'd say hi to me in the halls, and I'd say hi back. But that was the extent of it. Hearing her choke back a sob was like matches striking the inside of my chest.

I realized there was no conceivable way for me to get Jillian's pencil back from Paul. Not unless I wanted my face to look like a Picasso painting with a pepperoni pizza smeared all over it. There had to be another way to make her pain go away. My pain was enough for the whole school. For the whole world. No one else deserved to feel the type of torment that was crushing me from the inside out.

I reached into my backpack. I grabbed all my pencils—a fistful. I placed them in front of Jillian and sat back down. I stared straight ahead, trying to look as not-defiant as humanly possible. I concentrated on a small square of the chalkboard where the word *America* had been erased, so only a ghost of it remained.

No use. The can had been torn wide open, the worms were every-where. "Yo, meat!" Paul barked behind me. My attempts to pretend this was not directed at me failed when Paul got specific. "Slater!"

Slowly, I turned.

Fury lined his face. To him, it was as if I'd just smacked it. All there, written wordlessly in his furrowed brow. People who gain satisfaction from belittling others are oddly sensitive to people who don't condone such actions. It's as if they can do no wrong until someone stands up to accuse them of it.

Paul suddenly blanched, winking at me. "Yo, I always thought you were a faggot, Slater. I didn't know you had, like, a girlfriend." He laughed heartily at his own joke, several supporting laughs chiming in out of—I don't know—either similar cruelty or self-preservation. The laughter died down when Mr. Preston, our homeroom teacher, came in to take attendance.

I concentrated on staring straight ahead. The same faded, white marks on the same blackboard. I stared until the bell rang, when Paul's unmistakably powerful hand squeezed the blood flow out of my left shoulder. A ripped fragment of paper wafted down onto my desk, and he gave me a sarcastic thumbs-up and left the room.

I uncrumpled the loose-leaf to find two words in block writing: *YOUR DEAD*.

I didn't know what to be more upset about: Threatening my very existence on the planet was one thing, but not being able to discern the difference between *your* and *you're* was where I drew the line. I left the note where it was and got up. Jillian blocked my exit. We were the only two people remaining in the room.

"C-CJ," she said, barely a whisper. "I'm s-sorry." The hair plum-meted back down over her face, and she hurried off into the hallway.

This affected me in a bizarre sense, like the contents of my chest had been sucked into a vacuum. If Jillian had thanked me, I guess it would have been fine. It could have been for the pencils. But the fact she apologized? It revealed the mutual awareness that I might have just dug my own grave.

—

Second period, Advanced English. Mrs. Baker was nice; she reminded me of an older Diane Chambers from *Cheers*. Before the bell, she combed the room, collecting our reports on Hawthorne's *The Scarlet Letter*. I was the only student, in a room full of academic overachievers, with nothing to turn in. Mrs. Baker did not appear angry, more like I'd just let her down.

Defiance was not the cause of my avoiding the assignment. Quite simply, I despised the book so much I couldn't spend any more time thinking about it. Who cared that some chick in whatever century banged some dude who wasn't her husband? People cheated on people all the time. At that precise moment, in early November 1992, my mother could have been in another guy's bed. And my mother was not a bad person. Like so many other people, she was just a messed-up person straining to navigate a messed-up world. Having only experienced one romantic relationship, I had no idea if monogamy was even an actual aspect of the human condition. Either way, enacting vengeance against an unhappy woman seemed an impossibly stupid reason to write a book, much less read it.

As the class filed out the door, Kay Nguyen beelined straight for my desk. She stared at me in her peculiar, searing fashion. I always genuinely liked Kay—as the two recurring high-scorers on all diagnostic testing, we shared pretty much every class together. But again, I never saw her outside of school—Kay was far from a social being. She dressed like a businesswoman, despite being my age and five-foot-even, and she spoke like an overly serious documentarian. "CJ. You need to think of the big picture. High school reading lists are not meant to be enjoyable. They're meant to prepare us for the inevitable pain of adulthood."

Also in character, she walked out of the room without awaiting my response.

———

Somehow, I endured half the day, until fourth-period physics, the hour of my school day I looked forward to the most. Mrs. Levy was my favorite teacher. One of the younger teachers in school, she wore her hair down and used a backpack instead of a purse. She would do cool things in class, like setting magnesium on fire, and would quote Rush and Kate Bush lyrics in her lectures. Many teachers were prone to talking down to students, but Mrs. Levy gave the impression of actually being intrigued by what we thought and how we felt.

She chawed her gum as she discussed particle absorption. I suspected the gum was a diversion from cigarettes, which I'd often spied her sneaking in the recessed alcove outside the teacher's lounge. Several students were distracted in their daydreams and doodles, but I found Mrs. Levy's lecture gripping. What would inspire a proton to absorb one neutron while rejecting another? Why was science still unable to predict with absolute accuracy which atoms would attract and which would repel? Evidently, the same sordid fate that affected human beings was occurring simultaneously at a cellular level.

The bell rang too soon. Mrs. Levy prevented my exit. "How's that paper on time travel going, CJ?"

For some reason, I really liked when Mrs. Levy spoke to the entire class, but it made me uneasy when she directly addressed me. It wasn't anything stupid like a crush or timidity. Maybe just how she habitually singled me out as smarter and more interesting than I believed I truly was. Maybe I was simply afraid of disappointing her. "I don't know," I said quietly. "I think it might be too long."

"There's something you don't hear very often."

"Well, you wanted two to three pages."

"And how long is yours?"

"Um . . . I don't know. Like at least ten."

Mrs. Levy broke into laughter. "Is it finished?"

"Almost," I said to my shoes. "Half."

"My word."

I apologized, also to my shoes. "I know you have all those papers and stuff to grade, and don't have all that time to waste on mine . . ."

She cut me off with a gavel-like smack of her pencil eraser upon the desk. "I'm curious, CJ. What exactly were you writing about when you last left off?"

"I'm . . . struggling with relativity." I made the attempt to illustrate almost impossibly complex concepts with the simplest imaginable hand gestures but probably wound up looking like a mime on amphetamines. "Like, Einstein's theory states time slows down or speeds up depending on how fast you move relative to something else. But how is that possible, for time to change speeds relative to what we do? That would mean that if we could travel the speed of light we could just live forever, you know? That time isn't an absolute we exist within the confines of, but rather like a fluid prison we could somehow escape."

At once, the playfulness escaped her. "I'll tell you what, CJ. You just write whatever you want to write, and don't worry a bit about how long it is. You have no idea how much I'm looking forward to seeing what your fascinating brain comes up with."

I didn't know how to respond, so I thanked her. Mrs. Levy called out to me, stopping me in the doorway. "CJ? I know what day it is today. And I just wanted you to know that . . . I'm so sorry."

It felt like a wave, a tsunami, rising up inside of me. "I can't," I said.

"If you need someone to talk to about Carina . . ."

I kept my voice to a whisper, to keep it from cracking, to keep me from humiliating myself. To keep it all. "I'm sorry . . . I just can't."

"OK," Mrs. Levy said. "Just . . . just take care. OK?"

Nothing was OK. Specifically, not me.

—

No point in buying lunch. There was no way I could get food down. Instead, I walked to the football field. There was a hidden spot under the bleachers where you could smoke cigarettes, and no one would be able to see you or bug you. I wasn't sure what I needed, but I wanted to be alone.

I exhaled a funnel of smoke. I followed its trail through the bleachers overhead, finally dissipating into the backdrop of brightness. My attention was diverted by a flick of movement just beyond my cigarette—a swirling breeze shifting an aged and tattered sheet of paper, which partly blanketed a partially crushed soda can.

Lifting the stained page, I immediately recognized one of the many flyers that had been posted countywide just over a month prior about a missing girl from the next town over.

Under a bold headline of HAVE YOU SEEN HER? was her name, Alicia Russell, beside a grainy black-and-white photograph of a girl. Her face was pretty, but her eyes looked sad, encompassed by an overabundance of dark eyeliner, their focus on something slightly off from where the photograph was being taken. What really struck me was her age—eighteen, the same as Carina's when the cancer finally took her.

Cursorily, I'd followed the story when it was still the talk of the county. Alicia Russell had been hanging out with a bunch of friends at the Exxon station one weekend night, then decided to walk home and was not seen thereafter. For maybe a week it was all anyone seemed to discuss, but then the police determined pretty confidently that the girl had run away from home. Time marched on, and people found other things to talk about.

I wondered if it was the same after Carina died.

I was so caught up in the whirlwind, I had been unable to process what was going on around me. It was inevitable that Carina's death was what everyone was talking about in school and on the streets of my town in the immediate wake of her passing. But as time surges ahead, those initial waves calm to placid waters, and folks find other things to consume their thoughts and conversations.

For most of my town, Carina dying was just a sad memory, but one they had moved past. But for me? It was something I couldn't escape. It haunted me every single day. And on this day—precisely one year after the fact—the wake had churned into a violent tidal storm, drowning me from the inside out.

Did Alicia Russell have a brother? Did she have someone in her life who loved her as much as I loved my sister? Someone who was so consumed by the fate which had consumed her that they could barely struggle through days? For some reason, I couldn't stop staring at the grainy photograph, until I forced myself to turn the flyer over and place it back upon the dirty ground.

My introspection was interrupted by a pair of voices, laughing and happy, a guy and a girl. The girl's voice was what struck me. It was a voice I recognized all too well.

Natasha Walker. The first girl I ever truly cared about, and another person I cared about now lost to me.

The summer before middle school, the Walker family had moved in across the street from our house. My parents were thrilled about a new, nice family on the block. As for my happiness, it was more connected to the realization that they had an extremely pretty daughter, exactly my age.

Natasha was always quick to smile. As if there were an irrepressible joy welled up inside, constantly seeking excuses to burst out to the surface. She had an easy, sunny charm and a laugh like wind chimes. The two of us became fast friends, almost inseparable. And then during Christmas break, seventh grade, she kissed me.

We were bounding in from a snowball fight. Soaked with snow, I tore off my jacket and shirt to escape the cold. About to throw on a sweater I'd grabbed from the laundry room, I noticed Natasha. She was just standing there, watching.

"What?" I said, dumbly.

"Nothing. It's just . . . you're . . ." She reached out. Placed two fingers on the exposed skin around my collarbone and traced its expanse. Then she leaned forward. Her mouth met mine and opened, and mine followed. I wondered how her lips could be so soft and small yet pulse with so much electricity.

Then she pulled away. "Oh shit," she said. Then she laughed. That unmistakable laugh. Wind chimes. Before I could react, she was gone. The thumpity thump of her feet up the stairs, a slap of the kitchen door behind her.

Unable to move, I stood there, every inch of my body feeling hardened and vulnerable at the same time. Grasping for an idea of what just happened. Euphoria and terror jousted behind a cage of ribs.

Within days, we were happily going steady. For just over a year, we were "a thing." Until Carina grew sick, and everything changed.

To Natasha's credit, she called often. But she had a life too, and her life didn't need to fall apart because mine did. Between soccer and swim team and dance class and student council and social life—well, it didn't leave much time left over to spend at a hospital trying to prevent her jigsaw boyfriend from falling to pieces.

And once Carina was diagnosed terminal, my emotions just vanished. Like there was a vortex inside me, sucking away everything that once felt worthwhile. I couldn't bear to even answer Natasha's phone calls anymore. Those days became weeks, those weeks became months. A few months later, it got back to me that Natasha was seeing someone new. It didn't hit like my heart breaking so much as like an alarm clock going off.

Now, the situation was obvious: Natasha had brought her lunch to the bleachers with the new guy she'd been seeing, Terry Manilla. And lunch was not the focus.

In fairness, Terry was a nice dude. Friendly and engaging, well liked and good looking. Going from me to Terry was like a popularity promotion. It offered Natasha an immediate bump in social status. She was now a full-fledged in-crowder.

This did not bother me. Natasha deserved neither blame nor resentment. She was a good person. Whether she chose to date me or someone else had no bearing whatsoever on that fact. In my mind, she deserved whatever she wanted from life. She would still smile hello when she saw me around school or on our block.

But just then she did not see me at all. I was hidden below the bleachers. She kissed Terry freely, unaware of anyone's presence in the vicinity. Especially mine.

I wanted to run away. But I couldn't. What if they saw me? I crouched into a ball in the shadows below. I smothered my cigarette and tried my hardest not to look up.

"Terry?" Her laugh. "*Here?*"

"We've got a half hour, babe."

"But your hands are cold!"

"I know what'll warm them up, Tash."

Natasha moaned softly. I couldn't take it. I wanted to die. Being invisible was not enough anymore. I wanted to simply vanish from existence. Life was a vice, crushing me completely. My lungs were helpless, unable to seize the air. I watched as the world disappeared around me. I was an astronaut lost in space, slowly watching the world grow smaller and smaller, silently screaming as I drifted off into the endless nothingness.

Next thing I was aware of was sprinting away. I didn't know if Natasha saw me. I didn't know where I was running. Just away. Away from the school. Away from everything. Into the woods behind the football field. Away from them, away from myself. Just away.

Away. The only place left to go.

Chapter 2

WAITING FOR THE LIGHTNING

A FIVE-MINUTE WALK THROUGH THE woods led to the train tracks. For some time, I followed the rusty metal rails until I reached Hidden Lake. It was a popular weekend party spot for kids—a small body of water walled in by the tree line, out of view from cops or grown-ups. School days, the lake was typically barren.

I paced around the tracks, cursing myself. Idiot! Ditching school was certain to get me in heaps of trouble—the last thing I needed. Trouble at home meant upsetting my father. Trouble at school meant drawing attention. Drawing attention threatened my self-imposed invisibility. "Stupid asshole," I muttered out loud, despite the fact that I was completely alone.

Or so I thought.

In the vague hopes of calming myself down, I lit a cigarette. Then a noise startled me. "Hey, you!" said a girl's voice, emerging from the worn pathway between the tracks and the small, secluded lake. "Got another smoke?"

The sun sliced in from beyond the water's edge, making me shield my eyes. I saw the backlit silhouette of a girl. A hazy glow fissured around her lithe outline, like she was a corporeal ghost.

She stepped forward into a sliver of shade. The light surrounded her like it had been born inside her, somehow escaped, and was now trying to melt its way back in. Her hair was windblown and brown.

Her eyes were dark and unknowable. My train of thought completely derailed, careening off the tracks somewhere between dumbstruck and starstruck.

"Hey, kid—do you speak, you know . . . words?"

My voice surfaced. "Uh . . . yeah." I fumbled through my pockets and offered the cigarette. She placed it between her lips. "Um, do you need a light?" I asked.

"No, I'm just waiting for the lightning." She rolled her eyes and leaned in. I could smell her, like orchids and mystery. She took my hand, guided the flame to her mouth. A wave of vertigo overwhelmed me, gravity itself altering. Like a tectonic shift in the fabric of the earth beneath me.

"Thanks," she said, sending a twisting serpent of smoke up into the air. She appeared to be close to my age, maybe a year older. I hadn't seen her anywhere around town before, and this was certainly not a face you'd forget.

She sized me up, not bothering to remotely hide the fact she was doing it. "You're nice," she said.

I struggled to manufacture a reply. Unfortunately, I was a caustic combination of socially reluctant, depressed, and, most of all, in abject awe of an incredible-looking girl who was for some reason even there at all, much less paying attention to *me*. Any sense or sensibilities I once possessed softly floated skyward, like balloons broken off from their strings.

"I'm Isabel, by the way. People call me Izzy." She held out her hand. I didn't know what else to do, so I took it. A handshake seemed an oddly formal greeting for a lakeside meeting between two teenagers ostensibly skipping school, but again, not much about her seemed particularly run-of-the-mill.

Her grip was stronger than I expected. I watched our hands, conjoined. She watched me watching our hands. "I think you're supposed to tell me your name now, too."

"Sorry. I'm CJ."

"Thanks again for the smoke, CJ." Izzy's words carried an air of finality. Was she just going to walk away? *Start conversation, dummy*, I chided myself. My brain clumsily fumbled through a cornball array of things to say. "Um . . . how old are you?" I asked, like a moron.

"The number can't even begin to describe it."

"I mean, shouldn't you like . . . be in school or something right now?"

She grinned, balancing a moment on the train rail with her arms extended, like a trapeze artist. "Shouldn't *you*?"

"Well, I was." I booted a pine cone as I strategized a way to explain myself without explaining myself. "And then . . . I don't know. I split."

Izzy laughed lightly, puffs of smoke escaping.

"What's so funny?" I asked.

She dismounted her train track balancing act with exaggerated flair. "When I first saw you walking down the tracks, you looked like . . . like *a normal*. But then you started calling yourself an asshole, and then you whipped out the smokes, and now it turns out you're ditching school. So you're like, some stealth, rebellious badass type?"

"I don't know."

"You don't know why you ditched school. You don't know if you're rebellious. What *do* you know, exactly?"

It was a good question. Considering the best way to answer, I plucked the leaves off a fallen branch, like flowers off a petal. "I know, um . . . about time travel, I guess."

"I'm sorry. Did you say *time travel*?"

"Sort of."

"Oh, good then. Me too," she said. "It's funny. Most dudes who are rebellious try to *look* rebellious. You know, crazy clothes, dyed hair, weird piercings, and tattoos and shit. But you, CJ—it's like you're . . . what's the word?"

"Invisible," I answered.

"Innocuous," she said at pretty much the same time. "You're actually not invisible at all. If you're trying to be, that's totally your prerogative. But I feel the need to tell you that you suck at it. Like, I definitely see you right now."

I was shocked by how good the sentence felt. The first time in recent memory I did not want to be invisible. I wanted to be *seen*. Of course, I was incredibly fucked up in the head that day. I didn't have a clue how to feel something not directly associated with hurt, so I just said nothing and kind of stared at the fallen leaves shuffling between my boots.

It was curious why she was still hanging around. Why would a girl so confident and pretty and smart enough to know the word *innocuous* want to waste her afternoon talking to a self-loathing jackass like me? But every so often, things happen that don't completely suck.

"If you want to come with," she said, "I was going to hang by the lake." She did not wait for an answer. She just flipped on a pair of disconcertingly pink sunglasses, spun about, and strode toward the glimmering sheet of water.

My eyes followed before my legs. Izzy's frenetic hair wove a tapestry of shadows down the span of her jacket. The blue jeans, timeworn to outline every contour. A small hole just below the left back pocket. I felt small, as if in the presence of some cosmic grandeur. Or maybe it was just my world growing larger inside me, straining to burst free from a suffocating mask of skin.

—

We sat at the lake's edge. Reflections of clouds painted the water.

I held my knees to my chest. Izzy leaned back on her forearms, her head tilted back so that the tips of her hair brushed the blades of grass.

"So you're an aspiring time traveler, huh?" She swigged from a flask, then offered it my way. The contents of the bottle smelled like something halfway between house paint and diesel fuel. I forced down a gulp. I fought the urge to cough and lost. It was like being kicked in the uvula by a rabid mule. I handed back the bottle with a fabricated nonchalance that amused her.

"Actually, it's not physically possible for people to travel in time," I explained. "We'd have to go faster than the speed of light, and the human form is fragile—not equipped for such a journey. We'd like . . . dissolve into atoms."

"What if you could build, like, a dissolve-proof suit? Could you do it then?"

"Theoretically, it'd be possible. Think of it like this: Everything in space/time is bent. Einstein's theory of special relativity proved the curvature of the universe. So, the time line? It's not, like, a straight line going forever in either direction like most people think. It's like, um . . ." I stood up. From the outside of her thigh to her heels, I drew a slightly curved line in the dirt with the toe of my boot. "It's like *this*. So the possibility exists—to Einstein, anyway—of finding what's called a *wormhole*. Like a shortcut from here . . . to here."

"Across my leg?" We both glanced down to where my dirt tracing met her leg, jagged shadows from the overhead pine trees siphoning the light around the area.

"Yeah, assuming you're the universe."

Mock playfully, she stuck out her tongue. "*You're* the universe."

"There's one thing about the whole theory that really messes me all up, though." Continuing the curve with my toe, I essentially traced a circle around her, kicking twigs and stones out of the way as I went. "It's not a problem with the theory itself, so much as the nature of anything curved. Because, by definition, any curved line eventually must meet back with itself."

"Well, that's a whole new, big, fat philosophical conversation." She seemed very pleased by this.

"I guess it would mean that, in the long run, we're not really going anywhere—any*when*?" I sat back down beside her, smoothing out a pile of pebbles. "I don't know. We're just spinning around in great, big circles we're too small to even see."

We sat in silence, watching the lake. "You're quiet on the outside but loud on the inside," she remarked. "Anyone ever tell you that?"

"No."

"Maybe they're just not listening in the right places. I hear everything. I'm like a fucking antenna."

Despite enormous curiosity concerning what exactly she was picking up from me, I chickened out and instead just turned back to the shimmering water.

"You want to know what kind of stuff I'm picking up from you, CJ?"

This, of course, made me laugh, and Izzy asked why. I explained that she had just known what I was thinking about, wondering if she was knowing what I was thinking.

"See? You need to believe me if we're going to be friends. I have a set of twenty-three strict rules I use as criteria in order to hang out with folks. Believing me and believing in me is rule number one."

"Twenty-three strict rules seems like a whole lot of strict rules."

"You've already passed a few. Like rule number three, which states you can't be a blatant scumbag."

Izzy's brashness was dynamic. She had no compunction vocalizing any thought in her head; to hell with consequence. I was the opposite—always reinforcing the walls around myself with even more walls. Her way seemed better. "But what if I'm, like, a secret scumbag?" I asked.

"That's rule number nineteen, which states you can't be a secret scumbag. Usually takes a while to find out that one, so we'll have to cross our fingers and wait it out."

I was smiling more in that half hour than I had in the previous half year combined. "Any more rules I've already passed?"

"Rule number four: no dipshits. All that time travel shit was pretty sharp, so I think we're good. Rule eight: You can't smell bad. I mean, I'm a bit congested, but I'm pretty sure you're cool there, too."

"*Pretty* sure?"

"Man, you really want to pass my test badly, huh?" Her expression had a unique way of balancing intensity and mischief.

"What? No!" I collected myself. "I mean, *whatever*."

Izzy kicked off her boots, then flung her jacket. "Wanna go swimming?"

"You're kidding, right?"

Her sweatshirt went onto the discarded clothing pile next. She was wearing a tank top underneath, but still.

"It's only like fifty-something degrees out," I protested. "And I forgot to bring my wet suit to school today."

"Any outfit is a wet suit if you jump into a lake in it." She started unbuttoning her pants.

It was a Herculean effort to focus on only her face: the asymmetry of her grin, the sickle-shaped scar edging her orbital bone. Izzy rolled her jeans into a ball, leaning in to shove the ball into my chest. The way what little she remained wearing shifted with the action rendered all my efforts to focus completely futile. "Your loss," she said.

There was still some question as to whether she was bluffing until she spun, sprinting full throttle toward the lake. She dove in. There was a moment of calm before she emerged, mermaid style, a few yards deeper in. She screamed with the bite of cold water as I laughed from the safety of solid ground. Who on earth was this girl? She was like a whirlwind of whim, consequence be damned. I had never imagined the possibility of, much less met, anyone like her.

After a while she emerged from the lake, soaked through, her hair matted and her wet tank top clinging to her in a way that left few secrets as to how cold she was. I was scared even to blink for fear that I'd miss something important to remember for the rest of my life.

Izzy stood over me, dripping. She answered my attempt to avoid the cold droplets by shaking her head like a wet dog, freely spraying freezing water all over me. We laughed like kids as her cold became my cold. And for the first time I could recall in so, so long, I was completely happy in a moment. Not like in the previous year, when even when I could laugh it was like passing through a temporary mirage.

Until that moment, happiness had never *belonged* to me. This precise moment by the lake, however—it was different and new. As if the happiness around me was actually real, and inherently *mine*.

Shivering, Izzy struggled with her jeans, which were insanely difficult to put back on due to the untenable combination of her current wetness and their inherent tightness. Fighting the urge to gawk, I wondered where she had come from, what her story was—all of it. In a small, innocuous New England town like the one I resided in, every teenage male pretty much knows the name and backstory of every attractive female near his age. So who was this girl? Where did she live? What were the circumstances that brought her to a patch of woods near a lake off the train tracks when most kids her age were sitting behind desks in school?

Unwilling to overwhelm her with such a litany of questions, I settled on an obvious one. "Did your family just move to town or something?" I fixated my stare on the reflection of the tallest trees wafting on the lake surface, careful not to be too overtly distracted by an even more attractive peripheral view of a glistening section of skin between where her underwear ended and the spot she had fought her jeans up to on her thighs. "I'm just asking because, you know, everyone pretty much knows everyone around here."

Izzy jumped up and down three times, which had the magical result of finally getting her jeans over her hips but also the unfortunate side effect of completely obliterating an unsuspecting dandelion below her blue-polished toes. Battling her fly, she glanced sideways in my direction, eschewing an answer to my question in favor of a distraction concerning the nature of it. "Nobody really knows anyone," she said. "They just think they do."

—

We emerged at the clearing where the tracks circled down into the town center. The spot was known as the Overlook, for its panoramic view of pretty much everything. The winding pattern of twenty-four square blocks made up the downtown: the 150-year-old three- and four-story brick-and-wood buildings that housed a smattering of shops and restaurants, streets winding off in all four directions to the surrounding blocks of aging, colonial houses where pretty much everyone I knew resided. I pointed past the row of buildings a few blocks west of where the town ended and the bay began. "I live right through there," I said. "What about you? I can walk you home if you want."

Izzy told me not to worry about it. She thumbed back in the opposite direction, into the woods. "I live that way."

A weird answer. She lived through the woods? There was nothing that way but more woods. The next neighboring town was ten miles in that direction down the road. It seemed like a hell of a hike to arrive at Hidden Lake, where we met, and an even worse trek back in wet jeans.

"Welp, see you later, Ceej!" Izzy said.

I'd never been called *Ceej* before. It sounded like *siege*, like something was under attack. I liked the way it sounded when she said it. "OK."

She had mostly dried out, but her hair still hung damply over her dark eyes. "Aren't you going to ask when we're going to hang out again?" she demanded.

"Um . . . what are you doing tomorrow?" I was floored by the realization that Izzy wanted to hang out again.

"Tomorrow's too long. How about you meet me exactly here at exactly midnight?"

"Midnight?" Pigs would not just fly, they would pilot space shuttles before my father would let me out of the house at midnight, much less on a school night. Izzy's parents would just let her out at midnight? I fumbled for a way to explain this without sounding like the clown prince of lame.

"Midnight's bad?" she asked.

"It's just, you know . . . my dad can be weird. I'd have to, like, sneak out my bedroom window and climb down a tree or something."

Izzy stepped into my personal space, astoundingly close. Though I was four or five inches taller, I felt like a firefly in the presence of a supernova. With her toe, she traced a curved line in the dirt around my feet. "Let's say this is your time line, CJ." She then traced a similar line around herself. "And let's say this is my time line."

She stepped back, admired her work, and then smiled at me. "Where do you suppose they, you know . . . intersect?"

My eyes spun down to the fresh markings in the ground below. Her time line. My time line. Crookedly drawn in grass and stones and dirt. We stood between them, staring each other down upon the precipice, the sun sinking behind her down a haze of distant sky.

"See you at midnight, then?" Then she laughed like a madwoman and vanished into the woods.

Chapter 3

BETWEEN FLYING AND FALLING

IT WAS NOT QUITE TWO in the afternoon when I heard my father's car pull into our driveway.

Normally, my father finished work and returned home just before dinner time. Though he was actually a decent cook when he put his mind to it, the rigamarole of preparing an entire meal seemed to wear on him since our once family of four had been cut down to just the two of us. Dinners had been simplified to something from the frozen foods aisle that could simply be heated up, or some quick and easy takeout from one of the handful of restaurants and cafés downtown.

We'd grab some forks and plates and cans of Coke from the kitchen and go eat in front of the television. The TV provided distraction so that we could talk without really talking. It was strange how much the lives of my father and me had been whittled down to the reinforcement of imaginary walls to keep painful realities out, yet there we were.

Still, this was not a normal day—far from it—and it took little effort to guess why my father had come home so early. The school must have noticed I'd split. They must have phoned him and told him I was not in class like I was supposed to be. I was filled with dread, anticipating the inevitable conversation.

My father rushed through the front door. "Craig! Where were you?"

"I'm sorry, Dad. I just needed . . . to clear my head."

"You could've called! I would have come to the school. Everyone was worried! I was worried! No one knew where you were . . ."

I apologized again. "I just . . . I couldn't stop thinking about it. I can't stop thinking about it." There was no need to define what *it* was.

My father's eyes flashed away. "We can talk later," he said. "If I drive you back to school now, you can still make your last class."

The carousel was dizzying—always saying we were going to talk *about* something we always wound up talking *around*. "I can't go back to school," I said. "We need to . . . I mean, we should . . . go see Carina."

My father had not been to Carina's grave since the funeral. This was not out of callousness. Precisely the opposite. I guessed was he was emotionally incapable, that he was afraid he'd just collapse on her grave and melt on the spot like an ice cube catapulted into the sun.

After the funeral, my father didn't even speak of it. Instead, he just scraped for some return to normalcy, manifesting itself in intense overconcern for myself and my mother. This coping mechanism soon proved futile. When my grades spun down the drain, his lectures about my future rang hollow. When my mother began to relapse into the substance abuse of her younger days, my father grew irrational and erratic. When mom finally split on us, something broke inside him. He retained the facade, performing the necessary duties of a parent—providing, protecting, reminding, advising—but it was as if the person he'd always been was dissolving from the inside out.

When I wanted to talk about Carina—if I needed to talk about how lost I was inside—there was always a reason to put it off until some undetermined later. By now I knew that if I suggested we visit my sister's grave, I'd be lucky if my father even remained in the house, much less the same room.

Usually I'd go it alone, riding my bike the handful of miles to the cemetery. I'd sit by her grave, sometimes talking to her, other times just silent. I'd chain-smoke cigarettes even though I knew Carina would hate that I smoked. I don't know why I felt it so necessary to go there, I just did.

Earlier that year, on what would have been Carina's birthday, I was overcome with a need to visit her grave. Despite a huge thunderstorm raging outside, I begged my dad to take us there, but he couldn't even meet my stare to tell me no. Instead, he said there were some pressing things to take care of at his office, and he probably wouldn't be back until after I was asleep. I watched through the window as he rushed to his car and drove off, his car bombarded by sheets of water deluging from the blackness of sky.

I crossed the street to ask Mr. and Mrs. Walker—my ex-girlfriend's parents—if they would drive me to the cemetery. They said they just needed to get their coats and whisked me inside, out of the rain. I saw Natasha and Terry arm in arm on the couch. They were watching TV, something with a laugh track. I waved weakly, and they both forced smiles and said hi. The two of them being so nice to me made my stomach feel like it was being torn out of my body. I somehow managed to keep it together until Natasha's parents led me out to their minivan, wearing matching pine-green rain slickers and expressions of great concern.

But I didn't want to have to do that again now, and I didn't want to go alone. I was insistent. "Dad. We need to go see Carina. Both of us. Together."

All of my father's emotions were sucked off into some void I could not see. "I have to go back to work," he said, his voice barely a whisper. "I had to leave in the middle of an important meeting when the school called. I need to go back."

"Dad, please. It's been exactly one year . . ."

At once, emotion returned to him, in spades.

Beside the front door we had a small table, which my mother had found at an antique store off Route 1. Atop the table was a '70s-style lamp my mother had found at a similar antique store a mile down the same road. The lamp was what my father swung at, sending it rocketing into the far wall and shattering into countless pieces on the wood floor. "Do you think I don't know what fucking day it is?" He wasn't whispering now.

My father was not a temperamental man and rarely cursed, save for food spillages and toe stubs. This was different. I'd never seen any behavior like this. He stood there, red-faced, trying to scale down his breathing. When he spoke again, it was a minute later and decibels lower. "I'll clean that up later. You don't worry about it. It's my mess." He repeated the necessity of getting back to his job, finally repeating: "It's my mess; I'll clean it up."

The door clicked shut behind him, and I was alone again.

—

As soon as my father had driven away, I swept up the shattered lamp.

I tried to sleep awhile but wound up just staring upward, my ceiling fan spinning aimless circles and ricocheting formless shadows about the room. I tried to make myself a turkey and cheese sandwich but only made it through a few bites before I grew tired of forcing myself to swallow.

Some hours later, I heard the front door open with my father's return home. I wondered if he would come up the stairs, maybe just to talk. Maybe just to see me. Our house wasn't large, especially the upstairs. A small bathroom, my bedroom, and the room that used to belong to Carina, which neither my father nor I had ventured into in months. Just two small boxes of space—one to sleep in and one to clean up in—a small hallway connecting them, and, finally, a permanently closed door.

Maybe I was disappointed by not hearing my father's footsteps up the stairs; it's hard to say for sure. What I did know was that I absolutely had to get out of my house. The hurt in the air was static and suffocating. I needed any way to escape it. Fortunately, Izzy had given me just that opportunity.

Surveying my room, everything was good to go. In case my father did decide to come check on me, a pile of pillows had been shoved under my blankets in a me-like configuration. My escape plan was ready to execute. I'd decided to go to the cemetery on my own before meeting up with Izzy.

Clambering out onto the roof, I shut my bedroom window behind me. As quietly as possible, I scrambled down the steep expanse of shingles onto the top of the garage. My father's bedroom was in the back of the house and mine in the front, but he wasn't exactly a deep sleeper, and I wasn't taking any chances. I'd caused him more than enough grief for one day.

Now came the hard part. I kneeled at the edge of the garage roof, twenty feet off the ground and several feet away from the sturdiest branch of the oak tree that presided over our front yard. Not high enough that a miscalculated leap could kill me, though a broken leg was certainly a possibility. Fortunately, I was wiry and coordinated, reputedly one of the better athletes in my grade. I coiled my legs and took the leap.

When you're hurtling through the air—in between one thing and another thing with nothing beneath you—it's a pretty weird feeling. The dizzying limbo between flying and falling. I desperately reached for the swiftly arriving branch. The wood strained beneath the impact. The tree held strong, and within seconds I was scaling down the trunk onto the relative safety of my front lawn.

A female voice startled me, slightly raspy and newly familiar, emerging from the hedgerow that encircled the yard. "Nice moves there, Monkey Boy." Izzy sauntered into the glow of the porch light, clapping soundlessly.

I brushed some leaves off while motioning for her to keep her voice down. "How'd you know where I live?"

She shrugged. "I doubled back and followed you this afternoon. Reconnaissance."

"Reconnaissance?"

"Knowledge will set us free."

"You're not like most girls, you know that? You're like a ninja."

A steely light seethed from her stare, slicing through the darkness, as she considered how to reply. "I guess I have a few complexities."

As far as I was concerned, any pretty girl was a cauldron of mystery strictly on the basis of existing. What did they talk about when there were no guys around? Did they know how their butts looked in those jeans, or was it just fortuitous coincidence? How did they do that thing where they took their bras off beneath their shirts and then pulled them out a sleeve? Every aspect of a girl was enshrouded in endless enigma, and in the very short time I'd known her, Izzy had already vaulted to the top of the list as the most uniquely idiosyncratic person I'd ever encountered. She pulled a watch face from her pocket, missing the straps intended to attach it to a wrist. "You're early. It's ten. I thought we were meeting at midnight." She dropped it back into her bag next to an Anne Sexton poetry book she'd evidently been reading by penlight before bearing witness to my semi-daring escape.

"You're early," I countered. When she didn't seem to give a damn, I tried to vaguely explain that there was someplace I planned to go first before meeting up with her.

"Oooh! Exciting!" Izzy narrowed her eyes. "Spill the beans! Drug run? Late night tryst?"

"Um, the cemetery, actually." There was really no sugarcoating it.

"You really know where to take a girl for a good time."

Was she flirting with me? I had no clue. When any girl whipped out innuendo, I felt like a cat toy being batted around a linoleum floor. Izzy, in particular, seemed to relish watching me squirm. I hoped it was more playful than predatory, but she was impossible to read.

I grabbed my bicycle from the garage. Our garage door had broken about the time my mother started drinking again. She would hide her bottles in the litany of buried boxes then sneak out at opportune times to dig them out. On one of her benders, I guess she was having trouble opening the door, so she just ripped off the chain drive entirely. My father kept promising to get around to fixing it, but that time still hadn't come around. Now it wouldn't open or close unless one had the strength of the Incredible Hulk and the patience to know where and when to jiggle it. In a town lacking any discernible crime rate, we simply settled on just leaving the thing open all the time.

As quietly as possible, I wheeled my bike toward the street and told Izzy my reasoning was rather difficult to explain. But more than anything, I did not want her to take off elsewhere. So I added if she wanted to come with me, it was only a half-hour ride.

Izzy straddled the bike behind me, hands upon my waist for balance. She did this with startling ease. I hadn't initiated any physical contact with a girl since things had ended with Natasha. As I pedaled down the block, Izzy's grip coiled tighter on my hips. This spurred a strange stirring inside me, as well as a more familiar one outside. I prayed Izzy wouldn't notice either.

Pulling the corner to Pine Street, an El Camino roared toward us and swerved wildly. I jerked the handlebars out of the path of the car with barely a second to spare.

Apparently not even noticing, the driver swerved down the remainder of the block, overshot a driveway completely, and finally skidded to a stop on a front lawn. My bike careened and crashed into the flower garden of the house across the street.

"Are you OK?" I asked Izzy, catching my breath.

"Dude! That jackass almost killed us!"

"That's Remy Ward," I explained. "Sometimes he forgets to leave his car at home before hitting the bars."

True to form, an inebriated Remy Ward stumbled out of his vehicle. He was so plastered he didn't even notice us. He tossed the car keys back in through the open driver's-side window and zigzagged to his front door. Fumbling with the doorknob, he finally managed to stumble into his ill-kept shanty.

"I've got an idea," Izzy said. "And it could very well save my girl parts."

I helped her to her feet. "Come again?"

"I'm assuming you've never had a ya-ya and ridden on the back of a bike."

"I've never had a what?"

She pointed to the insinuated area as she spoke. "Cooter. Coochie. Girl zone. Female nether regions."

Failing miserably, I tried not to turn red.

"That drunken putz just chucked his keys in the car. You know how to drive, don't you, Ceej?"

Obviously, I'd taken driver's ed and had a permit. Unfortunately, I didn't have my actual driver's test scheduled until a few days after my sixteenth birthday, still over a week away. Though I was no legal expert, I was well aware that driving without a license and without an adult in the car just days away from actually being eligible to get a license represented an absurd risk with potentially devastating consequences. These consequences were probably nothing compared to the ones for getting caught doing it in a vehicle that didn't belong to you. Flabbergasted, I asked if she was suggesting just hopping in Remy Ward's car and driving off with it.

"I'd drive it myself, but I have bad depth perception," Izzy said.

"You want us to steal a frickin' car?"

"Borrow. We'll bring it back. It'll be fun!"

"It'll be *fun*?"

"Consider it a rental, only the rental payment is being waived on account of that guy being a drunken fucktard who nearly splattered us both on the blacktop."

By all indications, Izzy was not kidding. I searched her features for possible hesitancy, but it was no use. She was simultaneously the most complex and random individual I'd ever experienced. But I realized this was not about Izzy. No, it was entirely about me.

I was being tested by the universe.

I wasn't exactly the type of person to create ripples. Most people described me as quiet, and I rarely had disciplinary problems at home or at school. Any controversial opinion that popped into my head was a nugget I kept to myself. Clearly, this was in contrast to Izzy, who did not give two fucks what anyone thought about her and who had no problem saying or doing whatever she felt like. So I was flattered that she saw me as equivalently capable of rash action. I was shaken by the thought of disappointing her. I also wondered if, in fact, there was something formidable locked away inside me, some untapped animal wishing to be released and roar into existence. *Something more.*

I was also scared as hell. Getting caught driving would mean not getting a license until college, not to mention being grounded by my dad for a similar duration. Yet this fear was trounced by the way Izzy was staring at me—not like she was hoping I'd say yes, but more like she *expected* me to. I'd known her less than a day, and there she was believing in me more profoundly than I'd ever felt believed in before.

Believe in me.

Rule number one of Izzy's twenty-three.

I reached down inside myself to find the courage to go through with Izzy's crazy plan and found that it was right there. As if it had been waiting for me all along.

"What the fuck," I said, to her evident delight. "Why not?"

—

The El Camino's headlights sliced through the highway darkness, the only vehicle on the road. The darkened highway was canopied by twin walls of pine trees, a cavalcade of stars spiraling overhead.

Izzy dug up a case of cassettes from the pile of beer cans by her feet. She rifled through them in the light before tossing them bitterly over her shoulder. "Shit. More shit. Worse shit. Who the fuck listens to this much country so far north of the Mason-Dixon line? Christ—Slaughter? Stryper? Winger? No wonder this jerk off's an alcoholic."

I was only half paying attention. My eyes were glued to the road, my hands throttling the life out of the steering wheel. Staying exactly the speed limit. Fighting the possible consequences of getting caught out of my conscious mind.

Izzy popped the glove box and found a pack of Marlboros. She took one out and lit it and literally stuck it between my lips, her effortless eschewing of physical boundaries both surprising and thrilling. "Relax," she said. "You're pretty good at this driving stuff." She took the cigarette back from my lips. "Hey, you gonna tell me why we're going to a cemetery? Stealing body parts to build the monster, Dr. Frankenstein? I guess I can be your Igor, but it's gonna take a while to grow a hunchback."

I sought a way to answer without answering. "I need to . . . go see someone." Despite a desire to confide in someone—anyone—about all the emotional pain I had been dealing with, the words just all kept getting in the way of themselves. How could I explain to someone I wanted so much to accept me that I had completely lost myself in the year since my sister had died? Who would want to befriend someone so broken?

Izzy caught me off guard yet again by instantly catching on that something was wrong. Softly, she placed the cigarette back in my mouth. "OK, Ceej," she said. "Whatever you need to do. We've got all night."

Maybe if I was stronger and more confident, I could have told Izzy how much her unexpected display of compassion meant to me. And I could have told her I was pretty certain she was the most exciting person I'd ever encountered. But the courage it took to steal a car was far more accessible than the courage to reveal a piece of myself to the world.

Instead, I just used the Marlboro in my grasp to gesture toward the road ahead. "It's just around that bend," I said.

Chapter 4

SMALL SCATTERED CLOUDS

A HUGE, CAST-IRON GATE ENCIRCLED the sprawling expanse of tombstones. A full moon illuminated acres of graves. Tree branches bent like bony, arthritic fingers around countless headstones, some smooth in their newness and others eroding in neglect.

The North Fork Cemetery had existed for centuries. Cracked gravestones dated as far as the early 1800s. Carina's plot was through a crooked path of jagged crosses that led to the back of the property. But first, we needed to break through the gate and onto the graveyard grounds themselves.

Around the side of the property, I led Izzy to the spot in the barrier where rusted-through metal left a wide enough egress to squeeze through. Past that, we navigated the trail to a clearing that led to a small plot of Jewish burial sites. Maine was far from the most diverse place in the world, but there had been enough Jewish people living and dying in the area to warrant a small section of plots, nestled in the fractured shade of a pair of white spruce trees. This was where my parents decided to bury my sister. "Hey, Izzy," I said. "You won't be freaked out if I leave you alone here for a few minutes?"

"I like cemeteries. I find them beautiful, you know? Serene."

I attempted to fend off the heaviness of the moment with a weak-ass attempt at levity. "I'm just saying, because most people would be unhappy being dead alone, surrounded by a bunch of dead people in the dead of the night."

She answered in full sincerity. "I don't see them as a bunch of dead people. I see them as a bunch of people who were once alive."

Considering Izzy's words, I wandered off, alone, across a quiet expanse of grass toward my sister's gravesite.

Carina's headstone was simple gray limestone.

Her name, the year she was born and the year she died. Carved below, a big Jewish star, and above, three simple words: *You were loved*. A row of stones lined the top of the grave. They had all been placed there by me. At the end of the row, I set down a new one.

Leaving stones upon graves was in accordance with an ancient Jewish tradition. It's not like I was religious. I never recalled believing in God or even caring either way. My parents never subscribed to organized religion enough to justify driving forty-five minutes to the nearest synagogue. What my Jewish background represented to me was more like a constant sense of *difference*. Back before my family imploded, we were among just a handful of families in town who did not celebrate Christmas. My sister and I were essentially raised with a religious identity of Hanukkah presents. Seeing the Jewish star on Carina's grave always seemed alien to me. As if although she'd never been actively Jewish in life, it somehow existed as an important distinction for her in death.

Tracing my fingers in the grooves of her name, I kneeled. The air felt damp upon my skin, like rain was coming. Not cold, but the chill was enough that my breath emerged from my lungs in small, scattered clouds. A slight breeze brushed the longish hair across the tops of my eyes.

Hi, Carina. I guess you know why I had to come see you tonight. Maybe I'm just stupid. I talk to you all the time in my head; I don't have to be here. I can be anywhere. It's like you're everywhere. I'm always hearing you talk. It's weird how I would give up anything to hear your voice, but at the same time . . . it's like your voice is the only voice I can ever really hear.

I've been thinking a lot about time.

Does death change time? Like, do you get further and further from being alive with every day you're not here? I feel like that a lot. Like I'm this lost thing floating aimlessly through outer space, watching the world get hopelessly farther and farther away.

Everything's fallen apart. Mom's still gone on the outside, and Dad's still gone on the inside. Every day is just something else to somehow make it through, from one side to the other. I'm just so lost.

I realized recently what it means to miss somebody—it's that moment of awareness that their absence has become a presence. You know what I mean? I think you'd get it if you were still here. If you could still talk to me. I mean, I know I'm just talking out loud to myself. You're gone. You're gone and I'm lost. I'm so, so lost, and I don't know where to go or what to do . . .

Wiping the tears off my face, I was brought back to earth by the awareness of a hand on my shoulder. Oh shit, I'd temporarily forgotten about Izzy.

I turned, embarrassed and ashamed and worried that she would think I was completely pathetic. I apologized, wishing I could suck the tears back into my eyes. "I don't mean to . . . bring you here," I stammered. "It's just, you showed up early, and . . . I'm just sorry . . ."

She stepped toward me. "Hey," she whispered.

"You probably wanted to do something fun tonight . . . and I'm being totally lame . . ."

"Hey," she repeated softly. She wrapped her arms around me. We stood like that, in silence but for the wind through the pines. Izzy embraced me tightly: not like a hello hug or a goodbye hug. More like a tornado was swirling around us, and the only thing holding us both on the planet was each other, and if either one let go, we might simply blow away forever and never be seen again.

—

Outside the cemetery, I rallied as hard as I could. Fought to get my shit together. I worried that remaining in a dark place would repel Izzy—the least conceivable occurrence I wanted. If she was, in fact, new to town, the odds a girl as cool as Izzy would want to spend her time with a sad, brooding dude seemed remote. So, I tried to fake it. "Well, that was sure fun," I said. "What do you want to do next?"

"CJ, you can chill out. Just be yourself. I can see you're not like most people, but neither am I. You don't have to act like you do around the rest of the world. With me . . . well, we can make our own world. Just be yourself, OK? That's actually rule twenty-four."

"I thought you said there were twenty-three rules."

"Yeah, there were. I just added that one to the list. Life's like that: Sometimes you've just got to play it on the fly."

As we walked from the iron gate toward the car, she asked why Jewish people put rocks on tombstones.

I explained there were several interpretations. The custom was thousands of years old, and nobody knew for certain. The Talmud insinuated after a person died, the soul continued to dwell in the mortal realm. Putting stones on the grave weighed the soul down to remain in some way connected to life. Another explanation was simply that the stones lasted longer than flowers—in this way, you were com-memorating the dead with something lasting rather than something else destined to die. "I'm not really religious or anything," I confessed. "It just felt like the right thing to do."

"That's one of the things I like about you, Ceej. I think doing what's right is in your nature. At least, that's the feeling I get from you."

"Dude, I just stole a car."

"Borrowed," she countered. A leaf blew into her hair. She removed and examined it with passing interest. She waited for the next breeze and then set it free. We both watched as the leaf floated away in a suc-cession of semicircles. "How did your sister die?"

"Cancer. Leukemia."

"You know . . . I . . . I believe she actually *can* hear you. Somehow. I don't know for sure, I just believe. I just feel it."

"How long were you standing there? At the grave. Like, listening."

She lit another smoke. "Long enough."

"Wow, you really are like a ninja," I told her.

"Nah." She passed me the cigarette. "Ninjas kill because of, like, contracts or political motives or whatever. I'm more like a recurring angel of vengeance."

If that wasn't the strangest sentence I'd ever heard, it was in the ballpark. I was fumbling for a suitable response when a police car swung around the bend straight toward us, sirens silent but the lights flashing jagged blues and reds.

Spotlighted in the high beams, Izzy and I traded nervous glances. Pulsing lights illuminated the night in frantic spasms.

A young cop with light hair shouted at us not to move. His hand rested on his weapon holster, which struck me as both terrifying and an emphatic overreaction. Then, a second cop's voice emerged from behind the funnel of light. This voice—it was a voice I recognized quite well. "CJ? Is that you?"

Mr. Walker, Natasha's father, strode into view, brushing off his police hat. The reason the Walkers had moved to town in the first place was that her highly decorated father was transferred from the Bangor PD in the hopes of diversifying an overwhelmingly White Waldo County police force. I'd talked with him many times when I'd been to their house and thought he was a thoroughly good guy, if a bit intense. Now he waved off the younger officer. "I've got this, Phil. Do me a solid and radio HQ that we've got a false alarm."

The blond cop looked dismayed by the lack of action. There wasn't much enforcing for the law to actually do in our part of Maine— mostly confiscating of beer from underaged kids and chasing moose out of residential cul-de-sacs. "But there've been reports of vandalism, and they've probably been drinking . . ."

Mr. Walker cut him short. "I said I've got this, Phil." The younger cop clammed up. Natasha's pop cut an imposing figure, maybe 6'3", with arms like Greek columns. Back when we were dating, I'd always been sure to get Natasha home by curfew. "CJ—is that Remy Ward's car?" he asked.

"Uh, yeah," I admitted.

"I pull that drunken knucklehead over every other week," Mr. Walker said.

"Yeah, he almost ran us over tonight."

Mr. Walker flashed his Maglite from the El Camino to the two of us, putting two and two together. "So you thought it would be OK to steal his car?"

Izzy chimed in. "Not steal. *Borrow*. We were going to bring it back, of course. The only thing we actually stole was that dope's pack of cigarettes."

The flashlight beam settled upon Izzy. "And you are . . .?"

"Izzy," Izzy said.

"Izzy. I'm Mr. Walker. Or Officer Walker. I'll answer to either."

She shook his hand, very businesslike. "Pleasure to meet you, Mr. Officer Walker."

He asked Izzy if she had a license and seemed displeased when she admitted she did not. My ex-girlfriend's father pursed his lips, mulling. "You two mind following me to that bench for a chat? I'm pretty certain my job description suggests I take you both back to the station on a litany of charges, but I figure we could discuss things first."

"It was all my idea," Izzy said suddenly. "If someone's in trouble it should be me. CJ didn't want to borrow the car, but I talked him into it. It wasn't like a joyride. You see, CJ's sister . . ."

Mr. Walker cut in. "Izzy, I know CJ quite well. He lives across the street. He dated my daughter for a very long time."

Izzy shot me a sidelong glance. "The plot thickens," she said.

"There's no plot," I said. "Nothing's thickening."

"First off—Izzy? You're too young to smoke. Put that nonsense out." Mr. Walker turned to me. "And CJ? I'm disappointed in you. I understand your need to come to the cemetery tonight. But you're a smart kid, and you need to make smart decisions. What if I wasn't on duty? You two would be on your way to the police station right now."

Izzy nudged me. "I think that means he's not arresting us."

"Izzy?" Mr. Walker admonished her. He continued after she apologized. "You both need to understand that driving without a license is not a joke. More importantly, you kids need to be careful being this far out of town so late at night. It's . . . *not safe*." He went on to explain his plan of action, which was to drive us home in the squad car while his partner drove Remy Ward's El Camino, and then to pretend the whole thing never happened. Izzy and I agreed to this and promised to act more responsibly in the future.

Before we left, Mr. Walker asked Izzy if she would excuse us a moment so he could speak with me alone. Once she was out of earshot, he put his hand on my shoulder and mentioned Carina. "Natasha and I discussed it over dinner. She wanted to call, but she was concerned that hearing from her would only make this extremely challenging day more difficult for you. It's probably tough for you to understand, but my daughter still cares a whole lot about you."

"OK," I answered, unconvincingly and unconvinced.

"She truly does, CJ. We all do. You're a bright kid with a big heart. There are great things in your future if you can just fight through everything you're going through in the present."

I couldn't muster the strength to explain that it was not the present I was fighting through but rather the past. Instead, I just said thank you to my shoes.

"Your friend, Izzy? She obviously cares about you, too. She was ready to take all the blame back there to get you off the hook. People are always going to believe in you. But, CJ, you need to believe in yourself. You hear me?"

Mr. Walker gave a paternal pat between my shoulder blades as I nodded. He said it was getting late, and he should drive us home.

—

It was my first experience inside a police car, which felt weird. I sat shot-gun, quietly watching the road unwind in the headlights. Izzy sat in the back, behind the metal grating. She was the opposite of quiet.

"This is so cool; it's like I'm in a movie!" She imitated some trope of a crook's voice from every black-and-white film noir. "Ya can't make it stick, fuzz—I wuz framed! The dope ain't mine! And the blood ain't from the murder victim. It's unicorn blood, and I killed that bastard in self-defense!"

Mr. Walker turned to me. "Where'd you find this one, CJ?"

I shrugged. "In the woods."

She asked him to turn the "flashy lights" on, and I think he was try-ing not to laugh when he told her no. It quieted down a few moments before she asked him if she could ask him a question. "What did you mean *it's not safe*?"

"Come again?"

"Outside the cemetery, you said we shouldn't have been out of town that late. You said it wasn't safe."

He glanced back. "Nothing you kids need to worry about. Just cop stuff."

She leaned forward, fingers between the grating. "This wouldn't happen to be about Alicia Russell, would it?"

At that name, Mr. Walker became suddenly alert, perhaps even vaguely alarmed. His eyes locked with Izzy's in the rearview mirror.

I was dumbfounded. She knew the girl who'd disappeared?

Immediately, Mr. Walker voiced my inner question. "Izzy—did you know Alicia Russell?"

From the rearview mirror, Izzy's stare cut from Mr. Walker to me and back. "Our parents used to be friends. I guess you can say I grew up with her. I'm from Seamont."

I considered her words. Being from Seamont would explain why I didn't know who she was. Though Midcoast Maine is small, not every kid knows every other kid from every surrounding town. I suddenly felt sad for Izzy—it must be tough having a lifelong friend run away from home so suddenly like they said Alicia did. But something else bugged me right away—if the police were confident Alicia had run away from home, why would Izzy have brought her up in a way insinuating something . . . darker?

This last point didn't seem to escape Mr. Walker's attention either. "Is there something you know about Alicia's whereabouts, Izzy?"

There was a moment of silence. Then Izzy said, "I know it's . . . *doubtful* she ran away from home."

"As the officer who initially investigated her absence, I'm going to have to ask what would make you say that."

"Did Alicia leave a note? Did she pack a suitcase? She worked as a clerk at the supermarket—did she empty her bank account? These are the things that teenagers do when they run away from home. They don't just vanish without a trace."

A small degree of anxiousness fought through Mr. Walker's normally unflappable demeanor as he gestured with a forefinger toward Izzy's reflection. "Did her parents tell you she didn't do any of those things?"

"No, but I'm pretty sure you just did."

Mr. Walker seemed unprepared for Izzy's sudden assertiveness. "Again, I initially investigated—but the Seamont PD took over the case and determined Alicia ran away from home. The case is closed."

"Yeah, but if you agreed with that, you wouldn't have said it wasn't safe for CJ and me to be out this late at night, right? I mean, this is small-town Maine, not exactly the crime capital of the world. And don't say bears, because it's November and they're all hibernating."

Mr. Walker and I shared a glance. I just shrugged—I wasn't sure what Izzy's angle was either. "I mean, I'm pretty sure she's right about the bears," I offered.

Mr. Walker's two large fingers pinched together and rubbed the space between his eyebrows. He was clearly somewhat disturbed by the nature of the dialogue. "Izzy, I'm not sure what I can possibly tell you. The only violent crimes we've had in this town in the past two years basically amount to bar fights and spousal abuse. And this is the town I'm a police officer in, not Seamont—where Alicia is from." He spun his free hand in the air, as if a prelude to a magic trick. "Hopefully, she'll just turn up."

"She won't," Izzy said into the darkness.

Chapter 5

TONIGHT TOGETHER

DRIVING INTO TOWN, THE HOUSES were still, but the breeze was active. Autumn-darkened leaves swirled around the aging wood-and-brick residences that lined the sleepy streets.

Mr. Walker asked Izzy if she wanted to be dropped off at her own house. She said no, formulating a quick lie that her bike was in my garage, and she lived pretty close. Her ease in making things up was both amazing and disturbing. Usually, telling big lies in a small town is like trying to bury an elephant in a sandbox. Everyone has some idea about everyone else's histories and families. Izzy, however, did not belong to my town. It was curious to me why Mr. Walker didn't ask her about that. Maybe he was too caught up in the Alicia Russell conversation to wonder if he knew Izzy's family. Or maybe his knowing it was the anniversary of the darkest day in my past impelled him not to trouble me too much in the present. Either way, Izzy was far from the type to simply offer up information.

There was also an inherent quality that made it easy to believe her. Izzy was incredibly engaging, one of those people who, while talking to you, could make you feel like the only person in the entire world. Unconsciously, a few minutes in conversation was all it took for you to want to accept her simply because of that human condition where, by all indications, she had immediately accepted you. Though it's certainly possible to spend all day discussing the psychological particulars of initial human encounters, it might be simpler to say Izzy seemed aware she was smart, she seemed aware she was attractive, and she seemed aware how to instantly recognize what would either unsettle people or set them at ease. She was essentially a high school–aged kid with a master's degree in general human engagement.

At times, Izzy gave the impression of strategizing multiple conversational moves ahead. When she was playacting the noir role in the back seat of the cop car and cutely asking Mr. Walker to "turn on the flashy lights," she was quite possibly acutely planning how she would broach the topic of Alicia Russell. What better way to get his guard down than to nail down an instantaneously improvised role of a weird, funny, quirky girl? At the same time, painting her as some nefarious master manipulator doesn't work with the knowledge that when the cops initially caught us at the graveyard, Izzy's first reaction was to steer all the blame away from me and take it upon herself. How does one define a person who effortlessly wielded the self-serving, the self-sacrificing, and the just plain mischievous like she was juggling invisible knives?

As Mr. Walker parked the police car in front of his own house and directly across from my own, I wondered just how much of Izzy's demeanor was precision and how much misdirection. In just a handful of hours, she'd gotten us into and out of trouble without so much as seemingly breaking a sweat. Her stare was a vapor lock drawing everything in, but her skin was Teflon, all the consequences sliding off into the ether.

Thus far, she'd deflected any questions I'd attempted concerning her home life or family or school or background. She was a mystery wrapped in a paradox wrapped in an enigma wrapped in a cannonball and fired straight off into the sky.

Mr. Walker waved goodnight as he drove away from my street. We waited for the taillights to fade. Then Izzy tugged at my sleeve and asked in a slightly loud whisper what I wanted to do next.

I laughed until the precise moment I realized she wasn't kidding. I glanced at the slumbering shell of my century-old white house, all the light within extinguished. The only sound on our quiet block was the air cycling through the turning leaves and our own hushed voices. I turned back to Izzy, intermittently illuminated by the long-broken and ever-flickering porch light of the elderly couple who lived next door. "Um . . . don't you think we've had enough trouble for one night?"

She looked at me like I had four heads. "What do you mean?"

"Well, all right," I said, instantly realizing the word *trouble* likely had two completely different meanings for the two people involved in the current equation.

She unscrewed the cap of her flask, swigged, then offered it my way. By the time I'd finished coughing, Izzy had fished an old boom box from our stuck-open garage. "Is there any place we can go listen to music or something?"

Hoisting the stereo from a pool of junk, Izzy had inadvertently bumped into a stack of hastily piled boxes. I noticed the top one about to fall and sprang forward, catching it just before it fell. I looked into the box, filled for some reason with mason jars, which would have made quite the racket had my reflexes been slightly slower. "Jeez, Izzy—do we want to wake the whole neighborhood?"

"It's OK," she said with a wink. "I put a magical spell on the entire neighborhood, so they'll sleep through pretty much anything."

Taking the boom box from her so that it would reside in more cautious hands, I shot her a sidelong glance. "I get that I haven't known you that long, but with you it's still tough to tell whether you're kidding or if you're actually casting magical spells."

"Cool," she stage-whispered. "Then everything's going as planned."

—

I had a secret spot along the bay.

I'd often go there, to be alone and write in my journal, or just stare off at the water and think. Hidden away between two abandoned buildings that were once fisheries, decades before I'd been born. Out of earshot from where anyone lived and obscured from the view of anyone who might be driving on the surrounding roadways. And conveniently, just a ten-minute walk from my house.

It was quiet passing the houses, but we felt free to talk in our normal-volume voices once we reached the strip of locked-up small stores surrounding the edge of the bay. The air turned thicker as we neared the water, a slightly bitter sea brine in the crisp autumn mist.

Admittedly, I was trying to think of something cool to say. Something like a dude would say to a girl in, like, a Cameron Crowe movie or Elmore Leonard novel; something that sounded clever and carefree but was actually overflowing with profound hidden wisdom and maybe just a hint of bravado.

Unfortunately, my lack of carefreeness severely undermined my cleverness, and I was profoundly lacking anything resonating as wisdom, hidden or otherwise. I settled on slaking my own curiosity by asking, "So, do your parents let you out this late, or did you sneak out your bedroom window too?"

Izzy increased her pace so that she was ahead of me, then spun and walked backward so that we faced each other as we spoke. "I get that you're curious about where I live and what my story is and all that, but for tonight anyway, I'd just really rather have me be defined by me and me only." She thought a moment. "No offense and all."

The "no offense" part was a small jab. I wondered what I shouldn't have been taking offense to.

Izzy just sort of chuckled at the look on my face and continued her point as she continued walking backward, two steps ahead of me both conversationally and geographically. "I mean, society's always trying to define everything we are and aren't, fit us all into neat, little, easily labeled boxes. But life is messy, and we're all complicated. Who I am and what I want to be have less than nothing to do with, you know, what my parents do or what kind of house I grew up in or whatever. Think about it—how do you want to be defined?"

"I don't know," I admitted. "I guess I want to be a good person?"

Izzy stopped a moment, still facing me; an action that halted me in my tracks. "Me too, but like, how do we even know if we achieve that? I mean, I'd love to give money to charity. But not having any money kind of prevents me from doing that. When I read about shit like racism or war or natural disasters in the newspaper it upsets me, but it's not like I have the influence to save the whole world. If someone was drowning, I'm pretty sure I'd jump in and save them, but that hasn't happened yet, so maybe I'm not a good person but just someone who wishes they had the opportunity to be one."

"I suppose there's the obvious shit, like not stealing from people and not killing people and whatever. Not preying on people weaker than you," I said.

"Most of that shit is situational, CJ. I've actually stolen food because I was hungry, but I've never felt the urge to pick on innocent, little kids to feel somehow more powerful." She continued walking, still facing me.

As I considered why she mentioned the stealing part and the preying part but left out the murder part, I realized Izzy was about to back into a three-foot divot where the road ended and the gravel path leading to the bay shore began. Quickly, I grabbed her shoulders and steered her onto a surer path. She looked down and laughed when she realized she had just narrowly avoided an unceremonious plummet into a mini-mud pit.

"See? You *are* a good person," she said, grinning with an air of self-satisfaction.

"Seems to me that if your definition of good person-ness is not letting someone else fall into a hole in the ground, you're setting the bar kind of low," I said, before carefully remembering to add: "No offense and all."

The moon's reflection cast an amber glow upon the fluid black surface of the water. Across the bay, scattered lights twinkled from faraway windows along the far shoreline. Docks jutted out from rocky beachfronts, the boats tethered to them rising and falling in the wake.

Izzy passed the flask and set the boom box upon the plateau of a particularly flat rock. The more I drank, the easier it became to get the whiskey past my throat and into my body. A wave of pleasant warmth spread through my chest. My head weighed less on my body. Everything in view blurred at the edges, the brights brightening and bleeding into the darks.

She fished a mixtape from her bag and inserted it into the boom box. As "Ceremony" began playing, I remarked that New Order was super cool. She jammed on an imaginary guitar, then lowered the volume. "What happened between you and the police dude's daughter anyway?"

"Natasha? Do you really want to hear about all that stuff?"

Izzy narrowed her eyes conspiratorially.

I took a deep breath. "It wasn't her fault. It was mine." I stumbled over an attempt to explain to Izzy but gave up after a few stilted sentences. "Natasha tried her best to be there for me. I was just fucked-up after my sister died, I guess," I concluded.

"I think that's one of the reasons we connect," she said. "You've seen death. You've looked it in the eye. You understand it."

Facing the water, I could hear her exhaling cigarette smoke behind me. "I don't understand death at all."

"Maybe that's step one in understanding death."

The need to change the subject was abetted by the whiskey. A thousand small fists punching my caution away. "You're from Seamont, huh? So were you really close to Alicia Russell? Mr. Walker seemed really curious when you brought it up."

"Actually, I never met Alicia Russell. I made that up. I'm also not from Seamont; that's another lie. Truth is, I just recently arrived in Maine." Izzy squinted one eye. "I want to tell you everything. But I can't right now. You're just going to have to trust me, OK?"

Baffled, I didn't immediately respond. How could one person necessitate so much subterfuge? The uncomfortable silence was broken by a familiar guitar riff grinding from the mixed tape. Izzy bounded upright in syncopation with the opening measures of "American Girl" by Tom Petty and the Heartbreakers. She traipsed around me, dancing and singing. Her ecstatic reaction to the song smashed all preceding seriousness into smithereens.

Izzy's singing voice was sandy and pleasant. As beautiful as the setting was, her dancing eclipsed anything. There was something hypnotic and untamable about how her body moved, encircling me, like a pendulum in a cyclone. She reached out, guiding me to my feet. I was stiff and reticent—not typically the dancing type. But something about that moment swept all inhibition into the ether.

There we were, the two of us. Dancing and singing like lunatics by the water's edge, spotlighted by a maniac moon and forever framed in my memory. Nothing existed except the two of us. Nothing else needed to. Even with everything time had taken away from me, that specific moment, eternally, was mine.

—

At the murky point when late night began its dissolve into the ensuing morning, it was high time to head home. I would somehow need to dig up the resolve to survive a day of school on almost zero sleep. Packing up our stuff, I straightened to find Izzy watching me. "What?" I said.

She made me "double promise promise" to meet her again at the overlook at midnight the following night. I offered to walk her home, silently wondering if I could make it back to my bedroom before my father woke up for work. But Izzy flatly refused, insisting she'd be fine.

We walked a few minutes to the overlook. At the point where our paths diverged, she faced me. "Tonight was . . . a really awesome night, CJ."

"Yeah, it was. I had fun tonight. Together." I liked the way the words sounded, so I said them again. "Tonight together."

Her jaw dropped. "What did you say?"

"I said it was fun, um . . . tonight together."

She stepped toward me, almost impossibly close, like that game we played at parties in middle school where the guy and the girl would have to get as near to each other without touching, and the person who broke the invisible force field lost. "When I was little, my family was . . . not normal," Izzy said. "I was sent away to live with my grandmother. My grandma made a living as a librarian, but her favorite thing to do was write little folk songs on her acoustic guitar. You have to know that my grandma was probably the only adult in my life who was ever really good to me. My mom treated me like some burden, and I never knew my real dad. I was always scared I'd be a burden to my grandma too, because after that there was nowhere left to go. One winter, she asked what I wanted for Christmas, and I said she didn't have to buy me anything; maybe she could just write me a song. That Christmas Eve she walked in my room with the guitar and said she wanted to play the song she'd written, not just for me but for both of us. She told me her heart had been lonely since grandpa died, but every night when she would get home from work and see me it would make her heart fuller and fuller, so she wrote the song about those nights. The song was called '*Tonight Together*,' and to me, it was the most beautiful song I'd ever heard her play."

We stood there in silence a moment, on the precipice of a town which seemed distant and close all at the same time. The night was a panorama around us, that limbo of fading stars in the final hours of darkness before the light was destined to fight it back to the other side of the world.

"I used to always ask my grandma to play that song for me, '*Tonight Together*,' up until the day she died." Izzy turned and stepped to the edge of the encompassing tree line, where a lazy wind slapped the leaves together, a cacophony of clicks resonating like polite applause. Suddenly, she spun back to face me from across the overlook. "It's just weird you would think to say those two words to me, and after such a crazy night."

"So, uh . . . I'll see you again tomorrow?"

"Actually, it's well past midnight. So technically, it'll be tonight," she said. She whirled back, only for a moment, before disappearing into the shadows and tall trees, nothing left of her but a voice. "Together."

Chapter 6

FIRE'S ECHO

THE SAYING "*CHANGE TAKES TIME*" does not account for exactly how much time it's going to take. Something had been set in motion inside me, and I was no longer the same person I had been mere days ago. I kept counting down the hours until midnight, when I would get to see Izzy once more. When was the last time I had actually been psyched up for anything? When was the last time I had felt sincerely good about anything? Moments glistened around me with newfound relevance.

The previous night replayed on a loop in my mind.

Izzy. How she blurred physical lines between us like impressionistic paint strokes. How she looked at me, eyes like twin, black lasers searing into my skin. After so much time in self-imposed invisibility, Izzy's eyes were carving me into focus. Like I was actually real. Like I was part of a greater existence that I had so long been apart from. Like I was peeling away the gray, shriveled skin of a dead world and revealing a crystalline new one beneath.

Lost in the possibilities of a new reality, however, the old one tugged back: "Craig Slater? Craig Slater? Are you with us?"

My homeroom class suddenly reemerged around me—the bland, wooden desk, white words on an off-green chalkboard, posters of dead presidents looking something between bored and bellicose. Mr. Preston stood over my desk, displeased. "Mr. Slater. Attendance goes significantly quicker if you can simply respond you're here the first four times I call your name."

Everyone stared. Then, Paul Thurmond's voice behind me: "Maybe he's busy fantasizing about his main squeeze Jillian," he chortled. More laughter.

At the neighboring desk, Jillian buried her shame, unbrushed hair shading either side of her face from view.

"So Mr. Slater—I'm just going to mark you as present, if it's all the same to you."

"Sure," I said. "Why not?"

—

My school day was a struggle to find balance between the self-induced fog of numbness I'd forced upon myself for months and an incendiary new friction sparking inside me.

Colorful arrays of lockers clicked open and closed as I traversed the hallways, the chatter of scores of kids I'd known since the dawn of my memories like a slightly new rendition of a familiar symphony.

The familiar and the new were forging uneasy alliances in my swiftly shifting estimations. I strained to balance the curiosity of unrecognizably emotional reactions to the rote things that had passed before me, barely registered, school day after school day, until now. The cream-colored brick of the walls, the posters promoting school events and important reminders, the trophy cases and porcelain water fountains and scuffed tile floors. The school colors striping the point where the walls met the stucco ceilings, forest green and silver. The rows of doors, small, square windows atop each, leading into labyrinths of classrooms. The faces I knew but felt could not know me, their backpacks and books, their expressions and movements.

I wondered when the last time had been that I'd really seen anything. Not just "looked at" but really *seen*. Almost as if my own self-induced invisibility had somehow dimmed everything in my immediate vicinity.

As I reached the door to AP English, I almost collided with Kay Nguyen, who was entering from the opposite direction at exactly the same time.

"Sorry," she said, with an apparent awareness that she was the one who had been paying less attention to where she was walking.

"Hello, Kay," I said.

She gave me the once-over. "What's wrong?"

"Nothing. Just hi."

Visibly suspicious of my answer, she rushed past posters of JD Salinger, Harper Lee, and some Brontë sister to her desk in the third row.

—

A few classes in, my presence was requested at Vice Principal Brackerman's office. This was not surprising. I knew cutting school the previous day wouldn't be without consequence. A few minutes were spent marinating on an uncomfortable, plastic chair outside the door that simply read: "Vice Principal." The secretary tried to avoid eye contact with me, alternating between furious spurts of typing and reading over what she had just typed while tousling her extremely orange-dyed curls with a forefinger.

For some reason, I was agitated by the Muzak version of "Drive" by The Cars emanating lightly from an overhead speaker. The secretary's phone buzzed, and she picked up and hung up without a word before telling me Mr. Brackerman was ready to see me, never once looking up in the process.

A military veteran, Mr. Brackerman kept his crew cut despite being decades removed from any sort of service. Behind his desk were two shelves: one with photographs from his army days, the other with trophies from the school football teams he'd coached for years. He told me to sit down, then silently shuffled through papers for two to three minutes. Maybe some sort of deliberate interrogative strategy. As if it was somehow important for me to realize my overall relevance to him was dwarfed by whatever notifications he was cursorily glancing at. Finally, he shook his head slightly, removing a slightly crooked pair of reading glasses. "Craig Slater. Do you know why I called you in to see me?"

Mr. Brackerman's reputation was firmly entrenched in a schoolwide belief he was a humorless ballbuster devoid of empathy—unless you were on the football team or the cheerleading squad. Having steered clear of disciplinary action since I'd started high school, I'd fortunately made it that far without partaking in a single one-on-one conversation with him. As for his initial question, it was pretty clear why I was presently sitting in his office. "I'd guess it's because I ditched school yesterday."

"That is correct." Mr. Brackerman opened a file with my name on it. He put his glasses back on and leafed through. I wondered what could possibly be in the file. It didn't occur to me I'd ever done anything great enough or lousy enough to warrant some sort of scholastic dossier. "Normally, I employ a three-strike rule with student disciplinary action. It says here you played baseball and then quit the team, but I assume you know what *three strikes* means?"

"Um, you're out?"

"That is correct. Normally, I would just assign detention for your initial offense. The second offense results in suspension. And if there is a third offense—well, let's just say firmer measures are involved. One of your teachers spoke with me and put in a very good word for you, so I'm thinking we might even be able to do away with assigning you detention as punishment."

"Mrs. Levy?" I asked.

He nodded. "Still, I felt the need to call you in for a talk after I noticed some disturbing patterns in this." He spread his thick fingers upon my file for emphasis. "Quitting baseball was one red flag. But I also noticed your grades have dropped precipitously in the past year. This pattern has culminated in cutting school yesterday. In essence, there seems to be a lot of quitting going on with you lately."

I steeled myself. I knew what was coming next.

"Of course, I'm aware of the family tragedy you suffered last year. Your sister was a fine student, and the school mourned her passing. So it seems to me you're not just any student, but rather one who is facing significant adversity. Would you agree with that?"

"Would I agree I'm . . . facing adversity?" Usually I was pretty good at feeling out where a conversation was heading, but I was distracted by the irritation of Carina being summed up as "a fine student." If she was a C student, would her death be somehow less tragic?

"I know all about adversity, Craig. I fought in the Vietnam War. I've seen terrible things. Very bad things. So, believe me, if anyone understands the adversity you have been through, it's me." Mr. Brackerman squinted at me intently, using his index finger to point out the person in question when he referred to "you" and then "me."

I was getting very uncomfortable. I wanted this conversation to go away. I wanted him to go away. *I* wanted to go away. The air felt hot around my lungs and face.

"I'm here to tell you, Craig, there are two things you can do when faced with adversity. You can buckle under it and quit, or you can fight it and become stronger. It's like I tell my football players all the time: When I was in Nam, there were many times I just wanted to quit. But you know what I did? I *manned up* and fought. I beat the adversity and the odds, and that's why I'm here today. And that's also why I called you in here today. To halt this cycle of quitting and tell you—you can *man up*. You can look that adversity in the eye and stare it down. Do you understand what I'm telling you?"

"No."

"Craig, I'm saying there's a point where a man is defined not by the adversity he faces but by his ability to overcome it. When I was first deployed, I remember my sergeant said to me—"

Standing up suddenly, I cut him off before I realized I was even doing it. "Just . . . shut the fuck up already," I heard myself say.

His face twisted, lines of anger narrowing along the edges of his eyes and mouth. "Excuse me?"

I opened the door, my hand trembling with rage. I don't think I was exactly yelling, but I was definitely speaking rather loudly. "For the love of everything holy—just no more war stories or football analogies or bullshit like you understand anything. I mean, Jesus Christ!"

I stormed out of Vice Principal Brackerman's office as he yelled some pretty nasty things back. What they were, I don't really recall. The words didn't register; they just sort of buzzed past me like angry, little hornets.

—

My suspension from school was effective immediately, which was about as long as it took for me to realize that my choice of words for the vice principal might not have been the most prudent option. Even so, I considered myself justified. Shutting my locker, I noticed Kay Nguyen shuffling toward me.

"Hey," I said.

"You've been suspended."

"Does the grapevine really work that fast?"

"When you curse out the vice principal with the door to his office open, it does," she said.

"It wasn't that big a deal," I explained. "He was being an idiot, so I told him to shut up, that's all."

"That's all? He's the vice principal." Kay pressed each of her temples with a finger, as if to keep her head from exploding.

"We all need to shut up sometimes, I guess. Me included, but still."

She pointed to my chest. "Your fire is burning out of control," she said. Kay probably weighed around one hundred pounds even, but her intensity in that moment bore the weight of mountains. "You're burning yourself alive."

"Look, Kay, I know you always mean well, but I don't see how the whole speaking-in-metaphor thing is really supposed to help me out right now. Brackerman was being a dick, and I let him know. But he's the vice principal, so now I'm suspended. That's how the world works, and it's going to keep spinning whether or not some stupid kid is suspended from school."

Kay looked like she was exerting all of her mental energy not to slap me. "You are not stupid. I've known you since kindergarten, CJ Slater. I know what you are. It is not this. You've always had that fire inside you. But it used to come out in kindness and in creativity and intelligence. Now it's just all trapped inside you . . . and can't you see what you're doing to yourself? It's like you don't even care that you're alive."

For a moment, I was dumbstruck by Kay's sharp words. On the one hand, of course I cared that I was alive. Even in my darkest moments I had never considered suicide—that would not only absolutely destroy my parents, but it would be spitting on the memory of Carina's prolonged battle to survive. Conversely, prior to Carina's death I was always thinking about and talking about "the future." Once, I wanted to be everything: a major-league baseball player or a famous author or a visionary scientist or an FBI agent or a movie director or the next Jacques Cousteau or some combination of all of those far-fetched things. Now I couldn't even think about the future much beyond getting through each day.

Kay was breathing heavily, her hands balled into small fists. "This isn't you, CJ. I know what you are."

For some reason, I was overcome with a strange emotion. It welled up inside me and punched the air from my lungs and throat. I struggled to regain composure. "Kay," I said quietly. "I don't even know what I am."

"Then don't you think that's an important thing to figure out?" Before I could respond, she stormed off down the corridor, squeezing the life out of her hall pass. Just like that, she was gone, leaving her question unanswered.

In the wake of Kay's pointed words, I fumbled to find the meaning. Was there, in fact, a fire burning within me? Since Carina had died, I'd ceased to believe anything powerful or significant could come from inside me. I felt numbed, my entire chest hollowed out. As for figuring out who I was, this was even more difficult. I didn't feel like a person at all. More like just the echo of a person, the thing left behind when all the voices and profound words have gone away.

Even so, Kay had a valid point that wasn't lost on me. I was still alive, and therefore, by definition, still capable of those positive things Kay had once seen in me.

Then my thoughts turned to Izzy. Were those positive aspects what Izzy sensed in me? Clearly, she seemed eager to hang out with me, which had no small effect on my sense of self-worth. If someone as amazing as Izzy wanted to be around me, I had to be worth being around, right?

Unfortunately, this momentary positivity was immediately squelched by a more familiar reflex of self-loathing. What if Izzy was just hanging out with me because she needed someone at that particular moment in her life? It wasn't like she had revealed anything about her life. She'd only revealed what she had lied about to other people. She wasn't from Seamont. She didn't know Alicia Russell personally. Aside from the story about her grandmother, I really didn't know a single thing about her life, and there was no verifying that story, either. It was terrifying to me, the idea that Izzy could be just another temporary aspect of a callously spinning world destined to leave me—maybe as soon as something better came along.

But then again, there was also rule number one to keep in mind: Believe in her. The more I considered it, the more it seemed that whatever Izzy's actual backstory was, she was someone worthwhile and worth believing in. So this was exactly what I was going to choose to do.

But there was no time to wallow. My father had been called to pick me up from school, setting me up for a whole new minefield to somehow traverse.

—

My father stared straight ahead as he drove me home in silence. The walk from the driveway to the house was in similar silence.

It was only when we reached the living room that he finally spoke. "You need to get your priorities straight in order to survive in this world," he said.

In halfhearted protest, I offered an accurate recounting of Mr. Brackerman's monologue. "I'm supposed to just shut up through that crap because he's the vice principal? He's an awful person!"

"The world is full of awful people, Craig. And often in life, they'll have positions of power over you. You're going to have to answer to people who lack compassion and empathy, and you can't just tell them all to go to hell. You think I've never wanted to tell my boss to go take a hike? Of course I have, but I have to keep food on our table and a roof over our heads, and that's far more important than feeling like I've gotten my two cents in. Do you hear what I'm saying?"

I understood the gist of his words: Some battles were not worth the fight. And this was one of those times. Even so, my heart bled at the way he was telling me to accept defeat. Instead of arguing, I simply nodded.

"You're grounded for the week," he said, with more sadness in his voice than anger. House arrest until my suspension from school was over. He hoped I would learn from this. Then he walked out the door and headed back to work.

I sat there, alone in my living room, pondering the injustice of the world. There had to be a way to make it right. People like Mr. Brackerman would receive a paycheck for saying horrible things with no benefit but for a megalomaniacal reinforcement of his narrow worldview. Bullies like Paul Thurmond barely received a slap on the wrist for shoving another human being's head down a toilet bowl because he was good at football, while I was suspended a week for talking back to an authority figure who was essentially diminishing the significance of my own sister's death. Rotten people ran rampant in the world, free to wake up and see the sun and smell the air every day regardless of their cruelty, while Carina would never experience those simple joys again. Where was the justice in that?

That afternoon, alone in the house, I vowed to change it. I didn't know how or when, just that I would know when the time came. There was change brewing inside me. Now I needed to solve the puzzle of how to harness it. There had to be a way, and, like Kay had insinuated, it was up to me to find out what it was.

But not that night. On that night, I was going to defy the terms of my punishment. I was going to break yet another rule.

After all, I had plans to meet Izzy again.

Midnight.

Something lit up inside me with the thought. Maybe it was nothing.

But maybe it was fire, after all.

Chapter 7

FOR REAL

AT THE OVERLOOK, IZZY WAS nowhere to be seen. Getting comfortable among the ragged weeds, I lit a cigarette. Then everything went dark.

"Guess who?"

Easy enough, but Izzy's hands over my eyes felt good. Better to make the moment last. I could smell her, like autumn leaves and wayward angst. The front of her shirt brushed lightly along the back of my jacket. "Lizzie Borden," I said.

"If I was Lizzie Borden, I'd have axed you to death before bothering to ask you to guess."

"Technically," I said, "Lizzie Borden didn't kill anyone. In 1893, she was acquitted on account of all the evidence was basically circumstantial."

Izzy took her hands off my eyes and chuckled as she knelt beside me. "How do you know all that shit?"

I shrugged. "I read a lot."

Historians generally agreed that Lizzie Borden's father was a nasty man, possibly raping the family maid, I told her. Another school of thought intimated that Lizzie was a lesbian, secretly enamored of the maid. "There's no way to prove anything either way, but I can't swear I wouldn't be whipping out the axe if someone I loved was being hurt by someone evil."

Izzy nabbed the cigarette from my mouth and took a drag. "You really think you could do that? You know, kill a person . . . because they were hurting someone you loved?"

I was overcome with an image of my sister, of the intolerable pain she had suffered. I could not conceive of ever allowing such a thing to happen to someone I cared about. Never again. Not if I had any power whatsoever to prevent it. "Yes," I replied. "I do."

She released the smoke from the side of her mouth so as not to break eye contact. "Well then," she said. "That's certainly good to know."

—

Izzy claimed she hadn't eaten all day, so I biked us to the diner.

I was curious if she ate dinner with her family, like most people, but she deflected the question. It was weird how reluctant she was to speak of her background, especially considering she talked so freely about virtually everything else. Any question I asked about how she lived and where she came from was deftly deflected with a swift counterquestion or change of subject.

The N on the neon sign had burned out, so it only said DI-ER, the source of many jokes in town. Izzy ordered a cheeseburger and milkshake. I got coffee with a buttload of creamers and a half dozen sugar packets.

"Is that even coffee anymore?" she asked with a grin.

Watching Izzy wolf down her burger was like watching those nature shows with a crocodile savaging a wildebeest. I asked when the last time she ate was but, again, she didn't answer. "What about your family?" Izzy asked.

"Like, what do we do for dinner?"

"Well, you keep asking about me. I picture your family as super educated, moral people. Your parents brought you up well. You're a good kid."

"You don't know if that's true," I said to my coffee. "I don't even know if that's true."

"Most dudes I've spent this much time with have been essentially devising strategies to get into my pants the whole time. There's always an angle. But if you had an angle, I'm not sure what it might be. It's confusing but also sorta refreshing in a way. You've got no idea what it's like being a chick, CJ. Sometimes you feel like a walking vagina-shaped bull's-eye."

Maybe if I told her about my mom, I thought, *she'd reciprocate with her own backstory*. And stop saying *vagina*. I divulged what I could: that my family had been reduced to myself and my father, who ran the records department at the town hall. Dinner was usually takeout while watching TV. The only thing my father wanted to do less than cook was talk. And my mother—a whole different story.

Izzy's mouth fell into a small, silent *O*. I told her about my mom: the booze, the drugs, the physical abandonment to one-up the chemically induced metaphorical abandonment.

Somehow it was impossible for me to speak of my mother without offering a defense on her behalf. I didn't see it as my mother giving up on me. I saw it as my mother giving up on being a mother.

Were my parents good people? I believed they were, but who was I to judge? Were they good *parents*? Maybe, once upon a time. I supposed it must be the most difficult thing in the world to remain a good parent when half of the people you were parenting suddenly no longer existed.

Apparently, this wasn't what Izzy had expected to hear. "Well, there's an unforeseen plot twist," she said.

"There's no plot," I responded. "Nothing's twisting."

"Let me ask you something." She popped a french fry in her mouth. "Do you believe in reincarnation?"

"I don't know. Do you believe in sequiturs?" It made her laugh, which was good on the ego level of making an incredible girl smile while simultaneously giving me pause to consider the question.

Though I was fascinated by theoretical science, there was a fat line between the mathematical plausibility of time travel or teleportation or whatever versus the flat-out *supernatural*. Which is to say, the odds of my having been Abraham Lincoln or Jimi Hendrix in some past life seemed equivalent to my odds of coming home from school one day to find the Loch Ness Monster eating Pop-Tarts on my front porch with bigfoot.

As far as reincarnation in particular went, Carina's desire to believe in it forced me to give the possibility great consideration. My sister had stared down her own death every day for well over a year. Who was anyone to say that her belief that her soul was not going to be completely erased from existence was wrong? "If Carina believed she could live on after she died, then all I can do is hope she was right," I concluded.

Izzy shoved her empty plate aside and snatched the final cigarette from the pack. "In the remote mountainous regions of Nepal and Thailand, they have an ancient rite called *birthmarking*. Ever heard of it?" I shook my head no.

"Well finally, Ceej! Something you *don't* know."

She started to explain. "In 1982, some Princeton University anthropologists traveled to remote mountain areas of Tibet and Nepal to study the Indigenous people. They live at high altitudes, so far removed from civilization that they exist almost completely outside the fringes of society. The anthropologists were led by Dr. Owen Stevenson, highly respected in his scientific field. Deep in the mountains, they found several of these lost tribes. The scientists became particularly intrigued by the tribal death rituals." She grabbed my arm, then used her index finger to mime the act of drawing shapes upon my arm.

"In their ancient funeral rites, there's a ceremony where the corpse's body is marked with artistic configurations of lines or dots or shapes or whatever. The Princeton scientists learned of the belief that souls of the dead are transferred into future babies born to the family or tribe. Which means that the child receiving the soul will be born with birthmarks that correspond to the markings made upon the corpse during the funeral rite."

"That's pretty wild," I admitted.

"I'm just getting started," Izzy continued. "In 1990, Doc Stevenson returns to the regions of Nepal and Thailand he'd studied eight years before. And guess what: He finds a female child with strange birthmarks on her arm that look almost exactly like a photograph he has from a funeral birthmarking nearly a decade earlier. The parents explain it's because the man was the girl's uncle, and his soul was reincarnated into their daughter's body. When the doctor expresses his disbelief—mind you, he's an Ivy League professor and anthropological super-expert—the parents take him to the house where the uncle's widow still lives.

"The widow says that from the time the girl could first talk, she's been referring to her using the nickname that only her dead husband used. Something in Nepalese, I forget, but I think it translated into English as *sweet cake*. The little girl then sits down in a chair the family says was the chair the dead great-uncle used to sit in. So Stevenson begins to look for families of people he'd seen birthmarked the previous decade and finds multiple similar cases. Not only the birthmarks but also a tendency for weird behavior that supposedly mimics the dead person they allegedly reincarnated from."

"Is all this for real?"

"Stevenson gave a presentation on his study last summer at the University of Virginia," Izzy insisted. "I had to travel across the country to get there. I saw the photos and everything. It was fucking freaky."

She'd done *what*? "Wait, how did you—"

Izzy cut me off. "The dude is an Ivy League anthropology super-brain. I don't think he's going to gamble his entire professional reputation on some hokey bullshit."

"Um, let's just say all of this is 100 percent true," I began. "Even if everything the doctor professed was entirely factual, we still can't say without any doubt that it's reincarnation."

"That's exactly what Stevenson said! He had a long list of things that could explain it—coincidence and something called 'pregnancy imprinting' and personality coaching and whatnot. He was able to systematically disprove every theory he could think of *except* for reincarnation."

"So essentially, he wasn't saying that it *was* reincarnation, just that he could *not* prove empirically that it was *not* reincarnation." I wasn't sure what to think, or why exactly she was telling me all this.

"Bingo."

I polished off my last sip of coffee. "And what about you? Are you telling me this because you believe in this stuff?"

"What I believe," she said flatly, "is extremely complicated."

—

Izzy paused in the vestibule of the diner as we left, tossing her bag onto the cigarette machine. She asked if I'd meant what I said about killing someone if they'd hurt someone I loved. "You honestly believe you'd be capable of that?"

"The truth is, I've got no idea what I'm capable of." There may have been no truer words to ever come out of my mouth.

"Are you capable of keeping a lookout?" She fished a bent coat hanger from her bag and knelt down beside the cigarette machine. She inserted the hanger deep into the slot where the cigarettes slid out after you pulled the handles.

"Does that actually work?" I asked.

Nary a second after I asked the question, a colorful array of packs popped out, sliding out into the metal tray at the bottom of the machine. "We'll leave the menthols. I mean, I'm kind of trashy, but you've got to draw the line somewhere." The final pack wouldn't fit in her bag. She moved my jacket and shoved it into my front jeans pocket. It was more functional than sensual, but my physical reaction was stiffly predictable. There just didn't seem to be any lines to cross for that girl. Izzy just did whatever the hell she wanted, whenever the hell she wanted.

When we got on my bike, Izzy boasted how she was corrupting me. "Drinking, stealing cars, and now you're my willing accomplice to cigarette larceny."

I laughed. "Any other laws you want me to help you break tonight?"

"Well," she said, "since you asked . . ."

It just so happened, Izzy claimed, that she needed to break into the town hall in order to obtain some property records that she would be unable to procure upon request. And because my father just happened to be in charge of the town records . . .

"No way!" I protested. "Are you *nuts*?" If there were no limits for Izzy to cross, there definitely still were for me.

I pulled my bike over to the side of the road. "Seriously. What are you? A spy of some sort? You're, like, working for the KGB or something?"

"There is no KGB anymore. Glasnost."

I tried to calm myself down. "I *know* there's no! KGB! Anymore!"

"Look, Ceej. It's not like I need to *steal* anything. Let's just say I need to find someone. I just need to copy down some property records. I'm looking for something in a wooded area; a house with a lot of property that could be fenced off or otherwise obscured from public view."

My thoughts swam. Though I'd wondered why and how Izzy suddenly materialized in my town, I hadn't come close to solving the mystery. I still didn't know where she lived or came from or anything. Now—suddenly—it seemed she had some sort of motive, some murky modus operandi. Still, it completely escaped me how breaking into the town hall to look at property records could possibly benefit anyone for any reason whatsoever. My mind shifted to the one local aspect she seemed fixated upon—the missing girl from Seamont. "Is this about Alicia Russell?" I asked, trying not to sound too suspicious.

She appeared to be deliberating and then nodded slowly.

"My father could get fired," I said. "We could be *arrested*. I mean, this is, without a doubt, the craziest idea I've ever heard in my life."

"Life's a bitch," Izzy grinned. "And then you're born again."

Somewhat frantically, I explained how impossible it would be to even get inside. The town hall sat one story atop the police department. Even late at night, there would be cops in the station. In order to even reach the stairwell or elevator to the records department, you'd have to waltz right past the front desk. The only possible way to reach the records undetected would be a perilous climb up the fire escape in the back, followed by an even more perilous climb up the roof to the top floor, where we'd need to jimmy open the window from the outside and sneak in.

I knew the layout of the building and the location of the files Izzy sought because the previous summer, my dad had gotten me a job there, organizing myriad town records so that Janice the office manager could log them into the new computer system. But this familiarity didn't mean I wanted to take this kind of risk, not even for Izzy.

"And then there's the laser security system," I added. At that point I'd have said anything to dissuade her.

Izzy rolled her eyes and grinned. "Yeah, right," she said.

"OK, but the rest of it is 100 percent true! There's no way I'm going to take all those risks. Not just no, but hell no. I'm serious, Izzy. No way. Never. Not even when pigs fly."

Chapter 8

EUREKA

BUT THERE I WAS, SCALING the first tier of the fire escape with Izzy at two in the morning. As we climbed, she whispered something about flying pigs.

I ignored her. I refused to spend the final moments of my freedom conversing with the person who had talked me into the plan that would certainly end with us suffocating in some juvenile detention facility. Silently and sullenly, I led the way up the fire escape toward both the town records department and my certain doom.

Climbing to the second floor, she remarked that I had a nice ass.

Normally, this would have been excellent news, but at the moment in question, I was paralyzed by anxiety. *"Really?"* I whispered frantically. "We're breaking into a government building, and you're checking out my butt?"

"So?"

My response evaporated as the back door opened below us. A man in a police uniform walked outside.

Reaching down, I covered her mouth. We froze, directly above the policeman. It was the same policeman we'd seen with Officer Walker the previous night, at the cemetery. He lit a smoke and cracked his neck. If he glanced even remotely upward, he'd see the treads of Izzy's boots just a few feet over the crown of his skull, nothing separating crime stopper and criminal but for a few rusty, metal grates. "Frickin' cold out," he said, apparently to himself.

We froze like statues. Our bodies were rigid, belying our racing pulses. The officer smoked casually, spitting distance below us. *Please please please cop dude*, I said over and over in my head, *don't look up*.

He realized his shoe was untied. "Frickin' shoelace," he said, crouching down to knot it.

My stare slid to Izzy: mouth still covered, not moving a muscle. Izzy licked my palm. I shot my best dirty look. She winked.

A slight drizzle began to fall. "Frickin' rain," the officer said. Then he flicked his cigarette butt and disappeared back into the police station.

I wiped my hand off on my jeans.

"Frickin' hand-lickers," Izzy said, imitating the cop and poking fun at me in one fell swoop.

—

At the top of the fire escape, there were fifteen feet of sloped roof to the window. Five feet into an uncomfortably precarious climb, my foot slipped, and I slid several inches before catching myself on a pipe. Was I really risking death for this girl I had only just met? Then again, it seemed any night with her included a mandatory flirtation with compound fractures or a jail sentence. I gulped in air, relieved to still be in one piece.

"Don't fall," Izzy said.

"Thank you, Captain Obvious," I said.

"That's *Major* Obvious," she said. "I've been promoted."

We reached the window, but it wouldn't budge. Izzy told me to look out, again brandishing her bent coat hanger. "The Swiss Army knife of petty crime," she boasted.

I rubbed the part of my hand where the skin had scraped during my brief slide down the roof. My gaze shot back toward the downtown streets, suddenly below us. Despite my anxiousness, something strange occurred to me: Looking down upon the weathered concrete rooftops around me, the glow of the traffic light turning green to amber to red, the angle of the moonlight flecking the blacktop with gold, it suddenly struck me that even though I'd been in that small downtown countless times, seen those same buildings countless times, walked down that same tapestry of streets and sidewalks countless times—I had never before seen them from this overhead angle.

It struck me as strangely beautiful that something seen so many times as to fade into a simple, unremarkable backdrop could, with just the inspiration to change the perspective, resonate as suddenly and magnificently . . . *different*. Of course, the wonder was somewhat tempered by the fact that the reason I had the perspective at all was due to a precarious balancing act on the town hall roof, with the eventual goal of breaking into the records department. Still, it was a pretty cool view.

Izzy inserted her hanger in the space between the two halves of the window, fidgeting it around until she flicked the lock inside. "Eureka!"

I slid open the window. "I don't think you say *eureka* when you *do* something cool. I think *eureka* is when you *find* something cool."

"Oh. What do you say when you *do* something cool?"

"I think . . . *ta da*."

"Ta da!" she chimed. Then we both scrambled inside.

I shushed her as we entered the building, warning her it was an old building with creaky floors and thin walls and the police station just a few rows of aging wood slats below. Izzy offered a small flashlight, which I used to create a thin beam of illumination as I led the way. We slinked through a narrow hallway on tiptoe.

Much to my chagrin, Izzy began lightly humming the theme to *Mission Impossible*. "Dun-dun-DUNUNT, dun-dun-DUNUNT."

Stopping in my tracks, I turned with the most forceful whisper I could muster, the flashlight aiming square in her face. "Izzy, stop. Now. I mean it."

For a moment, she stared at me, expressionless in the column of fabricated light. Then, she lightly trilled in with a falsetto crescendo of the theme song. "Doo-doo-DOO! Doo-doo-DOO!"

I gritted my teeth. "Izzy!"

"Fine, sheesh," she said.

Once we got to the records room, it didn't take me too long to locate the real estate records Izzy was after. She copied down several addresses of properties in town that had been recently purchased. Shoving the notebook back into her bag, she grinned. "For someone who bitches so much every time he needs to break laws, you're actually pretty good at it."

All in all, I preferred the ass compliment. Our escape from the building had no close calls like our forced entry. Sometimes things get easier once you know what to expect. We hopped on my bike, and it was back to the overlook.

—

It was past three a.m. when we reached the edge of the forest. Our dividing point. The place where I'd head into town, and Izzy would vanish back into the darkness of the woods.

My father routinely set his alarm for five-thirty a.m.; he was an early-to-bed, early-to-rise kind of guy. So I needed to think about getting my butt back home. If Dad woke up and I was not home, all hell would break loose. I'd crossed enough lines for one night.

My ire toward Izzy had subsided, mostly because we got away with everything without getting caught. "Same time tomorrow?" I asked.

"Same time, same place." She made her fingers into a small gun, pointed at me, and fired before making for the tree line.

Another weird feeling overcame me. Like the best part of me was escaping into the forest with her. Like I would be missing some crucial, intrinsic part of myself until midnight the following night. And what if something changed? People disappeared all the time. They abandoned you when you least expected it. They moved away. They died. I had to get her attention. Turn her around to face me. Even one more second with her was better than the same second without her. "It was, um . . . great hanging again tonight," I said.

"Tonight." Slowly, she faced me, her face still in shadow. "Together," she added.

"Tonight together," I said. I heard her laugh lightly, and she was gone.

In her sudden absence, that buried piece of me fought its way out. I felt a greater aloneness than my usual sense of alone. Suddenly a wicked idea struck me. The previous night Izzy had followed me home. If she could pull such a stunt, why couldn't I?

I waited a minute to be sure she couldn't hear me. Then I pulled the hood over my ears and went into the forest. Silent as a cat, I followed the sounds of her footsteps through the leaves and sticks, trailing her deeper and deeper into darkness.

After about fifteen minutes, I began to doubt the wisdom of my decision. Branches and brambles whipped me in the face. I could make out the edges of Izzy's silhouette ahead of me. I was careful not to make a sound.

Wherever she was heading, I hoped she'd arrive soon. Getting home before my father woke up was imperative. Finally, we reached an opening in the dense underbrush. All at once, I realized where she was leading me.

But I could scarcely believe it was true.

—

Buried deep in the woods, the old logging plant had been one of the town's main industries at the turn of the twentieth century. It had shut down during the Great Depression and never reopened. Now, eroded into a decrepit shell, its only purpose was as a place for kids in town to go drink and spray-paint the walls. I'd been there a few times when I was younger, playing hide-and-seek with my friends.

By now the floor had rotted through, the windows all shattered. The walls crumbled. The infestation of insects and rodents had made the place unsavory, even for partying kids looking for a place to drink their beer without the cops finding them. It was nothing more than a filthy shell—and this is where Izzy had unknowingly led me.

She scaled inside. I watched, hidden behind a barrier of shrubbery. She emerged with a duffle bag and rummaged inside, removing some clothing. She stepped to the outside wall, where a hose had been affixed with what looked like wire and duct tape. She turned a spigot, sending water shooting out of the hose.

It was a makeshift shower. As she removed her boots, I tried to fathom what I was seeing. Did she actually *live* here?

And as her jeans followed her boots onto a pile among the rubble, the even more disconcerting thought struck me that I was watching her undress. The realization struck me like half a million lightning bolts.

The moonlight was focused enough that I could see that her underwear and bra were both a dark red. Maybe maroon. She turned to face the wall with the hose. Water sprayed out into a small pool in the dirt and gravel.

I should just leave, I told myself. I was supposed to be the kind of guy a girl could trust. Izzy had said so, earlier at the diner. I wasn't just another drooling dude trying to get some action.

But my hiding spot in the underbrush was barely thirty yards away, and any sudden move or attempt to rush off back through the woods would likely be something she'd hear. So maybe I was better off just staying put.

I was completely paralyzed, unable to do anything except witness my resolve and Izzy's outfit simultaneously unraveling.

Then her bra hit the discarded pile of clothes. And then her underwear.

Her back was completely toward me, but it was the first time I had ever seen a girl completely naked in any capacity. I mean, in movies, sure. But not real life. And I was maybe 50 percent certain this was real life.

The skin on her back turned a shade lighter where her spine met her backside. She quickly flung her hair under the flow of water—though not a particularly cold night, it was far from warm. And the water was probably cold.

I felt guilty spying. But was I actually spying? Izzy had followed me home; I was just doing the same. It wasn't like I'd planned to see her undress. And what was I supposed to do, close my eyes? Is it even possible for someone to close their eyes when they're witnessing the most magnificent sight they've ever seen?

As Izzy shifted under the water there was absolutely zero doubt—this *was* the most magnificent sight my eyes had ever seen. The Seven Wonders of the World were bungalow colonies compared to this. My skin felt hot and too tight. When I had been with Natasha, I had seen parts of her unclothed, but never all at once. It was like puzzle pieces my mind put together. This was different. It was a whole, naked girl. And not just any girl. Isabel. Izzy. The most beautiful girl I had ever seen. With no clothes on. And wet. Constellations exploded inside me.

She bent over to grab a towel. I lost my balance, plunging face-first into the jagged underbrush.

Izzy looked up.

I froze where I was. I crouched on my stomach in the dirt behind the brambles, my mouth dry but my body still sweaty and hot even in the cool night air.

After a few moments, she must have decided it was nothing. But it was not nothing. It was the opposite of nothing. Her hair wet, she escaped back into the run-down building. I could see her through the blown-out window, wrapping a tattered sleeping bag around herself upon a pile of cardboard.

In that instant I experienced shame like I had never known before—and not just for spying her naked. It was the realization that Izzy was in more dire straits than I could have possibly imagined. She was homeless, sleeping amid rubble and rats, while I was going home to a heated house and a warm bed. How had this happened? Why?

Turning from her, from the wreckage she lived in, and heading back home through the woods, I made a vow.

I would save Izzy. Even though she'd never asked to be saved, even if she didn't behave in any way like a person in need of saving. Still, seeing her, without a family or a home around her, living alone and in squalor, I swore it to myself. I would not allow her to suffer. I would save her, even if I died doing it.

Little did I realize I was spinning headlong toward both this goal and its potential consequence, a meteorite rocketing toward the sun.

PART TWO

Chapter 9

RICOCHET

SCIENCE HAD ALWAYS BEEN AN obsession of mine. I always thought of it as *magic explained*. Unique to science: The explanations of the natural world do not diminish the magic. Discovering the precise composition of sunlight and the mechanics of how it travels light-years to the earth doesn't make it feel any less good on your skin. The science of science itself offers nothing, if not endless opportunities for discovery.

Science is often split into *the theoretical* and *the applied*. The theoretical is, in essence, a hypothesized idea. Can humankind send a person to the moon? What are the requirements for a space vessel, what are the practical and mathematical possibilities that the people aboard such a vessel could survive such a journey? Then there is applied science, which is the physical and actual application of your theorized hypotheses. *All right, we've built the spaceship and provided space suits, let's blast some dudes to the fucking moon.*

When you think about it, growing up is a lot like a great big, tumultuous—often cruel—science experiment. So many of our experiences are initial, which is to say theoretical. With no experience to fall back upon, we have no idea what the consequences of our actions will be. We can listen to our parents when they tell us that if we drink an entire bottle of vodka, we're going to puke all night, then wake up with a nasty headache. But we have no idea exactly how bad the puking and headache are going to be unless we physically experience them for ourselves.

The first time I saw Carina drunk, she was fifteen and I was twelve. My parents were in the bedroom. It was Saturday night, my parents' date night, which meant stay clear of my parents' bedroom unless you wanted to hear bedsprings and sounds likely to traumatize you for the rest of your life. I was in the den watching *Die Hard* on VHS with the volume extra loud.

Even so, I could not help but hear a clamorous thud at the front door.

Carina had been out with her friends that night. Normally, she'd slink in quietly and head straight to her room—not on that particular night. That night, she sounded like a flight of stairs falling down a flight of stairs.

The front hall revealed a puddle of Carina on the linoleum floor. I softly shut the door. She smelled like turpentine and confusion. Her makeup had run from everywhere she'd applied it. "Carina? Are you, um . . .?"

"Waaaaaaasted!" she replied.

Frantically, I shushed her. If my parents found her like that, she'd be grounded forever and a half. My fears reared their idiot heads when I heard my father's voice. Was everything OK?

"Sorry! Stubbed my toe!" I lied. "No biggie, go back to bed!"

The door sounded shut behind him. I grabbed Carina, who was drooling on herself. I was always a strong kid, especially considering my size, but she was like somebody filled an air mattress with Jell-O and paperweights. "You gotta help me out here, sis!" I whispered frantically.

"Whoooo-eeeee," she said.

Miraculously, I got her mostly upright, wrapping her arm around my shoulder and struggling to the stairs. Each step was made as quietly as possible on my part, but Carina thumped like a drugged dinosaur. Shushing her and dragging her grew seemingly more difficult with each ensuing stair. Carina was slim, but a head taller—I thought we'd never make it. My reward for finally reaching the top of the stairwell was a slurred warning: She was about to hurl.

Somehow, we reached the toilet in the nick of time. The ensuing half hour was spent holding back her hair among a maelstrom of vomit and promises that she was never, ever going to drink again.

Thus, we come full circle to the sciences, theoretical versus applied.

The theoretical science is that my mother was, at the time, a recovered alcoholic who had completely sworn off drinking. Our parents knew—very well—the dangers of alcohol abuse, and as such often passed that knowledge on to their children.

The applied science is that Carina harbored some visceral need to test such theories for herself.

Realistically, not all experiences need to be personalized in order to be learned. If you tell a child not to jump in front of a speeding car or they can die—well, they're generally going to take your word for it and not test the theory empirically. But if you tell the same child that drinking too much leads to praying at the porcelain throne and feeling like dog shit the next day? That's not something they're going to take your word for until experience proves it firsthand.

What about this, though—what if you told a kid how much it would hurt when they fell in love?

What if you told them the pain of love was ten billion times worse than any hangover ever recorded? What if you told them that the chances of first love not ending in heartbreak were infinitesimal? What if you told them the pain of this first heartbreak—also lacking the perspective and consequence necessary to realize it does not last forever—was so unbearably excruciating it would feel physically worse than your heart itself being violently torn from your rib cage?

Worse than being hit by a car. Lost love was a worse agony than absolutely anything. Would anyone still fall in love knowing the inevitable pain it led to?

You bet they would.

And as a matter of fact—my sister did, indeed, drink again.

It was over a month later, and she was a lot smarter about it, but she had definitely gotten a pretty good buzz on. I could tell by the way she busted into my room, interrupting me from listening to The Clash's *London Calling* on my headphones while reading *Tiger Eyes* by Judy Blume. She pounced on my bed, sending me springing into the air while I called her a lunatic.

Carina removed my headphones. "I kissed a boy tonight," she said, a tremendous grin on her face.

"Gross," I replied.

"Not gross, CJ. The opposite of gross. He smelled like wood and tasted like smoke. He had this way of looking at me and past me at the same time, like he was everywhere at once. Like, scattered but in a cool way, like that modern art exhibit Mom took us to that one time in Portsmouth."

"You're drunk again," I told her.

"No, no," she said. "I'm fine. I mean, I've been drinking. But everything makes sense now. And do you know what the best part was?"

I didn't much care to know, but I also didn't care much to tell her I didn't care to know.

"When he kissed me?" she said. "His hands were shaking. Not like a lot, not like he was having a seizure. Just a little, you know? Like he was nervous. Like kissing me was something so big that it scared him. Isn't that cool, that I have the power to make someone feel so hard it makes them literally shake?"

"I don't know," I said, truthfully. "I guess."

She mussed my hair and stood up. "Someday, CJ. Someday, a girl is going to want to kiss you that badly. You just don't know what you're capable of yet, that's all."

—

That night, after seeing Izzy at the mill, sleep was impossible. All I could see was her. Beneath the hose. Water ricocheting off her bare skin and scattering around her, small sparks of moonlight.

Jousting that image was a darker realization—she was in trouble. Homeless, living in squalor, way out in the wilderness. There was no logic. She said she'd arrived in Maine recently, but why was she apparently living at the mill? Was it about Alicia Russell? It didn't add up. Izzy had confessed she'd never even met Alicia. Maybe she was delusional. Maybe a traumatic childhood, something dark in her past she was running away from. But what? And why would it lead her to some Podunk town in Midcoast Maine?

There had to be something I was missing. Izzy told me she needed time before she let me in. Fucking time. Always shutting me in or shutting me out. I recalled the circle I had drawn around Izzy in the sand, the night we had first met. The time line traced around her leg— if you could cut across time, you could escape it. Time could no longer hold you captive in its airtight grip.

I needed to know. There had to be a way. I resolved to go back to the abandoned mill, that day, regardless of the fact that Izzy and I were not scheduled to meet up again until—as usual—midnight. I wasn't even certain Izzy would be there.

Outside of when I met her at Hidden Lake, I had only seen her at night. I had no clue whatsoever how she spent her days. This resolution took some inner fortitude, as there was no guarantee Izzy wouldn't be pissed off at my intrusion. Of course, there was also the chance she wouldn't even be there—again, she'd never revealed to me what she was up to when the sun was out.

The way I figured it, if she wasn't at the abandoned mill, maybe there would be some clue lying around that hinted at the reason she was sleeping way out in the woods in the first place. And if she was around? Well, my eventual plan was to ask her some important questions—such as what had even brought her to town. And eventually, I planned to offer her an invitation to stay at my house instead of all alone in the woods and the cold.

If she was angered by the fact that I'd followed her last night? Well, she'd done the same to me, after all. I hoped she'd see it more as reciprocity than an invasion of her privacy.

—

When my father woke and shuffled into the kitchen, the coffee I'd made was already waiting for him. "Well, this is different," he remarked.

I told him I wanted to apologize—getting in trouble in school, all that nonsense. I was stressed out lately, and I was sorry. He eyed me with some uncertainty and mentioned it was more worrisome I was awake so early.

"Dad? If someone you know is in trouble, do you think it's your responsibility to help them?"

He set down his coffee and the newspaper. "What kind of trouble are we talking about?" He looked at me with one eyebrow raised and no small suspicion in his eyes.

"Let's say there's a kid. And that kid had to run away from home because . . . terrible things were happening there. Would it be the right thing to do to invite them to stay in your own home . . . you know, for a little while?"

In that moment, I watched my father become a father again. For a full year, our problems had centered on the loss of Carina, then the loss of Mom. Our own problems. But now something shifted in him, and he looked me in the eye. "I'm very proud of you for even bringing this up," he said. "Your friend—if he's being abused, I think the right thing to do is bring it to the police. They're more . . . equipped to handle these sorts of problems."

"She," I said.

"What?"

"Not *he*. *She*."

My father swallowed hard. "Oh. Oh."

"I think it would shatter her trust in me if I went to the cops. She's kind of between places to live right now."

"Between places to live?" My father set down his coffee. He was always a more literal man than a metaphorical one—that was more my mother's department. To him, you either lived in one place or another, and it wasn't exactly a thing you could be between.

"She just needs someplace to go for a little while and figure things out, I guess. I thought maybe the right thing would be to ask her if she wanted to stay here . . . you know, until we figured out the next step."

My father stood up. "If you know a girl who is in imminent trouble? Of course she can stay here, Craig. Of course she can." He gathered his things and headed to the front door. Before leaving, he smiled at me in a more genuine fashion than he had in a long time. "And again, I'm very proud of you."

Making my father proud was a warm wave. The day had started out pretty well. But I still had to sell Izzy on the idea, and I had a strong inclination this would be the tricky part.

—

After a hot shower, I picked clothes out of my closet. Something stopped me at the full-length mirror. Wet hair matted to my face, droplets sliding down my stomach. Again, I thought of Izzy. Showering beneath a hose, in the night. Naked. I wondered if it was even remotely possible that a girl could look at my body and feel anything remotely as affecting as I had, watching her. I tossed my towel on the bed and stood, exposed.

I was slim, wiry. There was definition in the musculature of my arms and stomach and thighs. The uneven patch of hair starting to sprout on my stomach and chest seemed awkward. Was my face attractive to a girl? It didn't help any that my mom's old friends would say things like "CJ—you're getting so handsome!" What did that even mean? I always figured it was just something people said to make you feel good. It wasn't like there were any girls in my high school who thought so, at least as far as I knew. Was I? Yet another problem with the science experiment of growing up: I had no reference point. What was the control group to whether or not you were attractive? I guessed Natasha thought I was OK, since she'd dated me, after all, but she was never the type of girl to shower people with compliments. Did other girls at school think I was attractive? I realized I really had no idea what people saw when they saw me. And Izzy—what did she think?

Carina had said that one day a girl would kiss me, and it would make her shake. Looking at myself, I had a difficult time conceiving such possibilities. I was me, that was all. It didn't feel like a whole hell of a lot. But, *if.* If Izzy felt half as profoundly about me as I did about her? Maybe whatever I looked like, maybe whatever I was . . .

Maybe, it would all be somehow worthwhile.

—

Halfway through the woods, I cursed myself for neglecting to check a weather report. The rain came suddenly. It was steady, drenching me even through the tree cover. By the time I reached the old logging facility, I must've looked like a drowned wolf.

Carefully, I went inside the decrepit mill. Izzy's "home." I saw a vacant sleeping bag, laid out upon cardboard and newspapers. There was an empty bottle of generic whiskey, a crumpled bag of salt-and-vinegar potato chips, and a half-empty box of chocolate chip granola bars. A duffle bag, zipped shut but for a navy-blue sock sticking out of it. A well-worn Anne Sexton compilation beside a dented flashlight. A small, battery-operated cassette player with her signature pink sunglasses, neatly folded atop a matching pink Joan Jett cassette case. But no Izzy.

Measuring each footfall, I penetrated deeper into the devastated building. There were broken bottles, cracked floorboards. Loose nails that had been collecting rust for years. I called Izzy's name—no reply. The corridor ahead was obscured in darkness.

Flicking my lighter, I navigated gingerly. Several yards deep, daylight seeped in. I followed it to a huge room, if you could call it a room. The entire side wall had crumbled so that you were pretty much inside and outside at the same time. Several rodents scattered under debris upon my entry. I scanned a slow circle, wondering how on earth Izzy could live in such a place. I did not even know how long she had actually been living there.

Then, I noticed it on the back wall. My eyes widened. A shocking discovery, just beside where I'd entered from the corridor. As was becoming the new norm, it defied anything in my imagination.

—

Large slabs of thin wood had been nailed to the wall, to emulate a sort of bulletin board. Upon that were pinned photographs of girls—thirty or so, it looked like.

All the photos were from newspaper photographs and *Have You Seen Me?*-type bulletins. All the girls were approximately Izzy's age. Their physical appearances were frighteningly similar. It was as if some movie studio decided to make a movie about Izzy's life, and these were the headshots from the casting call. All had dark hair, all thin. All shared features that could almost be described as *elfin*. Many wore dark eye makeup and rebellious expressions. This was not exactly the dean's list.

And all of these girls had disappeared.

Michigan, Minnesota, Idaho, Indiana, Oregon, Oklahoma, Washington, Nebraska, New York, New Hampshire, Pennsylvania. The arrangement appeared to be chronological, from the early 1970s until very recently.

At the very end of the bulletin board was Alicia Russell.

In her photo, Alicia could have passed for Izzy's cousin: the dark eyes and intense stare. Angular facial features somehow aligned into a configuration simultaneously beautiful and haunting. The hair, dark and wavy, somehow balancing unkempt with pretty. In many of the missing bulletins and articles, the height and weight and age were listed. All of the girls could have approximated Izzy: 5'1"–5'6", 100–130 pounds, 14–19 years old.

Alicia Russell had last been seen at the Exxon station on Route 9. I knew the place. Kids hung out there, mostly the burnouts or metal heads. I knew that crew, but it was never my crowd. The Exxon had a huge convenience store and two pinball machines. The parking lot led to a large back area that bordered the woods, out of view of cops or adults. Those woods were always littered with busted beer bottles and smashed-in cans and the occasional hastily torn condom wrapper.

There was one more photograph, xeroxed from a newspaper. Nailed a few feet left of the makeshift bulletin board. Something about this separation drew me in for a closer look.

It was a photograph of Izzy.

At least it could have been. The hairstyle was different: completely straight, almost hippie-ish. The girl's face lacked the peculiar, sickle-shaped scar atop Izzy's cheekbone. But the eyes and the facial features—it was Izzy, down to the slightest contour and detail.

It was an old newspaper article about a girl who had disappeared. The number for the police department was listed. The authorities were concerned she had been abducted and were actively seeking any information.

The photograph was tagged by the name of the girl: Isabel Ellison.

At the top of the page was the name of the newspaper: *The Oregonian*.

Just under that was the date: *October 2, 1971*. The photograph of Izzy had impossibly been taken before she had even been born.

The article was over twenty years old.

Chapter 10

THE GIRLS

A VOICE JOLTED ME OUT of my skin. "Shouldn't you be in school, young man?"

Izzy stood behind me amid the blown-out concrete. She was dripping with rain. She wore a button-down flannel, black jeans, and a raised eyebrow. She gestured at me with a half-eaten Slim Jim. "Normally, I'd be upset about this type of personal intrusion."

There was a lot I could have said, but thoughts of everything else between us were nothing compared to what I'd just seen. "These girls," I said hoarsely. "What the hell is going on?"

"They're victims," she said.

I pointed to the lone photo, set apart from the rest. Isabel Ellison. Her doppelgänger. The exact same face, the exact same name. It resonated with eerie impossibility.

"This could be you," I said. "I mean, I know it's not. The hair is different. Missing the scar around your eye. And of course, the fact that *she vanished two freaking decades ago.*"

"Yeah. It could be me." A resigned grin as she edged closer. She did that disconcerting thing (strangely what my mother often used to do), brushing the too-long hair from my eyes. Then, Izzy turned over an empty milk crate and set it beside me. "Here," she said.

I sat on the milk crate.

"My name isn't actually Isabel Ellison," Izzy began. "My parents named me Haley Blake, so I guess that's my real name. I decided to call myself Isabel for reasons that will make sense after you hear what I'm about to tell you."

I fidgeted uneasily, unsure of where this was going. My hands searched for a way to occupy themselves, but finding nothing, wound up just tapping a nervous rhythm on my kneecaps.

"You OK there, Ceej?"

"Yeah, yeah. I'm good," I replied. I pulled out two cigarettes. I lit them both at once. "Go on."

She snagged one of the smokes from my fingers and explained.

Isabel (or Haley Blake, or whatever) was born and raised in Coralville, Iowa. Her father was never in the picture. Her mother worked nights and brought home a litany of so-called uncles. Mostly, Izzy stayed with her grandmother, who worked at the Iowa City Public Library. She would go straight to the library after school and stay until it closed. "It was a normal, dysfunctional, American childhood," Izzy explained. "Until the nightmares began."

As a child, Izzy would experience disconcerting night terrors. This was not particularly out of the ordinary—many children are haunted by dreamed boogeymen. At eleven years old, she had her first period. With the onset of puberty, her nightmares exploded into a problem beyond comprehension.

In these recurrent nightmares, Izzy was being held captive in a cellar of some sort. Literally chained to the wall. Insects skittered through bloodstains on the floor. The smell was oppressive. On the walls was an array of weird, metal constructions that made no sense. A light would swing around, connected to the ceiling by a wire. In the center of the room was a metal table on wheels, like a hospital gurney. Welded to the table was a loop where her captor would attach her handcuffs when he came down to rape and torture her.

I couldn't believe the sheer tragedy of what I was hearing.

As Izzy explained her harrowing recollections, I found it difficult to focus on any one thing. My view ricocheted—from the emotional duress distorting her expressions to the cracked concrete on the decrepit walls behind and beside her. On the glassless corner pane of a blown-out window, an abnormally large spider tended to a tapestry of webbing. Sizable deluges of rainfall streamed myriad pathways through eroded sections of the ceiling. The light fought its way inside through various egresses in the crumbling construction, leaving certain sections illuminated and others completely obscured. It made sense that Izzy's horrific recounting took place in what could have doubled as a horror movie set. "You were eleven years old when you had these dreams?" I asked, horrified.

"When they started. They grew much worse as I got older."

Worse? What could be worse? I was shocked. "When did they stop?"

"They didn't," she said, softly. "I have them almost every night."

The dreams were visceral, she said.

Whenever she woke up, it was the conscious world that felt like the dream. By the sixth grade, Izzy began compulsively shoplifting NoDoz. By the seventh grade, she was briefly hospitalized for problems associated with lack of sleep.

The man haunting her nightmares was faceless. He wore a mask of some sort. She could scarcely go into the unspeakable intricacies of what this man would do to her. Torture. Literally.

My deepest fear was being helpless to save someone I cared about—and there I was, sitting on a crate in a dilapidated building, listening to Izzy describe a macabre torment that had plagued her without mercy. Helpless, her frightened eyes darted away from anything as soon as they hit them, like scared, little, black mice. I was savaged to the core.

"The dreams end," she said, "when he cuts out my heart. I watch it bloody and beating in his hand. And then I wake up screaming."

"Izzy," I said, "I'm so sorry. I didn't know. I should have . . ." I trailed off, uncertain of what exactly it was that I should have done.

"You didn't know because I didn't tell you. And I didn't tell you because . . . I'm just scared people won't believe me. And I get it, I know I sound crazy." Izzy turned and leaned against the wall, her hand on a distended brick under some spray paint too timeworn to tell if it was a Satanic symbol or a cartoon ghost.

"I don't think you're crazy," I said, sincerely.

But there was more.

At thirteen, Izzy was helping her grandmother at the library, unloading a box of new books. One hardcover caught her eye: *Serial Killers Among Us*, by Jeannette Wexler. On the cover was the silhouette of a girl, with a gaping hole in the area of her chest where her heart belonged.

Izzy read the book that night. It dealt with a series of murders around the continent that the author believed were the work of uncaught and unidentified serial killers. The final section was about what Ms. Wexler called "perhaps the most prolific unidentified serial murderer on the continent." A man she referred to as the Keeper of Hearts.

Ms. Wexler claimed to have found twenty-one separate cases of girls—coast-to-coast—who had disappeared. Their bodies had been found in shallow graves within a dozen miles of where they had last been seen. All of the girls shared certain physical likenesses. All of the bodies displayed evidence of torture and rape. All of the corpses shared a trait far more petrifying than humanly conceivable.

Their hearts had been cut out of their bodies.

The author believed the first victim of the killer to have been a girl from Oregon in 1971 named Isabel Ellison.

"Does she say who the killer was?" I couldn't help myself from asking.

Izzy shook her head. "Nope," she said. "And no one knows who he is, either."

According to the book, he apparently moved haphazardly around the country. An interviewed FBI profiler claimed the killer probably had a job that allowed for mobility—like a salesman or a trucker—and that let him blend in easily. He spent a great deal of time with each individual victim: Autopsies revealed that the girls had been brutalized for months—both before they were killed and even after. The killer was not impetuous. He chose his victims carefully, lurking under the radar. He prayed upon girls who had fallen through the cracks—like prostitutes and runaways and drug users. This combination made him an elusive target. Perpetrators with no definitive connection to their victims are apparently the most difficult to identify and apprehend. The lack of a confined geographical setting made it even harder. By the time police found one victim in Wisconsin, the killer was already stalking his next victim in Ohio. With criminal records only recently having been consolidated across state lines, at the behest of the FBI, the Keeper of Hearts had also exploited the lack of any institutional cohesion to find the cracks and slip through them.

After reading the book, Izzy decided to write Ms. Wexler a letter, basically saying how powerful she found it and asking if maybe a sequel was in the works with more information on the Keeper of Hearts. Weeks later she received a reply from the publisher, indicating that Ms. Wexler had tragically passed away only weeks after the release of her first book.

Further research at the library revealed the circumstances of Ms. Wexler's demise had been understated. In fact, she had been found stabbed to death in her suburban Washington, DC, apartment. The crime was still listed as "unsolved."

Izzy led me back through the corridor. She fished around in her duffle bag, emerging with the Wexler book. She opened to the identical photograph of Isabel Ellison, hanging in her makeshift crime lab. "That's when I realized what was happening," Izzy said.

"What was happening?" I asked. It was a ton of information, and I was having difficulty defining precisely where the connections were.

Izzy continued, explaining the hours spent in her grandmother's library, researching crime news from around the nation. By the time she was fifteen, she had identified thirty-four probable victims and four additional possible victims of the Keeper of Hearts's reign of terror.

"What I'm still having difficulty wrapping my head around," I said, "is how exactly this relates to you. Were you . . . related to Isabel Ellison?"

"Not that I'm aware of," she replied. "I researched it but couldn't come up with anything."

"Then what's the connection?"

"The connection is," she said flatly, "that I *am* Isabel Ellison."

—

My shock wave wasn't close to ending in that moment.

"CJ . . . remember at the diner, when I told you about birth-marking?"

I nodded.

Izzy began to unbutton her shirt.

Halfway down, she paused. I didn't know if I should say or do something. I didn't know where to put my eyes.

"Do you remember rule number one?" she asked.

I nodded again. In the light, fracturing in through the busted cement, I could see the outlined definition of her cleavage. She was not wearing a bra.

"You have to believe me," she said. "You have to believe in me." Her fingers continued down. Another button, then another. The flesh on her stomach seemed strangely aglow in the half-light. Then she pulled the shirt back entirely so that it was hanging limply off her shoulders, and all was revealed.

After a stunned moment, I caught onto what she was intending to show me. The darkened skin, like a scar or a very large birthmark. A brown patch staining the lush span of whiteness, about the size of a human heart, and located precisely over her own.

Birthmarking. I recalled in detail what she had told me in the diner. I stammered. "You . . . you think that . . ."

She placed two fingers over my lips, quieting me. Then her hand slid down my mouth to my chin. Then down my neck, to my collar-bone. It traced the outline to my shoulder, down my arm, until closing upon my own hand.

She lifted my hand. She used both of hers to gently open my fingers, a flower compelled to bloom. She placed my palm over her left breast. The light skin felt magic, like caressing a cloud. The darker skin felt somehow coarser, rougher. Older. She placed both hands over mine, my fingers captive over her heart.

"When I was a toddler, they told me this was just a birthmark, like many people are born with," she explained. "But now I know what it really means."

Spellbound, I continued listening as Izzy told me that when she was fourteen, her grandmother died. She gently pushed away my hand and used the other to hold her shirt closed. She moved back in with her mother, but the arrangement was toxic. All Izzy could think about was ending her nightmares: the constant torture and murder by a face-less, sadistic maniac.

Maybe if she found the killer, the so-called Keeper of Hearts—maybe she could lay it all to rest, she decided.

She worked various jobs, after school and on weekends, until, combined with the small amount of money her grandmother had left her, Izzy had put away enough to leave. Then she packed her bags and took off on her hunt. She threw away her ID and her past as Haley Blake and rechristened herself as Isabel.

She went state to state, retracing the news she'd amassed of van-ished girls, the possible victims of the Keeper of Hearts. She learned the Greyhound bus schedules by heart. She'd find the local libraries and spend hours researching. She became adept at finding local crime articles on microfiche. And she knew how to zero in on finding stories of missing girls. She found several that Ms. Wexler hadn't detailed in her book. Girls like Isabel Ellison. Girls like Alicia Russell. She learned to find the friends and families of the victims, to get more information from the people the missing girls knew. She learned to pose as a friend, or a cousin, or whatever she needed to be. Across the nation, Izzy tried to find the killer before he moved on to the next place, another victim. She'd stow away on trains, hitchhike, whatever. She'd pick up work here and there to make enough money to get by: waitressing, maid services, farm, and orchard work. She learned about the kinds of places that paid cash and didn't ask for ID. Sometimes food and shelter were hard to come by. Her fingers became nimble at swiping food off convenience store shelves. She learned how to break into KOA campgrounds. She learned to stop wondering if her mother was even bothering to look for her. She learned to never tell anyone her real name. She learned to never let anyone get too close. Many nights were spent cold or hungry. Suffering. She learned suffering. She learned that some strangers were kind, and when she found them, she accepted their help. Others were not kind. She stole a road atlas because she preferred hitchhiking on the scenic routes. She cried so many tears she wasn't sure if she had any left to cry. She'd been essentially a vagabond, completely on her own, for over a year and a half. She learned the difference between loneliness and solitude and that fleeting despair wasn't the same as hopelessness. She learned how to fight, even if she didn't know exactly what it was she was fighting. She couldn't say she was proud of everything she'd done to survive, but she'd gotten through the days.

It was a mind-blowing story. And I was riveted.

After a brief pause, Izzy continued.

"Just before coming to Maine, I was looking into a girl who disappeared in New Paltz, New York: Allison Flynn. A few inches taller, but otherwise could have been my cousin. Turned out to be a false alarm—she'd taken off to join some organic nature cult in Woodstock. While I was out there, the cult got busted for growing and selling mushrooms—not the kind you put on pizza, if you catch my drift. Allison got booked with the rest of them—mystery solved. So, I got a job working nights as a shot girl at some sleazy college bar and spent days in the library searching microfiche for the Keeper of Hearts's next victim."

Tracing unintelligible shapes in the dirt, I asked her where she stayed. Was there an abandoned logging mill in New Paltz too? I still wasn't sure what to think about all this.

"It doesn't matter. Some weeks ago, I found the article about Alicia Russell, and everything seemed to match up. I caught a bus to Boston and then another one to Portland. I hitchhiked up here and spent a day or two scoping things out until I found this factory. It was only a few days later that I found you. Ta da!" She said it fake cheerfully, a sharp turn from the crushing agony of what she had just relayed.

"Eureka," I replied joylessly.

Izzy stood and buttoned up. "I always feel I'm just missing the killer. Like he's just slipping through my fingers. Sometimes I don't know if I can do it alone. I always thought I had to, that no one else could understand. But then I met you, and it was like . . . *fate*. We both have these impossible missing pieces to ourselves. And you knew that cop who agreed with me about Alicia Russell. And your dad works at the town hall, and you knew exactly how to get the records I needed. The way our minds click. And we both love Tom Petty. And *tonight together*. All of it, you know? It's crazy, I've only known you two days and it already feels like forever. And I'm thinking maybe I was wrong believing I was meant to do this alone."

"I'm not sure what you're saying," I said, sincerely.

"What I'm saying is . . . I've been doubting myself lately. Like I'll never get him. Like I'll never be free of it. I just feel so alone. Not alone, but *alone* alone, you know? Not just alone like I'm the only one in the room. Alone like I was on a cruise ship, but it got walloped by a tidal wave and sunk and everyone died except for me, and now I'm floating on a big block of wood from a broken grand piano with no land in sight, and the only thing I can see is hundreds of sharks circling. What I'm saying is, I don't know if I can do this without you. What I'm saying is, will you help me, CJ?"

My mind was a maelstrom.

The most crucial fact was this: I was already breaking rule number one.

I did not believe Izzy.

I did not believe her.

Sure, I believed she suffered nightmares. And I believed her personal saga—born in Iowa, bad parents, mostly raised by a librarian grandmother, tough circumstances all around.

But I could *not* believe she was the reincarnation of a girl who was brutally murdered by a serial killer two decades in the past. At my innermost core, I did not subscribe to such supernatural beliefs at all.

Maybe Izzy had suffered a life of abuse—physically, sexually, I couldn't know. But whatever had happened, it had happened to *her*: Izzy, Haley. Not this Isabel Ellison, no matter how much she wanted to believe in birthmarking or reincarnation or whatever. I'd heard about psychological studies where people suffering abuse invented alternate past histories as an escape hatch. The mind was a powerful labyrinth that could do all kinds of things to our perception of reality and time. Whatever inconceivable adversities Izzy had endured—maybe they had given origin to a fantasy world of bombastic proportion; rebirth and recurrent murders and reinvention.

There was no reason not to believe that Izzy had stumbled across a book about the Keeper of Hearts, or that she'd written to the author, who just happened to wind up dead. Maybe Izzy saw the photo of Isabel Ellison, and the shock of recognition triggered something in her. And then the reincarnation thing was born in her traumatized mind, and she unconsciously concocted a fantastic tale about being the reincarnation of a two-decades-old murder victim in order to escape the actual abuses she had suffered in her actual life.

And maybe Izzy had really run away from home, and the hunt for a serial murderer had given her purpose. She was not just a lost teenage girl; she was on a quest to avenge the deaths of past victims and spare the lives of potential future victims. She was not just a victim of whatever she had truly endured—she was a protector of the innocent and hunter of evil.

Deep down, I believed almost everything about this Keeper of Hearts killer to be true. Izzy was extremely intelligent, and she'd clearly done her research. But all the reincarnation and birthmarking business was too much for my own mind to wrap around. To believe.

But.

Now she was pleading for my help.

Izzy was all alone in the world. And what if she actually *was* close to finding this murderer? I hadn't known Izzy long, but it was already quite evident that caution wasn't exactly one of her strong suits. Maybe it would be safer if I stuck by her. I couldn't stomach the idea of anything hurting her.

And then there was how I felt about her, and how that feeling wasn't like anything I had ever felt before.

Whether I fully believed her or not, the idea of being Izzy's confidant and coconspirator clobbered any other aspiration I had ever had. Everything and anything paled in comparison to keeping Izzy around. Just maybe—I could save her from a life of homelessness and hunger and whatever other nameless horrors might be lurking out in the world. And—just maybe—she could save me from myself.

She was looking at me intently, waiting to see what I'd say. It felt like ages had gone by, but all of those thoughts whirled around so fast in my mind that it could have been less of a pause than I thought.

"What kind of sharks?" I finally ventured.

Her eyebrows did a little scrunchy thing. "What?"

"Circling you after the boat sinks. There are only maybe five species of sharks that are dangerous to people. Most of them are docile or tiny or don't have sharp teeth or whatever. So I was just wondering what kind of sharks we were talking about."

"The biggest kind."

"Those are whale sharks. They can grow to the size of a bus, but they only feed on plankton and shrimp and shit. Not deadly unless one falls out of the sky and lands on your head. The odds seem low."

She laughed. "Does this mean you're agreeing to help me or not, Ceej?"

"I'm still thinking about it," I said. "Which felony are you planning to involve me in first?"

Chapter 11

STAKEOUT

LEANING UPON AN OVERSIZED TREE trunk, Izzy held the binoculars to her eyes. She confessed to having stolen them from an Army/Navy store in Saginaw, Michigan. She'd tried to trade the leery-eyed store owner a compass and a camera for them, but he kept gouging the price, finally saying he'd gladly give her the binoculars in exchange for "private arrangements." Not wanting to discover what those arrangements could be, she simply walked out of the store with the binoculars as soon as the owner was distracted by a new customer.

Now, the binoculars were inadvertently involved in a second illicit endeavor, being utilized to surreptitiously spy on a house. We were situated in a mostly concealed alcove a few miles north of Main Street. We were only hours removed from Izzy's earthshaking revelation regarding her backstory. The house we were, as she called it, "staking out" stood barely a fifteen-minute walk away from my own. It was one of the addresses she'd copied down from real estate tax records we'd illicitly procured from town hall.

Izzy was near certain that the killer was a man of at least forty (his spree of murders had begun twenty years ago) and no more than midfifties (most serial killers operate between the ages of twenty and sixty, she had learned in her extensive research on the topic). Izzy was convinced the killer lived alone, probably in a house that was fairly secluded. It was for this reason, she surmised, that the house we were staking out was not the one.

"You can see through the front windows from the street," Izzy explained. "The bastard we're looking for isn't the kind of guy who'd want pedestrians examining his living room. And look—the curtains are all up."

Taking the binoculars, I scanned inside. There was floral, yellow wallpaper and brightly colored furniture straight out of a 1970s sitcom.

"See what I mean, Ceej? We're hunting for a *serial murderer*. That living room looks like Norman Rockwell whipped his dick out and came all over it."

"That might be the single most disturbing sentence I've ever heard."

She shushed me when a car pulled in the driveway: a station wagon with wood on the sides. An octogenarian couple emerged. The man sifted through the mailbox while the woman opened the door with a key. Izzy declared we could cross the house off our list.

The bastard *we're* looking for. *We* could cross the house off *our* list.

It felt good to be a part of something, even if the aforementioned something was staking out newly bought houses illegally procured from stolen town hall records in order to find a possible serial killer lurking in the town where I had lived for my entire life.

"Where's our next stakeout, then?" I asked, careful not to put too much emphasis on the word *our*.

—

There was a row of old houses on the densely forested highway leading north toward Acadia: maybe a half dozen, situated in acre-wide intervals. Half-abandoned, no idea why. It was just past where the speed limit went back up to fifty-five mph, and trucks would often clamor past like roaring dinosaurs. Izzy and I counted several in our initial minutes of spying from a hidden spot in the underbrush across the road.

Fixated with her binoculars, Izzy explained the house was a solid possibility due to a concealed location, behind dense tree cover. Even with magnified vision, she could scarcely make out anything definite. I flipped through her notebook and asked what we knew from the tax records.

"Someone bought the house five months ago, which seems about right. Someone named Vandermeer."

I didn't know any Vandermeers. I lit a cigarette and scanned down to the aforementioned name in Izzy's haphazard handwriting, underlined twice. "I doubt that the man who is abducting and killing all these girls is a woman named Jennifer."

"Well, you never know. Maybe he has a rich mother who pays for his shit, and the house is in her name. I want to cover all of my bases. And you're not supposed to smoke on a stakeout."

"You're not?"

"Blows your cover." She took the cigarette from me, took a huge drag, then stubbed it out. I took advantage of the distraction to nab her binoculars.

"I don't think this is the right house either," I said, watching a woman walk onto her front lawn with painting equipment and a wooden stool. She looked halfway between a flower child and a tropical bird, with several randomly placed colorful braids and a chin so sharp it could cut glass. I guessed she was nearly sixty and likely named Jennifer Vandermeer.

"I really wish you'd told me that before we wasted the cigarette," she said, staring sadly down at the crumpled butt beside a crumpled beer can. The paint on the beer can was faded almost white. It had a pull tab, suggesting it had been resting there in that precise spot in the woods since possibly before I had even been born.

—

The third house was scarcely a mile from the second. The secluded location, off a winding dirt road, was promising, but was instantly canceled out by a front lawn filled with children's toys and a jungle gym. The Keeper of Hearts kept victims captive for months. Though there were sometimes serial killers with family lives, Izzy explained, that would be hard to pull off if you were keeping your victim locked up in the basement. The guy we were looking for was surely a loner and most likely didn't have 2.4 kids and a yellow, plastic swing set.

I stopped her from attempting to try out their trampoline and pulled her in the direction back toward town.

"Sorry," I told her. "I only have time for one more stakeout."

My dad came home early on Fridays. Sometimes we'd go out for pizza instead of eating it at home in front of the television. Afterward, he'd take me out to a movie. I found myself looking forward to it that night, and we'd talked about two different movies we wanted to see.

"Which reminds me," Izzy said, "shouldn't you be in school, or are you ditching again?"

"I sort of got suspended," I admitted.

"For cutting school the day we met?"

"Can we talk about absolutely anything else?" I pleaded. "Where's the next house we're staking out?"

"It's located right on our way back. I plotted the whole thing out perfectly. See, this is our route." Izzy unfolded a map.

Our exact route for the day was outlined in yellow highlighter. I guessed the orange and green marked trails were routes for future days. The houses were circled in red highlighter. On the bottom of the map were two crudely drawn stick figures, one stick figure boy and one stick figure girl. They looked like they were sketched by a second grader. She tapped them proudly with her index finger. "And that's us," she said.

—

We walked to the edge of town with the row of auto parts stores, a tattoo parlor, a 7-Eleven, and the only McDonalds within twenty square miles.

"Any chance you can meet up earlier than midnight tonight?" Izzy asked.

"No can do," I said. My father and I were deciding between a pair of films that both played around eight. I really wanted to see *Singles* but he wanted to see *A Few Good Men*. I knew I'd probably lose that battle, but even if I was creeped out by Tom Cruise, I didn't mind too much. Anyway, we wouldn't be home until around eleven at the earliest.

"Then I'm going to have to start our night mission without you," she said, frowning.

"Night mission?"

Izzy revealed that she had mapped out a list of three separate stakeout routes, drawn up to hit all the newly purchased houses off the list she had made using the town hall real estate records. The stakeouts of the houses were scheduled for the daytime. For that night and the next, she planned to stake out the Exxon station—the last location where Alicia Russell had been seen alive. "Alicia disappeared on a Saturday night about a month ago," Izzy said. "Apparently, she was smoking pot with her friends behind the Exxon until about one a.m., something she and her friends did pretty much every weekend."

I laughed at that. "That's what *everyone* does around here every weekend," I said. This part of Maine, I guessed, was like a lot of small towns: There wasn't much else to get up to.

Izzy ignored my remark. "The Keeper of Hearts chooses his victims carefully. They're all around the same age and look alike—you saw the pictures. I've read the *Crime Classification Manual* four times, and it says that he probably stalks his victims before abducting them. He's very methodical." Seeing as Alicia was regularly hanging out at the Exxon, Izzy reasoned, it was a very good bet that the killer watched her there. "Apparently, on that night she got in a fight with her dude about whatever, so she didn't get a ride home with him. She insisted on walking home, maybe a three-mile hike down the highway. And then she just vanished."

The part where Alicia Russell vanished after walking home from the Exxon I recalled from the initial news and gossip surrounding the event. I didn't remember hearing anything about her smoking pot or getting in a fight with her boyfriend, but Izzy seemed quite adept at digging up information surrounding her missing girls, so I decided against pestering her with too many questions. "All your logic and reasoning seem solid, but that still doesn't get me out of movie night with Dad. I'll do my best to make it, I just can't promise on an exact time of arrival."

"Fine," Izzy said, somewhat petulantly. "I'll just have to fly solo. But first, you're coming with me to the last house on today's stakeout list."

—

The aforementioned final house on our route was a run-down affair off the industrial road, beside a junk heap, behind a Jiffy Lube. The entire block smelled like rust. The house was wretched, the roof caving in two separate locations and a front yard carpeted by knee-high weeds. The porch swing had broken off at one end. The breeze rustled the loose chain in a creepy metronome symphony.

"Now *this* looks like the kind of place a serial killer would live," I said.

She shushed me, leading us to a pickup truck without wheels, propped up on cinder blocks. The hatch was covered by a tarp. She untied a section so we could crawl inside.

"Are you serious?" I was aghast at what lifting the tarp revealed: a collection of rusted gardening tools; a ripped-open, leaking, and odorous bag of fertilizer; at least three species of insects I couldn't identify and didn't want crawling on my leg.

"*Yes,*" she snapped back.

I wasn't happy about this, but she claimed it was a perfect stakeout spot. She broke out the binoculars while I sulked in musty filth.

After ten minutes of uncomfortable silence and silent discomfort, I was ready to quit stakeouts forever. It always seemed so glamorous when TV detectives did it, but I was getting bored with the inaction, getting sore with the contortions necessary to fit both Izzy and myself under the tarp, and getting grossed out by the thought of bugs burrowing into my socks.

Izzy spied like a hawk, the binoculars poking out of a crack between the tarp and the truck. Suddenly, she broke the quiet with a drastic change of subject. "So when you followed me back from the overlook to the factory last night," she said, matter-of-factly, "you saw me naked, right?"

I stuttered a syllable or two, unable to come out with anything like a reasonable answer or intelligible word.

She lowered the binoculars and turned to me. "It's OK if you saw me," she said. "I don't care."

A huge punch to my gut. If she had punctuated that comment with *I don't mind* or *it doesn't bother me*, it would have been fine. But *I don't care*—it made me feel small and insignificant.

On the other hand, she was also telling me in a roundabout way she knew I had followed her. If she did, then why had she undressed and showered anyway? Was it possible she *wanted* me to see?

My mind spun. I didn't understand myself, I didn't understand girls, I didn't understand people, and I most certainly did not understand Izzy.

Meanwhile, she just kept talking.

"Thank the stars there's that well outside," she went on. "When you're a homeless vagrant, personal hygiene is the number one biggest obstacle. Eating is a far, far number two. Anyway, at one point I heard a rustling in the bushes. I'm actually kind of relieved it was you. At first I thought it was a bear with a camera, and I didn't want to be caught on film."

In a world of possible reactions to being seen naked by a person you had met that very same week, suffice it to say this was not one I would have remotely expected. Not a shred of what I would have supposed—maybe embarrassment or modesty or even anger or curiosity—but rather a short treatise on vagabond hygiene and something absurd about bear photographers. "You might be the weirdest person on the entire earth," I said.

"At least I'm not a fucking Peeping Tom," she smirked, and I couldn't help but laugh a little, too.

Chapter 12

THE PIT

TOM CRUISE STRUTTED ACROSS THE big screen as my father munched popcorn in the aisle seat.

"He looks completely possessed," I muttered.

"*Shhhh*," my dad said.

"He doesn't even look human. He looks like an alien landed on the planet and stole a human's skin to wear as a suit, and this is the first time he's wearing it and it doesn't fit right."

"*Shhhh*," my dad said again.

"Look at his eyes. He's like an alien with a wedgie from his human skin suit."

"*Shhhh*," the couple behind us said.

On the drive home, my dad imitated his favorite line from the movie: "The truth? You can't handle the truth!" Of course, the realization didn't escape me that my father was trying to find a conversational connection based on the film we had just seen. And I appreciated his constant effort to find innocuous common ground. The problem was that all the mundane aspects of life we tended to discuss—well, they weren't *real*.

Sure, it was all real in the definitive sense that it all *existed*. The Red Sox were real, the Bruins were real, how I was doing in school was real, the weather that day was real, the movies we would watch together actually existed on actual screens. Yet, all of it existed as a diversion from our lives rather than things that actually impacted them.

It sounded stupid even to consider, but the very notion of bringing up anything that truly affected me to my dad was viscerally frightening. This is to say that I liked seeing him happy—I treasured his fist pumps when Wade Boggs hit a game-winning single or his cheers when Ray Bourque scored a game-winning goal, or his laughs during the funny parts in a film. He was a good dad and a good person, and he deserved these small reprieves. And I knew that revealing what was actually transpiring in my heart would only make him sad and quiet and distant again. Carina. Mom. These were the issues that consumed my inner world and ultimately why I felt the need to tuck that inner world as deeply inside of me as possible.

The way I saw it, my dad had been through enough. He didn't need to constantly worry about me, too. I was his son, and he was a caring father, and I was undoubtedly atop his list of life concerns. I figured the least I could do for him was let him think my life and mental state were mostly just fine, and he had nothing to worry about.

I'm not sure if this drove a wedge between us, but as the months went by, it just became harder and harder to talk with him about real things. It was whittled away to whatever we could share without actually sharing ourselves. And as lonely as it made us, at least it was more bearable than the raw, open wound of tragic loss.

In character, I just played along, responding to his Tom Cruise line with a Jack Nicholson line. Out of order perhaps, but it was the same scene and the only one in his courtroom monologue I was fairly certain I had remembered verbatim: "I have a greater responsibility than you can possibly fathom!"

As my dad chuckled at my response, my thoughts soared down the road, through the loose pine needles and the crisp coastal night—toward Izzy, lying in the underbrush outside the Exxon station, on a quest for evidence of a killer.

And what if she found the man? She was searching for a psychotic murderer, after all. What would she do then? Turn him in to the police? Break into his house and free Alicia Russell? I'd been scared to ask.

The day itself had ended in stalemate. After eliminating three houses from our list, the final house left us with no conclusions either way. It *looked* like a psycho killer's house, that was for certain. The secluded location behind a junkyard and tightly shut blinds also raised suspicions. The new owner of the house was evidently named Owen Laughlin. But in an hour of staking out the very creepy property, we had seen no signs of movement either in or around the location. Izzy resolved to return, maybe after the weekend.

—

My father parked in our driveway just shy of midnight. The Exxon was about a twenty-minute trek by bike. I was not only going to be late, but I was going to be late to being late.

Complicating the situation, my dad didn't yet feel like going to bed, instead challenging me to a game of Scrabble. But my dad was one of those Scrabble players who took at least five minutes per move, as if his brain were going through the entire *Webster's Dictionary* to triple-check if anything offered more points on double-word score than *aioli*. At that pace, I'd be fortunate to meet up with Izzy by the new year.

I was torn. We hadn't played Scrabble together since long before Carina died. The three of us would often play together while my mom sat on the chair, under a blanket, reading Stephen King novels and listening to Thin Lizzy or Led Zeppelin or whatever on her headphones. My dad convinced her to play with us once, but she quit forever after my dad wouldn't allow her to use curse words.

"You can't use *shitty*," he explained, trying to stay serious. "The *Official Scrabble Dictionary* doesn't allow for profanity. Normally you'd lose your turn, but seeing as you're my favorite wife and their favorite mother, I'll let you go again."

"*Shitty* is absolutely a fucking word," she replied, less amused than he was. My mom could be a bit volatile at times.

My father flushed a bit. Unlike my mother, he was never one to use swear words around my sister and me, Scrabble-related or otherwise. "Not according to the *Official Scrabble Dictionary*."

My mother just doubled down, folding her arms. "Here, I'll prove it. I'll use it in a sentence: *I think it's terribly shitty that you won't let me use shitty on triple-word score*. See? It's a word."

"Do you want our children to grow up cussing like sailors?"

At this point, Carina was laughing so hard she was almost falling off her chair, but I just sat there silent, always a bit anxious at my own inability to tell if my parents' arguments were genuine or just theatrical.

My mother stood up and gestured bitterly at the board. "You let CJ use *cock* before! Where was your precious no-profanity rule then?"

My father pleaded for calm with a double-handed gesture. "Rebecca—a *cock* is also a type of bird."

"No, I'll tell you what a *cock* is. It's what you're being exactly right now!" With that, my mother stormed out of the room as my sister actually fell off her chair laughing.

Anyway, that was the last time my mother played with us, but Scrabble still remained something for my father, my sister, and me to do together—right up to the time Carina began to get very sick.

Still, the thought of playing my father for the first time since our family was still a family was a powerful pull. Naturally, I appreciated his effort to connect with me, whether or not it was directly related to my recent struggles at school. It's also quite relevant that I really loved my father and loved spending time with him, regardless of the fact that, in all honesty, I was generally pretty bored by board games.

In the moment, I almost relented. But then my mind flashed to Izzy. She'd be all alone, staking out the Exxon station in the chilly night while I would be in a warm house, playing games. Would she wonder where I was? Would she be worried about me? Would she be angry with me? Would my absence somehow be a rift just as we were forging an *us*, instead relegating the parties involved to a separate *me* and *her*?

Beneath that existed an even stronger pull. What if there was a remote chance that Izzy was correct and a serial murderer actually used the woods behind the Exxon station to stalk his victims? Well, she would be in those woods too. She was certainly alone there at the very moment in question.

In the end, there was no decision to make. As much as it pained me to pass on my father's invitation, I had to get to those woods and find Izzy. And I had to do it as soon as possible.

The quickest solution I came up with was to feign exhaustion. I faked a yawn, which sounded to me like a really bad, fake yawn, though maybe that was just my conscience playing tricks on me. "Can we reschedule Scrabble? I mean it sounds great, but I'm just really tired tonight for some reason."

"Maybe it's because you woke up so early this morning," my father offered, reminding me that I had been awake early enough to make him coffee. It seemed a reasonable cover story.

"Maybe," I said. "I guess so."

"Maybe I'll pack it in early too. I've got some free time tomorrow, and the weather's supposed to clear up, so maybe we can throw a baseball around in the yard. You know, you've got to limber up the arm after taking off a season. Can't make those rocket throws from deep in the hole and move from shortstop to second base."

"Rocket throws?"

"Great throwing arms run in the family, you know."

"I know, you've only told me a kajillion times." I laughed a bit on the outside, but on the inside, I was stuck on the fact he said I'd "taken off" a season, as if it was some kind of planned vacation rather than my quitting the team in the middle of an at-bat because I felt like my chest was about to explode. Furthermore, my mind raced back to Izzy's map, her stakeout route for the following day clearly highlighted in orange.

What was I going to do about the rest of the weekend? How would I escape the conditions of my punishment with my dad at home? My father usually spent Saturdays or Sundays puttering about the house, watching sports, and doing odd errands and repair jobs. Lately, he'd even been building birdhouses in his basement workshop again— something else he hadn't done for a while. He didn't exactly have an active social life, so every weekend he was perpetually around.

Since my school suspension left me grounded all weekend, how would I sneak out for stakeouts with Izzy during the day? It was going to be impossible.

It might have been easy for Izzy to make shit up on the fly—she was an ace prevaricator, able to come up with something and roll with it. She lied with the same nonchalance as she told the truth. But lying for me wasn't easy at all. Sure, I could come up with creative things super quickly. But when any untruth left my lips, I felt gross on the inside and transparent on the outside.

But I *had* to see her, no matter how good it would feel to play catch with him in the yard and no matter how much I disappointed him by saying no.

I summoned my inner dice and rolled. "Oh shit, I forgot! I'm supposed to work a double at CD World tomorrow." I knew my dad would probably buy this and, with his relentlessly dutiful dedication to personal responsibility, that the terms of being grounded wouldn't extend to my weekend retail gig downtown. And it was a half-truth, after all—I was, in fact, scheduled at CD World for the night shift, but I had the day off and planned to spend it with Izzy.

He sat in his favorite chair to remove his shoes. "OK. Maybe Sunday, then?" He sat there a moment, eyebrows raised, hoping.

I wanted so badly for us to spend time together, to really talk, to connect on some core level that had been danced around for far too long. But how would I balance this with Izzy?

"Sure," I said. "Maybe." I started up the stairs, relieved. Not that getting away with it felt good. Actually, it felt awful. I took no pleasure in pulling a fast one on my dad. But what I needed to get away with was, quite simply, too important to me. As much as I reciprocated my father's want to do all these things together, he would still be there if I put them off awhile. With Izzy, there was no certainty. In the past year I'd lost Carina, my mother, and Natasha. I couldn't bear the thought of blowing it somehow and losing Izzy, too.

It was inconceivable how much my entire axis had shifted in the matter of two days. Time itself was becoming inconceivable. In the entire preceding year, I felt like I'd ceased to progress as a human being. Like I was trapped in perpetual stasis. Then, in the span of two days, I'd essentially gone completely renegade: talking back to authority figures, getting suspended from school, sneaking out of my house every night, breaking into town hall, being an accessory to stolen cigarettes and borrowed cars, staking out houses, and trying to track down an apparent serial killer.

It was because of Izzy, obviously. She'd exploded into my meandering, melancholy life like a hydrogen bomb filled with glitter and confetti, somehow beautiful but also cut from the pages of the obituaries. She was like nothing else but was rapidly eclipsing everything else.

More than anything, I was just glad she was there. And again, I was terrified she would disappear. So far, almost everyone I loved had disappeared. Maybe if I did everything right this time, Izzy would stick around. Maybe there was some complex combination of things I could do right or get right or make right to make her want to stay. If only I knew what. Or how.

The span of two days was toppling me like a tidal wave. I was feeling—*feeling*—everything. All the numbness behind my rib cage, bursting into flames. Maybe there really was a fire inside me, just like Kay had said.

It's funny. People who think a person can't fall completely in love in two days? Maybe they've just never been young. Or maybe they've never been people.

Thinking about it now, I've come to realize the time line itself it just as scarred as the people who live upon it. Some moments we just slide past like they never even matter, but other ones are carved with relevance, and we can never truly escape them. Births and deaths. Tragedies and triumphs. Profound connections and profound separations. These events dig into the time line like points on a map, scarring it like the stitches where we connect to time itself. Some points in time are just too big to pass over, and those are the points we keep coming back to again and again for the rest of our lives.

—

I waited until I was sure my dad was asleep. Then I shoved a bunch of pillows under my blankets and stealthily snuck out the window.

I pedaled like there was no tomorrow. Like I was in the Tour de France, except instead of being encouraged by screaming fans and other bikers, I was pumping down a pitch-black road trying to avoid broken branches, concrete divots, and the occasional vaguely startled raccoon.

Even making good time, the earliest I was going to be able to make it would be between one and one-thirty. Would Izzy still be at the Exxon? Would she think I ditched her? Was she angry? Would she leave without me?

A car barreled upon me from behind. I yielded, but it slowed just ahead. A voice from the back window yelled to me. "Yo, Slater!"

Shit. It was Paul Thurmond. On a list of conversational options, Paul ranked somewhere between lobotomized baboon and potted plant. And I was in a big-time hurry.

The car pulled over. Emerging from four doors simultaneously were Paul, Terry Manilla—Natasha's new boyfriend—and two older dudes from varsity football.

Paul laughed. "Slater! Just the dude I wanted to see! Shouldn't you be, like, home with your nose in a book?"

Caution was imperative if I wanted to get out of there as swiftly as possible. "Hey, Paul," I said. "Hey, Terry. What's up, guys?"

Paul stepped toward me in the way he always did to show how

much bigger he was. "Yo, I heard you got suspended," he said, laughing. "What the fuck, dude? I'm just saying, because I know you think you're so smart and . . ."

I had no time for this. "Whatever," I said. "Look—I have somewhere I really need to be right now."

Apparently, he didn't like that reply. He put his huge mitt on my shoulder, squeezing just enough to hurt. "What the fuck? I'm being all nice, and you're gonna turn around and be a dick about it?" He turned back to his friends to make sure they all would acknowledge how dominant he was. The two older guys laughed, probably just wanting to witness anything out of the ordinary on an autumn Friday night. To his credit, Terry looked uncomfortable.

"You want to talk?" I said. "Great, some other time. But *not now*." I knocked his hand off my shoulder.

Paul looked pissed but then Terry tapped him from behind. "Chill, dude. It's not worth it. Big game tomorrow. Last thing you need is to be busting your hand on some kid's face."

Paul backed off. "Yeah, whatever, man. As if someone like you would have anywhere to be."

I didn't respond, already pedaling away.

—

Using a small penlight, I ignited a small circle of visibility in the woods behind the Exxon and shuffled through the underbrush.

"*Izzy!*" I whispered her name a few times, just loud enough so she could hear me if lurking nearby, though not loud enough that the kids smoking pot behind the Exxon would be alerted.

She was nowhere to be found. I'd blown it. All this talk of *us*, and I'd ditched out on the stakeout. I'd let her down, and in my overactive imagination, she was growing more and more mad at me with every moment.

I should have been watching my step.

The ground became startlingly absent from where my foot anticipated it. All of a sudden, there was a steep indentation in the forest
floor, obscured by a patch of thickets. I plummeted into a pit of darkness, my face hitting a pile of dirt and sticks that were still damp from
rain earlier in the day.

Fortunately, my tumble produced only a few scrapes, nothing
bloody. I got up, and then it hit me.

The pit I had fallen into was the ideal hiding space for someone
who wanted to spy on kids hanging out behind the Exxon.

Between the surrounding brambles and where I'd landed, a thin
slit of space gave the perfect vantage point in the direction of the lot.
The indentation of ground level and the surrounding underbrush rendered me invisible to someone walking even just a few feet in front of
me. Spotlighting the surroundings with my penlight, I thought I could
see shovel marks, as if a person had come to that spot and dug it out. A
chill rocketed inside me, a cold current through my veins. Was I in the
hidey-hole lookout of a serial murderer?

Springing upright, I scrambled up and out, stumbling through the
underbrush. When I blindly collided with what was clearly another
human being, my heart nearly thumped itself out of my throat.

Izzy.

"CJ? Jesus!" She looked startled only for a moment, and then she
laughed. "You look like a tumbleweed," she said.

"I was late," I said sheepishly.

She'd been staking out the Exxon from a dozen yards down, apparently, when she heard the clamor from my falling into the hole. Then I
barreled into her like a jump scare in a horror movie.

As I explained everything that had just happened—my delay in
arrival and my blind search in the woods and my falling into a chill-
ingly suspicious hole—she picked the twigs and leaves out of my hair.
"Did I miss anything?" I asked.

She pointed to the group of kids circled in the parking lot. "The
redheaded girl with the whale tail apparently has a thing for the guy

with the mullet and the denim jacket, but he seems to be more interested in the girl with the tits and the allergies who seems to be more
interested in her compact mirror." Izzy tossed another twig before
narrowing her eyes at something she noticed on my face. "What the
fuck . . .? Don't move."

"What—" Before I could say anything else, she pulled what looked
like small, pale scraps of wood from the hair above my ear.

"What are these?" She squinted in the dark.

My penlight illuminated them on her palm. "They're shells," I said.
"Shells?"

"From sunflower seeds," I explained. "Trust me on this one. I've
played baseball since I was a little kid. You ever look on the bench at a
baseball game? Every dude in the dugout is munching sunflower seeds."

"Gross. I hate sunflower seeds. It's like there's little shell bits catching in your teeth and throat for two days after you eat one."

I was about to joke that kids weren't exactly allowed to chew
tobacco like the Boston Red Sox when a strange sound shut us up.

We both spun instinctively. Branches breaking, maybe a hundred
feet deeper into the woods.

At once, we turned to each other, all blood draining from our faces.

This time, it was most certainly not a jump scare.

This was real. Something else was there.

Something else was in those woods with us.

Chapter 13

PREDATORS AND PREY

THE WOODS AT NIGHT: IN the broken light of the moon, trees and undergrowth loom, their shadows eerie and intimidating. The banal realities of shadows and vegetation become nefarious, almost demonic, in the obscuring darkness.

So this made it all the more shocking when Izzy broke into a sprint—not *away* from whatever made the noise in the forest, but rather *toward* it. Straight into the blackness. Less shocking but equally stupid was the fact I took off myself, joining the pursuit. Chasing after Izzy, chasing after . . . *something*.

During those tense moments, I was consumed by the singular goal of *keep Izzy safe*. I simply ran, uncertain where my feet would land in the dark. Branches whipped at my face. There was no telling what lurked ahead. There's a reason why the woods at night have become an overused horror movie trope. It's fucking terrifying.

Up ahead in the distance, movement was audible. Someone or something was running away. But what? It could have been a deer or whatever. The night was pitch dark. Trees blocked out the moon-light. You really couldn't see a thing.

Our frantic pursuit ended when a tree trunk tripped Izzy up. She rolled into a heap of leaves. Skidding to a halt beside her, I asked if she was OK. She was more pissed off at letting whoever it was get away than she was with the scrapes on her arm.

"C'mon, Izzy," I pleaded. "We can come back tomorrow. Right now, let's just get out of here." Though I still had a good idea of our location, a few minutes deeper into the forest would have left me with no clue what direction was what.

She was petulant. "You seem almost glad that he got away."

"*He*? Did you see a person? It could have been a deer or coyote or whatever. You're being crazy."

"Well, everyone else always ends up thinking I'm crazy. I guess it wouldn't be a surprise if you wound up thinking that, too."

"I didn't say I thought you *were* crazy. I said you were *being* crazy. Sane people act crazy all the time, but that doesn't make them actually crazy."

"What the fuck do *you* know about sane people?" I wasn't sure if she was kidding or not. But also, a pretty fair question.

—

We walked back through the woods to the abandoned factory, pushing through the brambles in an uncomfortable silence. I was dwelling on what Izzy had said about how I thought she was crazy. It was so important to her that I believed in her. Rule number one.

Nagging guilt harangued me. In a sense, she was spot on: I did *not* believe she was reincarnated from a murder victim. I believed she'd invented the entire reincarnation scenario as an elaborate coping mechanism. Did that mean, in essence, I thought she *was* crazy?

"Are you mad at me?" she asked, breaking our silence. "I . . . I shouldn't have snapped at you like that."

"No, I'm not mad at you for that. Heat of the moment. Just forget it."

Ten tense minutes later, we reached the logging mill. Izzy stopped me between a trio of pine trees. "Are you going to tell me what you actually *are* mad at me about? You said, *I'm not mad at you for that.* That pretty much says that you're mad at me about *something*."

She was observant as hell, that was for sure. As for me, I wanted to clam up and let it pass. But Izzy was right. I was furious. All at once, I kind of exploded with it. "What the hell were you thinking back there?"

"What are you talking about?"

"Just running into the woods? What if it *was* the fucking killer? What were you going to do if you caught up? Bite him in the leg?"

For a moment, Izzy looked strangely sheepish, picking at some pine needles, with her stare wavering across the underbrush. "I'd cross that bridge when I came to it."

Incredulously, I pushed the branch out of the space between us, removing her newfound prop. "Are you kidding me?"

"Also, I think you're totally underestimating the human bite force. I read an article about this woman who was attacked in British Columbia by a mountain lion. While the lion was clawing her skull, she lunged forward and bit a huge chunk out of its neck. The animal took off in massive pain. The article had a picture of the mountain lion chunk; the lady kept it. It was pretty gross. The article quoted a scientist who said that humans have a bite force of 162 pounds, which I'm guessing is quite a lot."

"That's actually extremely interesting, and I'm probably going to ask you more about it later, but I'm still pissed off."

"It's like fifty-something more pounds than me, right?"

"Seriously Izzy, what if that was the killer and you caught up to him? He could have killed you too!"

She shot me a glance. Like she was making a big decision. Then she fished in her bag a moment. Her hand emerged with a small pistol.

The wind knocked out of me, I backed up against a tree. "You have a freaking *gun?*"

"Is this going to be an actual conversation, Ceej? Or are you just going to repeat the obvious in question form so I have to repeat the obvious about you repeating the obvious?"

"Is that your plan? Find the killer and kill him before he kills you?"

"There are several possibilities, I guess. But if it comes down to kill or be killed? Well, *be killed* doesn't really strike me as the best option there."

"If your plan is killing someone, I can't be a part of it, Izzy. I'm out." My fingertips felt somehow numbed as I dug them into the bark behind me. "You want me to help you out? Fine. We're going to find this guy. But then we're bringing everything we've got to the police."

"OK, great. Let's role-play. You be the police, and I'll be me. Excuse me, officer? My name is Isabel, but it's not really Isabel. It's Haley Blake. I'm a sixteen-year-old runaway with a rap sheet. I got expelled from school when I was fourteen for stabbing a girl through the cheek with a pen because she was going to beat me up for being a slut. At least with the dudes in school I could choose who to hook up with and when—not like that scumbag my mother dated who'd come into my room at night. I didn't have a choice then. My mom didn't even believe me, why would the school? Why would anyone? Why would the fucking cops believe me if I told them I was reincarnated from the victim of a serial killer? You know what they'd do? Think about it. They'd send me back home or to juvie or a psych ward. It would all be over, don't you get it? That fucker would just keep killing girls, and I'd be the one locked away. I get it, CJ, you're a good human being. You believe that human beings are good, and the world has some moral center that spins it on its fucking axis, like some righteous cosmic force. But it doesn't. Everything is just predators and prey."

Her words seared my skin from the inside out, ugliness billowing around me like a mushroom cloud. I'd only thought about sex in terms of wonder, excitement, and mystery. What Izzy had told me made it dark, an impossibly fast-coming and cataclysmic storm. How could anyone do such horrifying things to her?

I couldn't wrap my mind around it. Couldn't fathom the realization that Izzy's past was worse than even I could have imagined. I didn't even know her by her real name. Who was Haley Blake? Haley was Izzy, but Haley was Izzy as victim. As prey.

She'd stopped being Haley, so she could stop being prey. Izzy was born from the ashes to become a predator of the murderer, real or imagined, who haunted her dreams. Before, I felt fairly certain that Izzy had invented the reincarnation thing to escape a past of abuse. But after what she had just revealed to me? I just didn't realize how inconceivably bad it was. As tough as my life had been, Izzy's had been almost impossibly worse. The swell of emotion ground my mind to a near halt. I could barely come up with the words. Instead, I just stammered softly, "Jesus, Izzy. I . . . I didn't know. I'm so sorry."

"That's exactly what Jesus wanted, for people to be sorry. But you know what? Fuck Jesus. I'm more like God. I only exist if you believe in me. And the only person on this whole damned planet who believes in me right now is you. I mean, I wouldn't be surprised if you didn't anymore. You want to walk away? Then walk away." She looked at the gun in her hand. The metal on the barrel held a slight gleam of moonlight. "I suppose I could use this to make you stay, but that would totally defeat the purpose, right?"

Izzy's words and emotions stood out so strongly to me in the moment that time itself seemed to slow. Everything in that forest seemed ethereal, backlit by the moon. Her skin seemed to almost glow, while the deepness of her eyes kept them tucked tight in shadow. As I scanned the sharp edges around—the silhouettes of trees, the milky darkness past the brambles—my thoughts wrapped around every word she had just said to me.

She said she was like God, in that she only existed if someone believed in her. And truly, did I? Obviously, I believed every revelation she'd made about her actual life, but the reincarnation thing was not something I believed in my heart. Yet, I also felt this was not a *lie*, exactly—but rather a story she'd concocted as a survival mechanism to escape the pain of her actual life story. A device to give her meaning and purpose. To change her self-perceived state from prey to predator. In the end, was this a lie at all?

I didn't believe it was. Not if she believed it. Because my core belief was that Izzy was a good person. And I believed she'd endured a life of pain and somehow come out of it an amazing person—funny and smart and kind and empathetic and bursting with life. The most beautiful person—inside and out, in every conceivable way—I had ever encountered. So did I follow rule number one? Did I believe Izzy, and did I believe *in* Izzy? The answer was easy.

"This is going to sound insane," I said, "but I've never believed in anything like I believe in you."

Izzy stepped toward me. Her voice remained solid, but tears escaped her eyes. "Then promise you won't leave. Just promise. That you won't stop believing in me. Swear you'll believe in me always."

The wind had picked up again. Behind her, the moonlight illuminated the cracked concrete with an unearthly glow. The wetness in her eyes obscured the darkness behind them. My hands trembled for no reason. Everything she wished me to say to her was everything I wished her to say to me.

"I promise," I whispered. "I'll believe in you. Always."

She threw her arms around me and buried her head in my collarbone. "Even after that, CJ?" she asked. "Even after always?"

"Always," I said. I swore it. In my heart, I knew I would never mean anything more. Nothing would ever be more true. "And even after."

Chapter 14

TRACKS

THE NEXT MORNING, IZZY LAUGHED out loud when I met up with her. It had more to do with the shirt and tie I was required to wear, working a later shift at CD World. When she mentioned that my shift didn't start until five, I countered by reminding her that lying to my dad about working a double was how I even managed to show up at all. I had no choice but to leave the house in uniform in order to sell the lie to my father.

Izzy got the final word. "I just don't get why anyone would buy a Ramones album from someone dressed like a car salesman."

We spent the day staking out four more houses. The first belonged to a young couple, the wife about to pop out a baby. They definitely weren't serial killers.

The second housed a single man of appropriate age, but he had a prosthetic arm and leg. Izzy wondered if he had been attacked by a crocodile. I reminded her crocodiles weren't found in Maine. Either way, there was no way he was a serial killer either.

The third house was owned by a husband and wife with three kids and a trampoline. I wondered why so many parents bought their kids trampolines—every summer you'd hear about someone who broke their leg on one. Regardless, no serial killers.

The fourth house intrigued us. There were two large men in their forties. Both wore big, flannel shirts and hunting caps. They were drinking beer in lawn chairs in the front yard. There was a rifle in the cab of the pickup truck in the dirt driveway. The house was neatly tucked into the woods, obscured to any people who did not go out of their way to trespass. Except, of course, Izzy and myself.

Her pink sunglasses rested atop the binoculars. "They're definitely the right age, and neither seem like dudes you'd want to mess with. I wonder which one of them lives here."

"Take a break," I said. She stretched as I peered through the binoculars. The men were having an animated conversation. One accentuated his points with wild, asymmetrical hand gestures. The other just bobbed his head around on his neck a lot while sitting with his fingers in a little pyramid on his lap. When animated guy stood and leaned into head-bobbing guy, I worried they would fight or something. But that's not what happened.

"Neither of these guys is your serial killer," I concluded.

"What makes you say that?" She turned and rammed the binoculars back over her face. "Oh my god, are they making out?"

"It would seem so."

"Aw. It's actually kind of cute."

I chuckled. "Yeah, totally."

Izzy was impressed. "Very progressive. Most guys would be all grossed out by two dudes in love or whatever."

"I don't know," I said. "I guess it's cool for anyone to be in love."

In any case, Izzy's serial murderer preyed upon girls. This was not a search for John Wayne Gacy, so it was another house to cross off the list.

Izzy dropped the binoculars. "OK, it's getting a bit, uh . . ." She made a circle with her left hand and repeatedly jabbed her right index finger in the hole. The gesture was a common one, and it didn't take any time for me to catch on. "Let's bust out of here."

—

Our final stop was back at the Exxon, which Izzy insisted she needed to see in daylight, too. Maybe there would be something in those woods we missed the previous night.

Looking for the pit proved challenging. "It's probably well hidden," I said. Then I realized we'd walked past it twice and not noticed.

But not because it was so difficult to see beneath the brambles. Because someone had already been there and filled the hole in.

The dirt had been freshly packed down, probably with the back of a shovel. Leaves and sticks had been scattered atop and around.

Izzy and I looked at each other with no small amount of mutual concern. One night after we'd chased noises in the woods, not knowing whether it was man or beast making the sounds. The fact that just hours later, the hole had been filled in. It seemed rather indicting evidence that there was a person in those woods with us, and that this person had something to hide.

"Does this mean what I think it means?" I asked.

"It would seem," Izzy said with a frown, "that someone wants to cover their tracks."

—

As I biked us into town, Izzy plotted our immediate future strategy. Four remaining houses on our stakeout list. Also, we needed to revisit the creepy house behind the junkyard. That night, she'd start her reconnaissance of the Exxon, and I'd meet up with her after I got out of work.

Locking my bike in a downtown alley, I told her that her plans needed revision. As we weaved below a clothesline filled with a colorful array of dresses strung up between a pair of fire escapes, I explained how I was uncomfortable with the idea of her staking out the Exxon alone. If the killer was truly using the location as a stalking site, then it was unwise for her to be lying in those woods with her face stuck in binoculars. And the next day, Sunday, it was going to be tough for me to join her as well: I'd promised to spend time with my father, and I had work again later on Sunday night.

"Can't we put off the final stakeouts until Monday?" I asked.

"I'll have my people touch base with your people. Maybe they can pencil something in," she said sarcastically. "Anyway, what do you expect me to do tonight? Hang out with you at the CD store for six hours?"

I shrugged.

"Do they let you listen to whatever you want?"

I nodded.

"Do they have Tom Petty?"

Of course we had Tom Petty, I explained. It might have been a small-town CD store, but we weren't savages.

———

My manager at CD World was, for some reason, named Butch, but he wasn't a terrible guy. He was twenty-one and played bass in a Doors cover band. At first he wasn't too keen on Izzy coming with me to work. Then Izzy discovered the CD sampler along the far wall and slipped on the headphones. After watching her dance in place with her eyes closed and those jeans on for a minute or two, Butch said it was OK, and she could hang out.

Mostly she listened to music and popped outside for cigarettes and shot the shit with me. At one point there were a couple of metalheads checking out the new Warrant album, when she literally snatched it from their hands and replaced it with Iron Maiden. "You don't want to listen to that. That's not metal. That's wussy shit. This is metal, dudes!" They bought the Maiden CD, and she asked Butch if we worked on commission.

Halfway through the shift, I was caught off guard by the sight of my father entering the store. The previous night I'd suspected that he'd suspected I was breaking the terms of my punishment. Was he checking up on me?

He must have anticipated that question. "I was just picking up to-go food at the Chinese place," he said. "I figured I'd stop by and say hello."

With oblivious timing, Izzy chose that moment to bound over, grab my arm, and ask if I had a buck to get a pack of gum. Anxiously, I mumbled introductions.

"This is Izzy," I said, fumbling some coins nervously in my pocket while trying not to make eye contact with either of the parties involved in the introductions. "This is my dad."

"Holy shit! That's your dad?"

My father actually laughed out loud—not a particularly common reaction I'd seen from him lately. "Holy shit, I am Craig's dad," he grinned.

She measured us up. "I can totally see where you get the cool hair!"

My father ran his hand across his scalp. "Well, I um . . . never really thought of it as, you know, *cool* . . ."

"Well, it is," she exclaimed. "And I'm not just comparing you to *that* guy." She gestured at the dude in the corner in a Grateful Dead tie-dye looking through a row of concert bootlegs. He had long, stringy hippie hair on one half of his head, while the other half was being used to flop over the pancake-sized and -shaped bald spot at the crown of his skull. No one would be fooled.

My father laughed again. "Either way, I appreciate the kind words."

After a bit more small talk, during which Izzy bounded back over to a varnished brown standing rack of CDs that held rock T–Z on one side and R&B A–H on the other, I managed to get my father outside.

"Izzy seems really nice," he said. "Is she, um . . .?"

I cut him off. "I have to get back to work, and I swear to everything holy that if you embarrass me right now, I'm going to run away and join the circus."

"I do not miss being a teenager. Not one bit." He swung his car keys around his index finger. We glanced at Izzy, inside the store, now playing air guitar to whatever Motörhead song she was blasting on the sound system. "Try not to be home too late, Craig. Technically, you're still grounded."

—

Butch let me off an hour before close, and I biked Izzy and myself back to the Exxon. She complained about her girl zone every time I hit a bump. The same group of kids were hanging out behind the gas station as the previous night, maybe a few new additions.

Izzy showed me her foldout map of the United States. It was amazing: markings all over. Dates. Names of girls who had gone missing. Different colors were used to note where the disappearances took place and where the bodies had been recovered. She had the whole thing memorized.

"He likes the northern states," Izzy said. The farthest south he'd gone was either Missouri or Colorado. One victim was found at the border of Kentucky and Ohio. One near Wheeling, West Virginia. He didn't seem to be following any particular route, but rather zigzagging across the nation. Oregon in 1971, but not back to the Pacific Northwest until Washington in 1983–1984. The closest was Sacramento in 1975. Michigan was hit twice—Saginaw one year earlier but the Upper Peninsula way back in 1974. This was the fifth foray into New England: Vermont in 1977, Massachusetts in 1981–1982, Rhode Island in 1985, New Hampshire in 1989.

Each location had either one or two murders, and the killer would move on. Izzy guessed that if she couldn't catch him now, he'd head back west. The pattern was the lack of a pattern. A new location, and then the opposite direction.

"I have to get home," I said finally. It had been an hour, and nothing had happened. Izzy protested, until I pointed out that even the stoner kids were going home from the parking lot. "You can't have any stalkers when there's no one left to stalk," I explained.

"You're probably right," she relented. "Anyway, the killer's filled up his stalking hole, so maybe he's done with this location."

I agreed, then stressed that she allow me to walk her home. I was sure as shit not leaving her in those woods alone.

The temperature dropped precipitously. It felt like it was right above freezing. When we got to the mill, I helped Izzy get a fire going. It warmed up a bit, but I was uneasy about biking home while she slept outside in the cold.

"It's OK. I like sleeping under the stars."

"We all sleep under the stars," I countered. "Just most of us prefer a roof between us and them."

She smiled and lit a smoke. It was amazing how she could be so detailed about how to catch a murderer, who had eluded the authorities for two decades, while displaying a complete inability to plan out her own existence more than two days ahead. When I mentioned the upcoming cold snap weather reports were predicting, she admitted she was probably unprepared. When I asked if she had a warmer jacket or sleeping bag, she said she usually just layered up. When I asked how much money she had for food, she said enough to get through the week.

She preferred to change the subject. "Your dad seems nice," she said.

But I didn't want to change the subject. "I . . . may have mentioned something to him about having a friend in a tough situation who needs a place to stay for a while. Maybe, Izzy . . . maybe you could stay at our house."

Her eyes slid toward me, her head still directed straight ahead. "That's very thoughtful of you, CJ. But no. No way."

"We're in Maine, Izzy. It might snow next week."

"I can deal with the cold. What I can't deal with is having to explain my whereabouts and comings and goings to an adult. If you sneak me in for a hot shower while your dad is at work? I'm cool with that. But the last thing I need in my life is grown-ups asking questions: where I'm going. Where I'm from. Why I'm not in school. If it gets too cold,

I might bug you to snag me a couple blankets. But I'm here for a specific purpose, and it's not to play house."

"Play house?"

She stood to face me. There was an uncomfortable coldness to her expression, even as the flames from the campfire reflected in her eyes. "What do you think this is?"

"What do I think what is?"

"What do you think we are?"

"I don't know," I mumbled. "We're friends."

"We *are* friends. But what do you think is going to happen when this whole thing plays out?"

I stood as well, not wanting to look up at her as I considered her question. "I don't know," I admitted. The musty, cracked glass of a blown-out window reflected blurred orange-red reflections of the firelight.

"There are five potential outcomes. I've had plenty of time to think about all the options. All the potential endings. Five outcomes. No more, no less. One—I don't catch the killer, or I find out he was never in Maine. Either way, I pack up my shit and leave to try to catch him in the next place. Quite simply, I'm gone for good."

I attempted to interject, but she cut me off and demanded I let her finish.

"Two, I find the killer and we do what *you* want—we turn him in to the cops. The killer either goes to jail or the cops fuck it up. Either way, the cops aren't going to let a high school runaway back out onto the streets. They're going to contact my wastoid mother in Iowa, and when she doesn't want me, they're going to stick me in some institution or the foster care system or whatever. Likely, back in Iowa. Again, I'm gone for good."

"Izzy—"

"*Three!* Three, I find the killer and do what *I* want—put a fucking bullet in his head. The cops catch me. Best-case scenario, I only go to jail for a few years because I'm a minor. Maybe I tell them about the reincarnation thing so the authorities think I'm nuts, so they send me to a nuthouse instead. Closely related to this is four—I kill the bastard, and the cops *don't* catch me. But the last thing I'm doing is sticking around Maine, waiting for the cops to figure out whodunnit. Are you following me, Ceej? All four scenarios have one thing in common: I'm gone. I'm gone for good, and we're not going to be able to see each other anymore. I'm out of Maine, I'm out of your world, I'm gone for good."

"You said there were five possible outcomes."

"CJ . . . trust me when I tell you that you don't want to know five."

It was like someone had shoved an egg timer in my heart. I hadn't considered that it was just a matter of time until Izzy would be gone. Izzy would be gone, and I'd be stuck inside myself. Alone. Again.

It was all going to happen again.

Abruptly, I said I should go. This new pain I felt was cutting and deep, like nothing I had ever experienced before. Her words rang hollow but resonant in my head, in my chest: *gone for good*. As much as I needed to be with her, in that moment I also needed to get away. Would everything I ever cared about only exist to be taken away?

There was an icy uncertainty looming between us as I began to step away. We agreed to meet the next day before I went to work. I took off the fleece hoodie I wore under my jacket for her to sleep in. It was super comfortable and surprisingly warm. Now it was me who felt cold, but at that point, I scarcely cared or even knew if the chill was originating from inside me or out.

At the edge of the trail, I paused and called back to her. "What's number five?"

She sat down again, face aimed at the sticks crackling in the small circle of heat. "I told you, CJ. You don't want to know option number five."

"It's not *want*. I need to know."

Izzy stared directly into the heart of the fire I had started for her. "Five is . . . I find him, but he gets me before I get him." She considered this a moment, then simply shrugged. "Again . . . gone for good."

Chapter 15

PUZZLE OF SHARDS

OBJECTS ARE LIKE DREAMS: THEY take on meaning but only after we infuse them with this meaning.

My baseball glove, for instance. My dad had given it to me, a thirteenth birthday gift. Any time we'd throw the ball around, he'd wake early to oil my glove. He'd nestle a ball in the webbing and wrap large rubber bands around it. Over time, the leather softened around the shape tucked within.

To him, there were two secrets to a great fielder—a top-notch glove and a top-notch player wearing it. He would say my job was to be the top-notch player, but he made it his responsibility to ensure I had the top-notch glove.

Since Little League, I'd been a better fielder than a hitter. Every year I'd make the traveling team starting lineup. Usually near the bottom of the batting order, but all the coaches wanted me at shortstop. My middle school teammates called me "the human vacuum." A flattering nickname, if not especially catchy. But there was no guarantee that I would make the high school team, not after languishing in baseball inactivity for a full season.

That first year after Carina died, my entire world obscured itself beneath an impenetrable haze. I could scarcely inspire myself to hit the batting cages or prepare for the season. I trained with the team. I tried to keep my life together and remember the things I used to love doing. Things like baseball. But in our opening scrimmage game, I took a called strike one. The pitch was two inches high, but I didn't care. It didn't matter that the pitch was high. It didn't matter the bad pitch was called a strike. None of it mattered. I dropped the bat on the plate and just walked off the field. It was the bottom of the second inning. My season was over. Everything was over. I quit. This was all the way back in the spring, and I hadn't touched a ball or bat since.

My father actively encouraged me to try out again. To him, baseball was family heritage. His father taught him. He taught me. Nothing made him prouder than my turning a screamer up the middle into a double play or lining a base hit to the opposite field or stealing third base clean. Tryouts were months away, and already he'd broken out my mitt. Already he'd started the process of oiling the leather, of greasing the wheels for my return to the competitive world.

—

Sunday morning, I entered the kitchen to dueling aromas of coffee and glove oil. My dad pointed out my glove on the credenza, assuring me it was ready to go.

"Maybe we could go to the batting cages up in Bangor next Friday instead of the movies," he said. He took a sip from his mug and smiled optimistically.

My dad drank his coffee from the same mug every morning. All the rest of our dishes would be used once, then stuck in the dishwasher. But that particular mug was ceramic, a homemade Father's Day present from Carina. In her junior year, she'd taken a pottery elective and excelled. The mug looked as perfect as anything you could buy in the store. It was painted white with *DAD* written in red across either side. A big red heart separated the first *D* from the last in both words. Each time he used it, my father would hand wash it in the sink and carefully dry it before placing it back on the shelf. It even had its own shelf; the rest of the mugs, all uncomfortably stacked and cluttered together on the shelf above.

When he lifted the mug again for another sip, it broke clean off from the handle, splashing a small wave of coffee across his arm. The mug plummeted to the kitchen floor, shattering into a puzzle of shards.

My father sank from his chair. He kneeled on the floor beside the mess: pieces of broken mug, big and small, the perimeter of coffee extending slowly around it like a pool of blood around a shooting victim.

He lifted the largest piece and examined it. A large, mostly intact capital *D*, half a heart broken off beside it. His voice similarly broke a bit as he said, "This can be fixed."

"Dad," I said. The mug had literally broken into dozens of pieces.

He began to carefully place each fragment into a large, plastic sandwich bag. "Do you remember when she gave this to me? I was like, you bought me a mug? I was so impressed when she said she'd *made* it. Then she said she was thinking of majoring in art in college. I told her maybe she should make another mug, but instead of *DAD* she should write *unemployed*. She was always so impractical, you know? Like your mother. But so creative. Like you. There's that ceramics studio in Lincolnville. Maybe they can fix this."

My father held the sandwich baggie like it was filled with priceless gems. He strode past me and out of the house. He didn't bother to wipe the coffee off his arm or the floor, or even to close the front door behind him. I heard his car engine rev up and wheels backing out of the driveway.

My glove sat quietly on the credenza, wrapped in rubber bands, baseball hidden within. I looked at myself, barefoot in pajama pants and a Maine Hockey T-shirt, a big hole over my appendix.

The small pool of dark coffee spread across the white, tiled floor. I supposed I should clean it up or whatever.

I was kneeling with a roll of paper towels in one hand and a bottle of Windex in the other when I was startled by a knock on the screen door. From our kitchen, you could see all the way to the doorway.

"Mrs. Levy?" I was surprised to see my physics teacher standing there.

She asked if she could come inside.

I brushed myself off, tossing the Windex and stained paper towels into the kitchen sink. I must have looked like a hobo. "Sorry, just woke up," I said.

"It's fine. Is your father home?"

"No, he just left."

She looked around. My house seemed to fascinate her. If I had to describe our house, inside or out, I'd go with *relentlessly normal*. We were middle class, neither particularly neat nor sloppy. Our furniture and decor neither ostentatious nor haphazard. Just normal, normal, normal. Maybe this was the source of Mrs. Levy's fascination. Maybe she expected more eccentricity. She apologized for being there. "I suppose you weren't expecting a house call from your science teacher," she said.

My dad had left coffee in the pot, so I poured her one in a store-bought mug no one used anymore. For myself, a glass of orange juice. I asked if she wanted to sit at the kitchen table. She said no, maybe outside, so she could smoke?

In the backyard, Mrs. Levy lit a Camel Light. I always thought Camels tasted like licking cobwebs, but there was no pressing urge to bring it up. I kind of wanted a cigarette myself and asked if she'd mind. Could one get in trouble for smoking with a minor?

"It's fine," she said. "I won't tell anyone. I just came here to talk."

It felt a bit weird, smoking a cigarette in my yard with my teacher. But also, kind of cool. "I haven't gotten much done on my paper this week—"

"I'm not here about your schoolwork," Mrs. Levy interrupted. "I'm here because I'm . . . *concerned* about you."

"I'm OK, I guess," I said. I couldn't help but notice she was wearing blue jeans and a gray thermal. She looked more like she should be playing bass for a Seattle rock band than teaching AP physics. I found that cool too but kept it to myself.

She surveyed the yard and asked what I had been up to when she arrived.

I told her everything. I can't explain why, but all of the pain of that morning was like a knot behind my sternum I was desperate to be free of. I just spilled—the glove, the mug, my father. All of it. Then I felt terrible for telling her, because when I glanced directly at Mrs. Levy again, she was on the verge of crying.

"I'm sorry, I don't know why I said all that," I said. "Anyway, I should . . . thank you."

"Thank me? For what?"

"For standing up for me. To the vice principal. He wanted to give me detention but said you talked to him, and he decided not to. I mean, he wound up doing worse and suspending me anyway when I pretty much told him what a schmuck he was."

"You weren't wrong," she said. "Our vice principal just so happens to be a bit of a schmuck."

A new type of big shock. I was pretty certain Mrs. Levy was technically talking about her boss, right?

"The two things that seem to bother him the most are teenage boys who don't play football and adult women with convictions. You're clearly the first thing, and I'm clearly the second. I didn't *convince* him anything. I cut a deal. I had to agree to pass one of his defensive linemen who has not completed an assignment all semester in exchange for him going easy on you. You can't tell anyone this, CJ. I wish I could say that things worked differently in the grown-up world, but they don't. There are just as many bullies, only the bullies wear ties and titles. Then you went and told him off and got suspended anyway. So I'm left wondering if I'm still bound to my half of the deal. I've been thinking about this a lot. Despite the possible risk, I've pretty much decided not to pass the kid. It could end up costing me a lot. To be honest, I'm not really sure."

An even newer type of even bigger shock. "Why . . . are you telling me this?"

"CJ, there's something that you really, really need to know."

"What?"

Mrs. Levy turned her chair to face me completely. "You're worth fighting for."

"I'm . . . *what?*"

"You. You are worth fighting for. You might not see that, but I do. You're going to have to trust me, OK? It's why I'm here."

The moment made me claustrophobic—not Mrs. Levy, I liked having her there. The fact that she went through the trouble to come to my house, the words she was saying to me—they all felt good. But the moment—the idea that someone would risk something for me—it resonated like invisible walls closing in and threatening to crush both myself and my entire worldview. I was insignificant; invisible. Why would anyone care to fight for *me*?

"When I was your age, I was very close with someone," she explained. "It's not like he reminds me of you, it's not that kind of anecdote. I mean he was incredibly sensitive like you are. But the circumstances were different. He was gay. It's tough enough to grow up that way now, but believe me, it was even less acceptable in the 1970s. Anyway, his parents found out and kicked him out of the house. I was lucky. I grew up in a very open-minded family. I convinced my parents to let him stay with us."

I was mesmerized. As different as her past situation was from my current one, there were striking parallels. Mrs. Levy lit a new cigarette with the fading cherry of the one that was almost finished. How much did this woman smoke? I was only halfway through mine.

She continued, staring past me, as if the memory were replaying itself just past my shoulder. "Again, I don't want you to think I'm telling you this because he reminds me of you. He was completely unique, and so are you. I say this because it's true, but also because he killed himself."

"Oh shit," I said. "I'm . . . sorry."

"It was a long time ago, CJ. But I'm the one who found him. In my bathtub. It was . . . awful. I'll never get it out of my mind. Not for any of the cliché after-school special reasons. I didn't blame myself. I knew it wasn't my fault, and I knew I did everything in my limited adolescent power to help him. I was just mad at the world. He was a good person, who wanted to be happy. It was the world that was mean and unjust. What was the point of a world that would make good people suffer, a world that would then spin around to reward apathy and meanness? Why was my friend dead, while all the people who hurt him for no reason were still able to wake up every day and breathe and feel and laugh? For weeks I couldn't even get out of bed."

We sat in silence a moment before I asked what happened.

"My grandfather was a Holocaust survivor. He lost his entire family when Belgium was occupied by the Nazis. He would never talk about it. Once, he walked into my room and sat on the edge of my bed. He just sat there holding my hand. Finally, I asked him when the pain would go away. I figured if anyone knew, it would be him. I couldn't take it; it was eating me alive from the inside. Just . . . when would it go away? And he said, *Dana, the pain never goes away. You either succumb to it, or you grow bigger. You grow bigger than the grief inside you, too big for the grief to consume.*"

Mrs. Levy stood and inspected her cigarette. "You should probably quit smoking. I mean, so should I. My husband hates it."

I had to laugh. I was feeling overwhelmed by everything else she'd said, but I also didn't know quite how to respond.

She laughed too, but in a moment it dissipated. "I have to go, CJ. I just needed you to know: You're worth fighting for. Most of all, know this: The most important person who needs to be fighting for you? It's not me." She tossed her spent cigarette into the bushes. "It's *you*."

Chapter 16

THE JUNKYARD HOUSE

MINUTES BEFORE BUTCH AND I closed CD World, Izzy appeared at the door. She wore my hoodie under her jacket and the jeans with the hole below the ass. Butch was nervous about letting her hang after he locked the store, but then Izzy said she loved his David Bowie shirt. "*Aladdin Sane* is his third-best album."

"It's his best album, dude," Butch said.

"*Ziggy Stardust* then *Let's Dance* then *Aladdin Sane* then *The Man Who Sold the World*," Izzy insisted.

"*Let's Dance* second? You're off your rocker," Butch said. Then he turned to me and said he guessed it was OK if she hung out while we closed.

With Izzy helping us clean, it only took fifteen minutes to finish all our closing duties. Butch went downstairs to count the register and stick the money in the safe. Izzy took advantage of this time to recount the events of her day to me. She had staked out the remaining houses on our list. Three of them were quickly eliminated. One was owned by an elderly woman. Two she crossed off for racial reasons—an Indian man and an Asian family. She was certain the killer was White. "Not just because of what I see in my dreams, but also the empirical data collected on serial killers. They're almost all White dudes."

"What about the fourth house?"

She was on the fence about it. The house was neatly obscured from view but sprawling and well kept. "Almost a mansion. There were landscapers doing the lawn when I got there. I don't think our killer is hiring landscapers." She reiterated that the one house that truly nailed the profile was the decrepit one we'd found behind the junkyard. Appropriately enough, she was now calling it the Junkyard House.

"So is that where we're going tomorrow?" I asked.

"No," she said, "that's where we're going right *now*."

—

Izzy had sure done her homework.

She'd studied the map and told me she'd found a shortcut through the woods to the Junkyard House. Even I didn't know about that shortcut, and I'd lived in the town my entire life. Within twenty minutes of locking up CD World, we were sneaking to our vantage point behind the pickup truck on cinder blocks.

I whispered something about not climbing under the tarp this time. The moon was barely a mirage behind the cloud cover, nearly pitch-black out.

"Why, are you claustrophobic?" she asked.

"*Shhhh*," I said. The truth was more practical: If someone did catch us spying, I wanted to be able to make a quick getaway.

"OK, fine," Izzy snapped.

Instead of under the tarp, we huddled behind the truck, just a few yards in front of a pile of rusted and discarded car parts. She stared through the binoculars for, like, twenty minutes. I wanted a smoke, but Izzy reminded me of the "no smoking on stakeouts" rule.

"For someone who breaks all the rules, you sure have a lot of them," I grumbled.

Thankfully (and finally), in a hushed tone to match my own careful volume, she took the opportunity to explain more of her rules. To be precise, rule eleven and rule twenty.

Rule eleven was that you needed *grace*. I was taken off guard, because I associated *grace* with religious belief. To her, it meant someone who commanded a strong sense of dignity; someone who would not fall apart in the face of adversity or embarrass you in public when things were not going their way. "No one's probably ever told you this before, but you have a shit ton of grace. It might have something to do with the fact that you repress all of your emotions, but either way, I appreciate it," she said.

"I repress all of my emotions?"

"Chill, Ceej. You pass rule eleven. But now you're threatening to break the undebatable rule, which is rule twenty."

"The undebatable rule?"

"Don't be ridiculously defensive."

"I'm not ridiculously defensive!"

"See? Now you're being defensive about not being defensive."

I couldn't help but chuckle. "The undebatable rule. Genius. Because if you argue whether you actually broke it, then you're actually breaking it."

"Bingo." She handed me the binoculars and asked me to take a turn. Her eyes were getting tired.

Everything about the Junkyard House was suspect. For one thing, who would want to live behind heaps of trash? On one side of us was an actual pile of crushed-up car carcasses. I wondered what kind of machinery it took to pile them like that. A bit closer on the other side was a conical pile of myriad junk—gears and pipes and planks and such—about three yards across and a head taller than I was.

Contributing to the desolate nature of the entire sordid spectacle was the house itself. The roof indented, the siding and paint all cracked. Several of the windows were spiderwebbed, one even shattered. The surrounding grass was obscured beneath weeds, several thigh-high. It was not so much a lawn as a jungle.

The path leading from the road to the ramshackle garage was dirt and gravel. According to the tax records, Izzy said, the house had been recently purchased. Who in their right mind would look at that piece of crap and say they wanted to live there? It was creepy and gross.

Just when I was about to suggest heading home, a light turned on near the front of the house. "Wait a minute," I said. "Someone's inside."

She snagged back the binoculars. We waited in tense silence. After a minute or two, she whispered that there was a crack in one of the blinds. "I'm going to sneak up to get a closer look," she said.

"Are you nuts?" Worried my protest was too audible, I adjusted to a loud whisper. "What's there even to get a closer look at?"

"I'll know it when I see it." Izzy stood and took a few cautious footfalls alongside the back of the truck. All was quiet, but the lit-up window a few yards from the front door was ominous. My pulse accelerated.

The perception versus the actuality of time is a contradiction I'm certain exists exclusively within the human condition. And that next ten to fifteen seconds seemed to take place both within the span of a few blinks of an eye and yet last an eternity.

Izzy turned toward me, probably about to argue. Behind her, the porch light turned on. Before I could get the words out to warn her, the screen door slammed open as if kicked from inside.

"Izzy!" I yelled.

He was illuminated by the porch light. Tall and gangly. Late forties. A receding hairline, graying and matted, greasy and unkempt, and a face full of beard stubble. He wore huge Coke bottle glasses, a filthy undershirt, tattered jeans, and work boots.

And he was pointing a rifle at Izzy's back.

I grabbed Izzy's shoulders and forcibly flung her behind the truck. Her face was frozen in shock as I sent her flying. All I could think was that I had to get her out of range of that gun. She felt like she weighed nothing at all.

I spun back toward the house. I was exposed. The man looked down at his rifle, now aimed at me. He was yelling disconnected curses. None of it made coherent sense.

A sound like a thunderclap. A fiery light ignited around the man.

Inches from my hip, the tail light of the pickup truck exploded. The glass seemed to fly through the air in slow motion.

The next thing I was aware of was being on the ground. I rolled and faced the house. The man was still swearing. We heard him clambering down the stairs from his porch, cocking the release for another shot.

Izzy screamed my name as the man aimed his gun, this time at me.

My only thought was: *Take cover!*

Desperately, I rolled under the car.

Now I was behind the cinder blocks. Another patch of dirt exploded about five yards away. Were these warning shots, or was his aim really that bad?

After that, it felt like time had been literally affected by the terror of the moment. Like everything was occurring in slow motion.

The pickup truck was maybe one hundred feet from the Junkyard House, through an unkempt lawn. I hid under the car, behind the back left wheel. Maybe a military sniper could get me, but it wouldn't be an easy shot. Behind the right back wheel and farther from the house—that's where Izzy was. No one could have made that shot. For the moment, we were out of danger.

"Are you OK?" Izzy whispered to me.

"I think so," I replied. We waited.

Just off the front porch, the man hollered into the night. "You can't get me, you commie alien bastards!" Another shot exploded a patch of grass maybe thirty feet in front of us. "UFO satanists!"

I crawled along the back of the truck to a safer shelter beside Izzy. When I made it, she was brandishing the gun from her bag. I stopped her. "No, Izzy. No."

Izzy lowered the weapon. She looked vividly alarmed but not as frightened as you'd expect a kid to be when a person has just fired a gun at them. What was most frightening of all might have been her look of steely determination.

"I have a better idea," I told her. I called out across the unkempt lawn. "Hey, mister! My friend and I just got lost! We're sorry, OK? Just put down the gun, and we can talk. OK?"

For a moment, all you could hear was the wind.

Then, another shot exploded. It blew up a pile of trash behind the truck and to the left. "Fucking Martian devil worshippers!"

Izzy looked at me, creases of puzzlement bleeding into her expression. *"Martian devil worshippers?"*

This guy was clearly insane and dangerous, but now I seriously doubted he was the cold, calculating serial murderer we'd been searching for. "I don't think this is our guy," I said.

"I *know* it's not our guy," Izzy replied. "But right now that doesn't make us any less screwed."

"OK," I said. "Here's what we're going to do." My attention turned to the huge nearby hill of scrap metal, offering even better cover than the truck. If I distracted the gun-toting lunatic by making a break for it, Izzy would have the chance to escape. The guy couldn't hit a stationary target, so I figured his odds were pretty low of hitting a running one. I wasn't the second-fastest kid on the baseball team for nothing.

I told Izzy to run in the opposite direction, where the woods began. Once she hit the tree cover, she could escape back through the forest. I'd meet her back at the mill once I figured out how to escape from behind the pile of scrap metal.

Izzy glared. "You've figured out how to get me out of here but not how to get *you* out of here?"

"My brain functions incrementally," I said.

"What the fuck are you talking about?"

"Just run for the trees as fast as you can when I say *go.*"

"I'm not letting you make yourself a shooting target in order to . . ."

I ignored her. Instead, I stood up, waving my black jacket like a flag from behind the orange truck. "Hey, mister!" I said. "Let's just chill out and talk, OK?"

"Goddamned demon clones!" Another bullet, who knew where it landed. This was my chance. As he reloaded, I yelled, "GO!" and ran like no tomorrow. It was probably the fastest dash I'd ever run. I just hoped all my body parts would stay intact.

I dove headfirst for safety as another bullet ricocheted somewhere behind. My plan had worked—the shooter was focused on me. Off in the distance, Izzy had reached the woods.

She would be OK.

I saw her dip behind the trees to watch. I gave her a thumbs-up, but she didn't reciprocate.

"Stinking space spies!" Another shot exploded from the barrel, but I didn't hear it hit anything. What I heard instead was the sound of police sirens. Clearly, someone in the vicinity had alerted the cops about gunfire.

"Mister!" I yelled. "The cops are coming! Just put down the gun, or they're going to throw you in jail!"

Another moment of quiet. Then he yelled back: "I know a pretty good lawyer!" He shot at a muffler that was lying in the middle of a dirt path between his house and the junkyard. It would have been his best shot yet, had he only intended it.

The police car whirled onto the scene. Mr. Walker and his blond cop partner ducked behind their open doors, guns drawn.

"Mr. Laughlin!" Mr. Walker bellowed. "For the love of God, drop your weapon!"

The man obeyed. He raised his hands in the air—and started sobbing uncontrollably. The blond cop ran over and kicked the rifle out of reach. Meanwhile, Mr. Walker sprinted to me. He asked if I was OK.

"Yeah, I'm fine."

"You've got some explaining to do, son," he said.

I glanced back. Izzy was still watching from the woods. Mr. Walker's eyes instinctively followed where I was looking. He caught the same glimpse I did, of Izzy turning tail and sprinting away through the woods.

It was then I noticed Izzy's bag, lying behind the pickup truck in full view. Not just any bag—the bag in which she kept her gun. In all the chaos, she must have run off without it.

This bag also did not escape Mr. Walker's attention.

It was going to be a very, very long night.

Chapter 17

TRAPPED IN THE LOOP

ANOTHER POLICE CAR ARRIVED ON the scene, and two other officers searched the premises. They looked like they had been dragged out of bed and weren't even in uniform.

A pit rose from the depths of my stomach as I saw one of them emerge from behind the truck with Izzy's cloth bag, striped, with brown-and-yellow stitching. The other scanned the front porch with an oversized Maglite.

The sirens had been turned off, but the red-and-blue lights on top of the squad cars were still on. They flashed across the discarded metal everywhere in sight. The environs pulsed with colored refractions like some postapocalyptic discotheque. Eventually, they led the still-sobbing shooter into their car and took him away.

He turned out to be not Owen Laughlin, owner of the house and junkyard, but Chester Laughlin, Owen's younger brother. Chester apparently had a variety of mental illnesses and had been in psychiatric care. When he was let out, Owen decided to buy his brother the run-down house right behind his workplace, where he could keep an eye out. But Chester had stopped taking his meds. This was his third run-in with county police in a ten-day span.

Mr. Walker explained all this as he drove us back to the station. At one point, his blond partner turned back to face me. "The question is, what were *you* doing out there," he said. I didn't answer, and Mr.

Walker said nothing. His eyes flashed in the rearview mirror, meeting my own.

My mind raced through contingencies. Most pressing: The police had taken Izzy's bag, and I didn't know if the gun was in it or not. Had she put it back in her bag, or did she have it when she escaped into the woods? If the cops found that gun, the consequences would be dire.

An intense dread clenched in the pit of my stomach. Combined with the waning adrenaline rush of being shot at, I was overcome with a strange pins-and-needles sensation, like your arm when it falls asleep, only the feeling originated in my chest and behind my skull.

Before I'd met Izzy, the worst trouble I'd ever gotten in was negligible: a couple schoolyard fights in junior high. A handful of detentions. Now, in the span of mere days, I'd been suspended from school for telling off the vice principal, stolen a car, broken into a government building, and been shot at by a lunatic while trespassing. And now I was getting picked up by the police for a second time. Maybe I'd been better off before all of this.

Miserable, but invisible. What kind of trouble was I in for now?

—

At the station, I was led to a chair and told to sit down. Mr. Walker and the blond cop went into an office across the large, central room. One of the other cops entered soon after, carrying Izzy's bag. I was left alone in the room with the last cop who had arrived on the scene. He shuffled through some paperwork at a desk a few yards away, pausing at random intervals to shoot me judgmental sidelong glances.

I'm not sure how long I sat there, but it was quite awhile. There was a large clock on the wall, like the clocks in my high school, but the hands just seemed to spin around with no rhyme or reason, and I was too overcome with anxiety to pay real attention to what the numbers said. Still, the only sound aside from the rustling of papers was the ticking of the second hand, which seemed too loud for a clock that size. I rubbed my sweaty palms together as I wondered why the room had to be so brightly lit. The rows of ceiling lights cast the entire room in an unnatural shine.

After some time, the office door across the room opened, and the cop who found the bag emerged, no longer holding the bag. He paid no attention to me, instead heading straight for his partner to tell him they could call it a wrap.

The cop with the paperwork leaned back in his swivel chair. "Good. I've got a six-pack with my name on it; don't want to be stuck babysitting all night."

Maybe fifteen minutes later, Mr. Walker and his blond partner left the office. The two other officers wished them good night. Mr. Walker said a few things to his partner I couldn't hear from across the room, then approached me. "Don't talk, CJ. Just listen. Here's what you're going to say. You were just looking for a place to get alone and make out with that girl. Like an idiot, you took her to the junkyard, where Mr. Laughlin freaked out and started shooting. When they ask about what we found in her bag, you have absolutely no idea."

Oh, no. The gun.

"What . . . did you find?" I asked.

An older man in a flannel shirt and LL Bean vest slapped open the door to the office Mr. Walker had recently emerged from. Judging by his posture and demeanor, he was a person of authority. Mr. Walker's tone changed curiously and suddenly. "Just follow me, son. We need to ask you a few questions," he said as the LL Bean vest man approached from behind.

After being led to an interrogation room, I sat on a metal chair at a metal table. There was a metal loop affixed to the side, presumably for attaching handcuffs. They reminded me of something Izzy had told me from her recurring nightmares.

The man in the LL Bean vest entered, Mr. Walker in tow. He introduced himself as Sheriff Pfeiffer. He was obviously a no-nonsense kind of guy, but he didn't seem initially antagonistic. "First of all, we're glad you're OK. Mr. Laughlin will be taken to where he can get the help he needs. It's very fortunate no one was hurt. Secondly, we've called your father, and he should be here to pick you up just as soon as we ask you a few questions. And lastly, you don't have to answer any questions if you don't want to, but honestly, I don't see where there would be a problem."

I nodded slowly, still somewhat nervous what these questions could possibly be, and if they had anything to do with finding Izzy's gun.

"Officer Walker tells me you went to the junkyard to fool around with a girl. Again, it's technically trespassing, but I don't see why we need to make a big deal about it."

"I'm sorry, sir," I said. "It was a stupid mistake."

"Look . . . Craig?"

"CJ," Mr. Walker corrected him.

"CJ," Sheriff Pfeiffer repeated. "I need to know about the girl you were with, and I need to know about the contents of her bag."

Now I was terrified. It had to be the gun. I gritted my teeth. We were in deep, deep trouble. There was no way to wiggle out of this one.

I concentrated on controlling my breathing. I decided to play it clueless. "Izzy? She's really cool, but I've barely known her a few days. I think she keeps a bunch of girl stuff in her bag. She's always got cigarettes and binoculars."

"Yes, CJ. We found all that. But what do you know about this?"

Mr. Walker placed the bag on the table.

Here it was. The moment of doom.

It had to be the gun, right? We were dead meat.

The sheriff reached in and emerged with a journal. A great relief flooded my senses. Until Sheriff Pfeiffer turned the leather-bound tome to face me, flipping through the pages.

It was Izzy's case journal.

Inside, a litany of newspaper clippings, all about Alicia Russell. A folded up *MISSING* pamphlet, with a photo of Alicia. A hand-drawn map with red *X*'s where Alicia lived and the Exxon station she'd disappeared from. The main connecting road was highlighted yellow. Green *X*s were drawn in the surrounding wooded areas, under the words *BURIAL SITE*? The name and phone number of Alicia's boyfriend. How had Izzy gotten that information? I had no idea. Beneath that, she'd written notes from when she had apparently spoken with him—also something I had no idea about:

- *good-looking kid but kind of annoying*
- *lied & said I was journalism student*
- *says the cops were dicks but couldn't do anything because he had alibis—with people all night, went to diner after Exxon & then slept at friend's house*
- *suspects A. was fucking another guy but doesn't know who*
- *thinks other dude older cuz he found new jewelry in her room, totally expensive shit*
- *says I should ask her best friend, they told each other everything*
- *need to find A.'s best friend, but jackass bf wouldn't tell me more unless I agreed to go home with him—anyway, he def. doesn't give 2 shits about A. either way*

I shook my head. "I have no idea what all that is, sir."

"Then I need to know who this girl is and where I can find her."

My mind ricocheted from strategy to strategy. There was no way this man would even *believe* what was really going on. He'd probably believe a Paul Thurmond type of guy who was motivated by cliché guy things, like hooking up with girls and then spending the rest of the weekend bragging to his friends about it. So I decided to go that route. "Her name's Isabel," I said.

"We're going to need more information than that."

"Sir, I honestly don't know. I don't know where she lives. I don't even know her last name. I met her by Hidden Lake last week. She's superhot and was all flirty, so I told her where I worked, at CD World downtown. She met me at work tonight and said she wanted to hook up. I was like, cool. I couldn't bring her home. So I figured no one would be around at the junkyard and I could . . . *you know*. Like I said, sir, it was a really dumb mistake, and I'm totally sorry." As I fleshed out my hormone-infused lie, I watched Mr. Walker nodding along, as if approving my strategy. Hopefully, that was the case. I felt gross talking about Izzy that way, but it was the only strategy I could think of.

Judging by the sheriff's expression, this strategy was reasonably effective.

"Here's what's going to happen, CJ. We're going to let you off for the trespassing tonight. But we need something small in exchange." He cleared his throat. "We think your little lady may have knowledge about the recent disappearance of a local girl, and it would help us to know what she knows. So the next time you see her, I'm asking you to contact us immediately. Officer Walker says you're a good kid, and we can count on you. So we're counting on you. Don't tell her anything or let on. Just when you see her next, like if she visits you at work again or whatever, find an excuse to get to a phone and call me to tell us where we can find her. It's extremely important." Sheriff Pfeiffer handed me a card displaying his name, a police crest, and a phone number.

I gestured at the array of clippings on the table. "What do you think, sir? That's she's like, hiding Alicia Russell or something?" Playing dumb. I looked over at Mr. Walker, standing behind Sheriff Pfeiffer. It seemed almost as if he was avoiding my eyes. What the hell was going on?

"Sometimes," the sheriff said, "a girl is nice to you, and she looks great and seems great. Pretty girls can fool you; they wear all that stuff to distract from what they're really trying to get out of you. I get it, I was your age once. I don't think you're a bad kid because you went somewhere you shouldn't have been to get some action. But believe me when I tell you this, CJ. This girl? It's possible she's mixed up in things she shouldn't be. You just need to be careful."

His eyes shot holes through me across the table. I was beginning to feel extremely anxious again. Maybe I'd gotten him off our track, but there was still something I didn't understand. "Yes, sir."

"We just need you to do the right thing. Call us so we can talk with her."

"I understand, sir."

He stood. "Good. Then it's settled. I'm going to have Officer Walker explain the whole misunderstanding to your old man so no one comes down too hard on you. And don't sweat this girl, you're young! There's always a prettier one just around the corner, right? You take care of yourself and stay out of trouble. OK, buddy?"

Buddy? Definitely not. Though I was still overcome with relief that no one discovered Izzy's gun, I was equally overcome by unease in the aftershock of my "questioning." Why was the chief of police so interested in Izzy's notebook? Why were they so eager to find Izzy? Was there something in Izzy's notebook that could help with the case of Alicia Russell?

Something in Sheriff Pfeiffer's demeanor unsettled me. Something about his buddying up to me so quickly seemed extremely fishy. Combining that with Mr. Walker essentially *telling* me to lie to him immediately prior to the interrogation sent my head spinning in circles.

There had to be something, or several somethings, I was missing.

—

Once Sheriff Pfeiffer departed, Mr. Walker spoke in a hushed tone. "CJ, I need you to come over as early as possible tomorrow so we can talk. No questions now. Act normal. Your dad should be waiting outside."

What could Mr. Walker possibly "need" to speak to me about? Why was he acting like an undercover operative in a spy movie? What the hell was going on?

My father was plenty pissed off when Mr. Walker led me back into the station's main room.

"Don't be too hard on him," Mr. Walker said. Then Sheriff Pfeiffer reappeared to put his arm around my dad like they were old friends. Though I'm sure they were acquainted—they both worked in the same building, after all—my father was taken off guard by the sheriff's chumminess.

"Boys will be boys!" Pfeiffer exclaimed. "Now Seth, I know CJ broke a few rules, but let's not take this too far. Apparently, this girl's quite a looker, huh? Nothing we wouldn't have done at the same age!"

On the drive home, my father tried to make sense of things. "Look, I understand liking a girl. We've had that talk before. We can have it again. But the junkyard? Sheriff Pfeiffer said there's a mentally ill man who lives there, that he ran outside thinking he was being robbed and started firing his gun up into the air!"

Into the air? Why would the sheriff lie to my father?

"It was certainly loud," I said.

"Well, thank heavens he didn't shoot *at* you."

"Yeah," I said. "Thank heavens."

"I just . . . I know what age you are. If you want to . . . fool around with a girl? Just bring her to the house. Go to the basement. I can't say I'd be especially comfortable with the idea, but better the safety of our house than a junkyard or God knows where else."

I lacked the heart to admit the last time I'd hooked up with a girl actually *was* in our basement—more than a full year before, with Natasha Walker. It was almost funny. But what was *really* funny was that after a night where I'd been shot at by a mentally ill person while hunting down a serial killer, a bunch of grown men had somehow decided I was Casanova.

And where was Izzy now? I hoped she'd gotten away without being followed, and that she was safe out there in her abandoned mill all alone. She was nothing if not clever, so I wasn't necessarily worried about her safety so much as I was worried why the police apparently wanted to find her so badly.

Why would the contents of her bag make the police want her so badly? Thank the stars she still at least had the gun. But how could Izzy's journal be the cause of so much alarm when the Seamont police department had already decided Alicia Russell was a runaway? Could they possibly have some suspicion that Izzy was *right*—that there really was a serial killer running around the county? What was Sheriff Pfeiffer not telling me? Or was there something Izzy wasn't telling me? And Mr. Walker—why was he acting so strangely? Like a top secret super-spy. What was *he* not telling me?

As my father and I went into the house, he took his key from the door and stopped me with a hand on my shoulder. "I understand growing up is tough, and it's been even more difficult for you than for most," he said, placing his long, beige jacket on the highest coat hook. "But some of your decision-making lately isn't exactly making it any easier. I'm guessing you understand this."

"Yes."

"Anyway, I'm glad there was no bail money involved," he said with a grin. I followed him to the kitchen, where he began to fix himself a cup of herbal tea. Instinctively, he reached for his Dad mug. But the realization it wasn't there caused him to flinch, before reaching one shelf higher. "And—although we need to talk more about things tomorrow—this Izzy girl? She seemed nice. I'm, um . . . glad. You know, that you've found someone to . . . spend time with."

"Dad, jeez."

"I'm your dad. You can talk about these things with me."

"Izzy, she . . . I don't know." I thought about it a moment. "She believes in me."

My father did something curious then. In general, he wasn't the most affectionate man, but he put his hand gently on the side of my face and lightly rubbed my cheek with his thumb. It struck me he hadn't done this since I was much younger, and this was the first time he had ever done such a gesture without having to reach down to reach my face. It struck me we were finally pretty much standing at the exact same height.

"So do I," he said. Then he straightened up. "But it's been a crazy night. We can talk tomorrow. For now, you should get some sleep."

I plodded up the stairs, wondering if I would be able to get any sleep at all. My head was a constant, rushing current of the unanswered and the seemingly unanswerable. A million questions, all spiraling down to the same, stupid underlying one:

What the hell had I gotten myself mixed up in?

PART THREE

Chapter 18

LITTLE SECRETS

IN ORDER TO CALL SOMEONE, they need to have a phone. Izzy owned virtually nothing. What was it like, living outside something so basic as the ability to contact someone or have them contact you? It seemed lonely to me, though the more I considered it, the more I realized I probably had not spent more than a few minutes on a call with anyone since it fell apart with Natasha. In a year full of watching essentially all my forms of human connection with anyone whatsoever fray and wither away, the idea of speaking to someone on the phone wasn't close to the top of the list of things I was sad to lose. Still, it would have been nice just to be able to call Izzy—just to let her know I was all right and see if she was, too.

Watching the ceiling fan in my room turn slow circles, I imagined her, all alone, at the abandoned mill. I couldn't sleep.

I thought about sneaking out again to see her. But the night had been eventful enough already, and my best course of action was, obviously, laying low. I had to play this smart. So I slept fitfully, until sunlight finally pierced the blinds.

I met my dad in the kitchen for his morning coffee. I decided to act like the previous night was nothing worth mentioning. And also like it wasn't the weirdest thing ever to see him drink out of some old, navy-blue University of Maine mug instead of Carina's Dad mug. Perhaps as a diversion, I asked him about the Bruins tickets he'd bought us for December.

My father ignored my words, instead saying he thought we needed to talk about Izzy. "There's something I've been thinking about. Is she the person you brought up to me a couple of days ago? Your friend who is having troubles at home?"

I poured myself a large glass of orange juice. "Dad . . . it's complicated."

"Actually, wait. If I'm asking you to be honest with me, I owe you the same honesty back. I'm . . . worried that this new girl is somehow connected to the fact you've been . . . acting out lately."

"*Acting out*?" I hated that term. It was what parents said when they thought you were being a total asshole but didn't actually want to come out and say it.

"I can hardly be happy about having to pick you up at the police station," he said, opening a jar of pickles. It always seemed gross to me how he could eat pickles for breakfast, but it seemed to work for him. "And technically, you're grounded and shouldn't have been out necking with a girl in the first place."

"*Necking*?"

"You know what I mean."

"Dad, 1952 just called. They want you to stop hijacking their naughty phrases." As much as my father bent over backward to indicate how understanding he was, I would have generally preferred high-diving into a cobra pit than discussing anything sexual with him. Confounding this was the fact it was all a lie—I hadn't been with a girl in over a year. Confounding this even more was the abject impossibility of revealing anything remotely resembling the truth. Like, *Don't worry Dad, it's not sex that's going on, we're just hunting for a possible serial killer.*

He frowned at his now-empty U of Maine mug, placing it in the dishwasher. "What is it then? *Smooching*? *Tonsil hockey*?"

"If this conversation doesn't end here, I'm running away from home and joining a druid cult."

"Well, we should really discuss it at some point." My dad grabbed his coat off the back of his chair. "We can talk later, I guess."

As soon as his car pulled away, I snagged my jacket. I'd promised Mr. Walker I'd talk to him first thing.

——

Hurrying out the front door, an unfamiliar wave of paranoia wafted over me. I'd endured numerous feelings after my sister died. Paranoia, however? Not so much.

Yet there I was, peering in windows of parked cars. Could someone be following me? Sheriff Pfeiffer seemed desperate to find Izzy. Suspiciously so. And if I were him, the most sensible way to find Izzy would be to follow me to her doorstep. Little did they know, she didn't even *have* a doorstep. She barely even had a roof.

No one was following me. It was all in my head. Our street was boring and uneventful as ever. I crossed over to the Walker house.

I shouldn't have been surprised when Natasha answered the doorbell. Still, seeing her face managed to jab the air from my lungs.

"Um, hi," I said.

"Is everything OK?"

"This is going to sound strange, but I'm, um . . . kind of here to see your dad."

"You're *what*?"

Mr. Walker appeared at the top of the stairs.

"It's fine, Natasha," he said. "I just asked CJ to come by to discuss a few things." She glanced in confusion from her father to me and back again.

Mr. Walker came down and placed his hand on her shoulder. "Honey? Everything's fine. Go eat your breakfast."

Natasha turned back to me. "I was going to call you this week. Really. I'm so sorry." She offered a smile but not her real one. No teeth, lips pursed. Nervously, she brushed a stray lock of hair from her eyes.

"It's OK," I said.

"You swear?"

"I'm good." It was crazy how adept I was becoming at outright lying. Even to the people I most hated lying to.

She half-smiled again and went off to the kitchen. Mr. Walker led the two of us to his den and shut the door behind us. I sat down across from him, burrowing my work boots in the brown carpeting and eying the bookshelf behind him as he got comfortable in his chair.

Mr. Walker leaned forward and folded his fingers into an upside-down *V*. "I want to start by saying that I have the utmost respect for all the hardships you've been through," he said. "But now you're facing a new one."

"Yes, sir."

Mr. Walker had a very strong stare, but as difficult as it was to look away from him when he spoke, it was usually impossible to discern his emotions. I guess he was what people call a "man's man"—big, strong, and steely. "You don't have to *yes, sir* me. We have something of a situation here, but it's my strong conviction we're on the same side of it."

"I'm . . . not sure I understand, sir. Uh, sorry."

Mr. Walker pushed the air down with a pair of strong hands, a gesture meant to put me at ease. He paused a moment to think, then changed the subject to ask me a question. "Did my daughter ever tell you the reason I became a police officer?"

I shook my head no.

"Most people who've told you they understand the pain you've been through with your sister's death are being disingenuous—they don't. I feel it's important for you to see why I *do* understand. My family was originally from Philadelphia, but my father's company transferred him north to Portland. It wasn't easy for my brother and me. We grew up in a very tight-knit Black neighborhood, and then we found ourselves in, well . . . the Whitest place imaginable. We were no longer Warren and Walter—we were *the Black kids*. But eventually we made friends, found ways to fit in.

"One spring when I was fifteen years old and my brother was seventeen, we were playing stickball outside. We wanted to squeeze one last inning in before dinner. What we didn't know was that two blocks away a convenience store had been robbed, and the description of the thieves was *two Black kids*. When the police came, we had no idea what was happening. I was terrified. One of the cops threw me to the ground, screaming I was under arrest. My brother ran to help me. They shot him."

I said nothing, shocked.

"Four times. The first dropped Warren to his knees. The second dropped him to his belly. And then two more times after that, only God knows why." Mr. Walker stopped, taking a deep breath.

I could tell that part of him was always still there, in that horrific moment. To me it was inconceivable. How could any human being do a terrible thing like that?

"After that, I swore I'd dedicate my life to fighting for what was right, so something like that . . . couldn't happen again. Never. So after high school, I signed up for the police academy. Maybe *I* could give everything I had to make the world a better place—but Warren? My brother never had the chance. So I do know what your pain is. And this is why my heart broke when I saw what you were going through. How helpless you must have felt. This is why, CJ."

I was moved to the core.

"And this is also why we're connected," Mr. Walker said. "Why we're similar creatures. And why we need to help each other now."

Now I was on alert. Was he going to let me know why he'd done what he'd done last night at the police station? A litany of unanswered questions flooded me.

"*Nothing* I'm about to tell you can leave this room," he insisted. "I need to learn something from you, and you need to learn something from me—but no one else can know these things. Not a word. The consequences could be dire for both of us. For your friend Isabel. I saw how you acted at the police station to protect her. It was admirable.

I've never doubted for an instant that you're trustworthy, CJ. But I need your word."

I promised him.

"Good." He placed both hands on his desk and leaned in. With this, he launched into pretty much the craziest shit I'd ever heard.

—

In an unlikely fashion, Alicia Russell's disappearance had initially started out as Mr. Walker's assignment.

It began innocuously enough, when the Exxon clerk on the midnight shift called the police about a young couple having a screaming argument in his parking lot, which was giving him a headache and possibly driving away business.

Mr. Walker showed up probably under ten minutes later, but by that time the argument was no longer happening. All he found was the usual bunch of teenagers hanging out on the weekend, all smelling of pot and booze, and none seeming keen on talking to a police officer.

After a series of questions and threats to take them all to the station if he had to, a girl named Lisa spoke up. She pointed to another boy in the group of teens, a petulant but handsome long-haired kid named Brady. Lisa explained that Brady was dating her best friend, a girl named Alicia Russell. As Lisa told it, Alicia and Brady had gotten into a prolonged and very loud dispute about whether or not she was cheating on him, which only ended when she told him to go screw himself and stormed off in the direction of home—maybe a forty-five-minute walk down the road, into Seamont.

Lisa had offered to walk home with her friend, but apparently Alicia was the type of person to get mad at everything when she was mad at one thing and couldn't be talked into accepting the accompaniment.

It all sounded plausible enough to Mr. Walker, who then turned his line of questioning to Brady, the boyfriend in question. He asked a few questions until he was satisfied there was no physical violence between the couple or threat of any such thing occurring in the future. He then told the teens the party was over, that everyone should head home and sober up.

The group of kids all lived in my town, except for Lisa, who lived in Seamont. Mr. Walker offered to drive her home, figuring there might still be time to pass Alicia on the way and pick her up as well. Safe as it was in that part of Maine, the idea of a girl walking home alone down a highway past midnight wasn't something that sat well with him.

About a mile down the road, Mr. Walker saw something on the shoulder that caught his attention. He pulled over and picked up a red, leather glove. Immediately, Lisa recognized it as one of Alicia's. "It's not cold tonight," she had said. "Maybe it just fell out of her pocket."

After scanning the area by flashlight for a few minutes and not finding anything else of note, Mr. Walker herded Lisa back into the car and drove them to the neighboring town. Before taking Lisa home, he had her direct him to Alicia Russell's house. Apparently, Alicia's mother was working the midnight shift at a truck stop outside Acadia, and it was her stepfather who answered the door. He smelled strongly of alcohol, and his first question upon answering the door was to ask if "the brat had gotten herself in trouble again."

According to Mr. Walker, Alicia's stepfather was too drunk and ornery to answer any questions clearly, and repeatedly claimed that Alicia often didn't come home at night but stayed out for days at a time doing "who knows what."

Before taking Lisa home, Mr. Walker took down her phone number, gave her his card, and insisted she call him to let him know when she saw Alicia next to let him know everything had turned out OK. But unfortunately, Alicia was eighteen—legally, an adult. There wasn't anything to be done just because she got into a spat with her boyfriend and then didn't return home that night.

Maybe two days later, Mr. Walker was at the police station when he received a call from Lisa. She was freaking out and didn't know where else to turn. Apparently, there was still no sign of Alicia. Though it was true Alicia sometimes stayed out days at a time, this time she hadn't shown up for her scheduled shift at the Waldo Mart. Lisa insisted this was behavior she'd never seen from Alicia before.

Mr. Walker explained that if Lisa wanted to file a missing person report, she needed to do it with the Seamont PD; it was out of his jurisdiction. He was, quite frankly, puzzled when her reply was something to the effect that the reason she had called Mr. Walker in the first place was that she could not trust her own town's police.

Having a teenage child of his own, Mr. Walker realized that sometimes logic was not the strong suit of the adolescent mind. He agreed to go to Seamont to check things out at the Russell house. Was it possible that the stepfather, an utterly unlikable man, who held visible disdain for Alicia, had done something violent to her? It couldn't hurt to check, and afterward he could just call it in to the local PD and get things sorted out.

When Mr. Walker arrived at the Russell home, both parents were present. He was greatly disturbed by the mother's apparent apathy and the stepfather's obvious irritation concerning Alicia's whereabouts. Mr. Walker asked if he could look in her room, maybe see if anything there might indicate where Alicia could possibly be. Mr. Walker was distressed that this was not something Alicia's parents had thought to do for themselves.

It was a typical room: clothes, magazines, and posters of rock bands. Mr. Walker searched for hiding places, like out-of-reach drawers and under the mattress. Closet corners. What he found, he told me, raised some suspicion.

"Remember when I drove you home from the cemetery?" he asked. "Your friend, Izzy, mentioned a few things that also stood out to me that day in Alicia's room: suitcase in the closet, unpacked and untouched. Tangled in the bedsprings under her bed, I found a cigar box with a few hundred dollars in cash. That's a lot of money to leave behind for a girl running away from home. There was also a collection of jewelry that seemed extravagant for a teenager who worked part time at the Waldo Mart. One of the items was a bracelet. Though the bracelet wasn't garish, maybe just worth a couple hundred dollars, it was something an older man might purchase to impress a much younger girl. The bracelet had an engraving on the back that said *To my favorite little secret—D.*"

To Mr. Walker, this was more than enough circumstantial evidence to bring this case to the attention of the local police department. His next stop was the Seamont PD, to let them know they might have a missing person case. Again, he was a little unnerved when the officer he was reporting to immediately recognized Alicia Russell's name and . . . laughed. "Alicia's what you would call a *party girl*," he explained. "I don't think we have enough man power to check as many dudes' bedrooms as it might take to find her."

Thoroughly unnerved and unsatisfied by everything he had seen, Mr. Walker decided to make one final stop before leaving town. He recalled where Lisa lived from when he'd dropped her off after the night in question, and things didn't get any less unsettling once she answered the door.

Mr. Walker recalled that she seemed quite nervous, quickly looking around behind him and then ushering him into the house. She was convinced Alicia's disappearance wasn't an accident.

Lisa explained that she knew for certain Alicia was cheating on her boyfriend with an older guy. No, Lisa didn't know his name, only that he was older—and that Alicia had let it slip once that the guy in question was a cop. It had gone on for months, but she'd recently broken it off with him—for chilling reasons.

This officer had taken Alicia out drinking with a group of other cops on a boat. At first, Alicia thought it was awesome—drinking on the harbor, having fun, the center of attention. But things turned ugly.

The men had gotten drunk. Alicia had been drinking too, but soon she began to succumb to an unnatural dizziness. She recalled needing to lie down for a moment, and one of the cops saying something like, "I think the shit in her drink just kicked in."

The last thing she remembered was seeing two of the men standing up and starting to undo their pants. It was not until hours later that Alicia woke up, naked on the floor of the boat, her body and thighs covered in bruises. She began to cry. She stood up and looked around for her clothes. She realized it was well into the morning, and she was all alone on the boat, now anchored at the dock.

Traumatized, Alicia told Lisa that she planned to run away and never look back. She hated her parents and her life and wanted out of small-town Maine for good. She wanted to move to New York City. But she needed money. So she called the cop she'd been dating and demanded a large amount of cash, enough to get out forever. If he didn't pay her, she said, she'd tell his wife everything. Maybe she would even go to the newspapers.

And later that same week, Alicia Russell had gone missing.

—

The next day, Mr. Walker called into the Seamont PD, but they refused to handle Alicia as a missing person case, claiming the parents didn't seem concerned, so there didn't seem any plausible reason they should be.

Infuriated, Mr. Walker devised his own solution. Still having a couple contacts at the *Bangor Daily News* who owed him favors from his days patrolling up there, he asked if the newspaper would run an article about the missing girl. Maybe showing Alicia's photo to thousands of sets of eyes would result in the girl popping up somewhere.

He knew the Seamont PD wouldn't be thrilled, but they also would have no way of knowing it was him who alerted the local media. And thus the article ran in the biggest newspaper in northeast Maine, not coincidentally the same article Izzy would happen to dig up while searching through databases at a library in New Paltz, New York.

Due to the attention the article spotlighted on Alicia Russell, the Seamont PD announced they were launching a formal investigation.

Unfortunately, within two weeks, Alicia still hadn't shown up, and the Seamont PD announced it was their confident belief that because Alicia was unhappy with her home life and relationship, she had simply done what thousands of people did all the time: packed up and hightailed it out of her small town.

"But you didn't buy that," I said. Icy prickles sidled up and down my vertebrae as I fiddled with my keys to prevent my hands from balling into fists.

Mr. Walker leaned back in his chair and rubbed the back of his thick neck. "No, I did not."

I couldn't believe what I was hearing. "You think this policeman killed Alicia to keep her quiet? And that other Seamont cops could be in on it too?"

Mr. Walker stared at me. "I don't know what I think. I only know there's the possibility that Alicia Russell's disappearance is connected to something much . . . darker."

"Jesus Christ," I said. Then I thought of something he'd said. "Do any of those officers have a first name starting with the letter *D*?"

"I was getting to that," Mr. Walker said. One Seamont policeman: Officer Donald Pfeiffer.

The realization punched the air from my chest. "Like . . . like *Sheriff Pfeiffer*?"

"His son." Mr. Walker placed both arms in front of him and leaned in. "So obviously, this is a powder keg. I need to know what your friend Isabel's involvement is in this whole mess—she could be at serious risk. If a Seamont police officer did something to Alicia to protect himself, there's no reason to believe he would stop there. Does your friend, Izzy, have any discernible proof of what those police officers may have done to Alicia?"

Racking my memory, I couldn't come up with a tangible thing. I beat a rhythm on my left palm with my right fist as I fought to come up with something, focusing on the Walker family portrait on the back wall.

"Izzy doesn't know anything about all this—at least not that she's told me. As far as I know, she believes she knows pretty much exactly what happened to Alicia Russell, and it's nothing at all—and I mean *nothing at all*—like what you've told me."

This time, it was Mr. Walker's turn to be stunned. "*What?*"

The knock on the door caused me to jump. Then, Natasha's voice: "Dad? I'm going to school."

His eyes never departing mine, Mr. Walker directed his voice toward the door. "If you want a lift, have your mother drive you. CJ and I apparently aren't done talking just yet."

Chapter 19

ABOVE AND BEYOND

EXPLAINING TO MR. WALKER WHAT had led Izzy to Maine was difficult. Her upbringing, the nightmares, her belief in reincarnation, her discovery of a serial murderer known only as the Keeper of Hearts, and her ensuing quest to find him.

As a fail-safe, I omitted certain details—such as knowing where Izzy lived or how to find her. I said she'd just show up and throw a rock at my window. I also didn't tell him that I knew Izzy's real name. As a police officer with a high moral barometer, I was worried that Mr. Walker would feel impelled to report a homeless girl who was a juvenile. I walked a tightrope: I didn't want to betray Officer Walker's trust—or Izzy's.

He listened intently. Izzy had never said anything whatsoever about Alicia having any connection to a police officer, I explained. Izzy was on an obsessive hunt for a serial killer, one she believed had murdered Alicia Russell and—in a past life—murdered her as well.

When I finished, Mr. Walker just scratched his head. "I thought my story was difficult to believe," he said. "That version might be even more unfathomable."

"It's probably a pretty close call," I admitted. I couldn't tell if he believed me or not.

"I'm going to need some time to process all this," he told me. "In the meantime, I need you to make sure that—wherever your friend Izzy is hiding—she needs to keep her head down and stay hidden. We have reason to suspect a group of police officers sexually assaulted Alicia. Even if none of them is involved in her disappearance, it's possible they all suspect that one of the others is. It wouldn't matter who. Any one of them caught would potentially be catastrophic for *all* of them. This is a little secret these men will protect at any cost."

"What if you convinced those bastards that you believed it was a serial killer, like Izzy does?"

He shook his head. "Any involvement of mine would only arouse suspicion. This is Seamont's case, and officially, the case is closed. Also, the foremost perpetrator and suspect would be Donald Pfeiffer, the son of the sheriff in *my* precinct. We have to wonder whether Sheriff Pfeiffer has knowledge of this too. We have to be extremely careful here."

"Is there some sort of—I don't know—outside organization you could contact and let them know what's going on? Like the FBI or whatever?"

"This is why I asked you if Isabel had any physical proof. Everything we're discussing is completely based on supposition. If I go over the heads of local law enforcement and nothing can be substantiated, all I'm doing is sabotaging my own career and leaving Izzy in more danger than she started out in." Mr. Walker pleaded with me to report back to him with any new information. And he stressed I needed to lay low and keep Izzy hidden at all costs.

"Yes, sir."

At the door, he asked, "Why are you doing this? I mean, *all of this*? It's one thing to really like a girl. I understand that. But what you're choosing to do right now . . . well, it's kind of above and beyond, if you know what I'm saying."

I battled to assemble the scattered pieces of a true answer into a cohesive reply. "I don't know. It doesn't feel like I'm choosing. I *have* to do something. If I don't, I may as well have crawled into Carina's grave at the funeral and let them bury me, too."

Mr. Walker slowly nodded, his eyes never leaving mine. I told him I could see myself out.

—

Needless to say, my next stop was Izzy. Only this time it wasn't as easy as a hike through the woods. I had to escape detection.

First, I went home and turned on all the lights and played my stereo loud enough so that you could hear it in the front yard. Everyone knew I was still suspended from school, so it was imperative I create the illusion of being home all day. I pulled my hoodie completely over my head. Finally, I snuck out the back door.

I scampered from backyard to backyard until I was completely certain no one could have followed me. It occurred to me that I'd come full circle: right back to trying to stay invisible.

When I arrived at the mill, Izzy was outside. She was drying out some recently washed clothes on wood planks. She was wearing a beat-up, hole-pocked sweatshirt. But that was pretty much it. This time, the underwear was sky blue and her socks yellow. I stopped in my tracks.

She glanced up and saw me at the edge of the clearing. She dropped the sock she was wringing on the ground. She barely seemed to notice it. She was frozen.

"Uh, hey, Izzy," I stammered. "I'm sorry, just figured I'd come as soon as I woke and uh . . . I was hoping you wouldn't be mad and . . . well, I didn't know you'd be, um . . ."

She broke into a sprint. Even shoeless, on what must have been pretty sharp gravel and rocks, she really cooked across that clearing. I didn't get it. Was she mad at me about the night before?

Before I could react, she leaped up into the air, landing against my chest, knocking me two feet back, her arms wrapping around my shoulders, her legs wrapping around my waist. She buried her face in my neck. The only thing holding her up was me.

"Look . . . I'm, uh . . . sorry about last night and I guess, um . . ."

"Shut up and let me hold you," she said.

So that's exactly what I did.

—

Izzy wanted to go have coffee at the diner. But I was wary. Local cops often hung out there, and we needed to avoid all cops at all costs.

She frowned when I told her this. "It's not like there's an APB out on me." She stopped to think. "Or is there? You'd better catch me up on what happened last night," she said.

Instead of the diner, I took her to the used bookstore on the outskirts of town. It smelled like sawdust and was typically near empty. They had an espresso machine in the back and a seventy-year-old woman who fixed a super strong Americano. I thought it was a much better choice for us, because it wasn't in one of the strip malls or advertised by a neon sign. It was one of those weird Maine places hidden away in a former living room of a Victorian house.

Izzy and I sat at a corner table speaking in quasi-hushed tones. My first question to her was the obvious one: "Where's your gun? I was scared shitless the cops would find it in your bag."

"It was in my jacket pocket," she said. When she patted the pocket, I realized she was wearing that same jacket, the weapon still tucked inside. She pulled out a millimeter of the handle. I tried to hide my consternation. I didn't like guns. But we were both grateful the weapon hadn't been in her bag when the cops got a hold of it.

"Still, they got my case journal. And my binoculars. I mean, I've committed most of this shit to memory, but good binoculars don't exactly grow on trees." She frowned down at her Americano as she swirled it around her oversized, ceramic mug.

"My dad has binoculars. But I'm not as concerned about your case journal itself as what was in it that seemed to make them so interested." I tapped a nervous staccato on the chipped wood table as I relayed, to the best of my ability, all of the events from my previous night at the police station. "That sheriff sounded incredibly eager to question you. To be honest, it kind of creeped me out."

She blew in her mug, then took a sip. "I'm normally good at this kind of thinking, but to be honest, I have no idea what could be in my notebook that would be a big deal. I mean, Alicia's boyfriend's name and number. The fact Alicia was probably cheating on him with an older dude."

"Yeah, but what if the older dude she was cheating with was an officer of the Seamont PD?"

Her mug hit the table with a clank. "*What?*"

"I haven't gotten to that yet. I'm just trying to put the pieces together myself. To be honest, I didn't really sleep last night." I told her about lying awake in my bed, worried like hell. Watching the ceiling fan turn in slow rotations overhead, hoping she was OK.

"You're the best, CJ, you really are," she said. "But you don't need to worry about me. I've been through a lot, and I'm tough as fuck. I'm not worried about the killer finding me; I'm worried about me not finding him. To be honest, I didn't sleep much last night either. All the time I've put into finding this bastard, and I haven't found jack shit. We've staked out all the houses on our list, and none of them is the killer's. I'm trying to figure out what our next step should be, but I can't. I'm stuck. I was hoping to find this serial killer by finding his lair, but now it doesn't seem possible. I don't know what Plan B is at this point, I really don't."

Seeing Izzy struggling with self-doubt for the first time wasn't an easy thing. It hurt me. But how was I to break the news that, according to what I'd learned from Mr. Walker, there might not be a serial killer to find at all? "Actually," I said, "I may have figured out the next step. Only first I need to tell you about this morning. Because I'm not sure any revelations about where to find the killer even matter anymore."

It wasn't going to be easy to tell Izzy what Mr. Walker had revealed to me. Though his story of a corrupt local police force also stretched the limits of belief, it was still more plausible than Izzy's saga of reincarnation and serial killers. It felt weird that the thought of telling Izzy a serial murderer was probably not actually in the area was somehow going to disappoint her.

"Wait, what did you figure out? I need to hear that first!"

"All right," I conceded, deciding to tell her the good news first. I explained a revelation that had come to me the previous night. Initially, I didn't want to say anything to Izzy for fear of it sounding stupid. But the creeping despair in her prior admission was enough to make me grasp at straws. "You know that big, plastic thing with all the advertising pamphlets against the wall at CD World? I don't usually look at them, but I happened to notice this real estate guide—on the cover was an ad for a farmhouse for sale. So what if the killer is living in something like that? Seems like the perfect place for a serial killer who doesn't want people to know what he's up to. I'm pretty sure the tax records for farmhouses and commercial real estate are in a different file than the ones we looked at at the town hall—which could be why we didn't find it."

"Holy shit!" she exclaimed. "That's genius! We need to break into the records department again and find out what farms have been bought recently!"

"I already know of one. This kid Tommy Moorehead I used to play baseball with moved away early this year. His parents used to farm organic pigs and chickens for the local tourist trap restaurants. I've been there a bunch of times when I was younger: it's a big, old place, just outside town. Looks like something out of *The Wizard of Oz* or whatever. I remember someone saying Tommy's old farmhouse was bought by someone, but I guess I just didn't think of it until I saw the pamphlet."

"Oh my god! I love you!" Izzy sprang up, kissing me. On the lips. My mouth was open a crack because I was surprised by the action of her bounding up to kiss me. Her mouth was open because she was Izzy, which pretty much afforded her the right and the ability to do whatever she wanted whenever she wanted.

Giddy and excited, she said something about having to finish our coffee and get ready for our next stakeout mission. I was focused on a spot on my lower lip that still felt like maybe it was wet. Should I wipe it off? Should I not wipe it off? Should I never, ever wipe off my lips again for as long as I lived?

"Why are you just sitting there like a stiff, old statue? This could be a huge breakthrough! You're a genius!"

"I, uh . . ." There was no getting around it. I needed to reveal my meeting with Mr. Walker. It was the last thing I wanted to do. If there was no serial murderer in Maine, then there was no reason for Izzy to stay. She'd go somewhere else to track him. Telling the truth meant . . . losing her.

But *not* telling her the truth was far worse. She had to be made aware she was potentially in danger. Also of extreme significance was the fact that in all our investigating so far, we'd found absolutely zero evidence of a serial killer. At least Mr. Walker's story could be semi-corroborated by a witness (Lisa) and some suspicious behavior on the part of the Seamont PD.

It really was simple: After hours and hours of digging, Izzy and I had uncovered absolutely nothing of substance. While Mr. Walker's story was tenable enough to clearly concern an experienced police officer, Izzy's story was connected to a belief that she was the reincarnated victim of a serial murderer she'd read about in a book written by someone who ostensibly wanted to sell their book.

Ultimately, was it possible there actually existed a Keeper of Hearts? Sure. Izzy's research skills were really quite impressive, and the idea that a whole lot of physically similar girls in the same age group and general lifestyle were disappearing for no reason seemed quite a coincidence. But what were the odds that Alicia Russell was also a victim of his, if he even existed? Alicia had the right look and lifestyle and a shitty home life, but Mr. Walker's story was just a whole lot more . . . plausible.

Maybe I was best off keeping all options open, at least for now. While doubts were creeping in as to the existence of a serial killer in my town, it was still impossible to rule out *completely*. And since no serial killer meant no more Izzy, keeping this option open was imperative. She was not going to stay just for me. In a life of uncertainty, the one thing she seemed absolutely certain of was that she would never be free of her nightmares—or be free at all—until this serial killer was caught and stopped for good.

If he even existed.

And even if he did exist, only two people seemed convinced of it—a now-dead author and Izzy. The Keeper of Hearts was a theory, a ghost—not on any major media radar, much less the FBI's Most Wanted List. Therefore, if he did exist, he was very, very good at not getting caught. And if he did exist, how the hell would two teenagers be able to accomplish what the best of law enforcement in the United States couldn't? It seemed too remote a possibility to bank on.

Ultimately, the thought I kept going back to was Mr. Walker's warning that Izzy could be in danger. Not from some spectral serial murderer but rather from a far more mundane and believable threat—corrupt police officers trying to hide the secrets of their own wrongdoing. And if Izzy was in danger—even the vaguest possibility of being in danger—I had no choice: I had to let her know. I had to tell her the whole story. Even though the whole story meant potentially driving her away. Away, and out of my life.

Gone for good.

—

I swallowed hard, and then I revealed what Mr. Walker had told me.

Try telling a teenage girl she might have stumbled onto a murderous police conspiracy. Try telling *anyone* their life might be in danger. She listened intently, her expression almost neutral.

We fell silent. Then she said, "Holy fuck."

"Yeah," I said. "Exactly."

I was surprised she wasn't completely freaking out. Then again, this was Isabel Ellison, a.k.a. the self-declared reincarnation of Isabel Ellison, a.k.a. Haley Blake, a.k.a. the most unpredictable person I'd ever met.

Then she asked, "So, who do you think is gonna play us when they make this shit into a movie?"

"What?"

"I totally think they should get Johnny Depp to play you. He's really good at that face you always make. You know the one. Like, *I'm so pure of heart and innocent but also slightly insane, and PS your clothes might magically melt off if I stare at them for long enough!*"

"OK, that's totally not my face," I protested. "And also, did you just hear anything I just said?"

"They'll probably screw it all up and get Juliette Lewis to play me because she has brown hair and similar-sized tits."

"Izzy, listen to me. This is unbelievably serious." It was impossible to wrap my mind around her behavior. Hadn't I just told her, in no small terms, that there might be corrupt police officers who might have killed one girl already, on the hunt for her in the fear she might know something that could expose their crime? But it didn't seem possible to discern what she believed, because in that moment I didn't know what I believed either. Because the more I thought about it, if I really believed her to be in danger, I would have told her to get out of town that very instant. I would certainly not have been drinking coffee with her just a few blocks from downtown. Because sometimes, if what you want more than anything in the world is to believe someone, you will, even if all the logic in that world tells you otherwise. *"I'm* serious. We need to figure this out. What are we going to do now?"

"What do you mean what are we going to do now?" she said, standing. "We're going to go stake out that farmhouse."

Chapter 20

THE FARMHOUSE

SOMETHING WAS OFF ABOUT THE farmhouse.

Nothing overtly suspicious, just . . . suspect. It was in good condition. All was quiet; no one seemed to be home. No cars or trucks outside. The house was huge. Old and Victorian, brown and white wood. Two levels, a porch spanning nearly the entire perimeter. The lawn was in good condition, maybe a bit overgrown. I'd tossed a baseball with my childhood friend Tommy Moorehead on that lawn several times. It hadn't changed.

The house was a quarter mile down an unnamed side road, off the same main road that led to the cemetery where Carina was buried.

The barn and sty were off to the right. When Tommy lived there, there were always pigs and chickens running around, and they were fun to watch. They had also had a cat, a dog, cows, and some goats. Now the sty and the stable were empty and quiet. Barren. The only animal in view was a black bird giving me a vaguely dirty look from the biggest branch of the biggest tree overlooking the house.

"Weird place," Izzy said.

I couldn't quite put my finger on it. Why would someone buy a farm to do absolutely nothing farm related? It's not like there were any crops. The farm was meant for animals. Tommy's mother had a garden where she would grow root vegetables, but that was completely untended now too. "Why would someone who obviously isn't farming need to buy a farm?"

Izzy agreed it was strange—but that didn't mean a homicidal maniac lived there. "But yeah, I guess it's like buying an aquarium when you're allergic to fish."

"You can be allergic to fish?" I wondered aloud.

"But those tire tracks leading up to the garage look fresh, and the lock on the garage seems new. The blinds on all the windows look new too. So it certainly looks like someone is living here, anyway."

"Like, I can see being allergic to eating certain kinds of fish. But like, I'm not so sure you can just be around them in the water and just start sneezing and stuff," I replied.

She gave me a shut-up look but may have been hiding a smirk.

We reclined against the slotted wood fence that surrounded the property, the underbrush tall enough so that we were essentially hidden, out of view.

"I wish I had my binoculars," Izzy said. "Now the cops have them and everything else in my damned bag. I can't see if anyone is inside. Maybe I could creep up and get a better view . . ."

"The last time you had that idea, we wound up getting shot at," I pointed out.

She giggled so hard she snorted. "I'm sorry. It's funny because it's true!"

I finally worked up the nerve to say what I said next: "Izzy? Um, don't you think that, you know . . . Mr. Walker's idea of what happened to Alicia Russell might be a bit more . . . *plausible* than yours?"

She said nothing.

"I mean, people do bad things to people and try not to get caught for it all the time. Even cops. Reincarnation . . . though I'm not saying it's impossible . . . although I am saying it's less likely . . ." I trailed off, feeling like I was talking myself into a corner.

I'd noticed that when Izzy was upset, she avoided eye contact. Her gaze remained fixed on the farmhouse. "I *know* you're not saying you don't believe me."

"Izzy, I can believe everything you've told me—about the serial killer, reincarnation, *everything*—but it doesn't mean that Alicia Russell is one of his victims. It doesn't mean your killer is *here*. We've come up with *nothing*. Yeah, Alicia looks like all those other girls, and her disappearance fits the profile of your killer. But we need to face it: It could be coincidence . . . especially with this new information that those asshole cops may have actually had a compelling motive to do something bad to her. They *raped* her. She *blackmailed* them. You have to see the logic in what I'm saying, right?"

"Yes," she said, quietly. I couldn't tell what she was thinking.

Time passed before she spoke again. "I'll tell you what. Let's go to the library. We can research microfiche of newspapers to see if there are any other disappearances around the country that fit the profile. You might be right. Maybe this is the wrong place. Maybe the Keeper of Hearts isn't in Maine. But I don't think we should completely give up yet. I've been thinking about what you said—it is really strange that someone would buy a farm to *not farm* on. We should stake out this joint again tonight. Will you at least agree to that?"

"Of course. Whatever you want. I'll sneak out at midnight as usual, OK? Meet you at the overlook, as always."

"Tonight together," she agreed. "As always."

I was relieved—maybe because the weight of what I'd just told Izzy was finally off my chest.

I promised to grab my dad's binoculars before meeting her that night, but also reminded her I couldn't go to the library with her, just in case. Lastly, I insisted she avoid the library until after school let out at three o'clock. "It might arouse suspicion, a kid not in school on a school day. Keep in mind, the police are looking for you. What's going for us is none of them know what you look like except Mr. Walker and that blond cop. Even if he gave the rest of the department your description, it's probably just *thin, extremely pretty girl with long, brown hair* or whatever."

I saw her smile. "Did you just say you think I'm pretty?"

"What? No!" I stammered. "I'm . . . just saying that cop probably did."

"Because you can actually read people's minds, and you read his?"

"Izzy, shut up."

"Not just *pretty*. You said *extremely pretty*."

I changed the subject. "Uh, the point is, as long as you don't do anything to draw attention to yourself and as long as they don't catch you with me, you're going to blend in like any girl and be hard to find."

"OK," she said. "So I'll hit the library at three . . . *alone*. But first we have to go back to the mill. Which reminds me, you wouldn't happen to know where I could get a disguise?"

"A what?"

"Well, you said—oh shit!" Izzy exploded to her feet and shook her leg wildly. A small and very startled garter snake flew off into the tall grass. "Fuck!"

I laughed, rising to watch her jump up and down in circles, completely freaked out by the fact there was a snake crawling across her leg. "It's just a garter snake," I said. "They're harmless."

"I! Hate! Snakes!"

"All right, Indiana Jones, take a chill pill." Behind me, my eye was attracted to a sudden movement where previously there had only been stillness. In the farmhouse. In a front window. If only for a second. The curtains moved, what looked like a hand releasing them. There was no way to be sure, but I tackled Izzy to the ground.

"Jesus—there are *snakes*!"

"I thought I saw someone in the house watching us."

"You *what*?"

We stayed completely still for a few minutes. Nothing.

"Izzy, we need to get out of here."

"But you said someone saw us."

"What if they call the cops? Right now our biggest worry is the cops."

"All right," she said. "Let's go. But we're coming back tonight."

She suggested heading back through the woods, just in case. If the police were, indeed, alerted, they'd see us heading back on the road. So yet again, into the woods.

We had to head through a clearing—maybe fifty yards—to reach the tree line. Every few steps, I glanced back over my shoulder at the farmhouse. But I didn't see a thing. No movement, nothing. Was my mind starting to play tricks on me?

Chapter 21

THE SHARK THEORY

IN MY PHYSICS PAPER ON time travel, I talked about the conundrum concerning a person who is bitten by a shark, resulting in a permanent scar. Years later, this person builds a time machine to travel back in time to the day of the shark bite—to prevent it from ever occurring in the first place. After traveling to the past, the future self convinces the younger self not to enter the ocean.

So does the shark bite never occur? Does the scar just disappear? As far as I'd figured it out, my shark theory basically inferred that such a circumstance is *not* possible—which was also probably why my paper was lamentably still unfinished. That afternoon, after agreeing to meet Izzy at the mill, I set myself to the task of completing my paper on time travel.

If you were to build a time machine for the specific reason of going back in time in order to undo an event—well, it creates an impossible paradox. How could something that never occurred exist as a compulsion for building a time machine to prevent it from happening in the first place?

If the shark bite and scar never existed, neither would the time machine. The same time line can't contain the same two events occurring differently—getting bitten by a shark and *not* getting bitten by a shark—ending in the same singular result, which is to say, building the time machine.

My conclusion: The past is immutable.

Events cannot be undone.

Changing the past means changing whatever was the motivation to change that past, fracturing the very time line from its own self. No two differing events, no matter how similar, can result in a precisely identical outcome.

But what of the future?

To the past and the present, the future is still malleable. Anything yet to happen can still be altered by anyone's action, no matter how innocuous this action might seem.

The point is, there are three basic dimensions of time: the past, present, and future. The past can change the present and the future, the present can change the future but not the past, and the future cannot change the present or the past. Once something is done, it is done. Time can be altered, but only if it's ahead of you on the time line.

But. I also had to consider Einstein's theory that time is a curved line—and by mathematical law, any curved line will eventually meet back with itself. This would indicate nothing is really *before* or *after* anything else. It's all just some other point in an unfathomably large circle. So nothing can actually be ahead of you on the time line, because on a circle nothing can be technically "ahead" or "behind." Which creates yet another paradox.

It seemed certain that, like time itself, my physics paper for Mrs. Levy was never, ever going to end.

By the time my father returned home that evening, I was closing in on twenty pages. Instead of answers, everything I theorized led to an endless array of new questions. Not only was I trapped in time, now I was trapped in an inability to make any sense of it.

—

My father was in unusually good spirits, pizza in one hand and briefcase in the other. "I have good news," he said.

He set down the pie on the kitchen table. This was new: Since Carina had died and Mom left, we pretty much always ate in front of the TV.

Curious, I watched as he set out plates, napkins, and glasses. "I'll start at the end," he said, which made me think of my physics paper. "You're no longer suspended from school."

"What?" The suspension was supposed to last the entire week.

"Not only that, but the school is striking the entire episode from your record." He was positively beaming.

I was shocked. "How?"

"It would seem your dad has friends in high places." He smiled, looking proud of what he'd accomplished.

My father worked on the same floor as the mayor's office, and they often chatted about the Red Sox or Patriots or Bruins. Apparently, my father and the mayor had a conversation about me. When the mayor learned the circumstances surrounding my suspension, he was livid. He called Mr. Brackerman's insensitivity regarding my sister appalling. He instantly phoned the superintendent of schools, who accordingly called the principal, who angrily chewed out the vice principal, who reluctantly repealed my suspension, effective immediately.

"Dad . . . wow. I don't know what to say."

He swallowed. "Well, you can start by recognizing that you have an awesome father who will always fight for you, no matter what."

I just chuckled—but I also recognized the truth of what he said. It felt pretty darned good.

After dinner, my father sorted the mail. He handed me a large envelope addressed to me. My dad asked what I thought it could be. I shrugged and opened it.

I unfolded a sketch of myself, drawn in pencil. It was the work of Jillian Sillinger.

It was phenomenal: like a photograph but also kind of abstract, making it look like the image was in motion. She'd drawn it in blue and red pencil—maybe the very ones I'd given to her.

In the sketch, I was outside the school. There was a tree behind me. I was standing up and staring off into the distance. It looked like there was a slight wind blowing my hair a little, and autumn leaves suspended in the air around me. The expression on my face was somewhere between *there* and *far away*.

"We should get that framed; it's amazing. Who drew it?"

"Jillian Sillinger," I said. "That girl I told you about."

"The one with the learning disability? Maybe they were wrong about that. This should be hanging in a gallery. Look, she wrote something on the back."

Turning the picture over, it was strange how messy her handwriting was, especially in light of her artistic acumen. It said: "*CJ your always the nicest person ever and I needed to say thanx.*"

For a moment, I no longer despised anyone who confused *your* with *you're*. I was overcome by a sensation—maybe the world was not such a cruel and unjust place after all.

Maybe, under the dirt and mud, there was always a flower, just striving to push through toward the light.

—

Meeting Izzy at the overlook, we decided it wiser to take the woods to the farmhouse. The main road was risky. I was still worried about cops.

"Cops suck," Izzy said.

"Not all of them. Mr. Walker is the best."

"OK then," Izzy conceded. "*Some* cops suck."

After a short hike, we reached the farmhouse. From the edge of the woods, we crept to the wooden fence. Izzy used the binoculars I'd borrowed from my dad without asking. All was dark, no movement visible.

While I redirected the path of an ant through the grass with a twig, Izzy strategized and scheduled stakeouts for the following day.

"I have to go back to school," I told her, explaining that my father had somehow influenced the mayor to get my suspension repealed.

"Wow, the mayor himself!" Izzy sounded impressed. But I could tell she was also dismayed, because going back to school meant I wouldn't be able to spend days with her. She suggested coming to see me at lunch, but I shied away from the idea of my fugitive friend making a public appearance. Izzy insisted I was overthinking things. "C'mon, Ceej—what's better camouflage for a fugitive teenage girl than showing up at a high school—a building filled with hundreds of teenage girls?" *She should be an FBI profiler*, I thought. Or a lawyer. She could manipulate any argument or debate.

"OK, fine," I said. "Meet me by the football field for lunch." At least we'd have forty minutes together that way.

She lowered the binoculars. "I realize you have a life, but it bugs me we can't spend all our time together. Because, you know. If Mr. Walker is right. That I'm in danger. That the cops are looking for me or whatever. You realize . . . I might have to leave here soon. Really soon."

Gone for good.

The idea was unbearable. "I wish I could go with you," I said, quietly. "We could just travel the country together. See it all, sea to shining sea."

"Catching the bad guys," she said. "Every tonight together."

It was a beautiful thought. I envisioned us driving a convertible, blasting music, and streaming down some scenic highway through the mountains.

"Why don't you?" she asked suddenly. She looked at me.

"What?" My vision was suddenly deflated by reality.

"Just come with," she said. "It would be . . . I don't know. The best thing ever."

I shook my head. "I can't, Izzy. I couldn't do it to my dad. I just couldn't."

"Yeah, I get it," she said. "I'm not saying I don't. But did you ever think that if you live your whole life consumed with doing what's right for others you might never be happy yourself?"

"Maybe," I admitted, unable to shake the sadness from my words. She took the twig from my hands. "I mean, what do *you* want?"

"What do you mean, what do I want?"

"See, most people want a lot of things, and most people know what those things are. The fact you don't even pretend to understand the question proves my point completely."

"I want to find this serial killer before Maine gets too cold for stakeouts."

"CJ, you act like I keep all these secrets, but it's you. If I'm guarded with myself, it's only until I know I can trust the person. But I don't keep secrets *from* myself. It's like—at least one of us understands me, but neither of us understands you."

"I understand me fine," I said, not even understanding exactly why I said it.

"What do you want? I mean, you don't have to know right now. I'm just saying it's something you should . . . I don't know. Think about."

I felt dazed. *Of course I know what I want*, I thought. *I want my sister back alive. I want my mother back home. I want my father back the way he used to be. I want me back the way I used to be. I want Izzy to stay.*

"I . . . I don't know," I said.

"Well, then." Izzy's eyes were twin nebulas, somehow simultaneously pitch black and shining. "Let me know when you do."

———

Walking back through the woods, we were muted and pensive. Izzy finally broke the silence by asking me why my mother had left.

It was a loaded question, one I'd lost sleep over many nights. I gave Izzy my best stab at it.

My mother was fun and irreverent, self-deprecating and edgy. Where my father would lecture Carina or me for misbehaving, my mother would just say *you're being an asshole*. Like, when we were five. She cursed like a sailor, at home and anywhere else. She would ruin movies by yelling at characters who behaved stupidly. She only knew how to cook pasta. She'd talk shit to the opposing parents at my baseball games. Every summer, she'd lie out on the front lawn in a bikini and fight with my father about it. She never knocked before barging into our rooms. She blasted Aerosmith and sang off-key. She'd call herself *Hell Mom* and then go cry in the attic. At the grocery store, she'd open a bag of potato chips and eat the whole thing, forcing the clerk to scan an empty bag. She knew how to ride a skateboard. She bit the erasers off all our pencils. She'd walk into the room while we were watching TV and change the channel without asking, saying what we were watching sucked anyway. She once told us she couldn't take us to the zoo because she was allergic to giraffes. She'd call my father boring and then go cry in the attic. She drove like Mario Andretti. She'd read a Danielle Steel novel and complain it sucked and then go buy another one. She called my father *my handsome anchor*. She'd ask Carina if she was trying to single-handedly keep every eyeliner company on earth in business. She asked me if I was trying to dress like a miniature lumberjack. When Carina tried out for cheerleader in the fifth grade, my mother said pom-poms were a gateway drug to blow jobs. When I mentioned football tryouts, she asked if I was trying out to be the ball. She made fun of us all the time. Before Carina got sick, she'd gotten in the habit of referring to the two of us as *Teen Monster and Space Boy*. She told Carina her taste in boys ranged from dorky to total jackass. She'd walk in on Natasha and me kissing and say to her, *I don't know what you see in him, you're socially competent*. But she loved us. She loved us so much. Sometimes she'd just stare at me, and I'd ask her to stop, but she'd say she just couldn't believe she'd somehow made something so beautiful.

When Carina died, it took three people to hold my mother upright during the funeral. Halfway through, she just started uncontrollably sobbing. *Why couldn't it have been me instead?*

We were sitting shiva a day later when a couple who lived down the street said something to her about God's plan for Carina. My mother went downright ballistic, yelling *fuck your fucking god* and stuff that was even worse, until they pretty much dropped their casserole and ran out of the house.

And then she started drinking again. And the drugs. And then she left.

By the time I'd finished my sordid tale, we'd arrived at the logging mill. Izzy was visibly moved. "I'm so sorry," she said. "Your mother shouldn't have left you."

Immediately, I stammered out, "It's not her fault. It's not her fault Carina got cancer. It wasn't her fault she could not handle Carina's death. I should have . . . I don't know . . ."

"It wasn't your fault, either." Slowly, she reached for me.

Something in me made me pull away, something deep, which felt on the verge of shattering into a million pieces. "My brain knows it wasn't. But my heart can be an asshole."

"She's still supposed to be your mom. She's still supposed to be . . . there."

"It's my job to be there! That's my job! I have to be the strong one! Me!" I was crying. Why was I such a wimp? I hated myself for it, but I couldn't help myself.

"Why?" She took my hand in hers. "Why is it your job?"

"I don't know," I said. "It just is."

"It's not," she said. "And your mother shouldn't have disappeared."

I considered this. "Everybody disappears," I said. "You will too."

She thought a moment, her eyes glistening. "Name any place in America," she said.

"What?"

"Any place. We're going to make a pact right now. On this date, in three years when we're both over eighteen, we're going to meet there. So you can't say like *the Grand Canyon* because it's frickin' huge, and I might not be able to find you. Say something specific, like the top of the Seattle Space Needle or in the Statue of Liberty's left eyeball."

"OK," I sniffed. "The Statue of Liberty's left eyeball."

Izzy lifted our conjoined hands, so they were just below her chin. She lightly ran a finger along the lines of separation between our knuckles. Finally, she raised them even higher, softly brushing the backs of my fingers against her lips. "Good," she said. "And don't be late. Because, you know. I'm thinking I'm finally going to start taking punctuality seriously in my later teens."

Chapter 22

BRICK

I WASN'T EXACTLY LOOKING FORWARD to going back to school. I had no desire to discuss my suspension, even though everyone else would want to hear about it. I didn't want to run into Vice Principal Brackerman in the hallways—he was probably absolutely livid about the mayor overriding him. I simply hoped the day would pass as uneventfully as possible.

Homeroom proved a disturbing portent of the day to come.

Paul Thurmond brandished the cover of the sports page—a big article about him leading our high school team toward a first-ever state championship. A few friends high-fived him as I sat. "Hey, Slater! You see this shit? When's the last time you had your photo in the newspaper?"

"Any day now," I said drily. I mean, it was a local paper with a circulation of about jack shit. Not exactly *Sports Illustrated*.

"Coach B says Penn State and Miami are sending scouts to the next game. Unless you get Coach B fired by snitching like a little pussy."

I couldn't believe it: Had Brackerman actually told the football team about what happened with the mayor? Jesus! I might as well have been wearing a bull's-eye. I turned to the blackboard and squeezed the life out of my pen.

Paul was far from finished. "Hey, where's your main bitch Jillian? You bang her so hard she couldn't walk to school today?"

I glanced over to Jillian's desk. It was empty. I said nothing.

"You listening, Slater? I'm giving you advice." He slapped the back of my head. It hurt. "You should keep better tabs on your girlfriend."

Finally, I turned to face him. "I think we have different definitions of *girlfriend*. To me, it's not something you have to inflate first."

A couple of guys laughed, immediately stopping when Paul glared in their directions. Then the bell rang, and I was out of the classroom and halfway down the hall before it finished ringing.

—

In English class, Kay Nguyen kept staring at me. Not like the way a girl looks at a boy. More like the way a doctor looks at an X-ray.

After class, she blocked me in the hall. "CJ," she said, "I've been thinking."

"When are you ever *not* thinking?" I said. "Your brain is like a NASA supercomputer."

"I mean about you. I've decided you need to assert yourself more. College is only a few years away, but there's still time for you to make a top school, where you belong."

"I'm—well, flattered you think so. But I'm not sure I'm really cut out for all those straight A's. Maybe you're projecting your own future onto mine."

"This is exactly the type of nonsense that makes me want to sling-shot you to the moon."

I opened my mouth to protest and she shushed me, claiming we only had three minutes until our next class. "You haven't competed in math league for two years, even though you always finished second, only to me. You're the best writer in our grade, but you haven't contributed to the school paper since middle school. Yesterday, I pulled a few strings. You're now officially signed up for both activities."

I couldn't help but laugh. "Don't you think you should have asked me first?"

"Also the literary magazine," she said flatly. "And I forged your signature on the board for baseball tryouts, even though it's my personal belief that sports are for barbarians. I understand you were pretty good at them."

"Please tell me you're joking."

"I was only joking about wanting to slingshot you to the moon. Technically, it's impossible to slingshot a person such a distance. I thought you'd find it funny."

"I did."

"Thank you."

"But you, um . . . really signed me up for all that shit?"

Angrily, she poked me in the sternum with the eraser of her pencil. "It's not *shit*. It's exactly the type of extracurricular activity college admissions boards seek. They want incoming freshmen to be well rounded, not just overintelligent underachievers who always have headphones on and sit around brooding all day."

I scratched my head. "I'm . . . genuinely not sure if I should thank you or be really mad right now."

She drilled the eraser into my chest. "You should thank me."

I chuckled incredulously, pushing her pencil off my person. "And what if I'm actually mad?"

"Then I'm going to slingshot you to the moon."

For a moment we just stared each other down. Then suddenly, the bell rang. Kay balanced the pencil behind her ear. "This is the first class I'm going to be late for this year. It's all your fault." With that, she spun away.

Just before she reached her classroom door, I called her name. She turned to face me, somewhat impatiently.

"Thank you," I said.

Uncommon as it was for her, Kay smiled brightly. "You're welcome," she said.

She disappeared into her class, and I turned in the other direction, my own destination still a few doors away.

—

Mrs. Levy greeted me with a beaming smile. "Welcome back!"

"Hey, Mrs. Levy," I said.

At the blackboard, she discussed Richard Feynman and quantum physics—something in which I was already well versed. Mrs. Levy had given me two books by Feynman at the start of the semester when she realized how quickly I was burning through all the required reading assignments. Not even just to borrow, but to keep. I liked his writing style. And she'd scrawled a lot of cool, and sometimes funny, notes in the margins. A couple times during class that day she caught my eye and smiled. I suspected she was happier about my suspension getting repealed than I was.

After class, I approached her desk.

"Is this about your time travel paper?" she asked.

"Not exactly."

"How long is it now, anyway?"

"Twenty-two pages," I admitted.

"Whoa, nellie," she said.

"Maybe you can dedicate your entire summer vacation to grading it and then give it back next year."

She laughed. "Is it just me, or do you seem different?"

"Different?"

"I don't know. More . . . self-assured, maybe?"

It was a mystery how to answer such an observation. Was what Mrs. Levy said true? I wasn't sure about that. On the other hand, every single thought I had didn't feel stupid or pointless to me as soon as it occurred. Was it because I mattered to Izzy, that maybe I was beginning to matter to myself?

Instead of responding to Mrs. Levy, I shrugged and mentioned why I was there in the first place, which was to ask her if I could borrow some matches. My lighter had died.

She passed it stealthily. The students from her ensuing class were already filing in. "As long as I don't think it's for any illicit activities, like arson or, I suppose, underaged smoking? Well, I don't think there's a rule against it," she remarked.

I took the matches from her. "Breaking rules is the type of thing I would never, ever even remotely consider."

—

The teacher was late for my next class, which was history. After a while, students started wondering what was up. A girl in the back said maybe the teachers were meeting about Jillian Sillinger.

I spun in my desk. "What about her?"

"Oh my god, you didn't hear?" She leaped up from her desk and toward me. "You know how Sandy Manning does work-study nursing at the hospital? Well, she was there this morning, and she saw them taking Jillian out of an ambulance. The rumor is she slit her wrists."

"She . . . *what?*"

"From what I hear, her mother found her in time. They say she's going to be OK and live and stuff. But it's just so sad, isn't it? What would make someone do that?"

The teacher came in and class started, but I was in a haze. I was shocked and saddened by the awful news. Was there anything I could do? Should I visit Jillian in the hospital? Should I bring flowers? What was the right thing to do or say in such an awful situation?

I thought of the drawing she'd sent me. *I needed to say thanx.* Was it some sort of suicide note, and I was just too stupid to realize?

If I just made it through one more class, lunch was next. And Izzy was coming to meet me by the field behind the school.

She was the one person who would understand. The one person capable of understanding *me.*

Until Izzy, my pain had nowhere to go. I'd trap it inside and it would burn like acid, eating me away from the inside out. It hung inside me like a toxic, weighted mist. Now I had someone. Now I could release some of the pain, share it with someone who understood. It made all the difference in the world not to be alone.

Maybe I was no longer alone.

Maybe I hadn't been invisible all along. Maybe there just hadn't been anyone there to see.

—

For lunch, I'd packed two bagels with cream cheese and a pair of Snapple iced teas. I figured maybe Izzy would be hungry too. I hustled out of the building, barely conscious of my surroundings. All I could think was that I needed to see Izzy. Seeing her would make everything all right, if only for a little while.

Halfway between the school and the football field, something hit me suddenly and violently in the back. I almost fell on my face. The bag with the bagels went flying out of my hand. The iced teas soared through the air, smashing into an equipment shed under construction. They careened off the wall and shattered on some tools. I staggered to face what hit me.

It was Paul Thurmond. Behind him were three other guys from the football team. Filing behind them were about a dozen other students, probably along to witness the carnage. The football guys were all calling me a snitch. They weren't going to let some punk ruin their shot at a state championship. Who the hell did I think I was?

Any one of them could have kicked my ass. Their faces were all split by rage, yelling insults. Clearly, getting their football coach in trouble was a personal attack. I was somehow trying to ruin their championship. I was some nobody, trying to rob them of the glory they felt entitled to.

But I was even angrier. "When the hell are you going to grow up?" It surprised him. I was talking about Jillian.

"You mean your girlfriend, Slater? Do you think *that* would make the front page of the paper if she died? No one cares. *We're* putting this town on the fucking map! And you want to ruin it for everyone in town by trying to get Coach B fired? Who the fuck do you think you are?" He stepped toward me menacingly, pointing his thick finger at my chest.

I had to keep it together. I gestured toward the scattered students, eating their lunch outside. "So what now? You're going to beat me up with a bunch of witnesses and get suspended from school before the playoffs?"

Paul laughed. "Coach basically told us at practice yesterday: as long as you don't end up dead or in traction? Well, if nobody says nothing, then how do we know it even really happened?"

It stunned me. Bullies begetting more bullies. What the fuck was wrong with the world?

"A girl almost *died* today. Does that even register? Do you even care at all?"

He laughed again, uglier this time. "What's the world without one more fucking retard?"

Maybe Paul wasn't the only person who had a problem with anger. With everything I'd bottled up inside, I was a torrent raging inside a shell of skin and bone. Paul was just the lit match hitting the fuse.

The next thing I knew, I had punched Paul Thurmond in the face. Hard.

I was as surprised as he was. A hush fell over the people gathered around. Paul looked more insulted than physically injured. He reached up to wipe off his nose. He noticed the trickle of blood on his hand. Then his face changed.

The next thing I knew, I was flying through the air. Then I was rolling around the ground, the air knocked from my chest. It felt like a battering ram was slamming my stomach and ribs, and I tried my hardest to shield my face. I was getting slaughtered.

Nobody else joined in. Paul's friends laughed and egged him on. More people had gathered, but no one lifted a hand to stop the carnage.

I was pinned on the ground. Paul got my left arm down with his right hand and wrapped his left hand around my throat. I tried to pull it off my neck with my free hand, but he was too strong. I didn't even feel the physical pain at that point. I was just humiliated. Everyone watching me. No one helping. A strange rage roiled inside me. I was no longer pissed off at Paul because I wanted him to shut up. It was deeper. It was abject fury. He was holding down a stick of dynamite.

But he was just too much stronger. He turned to his audience. "Here's what's gonna happen, Slater. You're going to say you're sorry and that you'll never mess with Coach B or the football team again. Then you're going to say: *Paul, you are the king, and I am just a stupid, little pussy.* You do that? I get up and we're done here. But if you don't? I punch you in the face. You got that? OK, let's try it out for real. Say it."

I said nothing.

"I said, *say it.*"

My free fingers scratched through the gravel for something, any-thing. His fist crashed into my face. I felt dizzy and nauseous.

"You're really not too smart, Slater. Let's try again. Say it!"

"Fuck you, you piece of shit," I said.

"You got a dirty mouth, huh? I'll show you a fucking dirty mouth, Slater." He scooped up a fistful of dirt and gravel. He pinned my right arm down with his knee and shoved the dirt and rocks into my mouth. "Eat it!" he yelled. I was choking, I couldn't breathe. Small rocks grated against my teeth.

Paul glared. "C'mon, swallow, you dumb . . ."

Suddenly everyone turned to a commotion behind them. It was Izzy, sprinting over from the field, yelling. She must have come looking for me and then seen what was going on from outside the bleachers.

Paul's attention slipped. I felt his knee slide off my right arm. I took advantage of his distraction. I felt something hard and rough and wrapped my right hand around it. In an instant I spun free, using the rock or whatever to smash down on Paul's right hand.

"Get the fuck off of me!" I yelled, hammering the object onto his hand with every ounce of strength I had in me.

As I scrambled backward, away from Paul's grasp, I realized he was screaming.

He fell back, sitting on his haunches. He held his right hand tightly in his left hand. All at once, a geyser of blood started pouring over his hands, down both arms and into his lap and the dirt below.

I pushed myself to my feet—and then I noticed what had been in my right hand. It was half a brick, jagged where it was broken off, sharp as a knife at the edge, and now covered in Paul's blood. As I rolled out from him to spring to my feet, I noticed something strange, surrounded by a small, red pool on the gravel.

Paul's right pinky finger.

Everybody saw at once. Paul screamed. The crowd of now more than twenty people fell silent, their mouths open in shock.

I took off as fast as I could, staggering, coughing out dirt. I caught Izzy yards before she reached the crowd.

"What happened?" she yelled, looking at me.

"We have to get the hell out of here," I said, grabbing her arm. We sprinted off across the field toward the woods.

"Where are we going?"

"I don't know. Just hurry. I think I need to get out of town."

Chapter 23

SONICALLY REDUCED

EVEN THE SMALLEST CRUELTY OR kindness can change the course of time. It was an important lesson for me. And for Paul? Well, I certainly wasn't planning on cutting his pinky off, but again, everything might have been different if he had just given Jillian Sillinger her pencil back.

Izzy and I rushed back through the woods, toward the abandoned mill. We both agreed it might be a good idea to get out of town as quickly as possible. Could you be arrested for cutting off someone's finger with a jagged brick? And would the entire high school football team come after me now that I was responsible for disfiguring their quarterback and ruining their chance at a state championship?

It probably wasn't the most prudent idea to just wait around and find out. We formulated an escape plan as we rushed through the underbrush, rays of scattered sunlight illuminating our path beneath the pines.

First we had to get Izzy's stuff, and then mine. And then we had to figure a way out of town. As we hustled through the maze of trees, I explained to Izzy all the events that had just transpired. As Izzy was commenting on how bonkers it was that I had just chopped off someone's finger, I was undermined by a sudden spell of dizziness and nausea.

I stumbled, catching myself on the corroded bark of a beech tree. Izzy hurried to my side. She lifted my torn shirt, revealing a disturbing pattern of bruises. Gently, she placed a finger on what felt like swelling around my eye. "You look like you've been hit by a bus," she remarked.

"That's what it feels like."

"We're almost at the mill. You can sit down there for a while."

"There's no time." I was panicked. We needed to figure how to get me out of town—someone was bound to have called the cops, right? "I'm trying to figure out a plan, but my head really hurts."

She peered at my face. "Whoa, your retinas are doing the mambo. I think maybe you have a concussion."

"Thank you, Major Obvious," I mumbled.

"That's Colonel Obvious," she said. "I've been promoted again."

—

Izzy took the reins, planning everything. I was too woozy to think straight.

After getting her stuff from the mill, we rushed back through the forest toward my house.

I was scared to go home—wasn't that the first place the cops would come looking? She insisted we had some time to play with. Small-town cops weren't exactly lightning fast, and it wasn't like anyone had been murdered. We needed cash, and my money was at my house.

We cut through neighbors' yards until winding up behind a house diagonally across the street from mine. "Looks like the coast is clear," Izzy observed. "Let's motor."

We snuck in through the back door, just in case. I mentioned we needed to be quick, that school was bound to call my father at some point, and this was obviously the first place he'd come looking for me.

I led Izzy to my room, where I grabbed my money from a desk drawer and quickly stuffed a bag with some clothes. Izzy told me to go the bathroom and clean up and change, cautioning me to make it quick.

"Then what? Are we going to head to the bus station?"

"No way. That's asking to get caught. We don't know the bus schedule, and if I'm the cops, the first thing I do when trying to catch someone who's a flight risk is check the bus station."

In the bathroom, I peeled off my shredded clothing and jumped into the shower. The warm water felt good against my scraped-up skin, but I knew I didn't have the luxury of staying there long. I watched a moment as the water turned pink on its path down my body before escaping in a sanguine vortex into the depths of the drain.

Using my hand to wipe a circle of fog from the mirror, I was taken aback by my reflection. My left eye was completely purple and blue, swollen half-shut. The left side of my face, from my temple to my jawline, was discolored and bruised. I'd been hit, and I'd been hit hard.

After changing, I left the bathroom and grabbed my bag from my room. Izzy was no longer upstairs. At the foot of the stairs, I looked over and caught an anomaly in my sight line.

Carina's door had been left slightly ajar.

It was a door that hadn't been opened by anyone in one full year. Even in my concussed state, it was not much of a mystery who had thought to enter.

Something about it seemed wrong. The door that was always closed, now open. The door was in the wrong state of open/closedness and needed to be shut completely. I reached to the knob and was about to pull it back when something deep inside me gave me pause.

Instead of pulling, I found myself pushing. And I stepped inside.

The room was cast in a lavender glow due to the sunlight bleeding through the purple curtains. Purple was Carina's favorite color. I hadn't thought of that in some time. When my parents brought her flowers to liven up her hospital room, they always made sure that violets were part of the arrangement.

I glanced around. Her bed, neatly made. The comforter perfectly smoothed, purple to match the curtains, but with light dust scattered across it, highlighted by the sunlight squeezing in through the covered windows. The mirror over her desk, small light bulbs fixated in a square around it. The posters on the walls of her favorite celebrity entertainers—Prince and Madonna and Keanu Reeves. The print over her desk of her favorite movie, *When Harry Met Sally.* The black-and-white framed print over her bed—a school of dolphins leaping out of the ocean, in almost-choreographed unison. She'd loved that picture, which I'd saved up a month of allowance to buy her from the print shop for her fourteenth birthday.

As I closed the door behind me, I paused, noticing a framed photograph on her desk between a still-open tube of long-dried-up ChapStick and a purple ballpoint pen. A silver metallic frame of a six-by-nine-inch photograph, taken just months before she was diagnosed. The two of us at a carnival, arms around each other, both smiling ear to ear. She was holding up a stuffed elephant I'd won her by throwing five straight baseballs through a detached toilet seat, held up by a pair of ropes in one of the gaming booths.

I clicked the door softly shut and headed downstairs.

Izzy awaited me at the living room table with a paper and pen. "Now, write your dad a note."

"What?"

"Tell him you're fine and you'll call later, but you needed to go away for a bit. You told me he'd be a wreck if you ever left."

"Well yeah, but . . ."

She pulled her watch out of a pocket, the one lacking straps. "And hurry. The cops have probably made it to the school already, which makes your house the obvious next stop." She displayed a sheet of paper. "See? I wrote my note, now you write yours."

"What's *your* note?" I asked.

"Just another part of the plan," she said.

Once I completed the assigned task, she quickly placed my note obviously as possible, on the floor just inside the front door.

—

Outside Remy Ward's house, we hid in the bushes to make sure he wasn't lurking around anywhere.

"Please don't tell me we're stealing Remy Ward's car again," I said.

"Of course we're stealing Remy Ward's car again," she said. "But maybe I can stall him telling anyone about it."

She displayed her note: *You Hot Studly Beast Remy, I totally appreciate you saying it was OK if I borrow your car for a day or two. You were so amazing in bed the other night! At first I thought you'd be too drunk, but wow! Anyway, I'll bring it back with a full tank soon! XOXOX, Your Super Secret Sexy Baby Doll.* Before I could say anything, Izzy zipped up to the door and taped the note to it.

She surprised me by getting in the driver's seat of the car, where she found the keys dangling in the ignition. I got in the passenger side and asked, "You really think your note will work?"

"You said he's always drunk," Izzy shrugged. "I figure it's fifty-fifty, but fifty is better than zero."

She backed out of the driveway slowly, making as little noise as possible. Once we turned the corner, she hit the ignition. "Where's the highway again?" she asked.

I gave directions as I slid down in the passenger seat, aching and dizzy. "Didn't you say you had bad depth perception?"

She waved this off. "You've been looking out pretty much since you met me. It's my turn to look out for you."

I was trying to come up with a response, but everything kept spinning and spinning until it all just went black.

—

The thunderous blare of a truck horn woke me. Focus took longer than usual. We were on the interstate. The broken, white lines separating the lanes blurred together. The sun was almost down, a fading orange glow on the horizon. A light mist on the windshield fractured the headlights and taillights, leaving red and yellow trails in my vision. I blinked but couldn't read the signs, so I asked Izzy where we were.

"Somewhere in New Hampshire maybe," she said.

"Where are we going?"

"I'll tell you in a bit," she said. "But while you were out cold, I wanted to tell you I figured out the theme."

"Theme?"

"Of the movie. The one they're going to make about us some-day. With Johnny Depp playing you and, unfortunately, Juliette Lewis playing me."

I pushed myself up in my seat. It took more effort than expected. My ribs felt like they were made of wicker, and my head rang like a Jurassic gong. "Johnny Depp can't play me," I said. "He's like, super old. He's over thirty."

"Oh shit," Izzy conceded. "That *is* super old."

"It takes years to make a movie. They have to write the script, then there's preproduction, then they have to shoot it, then there's postproduction. By that time, Juliette Lewis will probably be over thirty too."

"You're totally right. You can't have it be like *Beverly Hills 90210* with a bunch of old people trying to act like teenagers. That always comes off hokey as fuck."

Out the passenger window, I watched the dotted lines separating highway lanes blur together in the wake of our speed. "So the people who will play us are probably, like, ten years old right now."

Izzy laughed bitterly. "I'm trying to, you know, even imagine this, but I feel creepy even going there."

I half-laughed, until I realized it made my entire chest feel like it was getting tap-danced on by a musk ox. I wondered if I'd broken a rib or two. "I know, right?"

"But the theme of our movie," Izzy continued. "It's about power, you know? How the people who want it badly are often the worst people. And then they use it to create pain and fear, as if keeping others powerless at their hands is somehow even more empowering."

"Sure," I said. It made sense to me.

Izzy lit a cigarette, and her words swirled around the smoke she exhaled. "Think about it: that vice principal douchebag who suspended you. Then that football jerk. If they'd just minded their own business, everything would have been so different. They could have had their power—a vice principal can do a lot of good for a lot of kids, right? And maybe that Paul kid had a future in sports or whatever. They just weren't smart or aware enough to realize the stupidest thing you can do with power is abuse it just to prove you have it."

She passed the cigarette to me. I tried a drag, but somehow my throat and lungs seemed to reject the entire action. I passed it back.

"Where it becomes a movie-like theme is: I'm chasing a serial killer. I read the entire *Crime Classification Journal* several times—that's what the FBI profilers use to identify and chase these bastards. Anyway, according to the pros, serial killers want control and power. Sure, maybe there's psychological and sexual dysfunction, but that's what it boils down to. It's almost a pathological form of bullying, if you think about it. One evil person getting the ultimate thrill out of totally controlling whether an innocent person lives or dies, or how much pain and fear they can inflict upon them, or whatever."

I nodded, agreeing with her.

"Meanwhile, we're the people society bends over backward to keep powerless, while we're bending over even more backward to save ourselves and each other from being abused by the people abusing the power. You fight your bully authority figures and bully bullies, while I escaped my bully authority figures and dedicate my life to hunting down the ultimate, ultimate bully of all: the bastard who hunts and kills girls like me—just to feel whatever rush he feels when he does it." She paused for a moment. There was no sound but the trill of the turned-down radio, car wheels on pavement, a light whoosh of wind.

Though my head still hurt, my thoughts were coming together enough to recognize some of the ideas she was presenting. After all, the whole thing started with Paul taking Jillian's pencil. He wielded it, mockingly presenting it to her before taking it away. A form of exerting and displaying how much control he had over her pain. The reason I stepped in and risked my ass to give Jillian my pencils was simply because I was essentially the opposite of Paul—a person who would rather feel pain themselves than see anyone else experience pain. But on another level, wasn't what I did just another method of exerting control over pain?

Something clicked about how she described serial killers as just a more pathological version of the common bully. I could see at least vague similarities in how Brackerman had to diminish my experience by insinuating his was more profound, or in how Paul needed to hurt Jillian and then hurt me in order to feel more profound, or how murderers will risk life imprisonment or even the electric chair to feel the profound power of literally holding another human being's life in their hands. "Are you saying the bullies create the system or the system creates the bullies?"

"I'm not really sure," Izzy said. "Can it be both? People who desire power chase it and often get it. People who don't care about power don't chase it because they're more concerned about actually important stuff, like friends and families and the world around them. Then they look up one day and find themselves at the mercy of some asshat who gets a boner from dominating them. I don't know what the answer is. I just hope it's not, you know, just the way everyone is."

"We're not like that, though."

"No. No, we're not. We're the people who die fighting that shit."

"We're also not dead."

"Speak for yourself." Maybe a minute passed, maybe many minutes. Izzy pointed to a sign advertising a truck stop. "I've gotta pee and probably so do you."

—

Inside the truck stop, I grabbed a couple of Snapples as Izzy asked for some gas money. I headed to the men's room and told her I'd meet her outside in a few.

By the time I returned to the parking lot, Izzy was at a nearby van, joking around with four hippies. Two dudes and two girls, maybe a couple years older. She sprang toward me.

She said the hippie kids were really nice. They were headed from Connecticut to a Phish show in Portland. They were showing her how they danced at jam band shows. All four of them laughed and started spinning circles, like colorful, stoned tops.

"Wait!" she said. "I have something, too."

She dashed to their van and slid a cassette in. "OK, it starts like this . . ." Extending her arms, Izzy circled slowly, like a small child pretending to be an airplane. The music began, a macabre, space-age-y guitar line that lasted maybe fifteen seconds. All of a sudden, a ferocious explosion of rabid energy infused the music, and Izzy started jumping and thrashing around like a maniac to a manic progression of power chords.

"What *is* this?" I yelled above the din. The hippies were clearly enjoying the show Izzy was putting on.

"Sonic Reducer, dude! The Dead Boys!"

Izzy started moshing and slamming into all four of them. The hippie kids loved it. Everyone started going nuts, bashing into each other and laughing, music blasting. Izzy a celestial ball of passion and joy. The night crackled around her like a live wire.

She flew into me and kissed me on the cheek. I threw her back in to the center of the little mosh pit as she laughed.

Izzy was an impossible gift to the world.

She was life incarnate, despite every cruel hand life had dealt her. She was a human power generator, infusing the air with electricity, wherever she was and whatever she did.

And she was accomplishing the impossible for me as well. Or, maybe, infusing the impossible inside me with infinite possibility?

There's really no easy way to describe it. I'd been as good as dead, and Izzy was bringing me back to life.

The song ended, and Izzy retrieved her mixed tape. We waved goodbye to the hippie kids, and they waved goodbye to us. I'd forgotten to ask where we were going, but at that moment, it didn't really matter.

—

It didn't take long to figure out we were heading toward Boston. Apparently, this was Izzy's plan all along: drive to Boston to find my mother.

"I think I've figured out where she works," Izzy told me, packing a new box of smokes against the wrist she was steering with.

"How'd you do that?" I asked.

Izzy shrugged. "You mentioned she was in Allston–Brighton. This morning while you were at school? I checked the yellow pages and made a few calls."

I considered this. "How did you know we'd be going to Boston? Are you psychic, too?"

She chuckled between closed lips, lighting a cigarette. "No. I thought it could be something you might want to do," she said. "You know, like, in the future."

The fact that she stated the Boston trip was something *I* would do—singular—forced me to pay more attention to the words she didn't say. Specifically, she thought it would be something I could do after she had left Maine forever.

There was no time to wallow in this. As we pulled around a bend, the bright lights of Boston ignited the distant night in an unnatural but mesmerizing glow.

Though I'd been to Boston with my family numerous times before, it was always breathtaking driving in, especially at night. The buildings seemed like huge arms, lit up from the inside, grasping at the clouds.

Highways twisted and turned, spiderwebbing the landscape as far as I could see. Billboards and neon, concrete and metal, headlights and taillights, streetlights and traffic lights. Everywhere I looked, something caught my eye.

We pulled up on a street lined with brick buildings, all filled with commercial businesses. Most of them were closed and gated up, but a few storefronts lit up with neon beer signs and bar lights. We passed a large, four-sided clock propped about thirty feet in the air by a large metal column, like the one beneath a streetlamp. "It's like a clock on a popsicle stick," I commented.

Izzy laughed. "A clocksicle."

She pulled off the main strip and drove a couple more blocks before parking. She gestured across the street to a large building. No sign lit up the entrance, and there were no windows. The front of the building was painted jet black. Something was inside, because a bouncer sat on a stool by the door, and a small line of people spanned the other direction from him.

"I'm pretty sure that's it," Izzy said.

My stomach tightened. Could Izzy really have found my mother? Was she inside that weird-looking building? What if she wasn't? What if she was? I stole a glance in the rearview. I'd cleaned up some, but it was still pretty obvious I'd been in a fight I hadn't won. "I can't go see my mother now!" I exclaimed. "I'm a total mess!"

"She's your mother, CJ."

What if she didn't want to see me? What if the reason she'd taken off from home in the first place was that she never wanted to see me again?

"You need to see her, and she needs to see you. It's important." She got out of the car and waited for me.

Three steps down the sidewalk, Izzy realized I was still at the car.

"My feet won't move when I tell them to," I said.

Izzy whipped around and stared at me impatiently. "CJ. I'm not going to tell you to grow some balls. I've seen you've got them. You risked getting shot to save me from that dude at the Junkyard House. You looked a police sheriff in the eye and totally bullshitted him. You fought a jerk off twice your size. If you can do all that, you can go see your mom. I've driven us all this way. Now let's move it."

This time I followed. But I wasn't happy about it. "You've never seen my balls," I muttered under my breath.

—

On a stool outside the bar sat a big, bald bouncer in a long trench coat. His muscles had muscles. He asked for IDs. Izzy had made me promise to let her do the talking, so I stood silently as she explained. We were looking for someone who worked there. Rebecca Slater?

The bouncer's expression floated in the purgatory between sympathy and suspicion. "I really wish I could help you kids," he said, "but I don't know no one by that name."

Izzy swiped my wallet from my back pocket and fished out the photo of my mom.

The bouncer's eyes lit with recognition. "Ah! Becky Z! She's the coolest! Yeah, she's working the back room tonight."

My jaw could have fallen off my face. *Becky Z*? Of course, I knew her maiden name was Zelig. But I'd never heard anyone call her *Becky*.

"Hey, you kids seem nice, and I'd be glad to pass Becky along a message. But the law says you need to be twenty-one to enter, so I'm really sorry, but I can't let you inside. How do you know Becky, anyway?"

Exactly at the same time, Izzy said, "*She's his mother*," and I said, "*She's my mother*."

Now, it was his jaw's turn to drop. He looked me up and down. "You've got her eyes," he said to me. "I mean, aside from the swelling." He opened the door and let us in.

—

This place was aiming high: snazzy couches and fancy light fixtures. The music was weird Euro-dance stuff, louder than it needed to be. The lights all filtered, red and purple.

Izzy and I were sorely underdressed in weatherworn leather jackets and jeans. The gray thermal shirt I'd hastily changed into at home had some blood spattered around the collar. Izzy had on a worn *Misfits* T-shirt over a black bra, visible in multiple places through the holes in the shirt. We received a few curious stares, and Izzy got some looks from dudes who were more than curious. We passed a tiled floor where three girls with super-short skirts danced with three guys with too much hair product.

"I don't see her," I yelled to Izzy over the music. She moved us along to a corridor off the dance floor that looked like it might lead somewhere. The corridor was narrow. We had to squeeze by a woman making out with a man and then a woman making out with a woman.

Walking into the back room, I saw her.

My mother wore a black pencil skirt. She was balancing a small circular tray in one hand, the other hand on her hip. She was talking to two men in suits. I'd never seen her wear so much makeup before. None of it seemed real. It was like I was trapped in some alternate dimension. My other-dimensional mother.

When she saw me, my mother immediately set her tray down on the nearest available table. Slowly, she stepped toward me. Then she broke into a run, and all of a sudden, her arms embraced me. In her heels, she was maybe an inch taller.

"Oh my god, Craig! What on earth are you doing here?"

"I don't know," I said. "I'm here to see you, I guess."

"How did you find me? What happened to your eye?"

"I'm fine," I said.

"Let me go see if I can get a break so we can go somewhere and talk." She rushed off.

Dizziness unsteadied me. Was it the concussion, or the emotion of seeing my mother for the first time in months, or both?

"Your mom's really pretty," Izzy said.

"I guess," I said.

Some guy appeared behind Izzy, wrapping his arm around her waist with a big, confident smile. "Hey, sexy thang!" he said.

Izzy cut him off, removing his arm. "I have anger management issues and a really mean right hook," she said.

As the guy hustled off in the opposite direction, Izzy turned to me and winked. Then my mother reappeared, waving us over to the fire exit. We followed her outside.

Chapter 24

BECKY Z

THERE WAS A HIDDEN AREA in the alleyway behind the lounge where my mother waitressed. One of those metal ashtrays on legs stood beside the metal door, but there seemed to be more butts lying on the ground around it than inside.

My mother brushed my hair from my eyes. It was something Izzy had done a few times, and something Carina used to do as well.

Izzy wandered off a bit to give us privacy, lighting a cigarette. I'd always felt weird smoking around my parents, so I held off even though I really wanted one. It was a casual habit that had accelerated after my sister's death, probably to cope with the omnipresent anxiousness. In the moment at hand, calming down was probably not possible under any imaginable circumstance. My heart was racing uncontrollably.

My mom said she only had ten minutes: Her boss could be a real pain. As quickly as possible, I explained the crazy circumstances that led us there. To Boston. To her.

She hugged me again. She didn't get out of work until very late. She scrawled her phone number down on the back of a receipt and asked if we had somewhere to stay the night. She could meet me the following afternoon.

"Mom . . . I'm not sure how long we can stick around. I left without telling Dad. I mean, I wrote a note, but you know how he gets. He's gonna freak."

She shuffled through her purse, offering a fistful of money. "Maybe you can go to the diner and eat something. I can try to get off work a bit early to meet you. There's so much I need to tell you. I miss you so much."

"Then come home," I said.

"Oh, Craig. It's not that simple."

"Yes, it is," I said. "Come home."

"I can't. It's difficult to explain. Maybe I can see about you staying with me. I'd need to ask, it's . . . not my apartment. It's complicated." She glanced anxiously at the door. "Shit, I wish I had more time . . ."

We only had a few minutes to talk, and there we were, not really saying anything. Making impossible arrangements. Alone together.

Across the alleyway, Izzy leaned up against a wall covered in a prism of graffiti. She looked like a movie still, her back foot up against the wall, slightly slouched, smoking a cigarette, watching me. Broken light illuminated broken glass all down the narrow, concrete corridor in either direction. A streetlamp distorted shadows from where the alley opened into the street, maybe twenty yards in the distance.

"You've had time, Mom. You said you needed time, and it's been months. As much as you needed time, I needed you even more. Don't you see that?"

"It's complicated," she repeated. She glanced a moment at the light of her cigarette cherry, as if the answers could be found inside the small, red glow. "Your father—he thought everything could just go back to normal. But nothing can ever be the same. How was I supposed to do anything? Everything in that house was Carina. Everything on that block, in that town. I tried to tell him. I swear I did. All of my dreams were buried with her. The only thing left to die was me."

"Mom, I'm still alive. Dad's still alive. And we need you."

She ran her fingertips across my face. She smelled like shampoo and whiskey. "I need you too. So much it hurts. But what you need . . . it doesn't exist anymore. I can't be that person anymore.

Here, I'm just Becky Z. It's simpler. Everything isn't a reminder. Do you understand?"

I fought the tears back behind my eyes with everything I had. I was losing it, and I hated myself for it. I hated myself for being the one left alive. I hated myself for not being good enough for my mother. I hated myself for being helpless to save my sister. I hated myself for running off and hurting my father. I hated myself for not being good enough to make Izzy stay with me. Why was I never enough?

The metal door opened, revealing a very tall man with slicked-back hair and a voice like sandpaper. "Drinks aren't gonna serve themselves, Becky," he said.

Becky Z. Who on earth was she? She was the person who used to be my mother but who no longer wanted the job. Maybe she hated herself the same way I hated myself. Why couldn't we just cross the divide between us? Why couldn't we just stay how we were meant to be?

Together.

Families belonged together, right?

No, Mom. No, I do not understand. But I didn't say anything. I just used both hands to wipe the stupid tears off my face.

My mother kissed me on the cheek and opened the door. "Craig, I love you so much. None of this was because of you. You need to see that."

Izzy stood behind me. "Mrs. Slater? I know it's not my business. But you need to know . . . CJ is the greatest person on the entire planet. He's brilliant, and he's kind. And he's awkward, but the more you get to know him the funnier he is. Your son is hilarious. He's weird and creative and so intense it's scary. He's brave, and he's like . . . what did they call the knights? Not like the opposite of days, but like the dudes with the armor in ancient England."

"Chivalrous?" I said.

"No, *gallant.* I meant, *gallant.* Mrs. Slater, your son is gallant. I thought gallant-ness was extinct, like the dodo bird or the unicorn, but then I met your son. Your son is a fucking miracle, and you should be there for him like he's there for everyone else."

Now my mom was crying too. Everyone was crying except for Izzy. Her eyes were small, black lasers slicing through the darkness.

My mother used the door as a shield between herself and the two of us. "Maybe someday. But right now . . . I just can't."

The door clicked shut behind her.

I turned to Izzy. She wrapped her arms around my neck and buried her face in my collarbone. It felt like it might be fractured, but I didn't care. I hugged her back. We stood like that there in the alley. A light rain had started to fall.

"Are you OK?" Izzy asked.

"I . . . I don't know," I said.

"I'm thinking you don't want to stay the night in Boston, then."

"I should call my dad. And I guess then we should head back home."

She pulled back a bit, the rain misting around her eyes. "What about the cops?"

I sniffed and rubbed my eyes, that post-crying moment where you try to hide the evidence. "It doesn't matter. My dad is probably freaking, and . . . I should just go back."

"OK, whatever you want, Ceej. We'll figure it out. We'll always figure it out."

We walked through the alley toward the streetlights. The shadows stretched out longer as we headed toward the light. "Izzy?"

"Yeah?"

"Unicorns didn't go extinct. They're mythological. It's different."

"No, it's not," she said.

———

On the way back home, we stopped at the first rest stop. At the pay phone, I called my father collect. I waited for him to calm down with the *what happeneds* and *where are yous* so I could talk.

"I found Mom," I said.

"You what?"

"I'm in Boston."

"How on earth are you in Boston?"

"I'm coming home, but I needed to do this. I guess I'll be back tomorrow."

"I'm trying to stay calm here, but it's very difficult. The school called, then the police showed up, and you're nowhere to be found, and now you're in Boston . . ."

"Dad, it's OK. I'm OK."

I heard my father take a deep breath, the way he always did when trying to level his emotions out. "Everything is insane here. There are people driving around looking for you. Officer Walker is here. Apparently, the boy you got in a fight with today is in the hospital. His family is saying all kinds of crazy things about pressing charges. You're apparently being expelled from school. It's like a circus. Officer Walker says he needs to talk to you."

I said OK, and my father put him on the phone.

"You're an exciting kid," he said.

"I guess I really screwed up this time," I said. Izzy was leaning against me, her ear pressed to the receiver, trying to overhear anything she could.

Mr. Walker explained that it was a delicate situation. Paul was at the hospital. I'd basically broken most of the bones in his hand, and doctors weren't sure they could reattach the pinky due to the damage. Paul's family was on the warpath, having already contacted a lawyer—swearing up and down that they'd prosecute me to the full extent of the law. The fact that I had skipped town wasn't helping my cause, although rumors were swirling that some of Paul's cousins were roaming through town with members of the football team looking to find me for revenge.

"I think the best thing would be for you to get back to town ASAP," Mr. Walker said. He told me to come directly to his house, and he'd take me himself to the police station.

I told Mr. Walker I could make it sometime the following morning, and he seemed satisfied with that.

"From what Natasha tells me, this Paul is a very cruel kid. When I was called in to the scene at the school, however, your vice principal seemed to have the opposite view. He painted it like Paul was a pillar of decency, and you were a predatory delinquent."

"That's because Brackerman is a lying asshole," I remarked.

"That's basically what Natasha said. The greater problem is, if the person in charge of school discipline has this view, it's certain to have significant weight if this whole thing winds up going to court."

I almost dropped the phone. What Mr. Walker was saying was disturbing as hell, but I also knew that the way things worked wasn't always fair. A truck blasted by ominously. "Well, I guess I'll deal with all that when I get home tomorrow," I said.

"Just make sure you come straight to my house or the station when you reach town. Paul's friends and family . . . well, they're not exactly the reasonable sort. You need to be cautious." Mr. Walker said he was giving the phone back to my father.

In the moment of respite, I looked over at Izzy.

"Quite the stir you've caused there, Ceej."

An understatement if there ever was one. A day that began with Kay Nguyen explaining I still had a shot at a top university was ending with the knowledge that I was expelled from school entirely and a very real possibility of winding up incarcerated.

Obviously, Paul had started it—but when the whole fracas began, only his friends were around to witness it. By the time other people had become attracted to the furor, it was me who threw the first punch. Was the combination of those things and any bullshit Brackerman testimony enough to get me convicted for—as ridiculous as it sounded—assaulting and seriously injuring a kid the size of a bear?

My father took the line. "The most important thing is that you're all right," he said. "And that you get home as soon as possible."

I told him I couldn't get home until the next day. When he protested, I steeled up, saying firmly, "Dad, you need to trust me."

I heard him take another deep breath. "OK," he relented. "The important thing is that you're all right."

Maybe I was all right, maybe I wasn't. Who knew? But there was really only one thing I needed to convey to him.

"I saw Mom," I said again.

"How was she?"

"I asked her to come home."

Silence.

"She's not coming home," I said.

"I know, Son," he said. "I know."

Chapter 25

EVERYTHING IN
THE HISTORY OF TIME

SOMEWHERE NEAR THE BORDER OF New Hampshire and Maine, Izzy suggested we should stop for the night. She steered off an exit after a billboard advertising the cheapest motel on I-95. We might as well use the fistful of money my mother had given me, she said.

From outside the motel office window, I watched Izzy ding the service bell. A minute or two passed, during which Izzy played with everything on the desk. A tired-looking older lady shuffled out in a robe. The lady shook her head, a clear sign of *no*. We'd discussed the possibility of motel clerks not wishing to rent a room to a pair of teenagers in the dead of night. I was counting on Izzy's twin superpowers of prevarication and manipulation. I saw her saying something and gesturing, and the woman glanced out the window at me. I waved, and she waved back. The next thing I knew, the woman gave her a hug and traded the cash for the motel keys.

As Izzy parked us outside a dingy room in the run-down motel, I asked how she'd pulled it off.

"You're my fraternal twin brother. The courts gave our asshole dad partial custody when our mother came down with muscular dystrophy, but he gets drunk and beats the shit out of you. I explained how he gave you the black eye. We barely escaped, and now we're driving home to our mom's house, but I'm too tired and you're too injured to drive the rest of the way so can we please, please have a room for the night? We'll pay in cash."

"Do you have this shit planned or do you just make it up as you go?" I asked, incredulous.

"Lying is like jazz," she said. "The true masters improvise."

—

The room was gross, but whatever. The overhead light didn't work, just the dim lamp in the corner. There was a desk with several initials hacked into it and two twin beds. Izzy used the bathroom while I sat on the edge of the bed, struggling to get my bruised and aching body in position to remove my own shoes. The mattress felt like cardboard. I tried turning on the TV, but the only station that came in was ABC, and it was some dumb mobster movie, so I shut it back off. Izzy shuffled in from the bathroom. She had changed into shorts. She was barefoot, tucking her toes tight into the cushion of the tacky, purple chair across from me and lighting a cigarette. "What do you think happens now?" she asked.

"I don't know," I said. "I might be locked up at the police station for a couple days, I guess. It's funny because it's in the basement, and my dad works upstairs at the town hall."

"That *is* kind of funny," she agreed.

"Why did you do this?" I said. "All of it. Risking getting caught, leaving your hunt for the serial killer, just to get me out of town. To see my mom. And then what you said to my mother, it was, well . . ."

"True?" she said.

"I'm far from the greatest person on the planet," I mumbled.

"To me you are," she said. "I've been so obsessed with how terrible people can be. My whole life. But you . . . you made me believe in goodness again. The world can be a monster, but it can also be . . .

I don't know. Something else. Something better. And you believed in me when no one else did. Maybe it was just my turn to believe in you."

"I just wish . . ." I said. "I just wish any time anyone I loved told me how worthwhile I was, it wasn't immediately followed by their leaving me forever."

"You know I have to leave," she said. "You know I can't stay." She never took her eyes off of me, exhaling a funnel of smoke out the side of her mouth, so she wouldn't have to turn her head.

"How long?" I asked. Worried my voice would crack with those two words, I just spoke them as quietly as possible, almost a whisper.

"I'll try to stake out the farmhouse another day or two, just to make sure. Something bugs me about that place; I can't put my finger on it. But most of all, I can't skip town while you're in jail or whatever. It seems, I don't know, tacky."

"*Tacky*," I repeated, a bit incredulously.

We stared at each other a moment in the darkened room. She ashed her cigarette in a plastic cup. "You know, you just said you loved me."

I thought back a few sentences and realized what had come out of my mouth, albeit in a roundabout way. "Shit."

"You realize we've only known each other a week."

"All I know is I'm terrified you're going to leave, and I'm just going to be lost again. I don't know shit about love. I don't know what I feel. All I know is that . . . with you? It's . . . everything."

"Stand up," she said.

"What?"

"Just do it."

I stood up.

"CJ." She stared at me a moment. "Take off your clothes."

"What?"

"Please. It's important."

The terror I experienced in the wake of her request was cataclysmic. But I didn't want to allow my fear to dictate my actions. Not this time.

I pulled my shirt over my head and dropped it. I peeled off my socks. I undid my belt and jeans. I paused to look at her. Her eyes pierced me. I pushed down my jeans, slowly and a bit nervously. I looked at her, but before I could ask if she wanted me to take off my boxers too, she said *yes*.

So I did.

Izzy watched me intently in the half-light. She made no pretenses about watching me. "You're beautiful," she said.

I didn't know what to say. Izzy was stunning. She was the prettiest girl I'd ever seen. I wasn't anything special. I was just a skinny kid with messy hair and a whole lot of emotional problems. I was just, well . . . me.

She stood. "You're so beautiful," she said again.

The blood typhooned in my veins.

She embraced me. Her head went where it usually did, in the crook between my neck and my shoulder.

I realized I was poking her in the stomach. I felt embarrassed. I tried to shift away. "I'm sorry, I . . ."

"It's OK," she said. "It's better than OK."

Izzy stepped back. She peeled off her tank top. She slid out of her shorts. She reached behind her and undid the bra. She lowered her underwear to the ground and stepped out of them.

"Izzy, I . . ."

She put her fingers over my lips, silencing me. She pushed me back on the bed. She climbed over me. She leaned down. Her lips brushed mine. She opened her mouth. I followed everything she was doing. Everywhere she was touching my body pulsed with indescribable energy.

"Don't think about it," she said. "Just feel." She reached down. My skin glowed. Galaxies of meaning. Everything in the history of time led up to a moment. The moment was us. Slowly, she began to move. Her eyes never left mine.

"I love you so much," I said.

"I know you do," she whispered. "I've always known."

—

The red, neon motel lights flickered intermittently through a crack in the dirty blinds. Our limbs tangled up with each other. In the half-light. In bed. Naked.

It was impossible to tell where one of us ended and the other began. She ran her fingertips lightly all across my skin. Anywhere on my body they wanted to go. I watched her face as her eyes caressed the length of me. At random intervals, she kissed my collarbone, just below where her face rested. I'd never been more alive. As if my entire previous existence was only a dream, a dream I was finally waking up from.

"Interesting day, huh?" she said, laughing at her own little joke.

"I guess so."

She flicked my ear. "You guess so."

"Well, I think I have a concussion, and I'm expelled from school and possibly going to jail, and Paul's family and friends are probably combing the streets with pitchforks and torches looking for me. But on the other hand, I lost my virginity. With you. So I'm not really sure if the right word is *interesting*."

"Don't forget the serial killer and the shit with your mother," she said.

"Oh yeah, the serial killer. My mom—I'm not really experienced with this stuff, but I'm pretty sure it's a bad idea to mention your mother when you're naked in bed with a girl."

"Fair enough," she giggled.

"Fair enough," I repeated.

"Hey, your life is more exciting than most fifteen-year-old dudes!"

"Maybe I . . . wait," I said. "What time is it?"

She tilted her head to see the clock, resting on the credenza beside her half of the bed. "Almost three in the morning."

"Shit," I said. "In that case, I'm turning sixteen in exactly one week."

"This week is your birthday?"

"Believe it or not, yeah."

"Well happy almost birthday," she said, kissing me on the mouth. Her mouth still on mine, she whispered a question. "What do you want for your birthday?"

"I mean, I can't think of anything else that would be better than this."

Her fingertips trickled down, past my stomach, past my hip bone. "I can think of a present I'd like for your birthday," she said.

I rolled her onto her back and followed atop her. It was easier this time. Like I was meant to be there all along.

"Sixteen years, huh?" Her words came out breathily, like little clouds. "If I weren't the same age, I'd think it sounded like a long time."

"I don't know," I said. "It's all led up to pretty much one thing."

She smiled. "And what would that be?"

"This," I said. "Us."

"Yeah." The air left her in a sigh. "I think you're right."

Chapter 26

FLOWERS FROM THE DIRT

I SHOT AWAKE TO A piercing, animal-like scream. One of the most jarring, horrifying sounds I'd ever heard.

Izzy was curled up in a fetal ball in the corner of the room. She hugged her knees and trembled like a small, scared animal in the half-light. Tears lined her face.

"No, no, no," she cried. "No, no, no, no, no."

I'd forgotten about her nightmares.

Or maybe I'd just never fully believed in them.

I rushed over to her. "It's OK," I said, holding her. "You're safe. You're safe. I'm here."

"Every night," she said, her voice quivering. "Every night. It never ends."

What does a person say when a person they love is gripped in the throes of an abject terror that is impossible to begin to relate to? "It's OK," I said again.

"It's not. It happens every night. It'll never stop. It'll never stop until I die. Until he kills me or I kill myself."

"We're going to stop it," I said. "We'll stop it, together."

She turned her head to me. Her eyes were wild. "You promise?"

What exactly was I promising? It didn't matter, not if it would help Izzy. Not if it would keep her going. Whatever I was promising, I'd figure it out later and hold myself to it. "I promise," I said.

Her breathing became a bit more even. She reached for my hand and squeezed. "You double promise promise?"

"Izzy, I don't break promises. That's rule number thirty-one."

She sniffled, pulling the blanket tighter around herself. "Wait, there's thirty-one rules now?"

I took her hand to my lips and kissed it. "You snooze, you lose," I said.

—

We checked out at noon. The motel desk clerk gave us startlingly warm hugs and wished us luck. We filled the tank and hit the interstate. Within two and a half hours, we passed the Waldo County line, mere minutes from town.

"Are you sure you want to turn yourself in?" Izzy asked. "It's not too late. We could just run away. You and me."

"I have to do this," I said. "It's the right thing to do."

"I knew you'd say that," she said.

I told her to turn off the main road; there was somewhere I needed to go first. She asked where, so I told her the truth: the county hospital.

"I need to see someone," I explained.

"Your friend who tried to kill herself?"

"Jillian. Yes."

"OK. Just tell me where to go."

—

Izzy waited by the car. At the hospital entrance, I realized I had nothing to give Jillian. There were two large planters on either side of the front door filled with yellow daisies. I looked in both directions. There were two orderlies down the hall, but they seemed more interested in flirting with each other than me. I waited for a nurse to wheel an elderly man inside and then surreptitiously ripped a half dozen flowers from the dirt.

Upstairs, the man at the front desk gave me directions to Jillian's room. It was down the hall and around the bend. I followed his directions, passing a few nurses and doctors and orderlies going about their business. An empty wheelchair caught my attention. It reminded me of the one I used to wheel Carina around the hospital. I counted down the door numbers until I reached Jillian's room.

I was about to knock when I was stopped by a young nurse a few doors down who saw me. She was sorry, but Jillian's parents had specifically requested no visitors outside immediate family.

I apologized profusely. "Um, could you just tell Jillian her friend CJ came to see her? And, um . . . could you give her these?" I handed over the flowers.

The nurse analyzed the daisies. "Did you take these from the planter in front of the hospital?" she asked.

We both looked at the flowers, then back at each other.

"What would make you say that?" I said.

The nurse smiled. "Jillian's mother is in the room. Would you like me to get her for you?"

"Oh, um . . . it's no big deal . . ."

"Just wait here, OK?"

She opened the door and went in the room. Moments later, Jillian's mother emerged. I'm not sure what I expected Jillian Sillinger's mother to look like, but this wasn't it. She was tall and athletic looking, with a short haircut that made her look like a CEO or some other kind of executive.

She recognized me immediately. "You're CJ," she said.

I nodded.

She placed both her hands on both of my shoulders. "Jillian has talked about you since kindergarten," she said. "It's a pleasure to finally meet you."

"Really? I . . . I never knew that."

"She's asleep now, but she's going to be so happy to hear you came to see her. It'll mean the whole world to her." She smiled. "I mean, the flowers are kind of pathetic, but she'll certainly appreciate them."

"I kind of picked them from the planter outside the hospital," I admitted.

"That's what the nurse said." I was taken off guard when Mrs. Sillinger followed this statement with a big hug. We said goodbye, and I started off down the hall. I was stopped by Mrs. Sillinger's voice calling my name.

"Yes, Mrs. Sillinger?"

"When your sister died last year, Jillian wouldn't stop crying for days. I thought you should know."

I felt strangely overwhelmed. I hurt for Jillian, who had only hours before attempted to take her own life. I felt guilty that Mrs. Sillinger thought Jillian and I were good friends or something, when I'd never even seen her outside of school. I just thought she was nice. I just didn't want her to suffer, because she was a person with a heart and feelings, and no person with a heart and feelings deserves to suffer.

But I also knew everyone suffers, and there was nothing I, or anyone else, could do about it. It's just part of being alive. Maybe there's no point to any of it. Or maybe, the only point is that when we do suffer, we're there for each other. Maybe the point is just that we don't have to suffer alone.

In the end, I really didn't know what to say. "Thank you," I said.

I left the hospital.

—

Izzy couldn't be seen in town with me or by any cops. And I had to turn myself in. And, we had to get Remy Ward's El Camino back to where we'd found it. There was just no way we were going to be able to pull all this off on our own—not at this point.

So we went to the pay phone in the hospital parking lot, and I dialed Natasha's number. By now it was after three p.m., so I figured the odds were pretty good that she'd answer. After three rings, she picked up.

"Natasha?"

"Holy shit! CJ! Where are you? Do you have any idea what's going on?"

"Yeah," I said. "But I need a favor, and I knew I could trust you."

—

Terry Manilla's beat-up Jeep Wrangler pulled into the parking lot. When he parked, Natasha jumped out of the passenger seat and ran up and embraced me. "I'm so glad you're OK. I mean, holy shit."

Mid hug, I asked if Terry was pissed off at me too. He was on the football team with Paul, after all.

Terry, behind the wheel, just laughed. "Not in the least, dude. I've told Paul a million times how whack it is to give people shit for no reason. You're cool by me."

"You think I'm cool?"

Terry laughed. "You want me to paint you a billboard? I'm dating your ex; I figured you don't want me to rub it in your face or anything."

"Point taken," I said.

Natasha fawned a moment over my shiner. Then she spotted Izzy, a few yards behind us, leaning against the El Camino and smoking a cigarette.

"Who's that?" Natasha asked.

"Oh, um . . . that's Izzy." I called her over. I introduced everyone.

Natasha looked the two of us over. "Are you two guys, like . . . you know?"

"I don't know," I said.

"Yes," Izzy said.

"Yes," I said.

"No," Izzy said.

"Maybe?" I said.

"Fuck if I know," Izzy said.

Flustered, I changed the subject to the plan Izzy and I had come up with. Terry was to drive the El Camino back to Remy Ward's house. Natasha was to drive Izzy back to the overlook and then drive me back to her house, where I could turn myself in to her father. Natasha and Terry couldn't mention having met Izzy to anyone, and of course nothing about Remy's El Camino. We were in enough trouble as it was.

Terry couldn't stop laughing. "Dude! I cannot believe you stole Remy Ward's car and drove it to Boston!"

"Borrowed?" I asked Izzy.

"Borrowed," Izzy said to Terry.

"Whatever, dudes. That dude is such a drunken fool. He almost ran me over when I was out jogging two weeks ago."

"See?" Izzy said to me.

Before Terry took off, he gave Natasha a kiss. I thanked him vehemently—I really owed him one now.

Terry shut me up by reaching down and putting his hand on my shoulder. "You don't owe me nothing, bud." He saluted us and took off in the El Camino.

I turned to Natasha and Izzy. Izzy flicked her cigarette butt and looked Natasha and me up and down. "OK, I totally get it," she said.

Natasha just smiled, her laugh like wind chimes. "I do too," she said.

—

Natasha drove to the overlook. She peered at the endless stretch of trees encircling the town below, twisting a path as far as the eye could see. "You live in the woods?" she asked.

"It's a long story," Izzy said.

"Give me a minute, OK?" I said.

Natasha nodded. She waited in the car as I walked Izzy to the edge of the forest.

"I'm not sure I can go through with all this," I admitted. "I'm terrified."

She reached out and brushed the backs of her fingers against the side of my face. "I'll see you soon," she said. "It's going to be OK."

"How do you know?" I definitely didn't. I had no idea what was going to happen once I turned myself in to Mr. Walker.

"I don't know." She leaned in and kissed me. Her mouth was sweet and smoky. "I just do."

—

On the short drive to my house, Natasha explained the situation at school.

Apparently, my exit preceded a pretty sizable spate of chaos. An ambulance came to collect Paul and his missing finger. The cops who showed up were Natasha's dad and his partner, who had to deal with Vice Principal Brackerman screaming bloody murder about their questioning of him when they should've been out looking for me.

"Jeez," I said, watching the road as we drove into town. With so much that had occurred in the past twenty-four-or-so hours, the downtown streets seemed as sleepy and boring as ever.

"Actually, Brackerman didn't say they should be out looking for, you know, *you*. What he said was they should be out looking for *that criminal CJ Slater*." Natasha giggled. "Can you imagine?"

"Well, in his defense, I did just steal Remi Ward's El Camino and drive it to Boston."

"Borrow. You borrowed it."

"Oh, yeah. I keep forgetting."

Natasha pulled the corner to our street, and I don't think either of us were expecting the situation we had just driven into.

"Holy shit," she said. "This is new."

There was a line of police tape around my front lawn. Six adults were being held on the outside of the line by Mr. Walker's blond partner. With Natasha's car windows open, we could hear them screaming stuff about me getting out of the house—apparently, they thought I was hiding inside. Our living room window was shattered; it looked like someone had thrown a rock or something through it. Mr. Walker was on the far side of the police line, gesturing like he just wanted everyone to calm down.

"That's Paul's family," Natasha said, recognizing them from some football function. "Not the nicest folks in town." She slowed the car to a stop one house away from her own driveway and asked if maybe she should just turn around and take me straight to the police station.

I considered this a moment. It seemed a sound idea. But Mr. Walker was right there, and in uniform. And the thought of being in the police station with Sheriff Pfeiffer—who creeped me out—and not Mr. Walker made me uneasy. So I rationalized. "It's OK, Nat. The police are right here. No one's going to do anything stupid."

Needless to say, I've always been stupid in underestimating other peoples' capacity for stupidity. As soon as Natasha had parked in her driveway, Paul's mother spotted me and yelled, "There's the bastard!"

Four grown men and two grown women then bum-rushed me as soon as I got out of the car. Mr. Walker ran over after them and got in between me and Natasha and the screaming adults. He told Natasha to get in the house as the blond cop grabbed me and tried to quickly hustle me into his squad car.

As he opened the door, one guy (Paul's uncle, I later learned) got around Mr. Walker and lunged toward us, throwing a wild punch. The blond cop shoved me in the car and used his body to block the man's path and wound up taking the man's fist straight in the nose.

Mr. Walker yelled something about the next person taking a step toward them or me going straight to a cell, and they backed off a moment. Mr. Walker and his partner used the opportunity to jump into the car and speed off, down the street and away.

The blond cop turned to me from the passenger side of the front seat. His nose was bloody. Just before he closed the door, he gave me a look. "You're really ruining my week, kid," he said.

"Sorry," I said, sincerely.

I saw my father run out the front door just as Mr. Walker peeled out around the corner. I felt bad. Dad must have had to call in sick to work.

PART FOUR

Chapter 27

LOVE IN THE TIME
OF RUNNING OUT OF TIME

THE TOWN HALL BUILDING HAD four levels. The first level served as the police station, while the second served as the town hall and the mayor's office. Then there was the attic and the basement. While the attic had no cute nickname, the basement was referred to as "the pokey" for the section in the corner where they built two small cells. After fingerprints and a couple photographs were snapped, I was taken there.

Each cell contained a bench, a toilet, and a small sink. They kept me in the far cell, the other cell completely empty. I found it slightly funny that they didn't even bother to close the cell door. They left the blond cop there to watch over me. I learned his name was Phil. He sat in a folding metal chair, holding an ice pack to his nose where Paul's uncle had punched him during the craziness earlier.

"I'm really sorry about your nose," I said.

"You're nothing but problems, kid," he said. "As if I didn't have enough problems."

Minutes passed. My mind was whirling from all the stress. I needed a diversion. "What are your other problems?" I asked.

"Why the hell would I tell you?"

"You never know," I said. "Maybe I can help."

"Jeez, kid. I've got a bloody nose, my rent just went up, and my girlfriend says if I don't spend all my free time reading books it proves I don't give a shit about her interests. I know the bloody nose is the only thing that's your fault, but you're going to pay my rent?"

"No," I said, "but what does your girlfriend want you to read?"

—

By the time Mr. Walker came downstairs to the cells, Officer Phil and I were too engrossed in conversation to properly greet him.

"Let me get this straight," Phil said, "Gabriel García-Márquez is comparing Florentino's love for Fermina to the plague?"

"Yep," I answered. "But García-Márquez is simultaneously insinuating love itself as the actual sickness."

"Wouldn't that make love, like, a bad thing?"

"Well, he's also saying that, although, to us, love can feel like a sickness, living your life without love is the more profound sickness."

Phil took off his police cap and scratched his head. "But how can being in love be a sickness and being without love also a sickness?"

I shrugged. "I guess he wants us to try to figure that out."

Mr. Walker glanced at us suspiciously. "What on earth are you two talking about?"

"*Love in the Time of Cholera*," Officer Phil said.

Mr. Walker rubbed his temples. "Well, it's nice to see the two of you have become all friendly."

"The kid's actually really smart," Phil said. "That is, apart from all the terrible life decisions."

—

Mr. Walker did his best to catch me up. My father was upstairs, posting bail. I'd be out by morning. The Thurmond family was threatening to press charges, but their case was proving problematic. The disparity in witness accounts, combined with Paul's enormous size advantage, greatly contradicted the version Paul's family was arguing, which painted me as the predator and Paul as the victim.

The violent encounter between Paul and me had turned into some sort of absurdist your-word-against-mine. As it happened, the only people who were present behind the school when Paul instigated the entire incident were Paul and his friends, who had all conveniently left that part of the story out of their accounts. About the time our argument started attracting bystanders was about the time I threw the first punch, which didn't help my cause one bit.

I could barely get the words out. "Are you saying . . . I can wind up in jail for this?"

"Paul's family has already brought in a lawyer. They're going to come after you hard—apparently his future as a quarterback is very likely over after serious permanent damage to his throwing hand. But it's not like you murdered anyone, so no one would be trying you as an adult. Unfortunately, a juvenile detention facility is not out of the question."

Even imagining such a fate made me feel physically ill. Not only would that completely destroy any future ambitions I had, but from what I had read about juvenile detention facilities, it would be something of a challenge to even survive. Knots of nausea ground against each other in my stomach.

Mr. Walker quickly caught on to whatever distress my face was conveying. He placed a hand on the dingy concrete over my head and leaned in. "Of course, I don't see that as a likely scenario given the disparity of accounts and situational events. This is to say, Paul's friends' enthusiasm to back up their guy has led to some, well . . . curious fiction."

Phil laughed. "One kid told us you had chased Paul around the parking lot with a brick before finally catching up to him behind the school. Another said Paul was scared to leave his house for weeks because you'd been sending him death threats."

Shocked, I grabbed a handful of my own hair. "That's . . . insane."

"Yes, it is," Mr. Walker agreed. "And your case is backed up by the fact you have no real record or history of disciplinary problems. With everything Natasha told me about him, I expected Paul to have a poor record. But according to the person in charge of disciplinary measures in your school—Vice Principal Brackerman—Paul's record is spotless as well. And before you say it, I know—Brackerman is also the coach of the football team for which Paul is—*was*—the star player."

"That's so messed up."

"Ultimately, your problem is proving you were the victim without any witness accounts of Paul's starting the fight and without any existing prior record of Paul bullying other high school students."

I reclined back on the hard, metal bench. "So, what's going to happen?"

"It's difficult to say how this all ends. But as for right now? First, there's a doctor here to examine you, as we need to make sure you don't require hospitalization for your injuries. As I mentioned, your father is posting bail, but with the erratic and threatening behavior of Paul's family, I've recommended to him that we let you spend the night here. It's not comfortable, I know, but at least it's completely safe. Your father will be allowed to take you home tomorrow, but I'm not entirely unconcerned. It's not like the town police have the man power to keep an officer at your house on guard duty very long. Maybe for a day or two? Obviously, we'll ask you to lay low awhile to let things settle. It's not as if school is an option anyway. Brackerman has suspended you and apparently already filed the paperwork for your expulsion."

I stood up and slowly walked to the corner of the room. I placed a hand on both sides and leaned into the concrete crack, facing away from the room. "This totally sucks," I said.

—

When the doctor came down to examine me, my thoughts strayed. Not surprisingly, the biggest concern in my mind was Izzy. How would we even see each other now? If I was being told to stay at home because Paul's family was after me, and if a police officer would be stationed outside my house for a couple of days, seeing Izzy would prove impossible. There was no indication Sheriff Pfeiffer had ended his search for her, so it wasn't like she could just come up and ring the doorbell with a policeman overseeing my house. At the same time, I couldn't just leave and not tell the officer where I was going. Sneaking out of my room would be impossible, too—my window led to the front yard, and beat up as I was, could I even make the jump from the roof of the garage to the tree right now?

As the doctor told me to cough, it hurt, but not as much as the realization of the growing situational chasm between Izzy and myself. We were running out of time. We had found zero evidence of her serial killer. Now I had an encyclopedia-sized list of my own problems that would preclude my seeing her at all. With no killer to keep her focused on catching, and no me to keep her around, would she just up and leave town forever?

The thought of Izzy leaving forever nearly made me hyperventilate while the doctor was taking my pulse. The thought of her leaving without even having the opportunity to say goodbye made me cough fitfully without even being instructed to do so. I worried the doctor would think I was dying of a heart attack or something.

He eyed me over the rims of his glasses. "What's wrong?"

"I'm, um . . . kind of scared of doctors," I said.

"Don't worry," he said. "I'd never beat you up as badly as this kid apparently did."

Somehow, it didn't make me feel any better. Nothing was broken, but the doctor thought I might have a bruised rib or two and possibly a slight concussion. I didn't seem to have any trouble breathing, which was reassuring. If it started to hurt when I coughed, or I felt dizziness or nausea, he told me, I should inform one of the officers so they could take me to the hospital, immediately.

After the doctor left, Sheriff Pfeiffer entered. He wore a bright, orange hunting jacket and look of general consternation. He stood outside my cell a moment, looking me over. "How tall are you?" he asked. Puzzled, I told him five-nine. "You're certainly big trouble for a guy your size."

Pfeiffer reiterated what Mr. Walker had said about my situation. He stressed that the fact I'd left town after the fight didn't exactly make me look innocent. Though my father had posted bail, they thought it best to keep me in custody overnight. Though they were letting my father pick me up the following morning, they were strongly recommending I stay inside my house, at least for the next few days. He explained that there were several witness interviews conducted at my school after the fight. There were a few things working in my favor, such as the fact that the kids who supported my version of the events all had consistent stories, while those supporting Paul were pretty much all over the place.

As I listened to the sheriff, I became strangely aware of how much darker it was in the cell area than upstairs, in the way-too-bright police station. The overhead light in my cell seemed to flicker a bit and was clearly in need of repair or replacement. I sat cross-legged on the bench, wrapping and unwrapping my fingers around the metal anxiously. "That's good, right?"

Pfeiffer leaned against the doorframe. He was barrel-chested and a bit imposing, and something about his demeanor seemed edgy. "There's one thing that concerns me about the stories confirming your account," the sheriff said. "All of them indicate you hit Paul with the brick when he was distracted by a girl who was running over to help you. All of those accounts indicate you ran off with that girl. And even though the girl was high school–age and it was a school day, none of the kids recognized who she was. I have a feeling that I know who this girl was, however."

I said nothing.

"This girl was your friend Izzy, right?"

My stomach dropped. I fought to keep my cool. "Why does it matter?" I said.

"It matters because you made me a promise!" Sheriff Pfeiffer hit the bars with an open palm. They made a bizarre, rattling sound that echoed a bit in the cavernous room. "You said you'd help us find her. And what did you do instead?"

What could I say? There was nothing. He had already caught me in one lie, so whatever I said would make him suspect it was another one. And the fact that his son was possibly involved in Alicia Russell's disappearance, however unverifiable, made him a very real threat to Izzy, who he seemed to believe had inside information on the whole Alicia Russell debacle.

What I had going for me was that, unless the police physically *saw* her, Izzy was pretty much untraceable. She wasn't even using her real name. She was, by all accounts, a literal living ghost. As such, I fished through my mind for the specific styling of bullshit most likely to get Pfeiffer off of Izzy's case. What was it that Izzy had said? *Lying is like jazz: The true masters improvise.*

"You don't have to worry about Izzy anymore," I explained. "When I left town and went to Boston, I dropped her off there. Apparently, she has a friend or something to crash with. I doubt you'll have to worry about her in our town again."

Pfeiffer righted himself and stepped in the room, clearly displeased with me. "And what exactly do you think it is I'd need to *worry* about?" He spat the word out like some sort of curse.

"I have no idea," I said, leaning back against the cold concrete. "*You're* the policeman."

He squinted a moment at me, as the light flickered overhead. Though clearly displeased with my answer, he seemed to consciously collect himself. He walked to the cell door but turned to me just before he departed. "I'm trying to figure it out, kid," he said. "Either you're really, really stupid or really, really smart."

"I don't know," I shrugged. "Probably a little of both."

When Officer Phil returned to watch over me, I was navigating the impossibly perilous terrain of second-guessing myself. Had I said the right things to Sheriff Pfeiffer? Would I wind up in juvenile detention? Was my future ruined? Was my father OK? Was Izzy OK? I was happy for Phil's return to the pokey, so I could ask a more definitive question: "How the hell is anyone supposed to sleep in here?"

Phil shrugged. "Only person we've had here overnight in the past six months is Remy Martin. Three times, actually. Normally he just passes out on the floor next to the toilet, but again, he normally has a blood alcohol content of 50 percent or whatever."

I frowned, looking down at the rigid metal bench. I rolled around a lot in my sleep and preferred lots of pillows and blankets to smother myself in. This was kind of the opposite. "That doesn't help me feel any better," I remarked.

Phil shrugged. "You're really into stories, right? Imagine you're like, King of Maine, and the cell is, like, a super comfortable palace bedroom."

Trying to make myself as small as possible, I curled up on the bench. I sighed. "Well at least like Mr. Walker said, I'm safe from all the people who hate me in here."

"Not so sure about that one, kid," Phil countered. "Sheriff really seems to have it out for you."

"Great," I said, my tone indicating precisely the opposite.

He put his feet up on a metal desk and folded his arms behind his head. "Just saying, you might want to hold off on entering any popularity contests right now."

Though something about Phil's forthrightness was endearing, I felt the hole just getting deeper and deeper. "But you don't hate me anymore, right?"

"Well, I called the girlfriend before. Remembered everything you said about the García-Márquez book. She was super impressed."

I shifted uncomfortably on the metal. "At least I've got someone on my side, then."

Phil leaned forward on his metal folding chair and rolled his eyes. "Well, she was so excited that she's running out tomorrow to get me another few books to read. So truth be told, right now no one on the planet hates you more than I do."

"Shit," I said. "Sorry."

Phil surprised me a bit by laughing it off. He winked. "Get some sleep, kid; you look like hell."

Chapter 28

TOO CLOSE TO THE SUN

FIRST THING IN THE MORNING, my father arrived to pick me up. Mr. Walker insisted on ushering me out the back door; apparently Paul Thurmond's mother was at the front desk filing a restraining order against me. No one wanted any sparks near what they considered to be a potential powder keg. The ridiculousness of everything did not escape us.

"A restraining order?" my father exclaimed. "That Thurmond boy literally weighs twice as much as CJ!"

"I'm assuming it's something their lawyer instructed them to do," Mr. Walker explained.

I just kept quiet. To me, the absurdity was almost symbolic in its backwardness. If Paul just left other people alone instead of feeding a constant need to exert his dominance, none of the chaos would have happened in the first place. The entire world needed a restraining order against people like him.

Mr. Walker led us out a short back hallway and saw my father and me into the car. He reminded me what a poor idea it would be for me to leave home for any reason for the ensuing few days, or at least until things cooled down. "There will be an officer outside your house when you arrive, in case Paul's family is still raising their ruckus on your front lawn," he informed us. "And Phil will be there to relieve him sometime in the afternoon."

I spoke for pretty much the first time all morning. "When will I be able to go back to, you know, having a life?"

Mr. Walker leaned into the passenger side window, glancing from my father to me. "Let's just take it one day at a time for now. I understand that's just a dumb phrase that doesn't really answer your question. But while my job is to figure out what truthfully happened in my town, Paul's family isn't concerned with such things. Neither are many of their friends or your vice principal. They're simply going to keep yelling louder in order to defend what they want to believe, and any actual evidence to the contrary is going to be fought tooth and nail, regardless of how damning or conclusive."

"That's messed up."

He nodded sadly. "Unfortunately, it's also how the world works. We think truth should be obvious, but often it takes a great deal of time for truth to come to light because so many people are fighting it in order to support whatever it is they believed or wanted to believe in the first place. People are fast to blame others but slow to take accountability for their own actions. Not all people, mind you. But mostly the loudest ones."

My dad turned the ignition and then patted me on the shoulder. "You heard Mr. Walker. Let's just take it one day at a time."

I wasn't exactly an expert on quantum physics, but at that moment, I recall thinking that maybe if Albert Einstein and Richard Feynman put their heads together, there might be a way to take it three days at a time, so you could just get all the bad shit out of the way in one fell swoop and get to the point on the time line where you actually wanted to be.

For some reason, this thought led me back to my physics paper. A pang of sadness wedged a crooked path through my throat as I suddenly realized that after being expelled from school, all my work on that physics paper had been for absolutely nothing.

—

Back home in my room, I played an old Replacements album. I
turned it up to the point where it drowned out my thoughts. I was too
exhausted to think. I closed my eyes and dozed off. At some point my
father came in and turned the volume down.

"How do you sleep with the music that loud?"

"I was asleep until you came in to turn it down."

My father paced a bit around the room, clearly having difficulty
trying to express whatever it was he'd come in to discuss with me. He
glanced around at the surroundings—things he had seen hundreds
of times, as if they held some new interest now that I was a felon
or whatever.

My room was painted forest green, a color I found simultaneously
calming and pretty cool. Mostly the decor amounted to posters of my
favorite bands, which I was allowed to buy at a generous employee
discount from CD World. The Pixies, Jane's Addiction, Pylon, Nine
Inch Nails, Led Zeppelin, Fugazi. The furniture was mostly a mis-
matched collection of items that had once belonged to Carina but that
she decided she no longer liked. There were a couple of really cool
black-and-white framed Ansel Adams prints over my desk: one creepy
woods scene and one mountainous landscape.

My father seemed to briefly consider sitting on the edge of my
bed but opted instead to lean against an old wooden dresser that was
missing a knob on every other drawer. "We need to figure some things
out, CJ," he said.

He wanted to talk about school. He'd been cautioned that my legal
situation could go on for months, and now that I was expelled from
school, we faced a conundrum. My father couldn't afford the expensive
private schools in the county. Maybe I could enroll at Seamont High.
If I was out of school for too long, there was a chance I'd be left back
to repeat the same grade again. My chances of getting into any decent
college seemed remote.

"At your age, it's difficult to understand the importance of education," he stressed. "Your mother never went to college, and it seriously

affected her life. She could never hold down a job. When she tried real estate, she was constantly passed over for promotions, which were given to people younger and less qualified, with college degrees. When she was unemployed, her job opportunities were severely limited."

"If you're asking," I said, "she's working as a waitress in a cocktail bar."

"Like in the song?"

"What?"

"You know the song." He winked at me and sang a line from the chorus, holding an invisible microphone to his mouth as if it was the only way to understand his joke. *"Don't you want me, baby!"* He was closer to on key than my mother ever was, but it was still nothing great. "Don't you want me, oh-oh-oh!"

"Yeah," I laughed, gesturing with both hands for him to please stop singing cheesy '80s hits. "Like the song."

"How did she look?"

I considered his question a moment, before ultimately deciding to simply tell him the truth. "Beautiful," I said. "But also, very sad."

—

Natasha and Mrs. Walker surprised us by coming over with dinner. They'd cooked a ginormous meatloaf and huge sides of broccoli and mashed potatoes. Mrs. Walker was an amazing cook.

"You can keep the Tupperware," Mrs. Walker said. "Somehow, I've collected so much of it we can barely fit the Bronco in the garage."

"That's a lot of meatloaf," my father joked. "I hope you're going to help us eat it."

My father panicked when he couldn't remember where my mother left the guest plates and silverware. They were like the regular plates and silverware, but the dishes had fancy designs around the edges and the silverware weighed twice as much. They'd been wedding gifts from my father's aunt. Anyway, Natasha knew where to find them right away.

My dad looked puzzled. "How do you know what's in my kitchen better than I do?"

Natasha smiled brightly. "It's almost as if people have forgotten how much time I used to spend at Chez Slater."

I'd almost forgotten how incredible Mrs. Walker's meatloaf was! I recalled when we were sitting shiva for Carina. The first few days I couldn't eat at all, but after that Mrs. Walker would bring me plates to my room, where I'd pretty much locked myself in. She'd tell me I had to eat. She said she'd cook up anything I wanted. On the fourth day, she brought meatloaf and said she wouldn't leave my room until she saw me eat the entire thing. So I did.

Over dinner, Natasha filled me in on what was going on at school. All anyone was talking about was that CJ Slater de-fingered Paul Thurmond with a brick. It was like half the student body had either aligned with Team Paul or Team CJ. Kids were arguing in the halls and in the classrooms and in the cafeteria. Rumors were flying rampant about the girl who ran off with me after the fight and where we had run off to for over a day. Was I living a secret double life, dating a college girl despite my unassuming exterior? Did Jillian Sillinger have a cousin from out of town who put me up to permanently injuring Paul as revenge for his incessant picking on Jillian?

At football practice, Terry and a few other kids had gotten in a big shoving match with Paul's closer friends on the team. After practice, Coach B said anyone snitching on a member of the team would be kicked off. Several of Terry's friends were really scared about this, but Terry was considering quitting.

"Terry can't quit," I said. "He's an all-county linebacker."

"He feels awful," Natasha said. "He's seen Paul do mean things to other kids. He feels ashamed that he wasn't the one to stand up to him, and you're like, half his size. I mean, maybe that sounds like an insult, but it's really a compliment."

I smiled. "Tell him I'm bigger than I look."

Natasha put her hand on mine across the table. "If we were judging people by the size of their hearts, you'd be as big as anyone."

It was certainly nice to hear.

I wondered why being told you had a big heart meant you were a good human being, but being told you had a heavy heart meant you were a sad human being. Maybe it wasn't an accident. Maybe the price of goodness came at the cost of sadness, and the people who made up these clichés knew what they were doing all along.

—

My father and I thanked Mrs. Walker up and down for the incredible dinner. We'd have leftovers for days to come. As Mrs. Walker headed back home, Natasha followed me upstairs to my room.

"I owe you an apology," she said. "Like, the biggest apology of all time."

"You don't owe me anything. I owe you. You've done so much for me. I don't deserve any of this."

"I hate it when you talk like that. When you were at your lowest point, I abandoned you. You were difficult to talk to—but I should have tried harder. And then when your mother left, I didn't even call. Believe me, I wanted to. But I was with Terry by then, and I was scared you were upset with me. And because of my own selfish . . . *bullshit*. Because I was worried I'd feel guilty, I didn't even call." Her eyes were damp with regret. "How can you ever forgive me for that?"

"Easy," I said. "I forgive you."

"I see what you did there," she said, smiling. "Do you think . . . do you think you can, like, be my friend again? Like, when this whole thing is over?"

"I *am* your friend," I said.

We hugged it out. It was really nice. Like, the nicest thing ever. I was overcome with the feeling of how much I loved Natasha. She would always know things about me no one else would. And I'd always know the same about her. She'd been my first kiss, and I was hers. You don't realize when you kiss someone for the first time how you become etched indelibly in their time line. That kiss is all it takes. You're carved into their life history forevermore.

Why is there only one word for *love* when there are so many meanings and layers and dimensions to it?

After the hugging, I looked for something for Natasha to wipe away her tears with. I didn't keep tissues in my room. I handed her a Sonic Youth T-shirt that was crumpled on the corner of my bed.

She dried off her face and laughed. "I have something else really important to tell you," she said. "Make sure your bedroom window is unlocked at midnight."

"What?"

Natasha leaned in conspiratorially, lowering her voice to a near whisper for the bits she found most crucial. "You-know-who may or may not have tracked me down today. You-know-who and I may have formulated a plan to get her in here to see you. At midnight, I'm going to the police car stationed in front of your house. I'll give the officer in charge of watching your house a coffee and chat him up to distract him. Then, you-know-who is going to sneak around from the backyard and climb into your window. I made sure to leave the ladder your dad uses to install his birdhouses—it's propped up against the house. Oh—and you know who you-know-who is."

I sat on the edge of my desk with my feet on the chair as I tried not to laugh. "Um . . . you can just say *Izzy*."

Slightly frustrated, she threw her hands in the air. "Oh, right! You get to pull all the top secret detective spy stuff, but I don't?"

"What do you think? The CIA has bugged my room?"

"It just all seems so exciting! Stealing cars, taking off to Boston, top secret drop-offs, and skulking around town. Is it true what Izzy said? That she's a runaway and if the cops find her, they'll send her back to Iowa?"

"More or less," I said. "How long did you guys talk for, anyway?"

"Oh, like a half hour. She's totally cool. We talked about everything!"

I squinted. "Define *everything*."

"Oh, you know. Life. Things. Stuff. What a great kisser you are . . ."

My voice went up seventeen octaves. "*What?*"

"I'm just busting you, CJ. I love it when your brain goes all kablooey like that." Natasha leaned in and kissed me on the cheek. "You take care, OK?"

"OK," I said.

The door closed behind her.

Then it opened again.

"Remember. Window unlocked. Midnight. Synchronize your watch."

"I never understood *synchronize* your watch. Doesn't everybody's watch say the same thing, anyway?"

She poked a finger into my rib cage. "Can I at least have *some* fun with your top secret detective spy stuff?"

"OK, OK. I'll synchronize my watch," I conceded.

"Over and out!" she exclaimed. This time she was really gone.

———

Around ten-thirty, I went downstairs to see if my father had gone to sleep yet. He was sitting in the kitchen, drinking what looked like whiskey.

"Is that whiskey?" I asked. "You never drink that stuff."

"I drink whiskey on special occasions," he said. "Today, I bailed my son out of jail, and he was kicked out of school. I think that's a special occasion."

I sat down next to him. "Can I get one of those?"

"No," he said. He took a sip and grimaced. "I don't know how your mother drinks so much of this. It's actually pretty disgusting. Was she drunk when you saw her?"

"I think so," I said.

"When I met her, she was the pretty bartender at our local bar. All of my friends would hit on her. She'd just laugh at them. It was like a game everyone had—first guy to get Rebecca's phone number is King of Boston University. But I wasn't like that with women. I was more like you: painfully polite. I'd just sit and watch while everyone else made passes at her. One night, she asked why I wasn't a jackass like my friends. I said I was more of a jackass because at least they had the guts to say what they felt to girls I was terrified even to talk to. She asked if I was terrified of her, and I said yes. She asked why and I said because she was mysterious and clever and funny and beautiful, and if you fall for a woman that amazing and she doesn't fall for you back? Well, it must mean that you're none of those things. She gave me her phone number and told me to call her."

"So you were the King of Boston University?"

"No. I never told my friends she'd given me her number. I think they found out like, six months later when we all went to an Aerosmith show together, and I bought her a ticket."

"They must have all gone nuts," I laughed.

"I never cared about that, Craig. I just loved her. I've always loved her. I still love her." It affected me in a strange way how when my dad relayed this to me, he just looked down into his glass. He swirled the whiskey around slowly. It was as if he was already resigned to never getting her back.

"I love her too, Dad."

"I think sometimes I failed her as a husband. Or maybe I failed her as a person. I worry I'm failing you as a father."

"No, Dad. *No*." My hands traded the Formica kitchen table for an emphatic gesture of protest.

"My job is to protect you. This bully Paul was picking on you for . . . how long? I didn't even know. It's my job to know. It's my job to stop it. And I was thinking—two nights ago when you were gone, and last night when you were in a damned jail cell—I was thinking how many times you tried to talk to me. And I kept saying we'd talk later. No matter how much losing Carina and your mother hurt me, I'm your father! I was too wound up in myself to remember that *you* were hurting too."

"Dad," I said. "It's not too late."

He patted me affectionately on the face and stood. "It's funny. All this craziness going on, and I still can't help but think how lucky I am to have a son like you."

He kissed me on the forehead and shuffled off to bed.

—

Around midnight, I heard scuffling at my window. I quickly hit play on a CD to drown out our voices and popped the window open. Izzy's arms reached in, and I grabbed them, helping her land as noiselessly as possible.

Izzy brushed herself off. She was wearing black jeans and a black sweatshirt. She looked like a punk rock cat burglar, and in a hushed tone, I told her as much.

"Thanks," she said, for once thinking to keep her voice down without my even asking her to. "Not exactly easy sneaking in here. I'd guess it's even tougher than sneaking out."

"You at least had a ladder," I said. As she stepped from the window into the light, something about Izzy's expression gave me pause. She didn't seem as cheeky as usual—a bit pale, in fact, with lines of concern encircling both eyes. She looked like she'd seen a ghost. Instinctively, I asked if she was OK.

She looked like she was about to confess something, then stopped herself and pointed straight up in the air. "What is this?"

"It's from the new Rush album," I explained. "'Bravado.'"

Izzy nodded. "It's really great." She looked around my room, inspecting everything. She was certainly less talkative than usual, although that was quite a high bar to fit under.

"Seriously, Izzy. Are you OK? You seem . . . weird."

She turned to face me from the corner of my room. I only had the desk lamp on, with the overhead light off, immersing her expression in shadow. "Are *you* OK? I mean, Natasha told me you spent a night in jail. That had to be tough."

Smoothing out a place on my bed, I sat down. "I mean, the toilet was in the middle of the cell, which was weird. But it wasn't like I was there very long. Problem is, now I'm not supposed to leave the house for a while."

She used the back of her hand to wipe something off her face. Was she crying? In the half-light, it was impossible to tell. "Ceej—I need to say something to you."

Though I had just sat down, suddenly I needed to stand. Any levity or joy I had in seeing Izzy when she first climbed in my window was quickly evaporating into an anxious concern. "What?"

She took a deep breath and turned to my dresser. Her fingers skirted across the wood surface before finally arriving at a small, framed photograph of my family. All four of us—Mom, Dad, Carina, and me at a scenic overlook in Acadia. It felt like a lifetime ago, all of us smiling with such carefree bliss. I recalled the woman my father asked to take the picture and how she told us what a beautiful family we had.

Izzy ran her fingers down the frame, lightly caressing our faces. "I've done a lot of investigating without you in the past two days."

"That's fine," I said quietly. "I get it. You've gotta do what you're here for, even if I'm not around to help."

"No, that's not it. Just listen."

Despite my shifting unease, I shut up as she explained that she'd gone back to the farmhouse twice to stake it out. Though she didn't see anyone, she heard some strange sounds from inside, like someone working in a metal shop. So someone definitely was living there, but aside from that she had pretty much been unable to learn anything whatsoever. "Also," she added, "I was finally able to track down Lisa."

"Alicia Russell's best friend?"

"Yeah." Apparently, Izzy had gone to Seamont and asked around, learning fairly easily that Lisa worked at the same Waldo Mart as Alicia. "She said she couldn't talk until after work, but when I introduced myself as Izzy she freaked. She said the cops had been to her house asking about me and that I might know where Alicia ran away to. She took a smoke break and we went out back to talk. She kept asking if I knew what happened to Alicia and how I was involved. I had to come up with this huge lie about how I was the sister of another girl from another town who that Pfeiffer cop messed around with, so I was trying to get to the bottom of it. Lisa bought my story enough to tell me all of Alicia's. Needless to say, she's 100 percent convinced that it's the Seamont cops who are 100 percent responsible for Alicia's disappearance."

Added together, that equaled 200 percent. Pretty irrefutable. I leaned on my desk, squeezing the wood in a death grip. "And . . . you believe her?"

"I don't know what to think anymore. Maybe . . . maybe I was wrong about this from the get-go. Maybe I'm just . . . lost. Maybe I'm just chasing a ghost." Izzy stepped into the center of the room. The light reflected in the glassy wetness of her eyes. Her usual gaze of intensity and confidence had vanished, replaced by a shifting and disturbing doubt. "Maybe I'm just a ghost chasing a ghost."

I shifted toward Izzy, who had stepped toward the middle of the room. There was now nothing between us but two feet of space. Somehow, in that moment, such a small distance felt like an impassable chasm. "You're here to tell me you're leaving."

She looked away, at an empty spot on the floor, as if her eyes could not meet mine while speaking the word. "Yes."

"When?"

"Soon," Izzy said. "I just want to stake out the farmhouse one more time. There's just something that sets my stomach off when I see that place. Normally, I like to have my next town scouted out before I leave the one I'm in, but I have a couple ideas I need to double-check at the library tomorrow. And also, I need another day with you before I'm gone. We need . . . I don't know, one more day."

"I don't know when I'm going to be able to get out of the house," I admitted. "If I leave, I could wind up in seriously deep shit."

"We'll figure it out," she said. "We always do."

"I guess we do," I said. She hugged me. It was weird how I'd known her for such a short time, and yet when we said *always* it just felt so natural.

She shifted back, releasing one hand from her grip around my waist to brush the hair from my eyes. Tucking the lock behind my ear, her fingers unfolded, lightly clasping the side of my face. "You get I can't stay, right? Even if I wanted to."

Did she want to? It was difficult to imagine. Izzy wasn't exactly a person I could picture settling down to small-town life. Going to school every day, doing homework. Curfews and part-time jobs, mundane social activities with the rest of the kids. Keg parties by the lake, smoking joints outside the Exxon. Navigating some vague present in order to arrive at some amorphous future.

Could Izzy even exist in a normal life, like the rest of us? Whatever "normal" was. To me, she was less a typical teenage girl and more like some elemental force of nature. "I get it. The cops might be after you. It's not safe for you here."

She laughed bitterly. "You can't go, and I can't stay. The world is so stupid sometimes. Keeping us apart, when we're the only thing in it which has really ever made any sense to me."

Izzy broke the moment, gently pushing away to reopen my window. "I've got to motor. Natasha said I could probably only count on her to distract the cop for, like, fifteen minutes. I'm meeting up with her after school with plans for you and me to meet up again. But I have a ton of shit to figure out tomorrow and . . ." She pointed her thumb toward the open window. "You know."

I knew.

She climbed half out. Was I going to see her again? What resonated in my chest would be best described as not emotional pain, but rather seismic cataclysm. Everything was shattering. I choked out her name.

Both legs outside, she poked her head back in. "CJ, this is what it has to be right now. It's not forever. Remember what we said."

"I know, I know," I mumbled, trying to force the words out while forcing the tears to stay in. "Three years. Statue of Liberty. It's not forever."

"There's only one thing I know for sure is forever." She smiled. It wasn't a smile I recognized. Not her mischievous smile, or her electrifyingly joyful smile, or her self-satisfied smile, or her playful smile, or her confident smile, or her wild smile of impossible whim. It was a new expression, somewhere between sad resignation and hope. Between a beautiful dream and waking up from it. "And you know damned well what that is."

Chapter 29

THE PRESENCE OF ABSENCE

THE NEXT DAY, FRIDAY, MY father took a second straight day off work. I was feeling a bit guilty that he was using all his paid vacation days on damage control for me.

We had leftover meatloaf and eggs for breakfast. Again, it was weird seeing him pour coffee into the University of Maine mug. I couldn't remember how we'd even gotten it. No one in the family had gone there, and before Carina got sick, she had refused to even consider applying. "One-third of our town goes to Orono," she had complained. "It's not even college so much as a sequel to high school." She had her heart set on Boston University, where our dad had gone.

My father gulped down the coffee, explaining he had an appointment with a lawyer downtown. He said if I needed anything, Mr. Walker was across the street, and there was still an officer stationed outside the house. Once he had gone, I fell asleep again, trying to decide whether to finally finish my physics paper for a school I was apparently being expelled from or to read *Love in the Time of Cholera* again.

After maybe an hour, I woke up and decided to clean up the house a bit. If I was causing my dad so much aggravation, at least he could be aggravated in a freshly vacuumed living room. As I spruced up, my thoughts repeatedly drifted into a fitful state of worry—what would my life be like in the inevitably impending scenario?

Izzy was leaving. There was no preventing this. And everything after that loomed as incredibly daunting. It was tough to imagine even getting out of bed with nothing of real consequence to even look forward to. Combining that with the uncertainty of my practical future complicated things further.

Expelled from my own high school meant having to start again somewhere new, whether I was enrolled at Seamont High or maybe some affordable private school along the coast. Though I guessed it would be nice to be around a group of kids who weren't painfully aware of my family tragedy, I wasn't exactly a social butterfly who met people easily. Though there were not a great number of people from my own school I would miss, I experienced a tangible sense of loss at the realization that I wouldn't get to see the people I actually liked anymore, like Kay Nguyen and Mrs. Levy and a few guys from base-ball I always thought were cool.

If there was a bright side, it was that the more I stressed, the harder I cleaned. By the time my father returned home a few hours later, the entire downstairs was shinier than it had been in years. As I heard him opening the front door, I was really hoping he would notice and be pleased, but instead he just hustled over to me barely even noticing his surroundings, wildly waving a VHS tape in his hands. "You're not going to believe this!" he said excitedly.

I was surprised to see Mr. Walker follow my dad into the house, also seemingly in fine spirits. It was nice to see everyone in such a good mood, though I was a bit confused as to what was at the root of it. My dad didn't answer verbally, instead just grabbing my arm and yanking me toward the nearest television set. "You've got to see this," he exclaimed.

"It's from today at your school," Mr. Walker added.

My father started up the tape, which started with the camera set up on a small dais set up in front of the high school. Soon after, the bell rang and dozens of students began filing out of the building and gathering around the dais.

As I was asking what the tape was, my father shushed me to explain that Kay and Natasha had organized a walkout of school to protest my expulsion and what they had called "corrupt school leadership that had led to an epidemic of bullying."

"They did *what*?" It was a lot to take in. Both Kay and Natasha were quite possibly risking disciplinary action against themselves by heading such an endeavor. It seemed a long way to stick their necks out, especially Kay, who had never even skirted trouble in her entire scholastic life.

But sure enough, both Natasha and Kay gathered behind the microphone as a couple kids from the AV Club tested it out until satisfied with the sound. They tested *one, two, three* a few times, and then Kay stepped up to the microphone, brandishing a notebook. "This notebook contains evidence of a huge problem right now, not just in our town but probably in towns all over the country. And it needs to stop. This week, CJ Slater is being expelled from school. The reason given was that he injured Paul Thurmond, a boy two years older and one hundred pounds heavier, in an altercation. When, representing the school newspaper, I asked school administrators why Paul had no disciplinary actions against him while CJ is being punished to the extreme? Well, I was greatly disturbed by the responses I received. My answers ranged from an absurd statement that CJ was menacing Paul to several veiled threats to mind my own business. Well, I'm here right now because it is my business. It's all of our business. This is our school, our town, and a place we deserve to feel safe." Kay waved the notebook in the air. "In this notebook are the names, phone numbers, signatures, and brief accounts of seventeen students who have come out to attest to being bullied by Paul Thurmond in the past. Kids who had their heads stuck in toilet bowls, kids thrown into lockers, kids hung by their underwear in the gymnasium showers, kids beaten and threatened and humiliated. Kids! Kids who never had the courage to come forward before but finally have the courage to stand up to a bully because CJ Slater had the courage to, and now they know they will not be alone."

Dozens of kids gathered around the dais cheered Kay's words. I watched the VHS tape in shock. Kay deferred to Natasha, who stepped up to the microphone brandishing a different notebook. "In *this* notebook? It's the names, numbers, and signatures of everyone who attested to CJ Slater being a bully, or a dick, to anyone else pretty much ever." She opened the notebook, flipping through dozens of completely blank pages. "The first thing you'll notice about this notebook is it's totally empty. Go on, ask around yourselves. I guarantee you won't find a single story of CJ being mean to anyone. So we kinda need to ask, why is CJ the one getting expelled and Paul the one being treated by school administrators as the victim? I mean, I'm no Sherlock Holmes, but I think people might want to look into the fact that Paul is the star of the football team, and the guy in charge of school discipline is the coach of that very same football team. And that's just not good enough. It's not OK. It's not OK to allow all those bad things to happen to all those kids and then punish the one person willing to stand up to the bully who did all those bad things."

There was more applause, then some kid in the crowd yelled, "Free CJ!" As soon as it happened, it took off like wildfire, with pretty much the entire crowd chanting "Free CJ" over and over again.

My father stopped the tape. "Can you believe it?"

I was speechless.

Mr. Walker placed a hand on my shoulder. "I'm no lawyer, but apparently the whole case being made by Brackerman to expel you from school and by the Thurmond family with the lawsuit are contingent on the idea you're a delinquent and Paul is an angel. If this tape gets out—and I'm pretty sure my daughter and Kay will make sure it will—well, it certainly casts significant doubt on what those people are claiming."

My father expounded further, saying he had also been informed that several teachers were apparently trying to meet with the school board to file an official complaint concerning Brackerman's penchant for using strong-arm measures to coerce them into passing his football players regardless of whether passing grades were earned.

I was overwhelmed. "What does this all mean?"

"Well," my dad beamed. "For starters, your school is going to need to seriously reconsider the idea of expelling you. And I'd guess an investigation will be done into Paul's bullying and the whole grading scandal, which would certainly lead to an investigation of Mr. Brackerman."

Mr. Walker shrugged. "If everyone's argument was that you threw the first punch, it's not carrying a lot of weight when a whole bunch of kids are saying they've literally been dodging punches for years while the people who had the power to stop it turned a blind eye."

—

After a long and eventful day, my dad had his heart set on a good night's sleep. But he insisted he had just enough energy for a cup of hot chocolate, if I was game. We brought the steaming mugs to the living room, where we sat on opposite chairs with two sets of feet sharing the padded footrest.

My father took a noisy sip and raised his eyebrows. "Man, I make a good cup of hot chocolate, if I do say so myself," he boasted.

"It's Swiss Miss," I countered. "You just open the bag, pour it in, and stir."

"True, but there's an art to it."

We sat there for a couple of minutes, silent but for the occasional slurp, until finally I spoke. "Dad . . . I'm sorry I had to put you through all this."

"You have nothing to be sorry for," he said. Then he thought a moment. "Well, you have a couple of things to be sorry for, I guess. But I noticed you really cleaned up the house today, so I'm willing to let most of them slide."

—

At midnight, Izzy crawled inside my window.

Excited to see her, I began to relay the events of the day.

Izzy cut me off immediately. "Natasha told me. I . . . I think it's great. It sounds like everything will go back to normal for you, in time." There was a weariness in her voice and palpable sadness in her eyes. Something was wrong. It wasn't difficult to decipher what.

"You're leaving," I said.

"After tomorrow," she said.

I sat down on my bed. Izzy remained at the window.

"At the library I couldn't find much. There might be a disappearance that matches in Connecticut. It's not ideal, but worth checking out. Anyway, it's not far, and less risky to start again there than to hang around here. I staked out the farmhouse again today, but nothing. I've been here over a week with no evidence the Keeper of Hearts is here. I need to change something. I can't stop, but nothing I do is getting me any closer."

"What if you didn't have to leave?" I asked. "What if you could stay here?"

"I'm not sure you understand," she said. Her eyes were cold, black steel. "Every night. Every night, the nightmares. Every night, he tortures me. Every night, he tears my heart out of my chest while I scream. You saw it, at the motel. You saw what I go through. You think it could go away because you care about me? Nothing will make it go away. Nothing except finding him. I think you've forgotten that. That's why I'm here. Not for you. Meeting you was lucky, and I'm happy I did. But until I catch him, it will never go away. I'll be living this nightmare until the fucking day I die."

"We can see someone . . . we can . . ." I stepped toward her, but she backed away.

"CJ, I care so much about you. If you live for a million years, you'll never know how much I care for you. But sometimes I think you don't really believe me. And it's not like I don't understand. I get it. But I'll never be normal. I'm a fucking freak. My entire life has been a nightmare. I've had a few good things happen to me—and maybe the best one has been you. But I don't belong here. I don't fit here. You have your father, and your home, and you have a future. I don't have anything but surviving through a day to get to the nightmares every night. You're going to get your life back. You'll go back to school, and then you'll go to college. You're good, you're destined for all the good things. But I'm . . . I'm not. You need to understand."

"I don't. I don't understand. What about *tonight together*? What about all of it?" I reached out to her. "What about us?"

"I told you," she said. "Left eyeball of the Statue of Liberty. When I say something, I mean it. Don't be late."

Did I believe her? People changed. The world spun quickly, and there was no way to slow it down. Izzy and I had only had a handful of days together. How deep were the bonds between us, really? She'd go to new places and meet new people. Maybe she'd find her killer, maybe she wouldn't. Maybe she'd keep her irrepressible aliveness aglow, or maybe it would dim down with the inevitable difficulties of the harsh way she was forced to survive. Maybe this small window of time was all we were going to have, and thereafter, everything would be different forevermore.

She sat in the windowpane, ready to spin out and away.

"So," I said. "This is it." I felt hollowed out completely. It was happening, again.

"No. We need one more night together, but not like this. We deserve that much. I'm pretty sure we both have shit to take care of during the day. But I'll be staking out the farmhouse tomorrow one last time, sometime between sundown and maybe midnight. Just in case. If I don't see anything new, I'll just go back to the logging mill and pack up my shit. I'll wait for you there until sunrise, but there's a bus leaving for Portland pretty early in the morning. From there I'll be able to get another bus to Hartford."

I didn't know what to say. I asked her if she needed money. I had a hundred or so left over from our road trip.

"I have enough to get where I need to go. Just make sure you get out and meet me tomorrow night. I'll either be at the farmhouse or the mill. Natasha said they're taking the cops off watch, so I'm confident you'll figure out a way to get out of your house. Just make sure you do. Because after tonight?" She crawled out of the window. I heard her voice with her footsteps as she scaled down the expanse of the roof. "I'm gone for good."

Chapter 30

GONE FOR GOOD

TIME DOESN'T DEFINE US. INSTEAD, time gives us a window in which we can define ourselves.

That's it.

Nothing unbelievably profound. No brilliant revelations. That's it. It's there, then it's gone, and there's nothing you can do to change it once it's past.

At some point, we'll all get those chances to define ourselves. Who are we? Do we ever even really know?

No time to think about time. Clock is ticking. Blink, and it's gone. Gone for good.

I needed to give Izzy a parting gift to remember me by. I turned my room upside down for something suitable, but everything I owned suddenly seemed stupid and childish.

Dumping out a drawer, I glimpsed a small box. It was a Swiss Army knife that my sister had bought for me for my thirteenth birthday. My parents immediately took it away, before I'd even had a chance to tear off the wrapper. They said I was too young for something so dangerous.

After Carina died, my mother decided it didn't matter anymore. I should have it, if only because my sister wanted me to. She took it from my father's closet and left it on my desk. I didn't have the heart to open it then and just stuck it in the drawer.

So now, it was still brand new. I figured Carina would be fine with me regifting her gift to someone I loved. And knowing Izzy, she'd love it too. After all, what vagrant serial-killer hunter didn't need a knife?

—

Natasha and Terry came over as soon as they'd heard all charges against me were being dropped. Operation Free CJ had been a full success.

"Latest rumor is you'll be allowed back at school sometime next week," Natasha said.

"Second-latest rumor is Paul might *not* be allowed back to school once he's out of the hospital, because of all the accusations," Terry added.

With Paul's family worried about a new series of problems, they were unlikely to spend their time harassing me. The police would no longer be needed to watch my house. I could leave whenever I wanted to. Free CJ!

"So, it's Saturday night and the weather's supposed to hold up," Natasha said. "A bunch of kids are throwing a kegger at Hidden Lake. You wanna come with Terry and me? It would be cool now that this is blowing over to, you know, all hang out."

I thanked them for the invitation, but said I had to decline. "Next time, definitely. But tonight, I kinda need to ask for one more favor. You think on your way to Hidden Lake you guys could give me a lift to the cemetery?"

My father didn't like the idea of my going out at all; he was still worried there were people in town who had it out for me. I said it sounded like all the furor was finally settling down, and I'd be careful. I didn't reveal my real plan. Yes, I wanted to see my sister. But the cemetery was located extremely close to the farmhouse, where I was to meet Izzy on her stakeout. And the farmhouse was not too far from Izzy's abandoned mill, where I could, at the very least, help her pack up her things.

One final time, together.

—

I toyed with my father's binoculars in my lap while Terry drove. Izzy would be happy I'd remembered them for our final stakeout. Natasha talked a mile a minute about how cool the party was going to be.

Pine trees and evergreens streamed by in the darkness. There was almost no moon. I'd witnessed the same scenery on countless occasions, yet this time it felt crucial to remember. I had to face the possibility it was the last night I'd ever spend with Izzy.

Tonight together, and then time offered no promises.

Terry helped me pull my bike out of the back seat and gave me a handshake.

"Are you sure you're OK?" Natasha asked. Behind her, Terry wiped some dirt off his windshield with his sleeve.

"Yeah," I said. "It might seem weird, but this is just something I do. I just feel better if I talk to Carina, you know?"

"It doesn't seem weird," Natasha said. She fiddled with the zipper on her jacket. "Tell her I say hi."

"I will," I said. We hugged good night.

I watched their taillights disappear. I leaned my bike against the iron grating and snuck inside the cemetery.

—

Kneeling at Carina's grave, my index finger traced along the grooves of her name. I remembered the day my sister had been diagnosed with cancer.

There must be a mistake, I remember thinking. The diagnosis had to be wrong. Carina was beautiful and young. Maybe they'd mixed up her diagnosis with someone else's.

My mother was crying in my parents' room. Their door was closed. My father spoke reassuringly in low tones. The hospital had a great reputation. They hadn't caught it too late. We'd fight this together, as a family.

I padded up the steps to Carina's room. I knocked. No one answered. Normally I wouldn't dare enter my sister's room without permission, but this was different. I turned the knob and went in. Carina was lying on her bed in the fetal position. The only light was from a desk lamp. She was listening to "Just Like Heaven" by The Cure, staring straight ahead at nothing.

She didn't look up. She just said, "I love this song so much. Isn't it just magic?"

I sat down beside her. She squeezed my hand. She said she was thinking about the year before, when Tina Jacobson died in the car accident. "At the funeral, it was all the same thing," Carina said. "She was *so full of potential*. She had her whole life in front of her. She could have been anything she wanted to be. I felt guilty, because I kept thinking how crazy it was that when someone dies young no one really talks about who they actually *were*. Because no one really knows. So they sit around and talk about who the person could have been. It's like you die unseen. I want to be *seen*, CJ. I don't want to die. I don't want to die unseen. I want the whole world to see me."

Then she just wept quietly.

"I see you, Carina," I said.

But even then, I knew it wasn't enough.

Rising to my feet, I placed my hand on the rounded edges of Carina's tombstone. I ran my fingers through the row of rocks atop it, each one left there by me during previous visits.

Hey, Carina. I'm almost sixteen now. You wouldn't believe the week I had. Within twenty-four hours I found mom, lost my virginity, and wound up in jail. I mean, it sounds ridiculous. You'd laugh so hard if you were here. I can picture it.

Mom's not coming back. Come to think of it, neither is my virginity. I'm sorry, I shouldn't be joking about these things. But I needed to tell you. You were right. At one point, Izzy's hands were shaking. You were right. I told her I love her. And I know it. I know I really love her more than

I've ever known anything. I've never felt anything so . . . I don't know. So big? It's like the whole world is different now. It's like everything that exists has a bigger meaning than I ever imagined. But you should know. You were right, Carina. You were right.

I hope you were right about a lot of things. I hope you were right about reincarnation. I hope you're a dolphin right now, slicing through the waves.

Izzy believes in reincarnation. I want to believe she's right, too. For you. For all of us. I don't know what to say sometimes. I don't know what to believe. I guess I just wish you were still here. I just wish that more than anything.

I stood up and placed another rock on the grave. It was a nice one, perfectly oval and smooth on all the edges. It had a nice weight. It felt good to hold in my hand.

—

It was a ten-minute ride to the farmhouse from the cemetery. I left my bike behind a few trees. I snuck through the field. At our stakeout spot, outside the slotted wood fence, Izzy was nowhere to be seen. I glanced at my watch. It was pretty early, the sun barely down a couple hours.

Why had she given up her stakeout so early? Or maybe she was still at the logging mill, packing her stuff.

Should I wait for her at the farmhouse? Or should I go find her at the mill? I didn't want to guess wrong—it was a pain-in-the-ass hike through the woods, and I didn't want to miss her. So I decided to start the stakeout without her and hoped she'd show soon like she promised.

I peered through the binoculars and saw something peculiar right away. It was dark, with just a sliver of moon and no lights anywhere in or around the farmhouse. What I could see was a smoldering pit between the house and the area where the farm animals were once kept. A lawn chair was set up a yard or two away, as if someone had lit a campfire and then sat to watch it burn.

I focused the binoculars to their highest resolution. There were still embers burning at the base of the fire. Whoever had put it out had done it very recently. There was just enough glow from the embers to let me see that there seemed to be several melted items in the fire. Whatever was in there wasn't just wood and kindling. I couldn't see precisely what, but I thought I saw something weird poking out of the pit. At first, it almost looked like a hand. But then, it occurred to me—it looked more like the fingertips of a glove. It looked red, or maybe that was just the darkness mixed with the glow of the embers. Why would someone be burning a glove? Did it fall in the fire? I lost my view of it as the wind shifted. Smoke wafted into the air.

My attention was diverted to debris under the lawn chair. Something glistened through the tall grass, but it was obscured behind the blades, and I couldn't make out what it was. I scanned to the left with the binoculars and saw something else: a small pile, just below the arm of the chair. At first it looked like wood chips. And then I realized I was not looking at a pile of wood chips.

I was looking at a pile of shells. From sunflower seeds.

The hair on my neck stood up. Every cell in my body froze. An acrid taste burned the back of my throat.

I've just found the fucking murderer, I thought.

—

As fast as I could, I sprinted through the woods. By that time I knew the path like the back of my hand, but branches and brambles still whipped me as I ran.

My mind was spinning. We didn't know shit about the serial murderer. All we really knew was that *someone* had staked out the Exxon. The Exxon was where Alicia Russell had hung out on weekend nights.

It was the last place she'd been seen alive. And it was where I'd stumbled into the pit and found the sunflower seeds.

Someone at the farmhouse also ate sunflower seeds while watching the fire burning. A fire that could have been burning evidence. Including a red glove, like the gloves Mr. Walker said Alicia had with her the night she disappeared.

Was I right? Or was it just a coincidence? Either way, it might be enough to convince Izzy to stick around town. Maybe I could even convince Mr. Walker to go visit the farmhouse and see if he found anything suspicious.

It was *something*.

So I ran through those woods toward the abandoned mill, toward Izzy. My heart throbbed through my ribs. I was dying to tell her maybe she had been right all along. Maybe the killer was living at the farmhouse, and maybe we were the only ones who knew. Maybe she had been right all along, and maybe she didn't have to go.

But when I reached the mill, Izzy was already gone.

Everything had disappeared: her sleeping bag, her duffle bag. Her clothes. Everything.

No, I thought. How could Izzy have gone already? How could she leave without even saying goodbye?

I felt a burning in my chest. My legs were weak. I could scarcely even breathe. She wouldn't do that. Would she?

But Izzy—we found him!

We found the killer!

There was no way to find her. No phone number, no address. If she was gone, she was gone for good.

But wouldn't she have stayed for one last night with me, like she'd promised? She'd promised! Didn't she need to say goodbye to me like I needed to say it to her?

How could she just leave?

I stumbled through the corridor, tears blurring my vision, toward the busted-up back room where Izzy had set up her makeshift crime lab.

The wood was still nailed to the wall, but all the articles had been torn off. All the pictures were ripped off, many of the corners of the photos still stuck in the pins and tape that once held them up.

All of the girls were gone.

I felt a chill. Izzy had taken those photos with her all across the nation. They were her life. Why would she just tear them down, leaving pieces of them torn off like that?

Maybe she'd gotten so frustrated with our inability to find the killer that she just rushed out of town in anger.

Maybe she just wanted to avoid me.

Maybe the whole thing was a lie. Maybe she never cared about me at all. Maybe she'd just been using me.

No. *I knew her.* She wouldn't have done that to me. Izzy was warm and kind and beautiful and brilliant. She wouldn't have done such a thing to me.

Would she?

Staggering back into the front room, I spotted something in the corner. I lifted up Izzy's book, the poetry collection by Anne Sexton. Of all things to leave behind, why this?

Then I thought: *Maybe she left it for me. Maybe she left a note in the book.* Flicking my lighter so I could see better, I flipped through the pages.

There was no note. Nothing.

But there was something else. There was a small, wet streak on the side of the book. On the spine. Something sticky. I held it up to the light: It looked like blood.

Nothing made sense. My head spun. All I knew was that Izzy was gone.

I screamed out her name.

I searched the area around the mill frantically. Surely there was a note, a sign. Something, anything.

There was nothing.

She was just gone.

A light rain started to fall.

I fell to my hands and knees at the edge of the underbrush. I screamed her name over and over again. *Izzy. Izzy. Izzy.*

I grabbed my head in both hands. I wanted to tear it off my neck and hurl it into outer space. She was gone. She was never coming back. I loved her so much, and she was gone forever.

My hands were trembling. I held them in front of me.

And then I saw something sticking to the corner of my palm. From the dirt where my hands had been, in the slightly dampened ground.

A shell.

Images flashed.

The corners of the pictures, ripped out from the wall. The poetry book, left behind. The blood on the spine.

I knew her.

She wouldn't just leave. What we shared was too strong.

Everything is now.

Now is always.

It's all the same.

Frantic, I tossed the leaves and branches out of the way. A small hole had been dug out. A place where someone could see the abandoned mill where Izzy had lived all week. But a place that would be out of view to someone just a few feet in front of the pit.

Inside the pit were small white flecks, like wood chips. Shells. Shells from sunflower seeds.

Izzy had not left me.

She had been taken.

She'd been taken by the Keeper of Hearts.

Chapter 31

NO TIME LEFT

THE RAIN CREATED A SLIGHT mist, almost like a fog. I sprinted through the trees. I had never run faster. No one in the history of time had ever run faster.

Back. Running back. Back to the farmhouse. To where the killer had Izzy. Where he had taken her.

I strained to will my legs into moving even faster.

There was no time left.

There was no time.

———

Ducking down, I hurried from the edge of the forest to the wooden fence that surrounded the farmhouse.

The grass around the farmhouse was shorter. If he looked out a window as I approached, he'd see me. There was no way around it.

I had no choice. Izzy was inside. If he saw me, he saw me. He could have a gun. He could shoot me twenty times. Twenty thousand times. I would not die. I swore I would not die until Izzy was safe.

There was no time.

I sprinted through the open field to the firepit. In the pit, I could make out some of the items in the fire. A red leather glove, two of the fingers burned away. Half of a sneaker. The strap that belonged to a girl's purse. Most of it was burned beyond recognition.

Under the lawn chair were the shells from the sunflower seeds. In the darkness of the too-long grass, a few feet away, something glinted through the haze. A reflection of light that caught my eye.

I reached down to pick them up and immediately recognized them.

Izzy's pink sunglasses.

Images flooded me.

The first time Izzy and I had staked out the farmhouse. The snake—Izzy had jumped up and shrieked. I thought I saw a hand behind the window; someone had seen us.

Puzzle pieces connected in my mind. Into the very picture of a nightmare.

Is it possible that the killer had been watching Izzy the whole time she thought she was watching for him? Did he know he was being watched all along?

It would have been easy. He could have waited for her to walk back home through the woods and followed from a safe distance. He could have found her living space at the abandoned mill. And then he could have staked her out, the same way she was trying to do to him. For someone so practiced as a serial murderer, with two decades of experience, it would have been easy.

Wouldn't it?

All I knew was Izzy was trapped inside the house. The shells. Her sunglasses. I felt it in my bones. Ice shards digging along my spine.

Izzy had said that the killer kept his victims for weeks. Torturing them. Raping them. Before finally cutting their still-beating hearts from their chests.

Should I find a pay phone? Call the police? There was no time. Izzy could be in pain. That monster could be torturing her, even as I stood there. I could not walk away.

I had nothing to defend myself with. Then I recalled the Swiss Army knife. I tore off the packaging. I opened the blade. It wasn't much, but it was something.

As if possessed, I approached the farmhouse. The mist fell down from the sky. The night was dark. There was barely any moon at all.

Behind the house there was a window—open, barely a few inches. I glanced through. Darkness inside. My eyes strained. It seemed to be a laundry room—very small, with just a washer and dryer.

With the knife, I sliced away the screen. I reached in and pushed the window all the way up, as far as it could go. The opening was just large enough to squeeze through. For once, not being a large person worked to my advantage.

I landed on top of the washing machine with a slight metallic clang. I hoped it wasn't loud enough to hear. I waited a moment in the dark, the knife in my hand.

I didn't hear anything.

Terror sliced through me. Every breath I took stabbed me from the inside out. But I couldn't allow the fear to slow me down. There was no time left.

Cautiously, I opened the door. The hinges creaked slightly. The hallway was dark. What was I looking for? How would I know if I found it?

A cellar. That's what Izzy had spoken of from her nightmares. I'd never been in the basement of the farmhouse. Where was the entry? The house was huge. Pitch black. All I had was a two-inch-long blade. It was too late now. There was no time left.

Quietly as possible, I crept down the hallway. I could hear no movement except the slight sounds of my own footfalls. Every shadow played tricks on me. The house was cold, but I had to wipe the sweat off my forehead and temples. It was so dark I could barely see.

A doorway. I slowly turned the knob and deliberately pulled it ajar. A room full of cleaning supplies, brooms, and mops. I shut the door. More steps forward. Another doorway. This time, a small room filled with boxes.

One sound, one wrong move, and the killer would hear me. The killer would find me.

All I had was a tiny knife and the element of surprise.

I peered around the end of the hall. A kitchen. It led into a dining room. The walls were barren. The furniture was sparse and old. The shades were all drawn. It was dark as hell, almost impossible to see.

I stepped into the kitchen. And then I saw it, on the wall.

A telephone.

I reached for the receiver. Then I froze. What if he was on another line? What if the killer heard me?

It was a chance I had to take. I lifted the receiver. The dial tone seemed too loud in my ear. Silent as possible, I pushed the phone's buttons for the number of the Walkers' house.

A ring. Then another.

"Hello?" It was Mrs. Walker.

I whispered. "This is CJ. It's an emergency. Is Mr. Walker there?"

"He's out in the backyard. Are you all right?"

"I'm in danger. Tell him Izzy was right. Tell him the old Moorehead farm off Route 9. Tell him I'm inside the house."

"CJ, my God! What's going on?"

"Please! Tell him! The Moorehead farm."

"Yes, but . . ."

Terrified I'd been overheard, I hung up.

Cautiously, I stepped through the kitchen. The dining room led to another hall, two doors on either side of it. As I stepped carefully, I thought I heard something. Movement? I stopped cold. No other sounds. Just silence.

A few more steps. Gingerly, I pulled a door open. It was pitch black inside. I flicked on my lighter. It was a small den with a couch and a television. I closed the door. It clicked shut.

I turned. Another door. I opened it. Again, darkness. Again, my lighter. The weak, small flame barely illuminated a room filled with packing materials.

I pressed on, one step at a time. The floor creaked, and I froze. Silence, again. Another door. I twisted the knob. Blackness within. My lighter. A small flame.

A wooden stairway led down: the cellar below, obscured by a lack of light.

Straight down, into nothing but blackness.

—

The walls were wooden. The stairs seemed ancient, the steps groaning under my weight. I had to go slowly, remain silent. Touch down with a toe, then release the full weight of my foot. Then my other foot. Then the next step. Then the next.

I had to hurry, but I had to remain silent. He could be down there. The killer could be down there. And there was no time left.

I reached the bottom of the stairs. Complete darkness. There was no choice. I needed my lighter to see even two inches in front of my face.

The lighter in one hand. The knife in the other.

A narrow hallway. Old, battered wood on either side, like I was in an old mine shaft or cave. I could see maybe twenty feet ahead until darkness enveloped everything once again. A vague light emitted from a doorway on the right.

As I neared the doorway, the flame trembled, my hand shaking too. The fear was visceral. It was a virus, consuming me. A sickness I had to fight with every footfall forward.

The lighter went out. I couldn't see my hand holding it, barely before my own face. I flicked it on again. I reached the first door on the right. I paused. Listened. There was no sound coming from within.

A dim light escaped from cracks around the wooden door. I motioned to push the door open, but the hinges strained with sound. I pushed it slowly, a millimeter at a time. Just far enough to squeeze through. A small, weak light pushed into the hall. I could now see down the hallway. There were two more doors to the right, maybe twenty feet apart. The end of the hall was another twenty feet down from that. A wooden wall at the end. There seemed to be another hallway bending around to the left.

I froze but could hear nothing.

I squeezed through the crack in the door and slipped into the first room.

In the corner, a lamp sat on a large table, the only light in the room. The room was filled with what looked like metalworking tools.

Strange tools—cutting torches, welding devices, vices. The sides of the room were lined by piles of scrap metal. In the half-light, a creepy ambiance. But that wasn't what stopped my heart in my chest.

It was what was hanging on the walls.

Row after row of bizarre metal art pieces. Several demonic metalwork masks.

They were horrifying. And straight out of Izzy's nightmares, where she was trapped in a cellar. Chained up against a wall, in the cellar of a killer who wore a mask. Like these masks. In this room. In this cellar. Along these walls.

How?

And where was she?

On the large table, I saw a flashlight. I lifted it up. The batteries seemed to be dying, but it still gave off a dim, flickering light. I took it.

I squeezed out through the small space in the doorway. Illuminating a thin path with the flashlight, I reached the next door. There was no light coming from inside. Slowly, I pushed the door open a crack. I listened but heard nothing.

Carefully, I pushed my way inside.

The flashlight went out. I was in utter darkness. I shook it lightly to get it working. It flickered back on, but the light seemed even dimmer than before. I lifted the weak beam toward the center of the room.

And I saw the most horrible sight I would ever see.

It could not be Izzy.

It just could not be her. *Please, please.* It could not be.

There was metal table in the middle of the room.

A girl lying naked on it. She was not moving.

Right away I knew she was dead.

I just felt it. Like an animal instinct. It was not that she wasn't moving or breathing. She was just dead, and I felt it on my skin, along my spine. In my very veins.

I lifted the flashlight an inch higher and saw that her chest was covered in blood. And in the middle of her chest was a hole.

Someone had cut her heart out of her chest.

It could not be Izzy, I told myself.

But her body was the same size. The same shape. Her hair matted over her face was the same length and the same color.

It could not be her.

A sound escaped me, but I did not recognize it. It was not a human sound. An animal sound. A deeper grief than a human was capable of feeling.

It could not be Izzy.

But it could.

The dim beam of light trembled with my hand.

My breathing was erratic. My heart was a shard of broken glass in my chest.

I stepped toward the girl. The dead girl. The dead body. The body that was once a girl. The heart torn out of her.

It could not be Izzy.

Chapter 32

INTO DARKNESS

IN THAT MOMENT, I DIED.

I died a death more powerful than actual death.

I stifled a sob as I stepped toward the table.

Toward the body.

Toward the girl. Who was dead.

The girl who was dead.

"No," I whispered. "Please, no."

My trembling hand brushed the matted hair from her face.

And then I saw her.

Her eyes were open as if they were looking at me. As if they were looking through me. Forever open. Staring eternally, into death.

But it was not Izzy.

It was Alicia Russell. I recognized her face from the photographs.

I couldn't cry. There was no time to cry.

Where was Izzy?

I had to find her.

The killer must have taken her recently. Just an hour or two before. She had to be in that house. In that cellar. Somewhere.

"I'm sorry," I whispered. "I'm sorry, Alicia. I'm so sorry."

I lifted my fingers to her eyes. Then I gently pressed them shut.

There was no time left.

—

I slid softly into the hall and along the wall, toward the final room leading from the hallway.

Another wooden door. There was a light emerging from the crack underneath. I reached for the knob. Then I heard movement from up ahead. I froze.

I stood there. A statue. But nothing. Silence reigned once more. Inch by inch, I pushed the door, just wide enough to fit through.

I went into the room.

A dim light bulb hung from a wire in the center of the room over a metal table. The bulb offered the only light in the room. The light faded toward the walls, which were barely visible. The walls to either side were wood, and the back wall looked like concrete.

I heard the sound of metal moving.

In a panic, I aimed the flashlight at the far corner of the room. There was a chain attached to a concrete wall, extending to the floor.

To a bare arm, chained to the wall.

To a girl. Her skin glowed yellow in the flashlight beam. She was caked in blood. Stripped down to a dirty, torn tank top and jeans, torn to shreds, her hair matted over her face. Her eyes glowed black from behind it.

Her head tilted upward. "CJ?"

I raced over and slid down to my knees beside her.

"Oh my god. Izzy. Oh my god."

Her face was frozen in absolute terror.

She spoke in a hoarse whisper. "Get me out. You have to get me out." She was frantic. Her eyes darted everywhere at once. "He's here. He'll kill you. He'll kill us. Oh god oh god oh god. He's fucking here."

I didn't know how to free her.

The chain was affixed to Izzy's wrist by a thick, metal cuff. Then the chain went through a fat metal loop that was bolted to a metal square on the wooden wall. There was no way I could get that square off the wall. There was a keyhole, over her wrist. It was clasped too tightly to pull her hand from.

"Please," she whispered. "Hurry. He'll come back. He'll kill us. He'll kill us both."

I put my hand over her mouth. "There's a metal workshop just down the hall," I whispered. "Maybe there's some tool to break this. Or a key. Or something."

I stood up.

"No. Don't leave me. Please don't leave me. You don't know what he'll do to me. Please. Please."

"It's the only way," I told her. "I'm going to get you out of here, Izzy."

Her eyes were wild. Her face was bruised. Dried blood on her cheek and jaw. She was reduced to an animal state.

"Izzy. I promise."

"Please. Please. Please . . ."

I crept to the doorway. "Just stay quiet," I whispered. "I'll be right back."

I pulled the door open.

That's when I saw him.

He wore a mask made of metal: two eyes, covered by amber glass. Two holes over the nose. A thin, blank slit over the mouth, open just enough to see yellowed teeth.

He was a head taller than me. His chest and arms were thick.

In his right hand, a blowtorch shot on. A blue flame shot out of it as he turned it on me.

Instinctively, I dodged and swung with my right arm, knocking the torch away from my face. But the intense flame shot across my left shoulder and upper arm.

The pain was excruciating. Unbearable. Unreal.

I fell to the ground. The leather from my jacket melted into flesh. A smoking, bloody gash extended a few inches down my shoulder.

I heard Izzy screaming my name.

I tried to move my left arm but felt a shock wave of agonizing bolts of pure pain.

The man stepped toward me again. I rolled toward him, out of the path of the torch. I reached up with the Swiss Army knife, slashing him across the thigh. He made a strange sound as he staggered back. I rolled to my feet and stabbed him in the arm holding the blowtorch.

The torch flew from his grasp, still on, skidding into the far wall. Flames licked at the fringes of the wooden wall.

I felt a vicelike grip on my right wrist—my hand with the knife. With his thumb, he stabbed at my fresh wound near my left shoulder.

I screamed.

His fist went across my face—once, twice, then again.

I fell.

I felt his boot in my chest. I sailed across the floor into the metal table. The knife flew out of my hand.

He kicked me again. As I rolled to escape the blows, I saw the fire spreading from the wooden walls to the ceiling.

From the ground, I turned over the metal table. It hit his leg near where I had stabbed him. As he recoiled, it gave me the opportunity to regain my feet.

My body burned with pain. My ribs felt cracked. I gulped in air. My shoulder and upper arm pulsed with debilitating agony. Izzy screamed my name, again and again.

I reached behind me as he approached. For something. Anything.

A folding chair. I swung it and cracked it across his face.

The mask flew off.

His face was strangely expressionless. Just blank. His right eye was blank, too—glassy and dead, like a dirty pearl. Scar tissue webbed the area surrounding it.

Aside from the dead eye, he looked almost bizarrely normal. A round face. A slightly receding hairline. White skin. Yellow teeth. He was breathing heavily. Otherwise, he made no sound.

I was cornered.

He stepped toward me again. I threw a punch, right across his jaw. It barely slowed him. His fist shot out and sent me flying into the far wall into a shelf.

I looked behind me.

There was row after row of glass mason jars. Inside all of them, human hearts. Dozens of them. They were labeled with numbers.

I grabbed number thirty-two and swung it at him, hoping it would shatter across his face.

He caught my arm and pushed me back against the wall, forcing the jar from my hand. He placed it gently back on the shelf.

One of the jars rolled off the shelf, across the room. Over toward where Izzy was chained up.

Then he picked me up, as if I weighed nothing. He threw me across the room, away from the shelves. Away from his prizes. His collection.

The flames were growing. Like a tinderbox.

I tried to struggle to my feet, but my left arm crumpled beneath me. My jaw crashed against the floor.

He kicked my chest and stomach, again and again.

I felt blackness creeping up around the edges of my vision.

I looked up and saw Izzy. I was just a few feet away from her. I could almost reach her. She was screaming my name.

Suddenly, the man stopped kicking. He turned to Izzy. It was the first time his face showed any expression. He looked . . . almost hurt.

"He is nothing," the man said. His voice was slow and uncertain, like he had a slight speech impediment. It was hard to define in the moment. He raised a finger and pointed at her. "We're destined to be together! You came back for me."

"Fuck you!" Izzy shouted.

He forgot me in the moment. He stepped to Izzy and kicked her, impossibly hard, in the stomach. Izzy cried out and doubled over into a small ball.

I struggled to get up and failed. I struggled and failed again. I never knew such pain was even possible. I thought of Izzy and made it to my knees.

Flames were everywhere.

What finally got me to my feet was not me, but him.

His fingers wrapped around my throat. He lifted me up by my neck to his level. My toes barely scraped the ground. He was huge. His strength was immense. I tried to pull his hand off my neck, but my right hand was slick with blood, and my left hand wouldn't respond.

I glanced down at his other arm. He had the blowtorch again.

He looked at me. "He is nothing. We are fate." He seemed more curious than anything else—not angry, just curious. He lifted the blowtorch, flicking the switch until the flame reappeared.

Then he made another sound and staggered back.

I saw Izzy on the ground. She had crawled toward us, extending the chain that bound her to the wall to its full length of a few feet. She was holding a large glass shard in her bloody palm. She must have broken the mason jar. She stabbed him in the leg. On the inside of the shard, in the light of the fire raging around us, I saw the number one on a label.

On the floor beside her was a pale human heart, drained of color or life. Lying on the floor amid a puzzle of glass.

The man's grip loosened on my neck. Blood flowed out from where his right boot met his pants. I had only a moment to act.

With my right arm, I knocked his hand away. I lunged forward, breaking free.

My face collided with his collarbone.

I pulled my head up.

Then, with every ounce of strength I had left in me, I bared my teeth and bit down.

He screamed.

He released his grip, both of us staggering back in opposite directions.

I spat out the large chunk of flesh I had bitten out of his throat.

He tried to come for me but stumbled. His neck filled with crimson. He grabbed his throat with a hand, but the blood spilled around it and over his hand and down the front of his shirt.

The blowtorch was still in his hand. He stumbled toward me, torch in one hand, holding his bleeding throat with the other.

Flames were everywhere.

I fought to stand. I could not.

He aimed the torch at me. He was staggering, like a drunk man. I had to get up. I had to summon the strength.

Over and over, Izzy screamed my name.

He lowered the torch toward my face. I felt the heat in my eyes.

It ended in an explosion.

Then another. And another.

Chapter 33

THE BURNING DOWN

THE MAN LOOKED DOWN AT his chest. Three small red spots. They grew and grew.

The blowtorch fell from his hand to the floor, just beside my leg, still spitting out sparks.

He looked at me, almost childlike. Like something just happened that he didn't understand. Then he fell to his knees and crumpled, lifeless, at my feet.

I looked beyond him. There was a wall of flames.

Beyond them, in the doorway, was Mr. Walker. His gun was in his hand. Raised. Smoking.

He leaped through a wall of flame to my side. He pushed the dead man away.

"CJ! Can you move?"

"Izzy," I said. "Izzy."

Everything was blurry.

Mr. Walker glanced around. His eyes met the shelf, rows of mason jars filled with human hearts. "Jesus God in heaven," he said quietly.

He turned to Izzy and fought for a moment with the chain binding her. He struggled to pull it from the wall, but it was useless.

"CJ's hurt," Izzy said. "He needs help."

Flames were everywhere.

He nodded. "CJ, I'm going to get you out of here."

"Not without Izzy."

"I'll come back for her. I promise you. This place is burning down around us."

"Not without Izzy," I repeated.

Fear lined his face. "OK. I'm going to look. There has to be a key or something."

He jumped back through the flame and left the room.

"CJ," Izzy said. She was groggy. "You came back for me."

There had to be a way. I fought the pain. I fought to my knees. I couldn't breathe. My skin was on fire.

Then I saw the blowtorch on the floor.

I fired it up and aimed it at the chain. Sparks flew out and Izzy screamed when they burned her neck.

The mask. I grabbed it. "Put it over your face!" I yelled.

I shielded her body with my own, aiming the blowtorch at the chain. Bits of flame shot out, cutting through my clothes to my skin. But I kept on until the torch fizzled out completely.

The chain was thinner now. It looked almost fragile, maybe a millimeter of glowing metal left attached at the point where I had torched it. I tried prying it apart, but it was still too strong.

I turned to Izzy and took the mask from her. Her eyes were rolling back in her skull. The flames were all around us. The mask was metal—it was all I could think to use.

I smashed the mask down on the damaged part of the chain. Metal on metal. Again. And again. With both hands, even with the pain splitting my left arm from my body. And again. With everything left in my body and soul. And again.

Mr. Walker burst back into the room. "There's no time, CJ! There's no time!"

As I smashed the mask down again, I screamed. *"Fuck!"*

And again, even more violently. *"Fucking!"*

And again, with a strength I did not know I could even possess. *"Time!"*

Suddenly Izzy fell face down onto the ground, unconscious. The chain slid along with the momentum of her fall.

It was broken off completely from the other half of the chain, still extending to the wall.

I had done it. I had broken the chain.

I had broken the chain, and now Izzy was finally free.

I fell beside her. I looked up into the flames.

And then Mr. Walker was reaching down to lift me.

"Just get me up," I groaned. "I can go. Carry her. *Please*."

He helped me to my feet. I staggered, using the wall to brace myself.

Mr. Walker wrapped his jacket around Izzy. He scooped her into his arms like a small child. She was small and vulnerable in his arms.

She mumbled something unintelligible. She was delirious.

He looked down at her in his arms. "Don't worry, baby," he said softly. "I'm going to get you out of here. I promise you."

He turned to me, intense beyond belief. "CJ, you have to follow me. You can do this. Just do what I do."

"Sure," I said.

A raging wall of flame in the center of the room. He plowed through it.

I stumbled after him.

The doorway had partially crumbled. He ducked under it. I followed.

Flames surged along both walls and the ceiling in the basement hallway. He ducked down and ran through. I followed.

The walls of the stairway were scattered with flames, but not as intense as the hall. He ran up the stairs. I followed.

At the top of the steps, I stumbled and fell.

I tried to get up and couldn't. I crawled to the end of the hall. From there, I could see the doorway.

Mr. Walker stood at the entrance with Izzy in his arms.

He turned to me. "CJ, get up, *right now!*"

"I'm trying," I said.

"*Now*. I'm not going to tell my daughter I watched you die. You're going to do this!"

With all my strength, I pushed myself up. I took a step before falling back to my knees.

"I can't," I said. It felt impossible. They had to go without me.

I saw Izzy's eyes open, her head turning toward me. "Yes, you can," she said.

I placed one foot below me. I held myself up with my good arm. Then the other foot. Then I stood. I took a step. Then another step. Behind me, the inferno. Ahead of me, the front yard. I felt the floorboards crumple under my footfalls. And then, with everything I had left, I jumped.

When you're hurtling through the air—in between one thing and another thing with nothing beneath you—it's a pretty weird feeling. The dizzy limbo between flying and falling.

The moment I jumped—at most, it was a fraction of a split second—but it would be impossible to remember as anything other than the lifetime it contained. As if that moment were a fissure in the time line itself, a moment when everything in the history of two human beings was imprinted, for always.

There was no weight below me. Weightless, the pain was gone. And the fire was gone, and the horror was gone with it. And this is what I saw:

Izzy, emerging from the lake, the sunlight fracturing around her skin.

Izzy, laughing like a madwoman as she vanished into the forest.

Izzy, dancing to "American Girl."

Izzy, giving me a sidelong glance over her cigarette.

Izzy.

Unbuttoning her shirt to show a scar. Saying *tonight together*. Shoving the cigarettes in my pocket. Her tongue out the side of her mouth as she sat on a rooftop, breaking into a window with a coat hanger. Staring through her binoculars. Showering in the moonlight outside an abandoned mill. Starting a mosh pit in a truck stop parking lot. Setting a leaf free in the wind. Running barefoot across the gravel and jumping into my arms. Telling my mother I was the greatest person in the world. Kissing me. Saying my name. Believing in me. Just believing. Just Izzy.

Izzy.

In that impossibly long moment, the impossible stopped being impossible. Because of her. Falling became flying. Because of her. Time was broken.

For us.

I flew through the flame. I felt my foot strike the wood on the far side of the doorway. I stumbled and rolled. I regained my footing, inches from Mr. Walker and Izzy.

"*Go!*" Mr. Walker screamed.

We ran across the porch. We didn't stop running until we were halfway across the lawn. Falling to the ground together as the farmhouse folded and crumbled into itself and into flames, cataclysmically, but still safely far behind us.

—

I found myself on my back in the grass. I managed to turn my head. Mr. Walker sat a couple feet away from me. Izzy was still tucked in his arms.

He brushed her hair from her eyes. "It's all over, honey," he said. "Everything's going to be all right."

Her eyes fluttered open. Small, fragile butterflies.

"CJ," she said. "Where's CJ?"

"He's right here. He's OK too. Everyone's OK."

Izzy literally crawled out of Mr. Walker's arms. The metal cuff clinked down her wrist as she crawled, the chain broken off after a couple links.

I heard sirens in the distance.

I propped myself up on an elbow. I saw a fire truck and police car speeding toward us.

Izzy crawled into my arms. She wrapped her arms around my waist and pressed her head against my stomach.

"We did it," she said, almost a whisper. "It's really over."

"Yeah, Izzy," I said. "I guess it is."

Chapter 34

A SOUND AWAKE

THE KEEPER OF HEARTS WAS actually named Tucker Isaac Donaldson. He was raised a couple hours outside Portland, Oregon—and died a couple hours outside Portland, Maine. The FBI eventually connected him to a total of thirty-seven murders, starting in the early 1970s. They believed his first victim was Isabel Ellison. His final victim would be Alicia Russell.

Mr. Walker reluctantly became a bit of a national celebrity: the brave, small-town cop who took down one of the most prolific serial murderers in American history. It took almost a year before the national media started forgetting about the case enough to leave him alone. He insisted up and down he wasn't the hero. The true heroes were the kids who had tracked down the killer and barely escaped with their lives.

But I didn't feel like a hero. All I felt was pain.

I spent weeks in the hospital. I had first-degree burns all over my body and nasty third-degree burns on my shoulder and upper left arm that would leave lasting scars. I also had four cracked ribs, a fractured collarbone, a fractured shin, and six broken fingers. When people visited me in the hospital and I'd say, "It only hurts when I laugh" they'd pretend I'd said something much funnier than I actually had. More people visited me than I would have initially assumed.

Natasha and Terry visited me. Mr. and Mrs. Walker. Kay Nguyen.

Kay came with her mother and father. I'd never met them before. I waved and apologized for looking like hell and made a joke about first impressions. They laughed harder than the joke warranted, furthering my belief that hospital visitation can transform just about anyone into the ideal comedic audience. They left to give us a moment to talk.

Kay stood by my bed a moment before finally opening her mouth. "You should really consider taking better care of yourself in the future," she said.

"Thank you, Kay," I replied. "Not for, you know, kind of just stating the obvious. I mean, for everything. If it wasn't for you and Natasha risking your necks to speak up for me? Well, it could've gotten pretty bad for me, I guess."

"Worse than this?" Kay paused a moment, rubbing her eyes. "CJ . . . you're not alone. You were never alone."

"I think I know that now," I said quietly. "But sometimes I'm just a bit slow on the uptake."

"Well, then, that's sorted out," she said, straightening up. "I'll look forward to seeing you back at school."

—

Toward the end of my hospital stay, Jillian Sillinger came by to visit me. She came with her mother, who put a bouquet of flowers on the shelf by the window. "We actually paid for these at a flower shop," Mrs. Sillinger joked.

"However else would someone get flowers?" I shrugged, grinning.

"I-I'm really glad y-you're OK, CJ," Jillian said.

"I'm glad you're OK too," I agreed. "But maybe we should hang out sometime when neither one of us is a patient at a hospital."

Jillian smiled. "I th-think I'd like that."

—

Everyone who came to see me was greatly appreciated, though most of these visits occurred after I'd been in the hospital awhile. But I had only been in the hospital a little more than a day when my mother returned to Maine to see me.

I was still weak and a little woozy at that point and, in all honesty, I'm not sure I would've known how to react even if I had been 100 percent healthy. My mother stood in the doorway a moment, just looking me over. I could see my father, a few feet behind in the hallway, watching her watch me. She turned to him and he nodded, then she walked inside and lightly closed the door behind her. She tried to smile and it didn't work, so she just stepped over to my bed and started using her hand to brush the hair out of my eyes.

"You didn't have to come all the way from Boston," I said.

"Don't be stupid," she said.

"OK," I said. I tried to shift up in bed, but at that point I was still pretty beat to shit. I reacted accordingly, with a wince and a groan.

"What are you doing?" my mother asked.

"I'm trying to get a better conversational angle. From here I have to bend my neck all weird and then I'm still looking up at you."

My mother thought a moment. Then she sat down, cross-legged, right in the middle of the floor. "How's this?" she said. "Better?"

"Now I can only see your forehead and the fact that you probably forgot to brush your hair."

"I left the window open on the bus," she explained. "Guy next to me was wearing enough cologne to toxify a city block."

"That's a lot of cologne," I conceded.

She stood up, weirdly half-squatting, so we were at eye-level. "How's this? Better?"

"Mom, you're being ridiculous."

She straightened up. "I was like, who the fuck do you think you're going to attract with all that cologne? Women? Not human women, that's for sure. Bees, maybe." My mother finally noticed the chairs along the far wall. She flipped one around and sat on it, backward, leaning her chin on the backrest. "How's this?"

"Better," I admitted.

"Good," she said.

"Good," I said.

"Because I'm hoping that's just the thing when two people love each other a lot. That one of them can fuck up again and again and the other one can still find a way to forgive them."

"Mom . . ." I said, but my voice cracked, and I just couldn't talk anymore.

She looked around for a tissue but couldn't find one. Instead, she balled up the sleeve of her black cable-knit sweater in her hand and used that to wipe my eyes. She explained she was planning on staying in town for a while, at least until I was better. She couldn't promise she knew what she would do after that.

Some amorphous combination of head injury and emotion locked me all up, so I just mostly nodded.

My mother looked around, then back at me. "So there I was at work, and I guess your dad looked up my bar's number after your friend Izzy told him the name of the joint. And right away he told me you were in the hospital, and then probably less than a second later he said, *but he's fine*. But what I felt in that moment—between *in the hospital* and *but he's fine*—it was like forever, you know? It was like, in that second, my heart exploded a million times. You know what I mean?"

I just nodded.

She lifted my hand gently and found a space lacking bandages to kiss. "Oh, and even though I'm a lousy mother, I haven't forgotten it's your birthday in two days. What do you want me to get you?"

"You're not a lousy mother," I said. We sat there a moment, looking at each other, my hand still clasped in hers. "I mean, there are some areas of improvement we can go over if you'd like me to itemize a list . . ."

She laughed, her head whipping back like it used to. And despite the uncertainty of what the future would bring, in that moment we were exactly how we used to be. Because in that moment, we were together. And in that moment, we were happy.

—

Mostly, my time in the hospital was awful. Everything on my body hurt, and the food sucked. I begged everyone to bring me pizza or something, but apparently the hospital had strict policies.

Of course, my dad was there every day. We watched Bruins games during the week, and on Sundays we watched the Patriots. He read me chapters from *Love in the Time of Cholera*, even though he always said he was more of a nonfiction guy himself. He bought a VCR to attach to the TV in my room, and we watched our favorite sci-fi flicks, like *Empire Strikes Back* and *Alien*.

Mr. Walker apparently dug those movies too. He came by one night, and we watched *Return of the Jedi*. My dad hated the Ewoks, but Mr. Walker didn't seem to mind them so much. When my dad stepped out to use the bathroom, Mr. Walker paused the film.

"Phil keeps asking me about you," he said.

I laughed until it hurt, which didn't take very long. "Man, that dude couldn't stand me at first."

"I think a lot of people misunderstood you at some point," he said.

"You never did," I said.

"No," he replied. "I guess I didn't."

"Well, that's good," I said. "I'd be dead if it weren't for you."

He looked at me as if I were his son and not someone else's. He said, "Izzy would be dead if it wasn't for you."

I knew that was true—and yet we hadn't been able to save Alicia Russell. I knew I'd never be able to quite forgive myself for that. But the revelation that Alicia was the final victim of a serial killer surely answered a lot of questions one town over in Seamont.

As far out as Izzy's theories had first seemed, and as plausible as Mr. Walker and Lisa's theories had seemed, it was Izzy who turned out to be on the right track about Alicia Russell's disappearance after all.

No, the Seamont PD had nothing to do with Alicia's sad fate. But they would also never be punished for the crimes they had evidently committed against Alicia. Similarly, Alicia's mother and stepfather would never experience any consequences for simply shrugging the poor girl's disappearance off. I couldn't help thinking how gravely they had all failed her. Maybe if they'd all been doing what they should have—turning over every stone in a tireless search for her—Alicia would still be alive. To be honest, I'm pretty sure it's something I will never get over. I'll never forget the feel of her face, the lifelessness, as I reached out to close her eyes for the final time.

It's something that will haunt me forever.

As for Izzy's story, it can probably be said that it was true and that it wasn't. I considered it for hours in my hospital bed, the parallels between what she had dreamed and what I had experienced for myself in that farmhouse cellar.

In retrospect, there were a lot of details Izzy claimed to know from her dreams that could only be described as downright eerie in their accuracy. Specifics I was destined to see for myself on that fateful night in the cellar of the old Moorehead farm.

The fact that the sordid events even took place in the cellar at all. The metalwork on the walls. The metal table, with the overhead light, suspended from the ceiling by a wire. The fact that the killer chained Izzy to the wall, as well as the fact that he wore a mask.

This isn't to say that Izzy's dreams were proof positive of rein-carnation, of course. My first week in the hospital, I read the entire Keeper of Hearts section in Elizabeth Wexler's book about unsolved serial murders. What I learned is that all the bodies of girls who were found showed evidence of being chained by their wrists. All the girls had evidence of concrete and metal fragments under their nails. These details could have wormed their way into Izzy's subconscious, spurring on nightmarish aspects like the chain, the cellar, the metal table. And when I'd asked Izzy outright whether she'd read the book or had the dreams first, she said, in all honesty, she couldn't rightly remember. It only made sense that Izzy's horrifying dreams would end with the killer cutting out her heart—after all, he was given the moniker Keeper of Hearts in the book where Izzy first discovered the idea of him.

But the overhead light. And the killer's mask. Though both of these facts struck me as chilling in their accuracy, both could be attributed far more to coincidence than as incontrovertible proof of reincarnation.

Or, as I confessed to Izzy at the hospital: I never necessarily believed in reincarnation, but I didn't have to. Because I always believed in *her*.

She seemed perfectly satisfied with that.

—

Izzy's room was on the same floor as mine.

Every moment we were allowed we spent together. Sometimes we talked seriously, and sometimes we joked around. Sometimes we just sat quietly, holding hands.

She complained even more than I did about not being allowed to smoke. A nurse tried explaining once to her that it was a hospital—but when this just revved up Izzy more, I had to explain to the nurse that sometimes logic just didn't work on Izzy like it did with normal people.

Izzy's injuries weren't as bad as mine. She had a concussion, multiple contusions, and a couple of bruised ribs. Apparently, I was right about how he'd tracked her back to the abandoned logging mill.

That fateful night, she'd been reading Anne Sexton and waiting for me to arrive when he snuck in and beat her into unconsciousness. Then he dragged her and her duffle bag back through the woods to his farmhouse. He locked her up in the basement before going out—the cops assumed to build the firepit and burn all her stuff.

The good news is that I arrived at the house before he could really do the worst. Her only injuries were from the beating, plus a few minor burns from the fire. She needed several stitches on her palm from when she'd shattered the mason jar to stab the killer in the leg with the broken glass. She told me she'd call the scar her second life-line. But really, it was my life she'd saved when she got that scar.

I didn't tell her about the numbered tape I saw on the glass shard in her hand. If the numbers corresponded to the order in which he'd killed his victims, then number one apparently meant Isabel Ellison. The *real* Isabel Ellison. Or the first one, anyway.

I didn't think Izzy could handle knowing that she'd shattered the jar containing the heart of the girl she thought she'd been reincarnated from.

But it's a good thing she had—or I'd be dead. That moment gave me the chance to break free of his grip. The chance to use 162 pounds of human bite force on his neck, which gave us the extra few moments we needed for Mr. Walker to bust in and shoot him three times, in the heart and both lungs.

To be honest, I don't know if I'll ever tell Izzy this.

Who knows? Maybe one day.

Maybe one day soon.

After all, almost three years have passed to the day.

———

Hey, Carina. I can't stay long. The hospital only let me out for a few hours since it's my birthday. And I don't know what to feel when people say it to me. "Happy birthday" doesn't seem right.

I try all the time to remember you happy. Because that's how anyone would want to be remembered, I guess. Not dying in a bed, in a room that's not yours, surrounded by machines. But . . . happy.

Happy is weird, isn't it? It's not always what you think it is. Some memories are of times that were painful, but when you think of them, you realize how happy you were deep down.

Like, remember the time when I was ten, and I fell off the bike and tore up my knee? I cried like an idiot. But you picked me up in your arms and carried me two blocks home. The whole time you kept calling me a fat shit, until I had to laugh. I was skinny as hell! And then you said you were going to get some peroxide and bandages, but instead you came back into the living room with the axe Dad used to cut firewood and said you were going to have to cut my leg off. What I mean is it was a really shitty day for me at the time, but now when I think about it, it was really a wonderful day. Because every time I see the scar on my knee, I'm reminded of you.

You never said you loved me. Maybe when we were really little, but not when you got older. You used to tell me I was a pain in your ass, but you were stuck with me because I was your brother. When you said that I'd imagine you were saying you loved me in some kind of supersecret code.

I told you I loved you all the time. You'd tell me I was mushy or sappy or lame, and I'd get really upset.

But I look back on all that now and realize I was happy. Because you were there. Because as long as you were there, I was never alone.

I think after you died, I forgot how to be happy. But I'm learning again. I'm trying. There are all these people around me who tell me I'm something worthwhile even though I'm still always scared deep down that I'm actually a complete mess. There's a beautiful and incredible girl, Izzy, who I think might love me, even though she never tells me that either.

Anyway, I've got to go. I'd say I'm running out of time, but I'm not. There's so much of it left for me. I wish more than anything there was more time for you too. And for you, I'll try to have a happy birthday, Carina. Not just for me, but for the both of us. Because you'll always be with me. Always.

I found a really good rock near her grave—like a triangle, with an indentation in the middle. It almost looked like a heart. I placed it alongside the others and then turned from the tombstone.

My father was standing there waiting for me. He put his arm around me. He said he thought what I said was very beautiful, and he was proud of me.

"Dad?"

"Yes, Craig?"

"Do you think . . . do you think she can hear me?"

"Yes, Craig. I do."

I tried not to cry. But as strong as everyone kept saying I was, it wasn't true. I was weak and stupid. I bawled like a freaking baby.

My dad just hugged me. As hard as I remembered him hugging me since I was just a little kid.

"If you want to talk about it," he told me. "I'm right here."

EPILOGUE

REALLY, THE END HAS TO be about Izzy. It's not my story; it's hers. It will always be hers.

I will always be hers.

I know that now. I knew it then, and everything since has been there to remind me.

The first years she was gone, we would write to each other constantly. Then I received a weird letter from her saying "some things were changing," and she might not be able to contact me for a while. She told me not to worry, but I did—especially when several months passed without so much as a single word from her.

A month ago, I received a postcard. Nothing was written on the back. On the front was a photo of the Statue of Liberty. The left eye was circled, with two arrows pointing at it, like lost little clock hands.

Those little clock hands sent me spinning back through all the time I had known Izzy. Just a few weeks in the greater sense of time immemorial.

But then, the lines of time are curved, after all.

For me, those days with Izzy are the center of my life, all the rest of my days forever fated to spiral around them. From the day I met her, a silhouette by a hidden lake who told me she was just waiting for the lightning, until the last time I saw her, on a snow-crusted Maine morning outside a hospital, when she wouldn't let me say goodbye.

—

Pretty soon after Izzy and I were admitted into the hospital, the Child Services people learned that Izzy wasn't Isabel Ellison at all, but rather Haley Blake.

Isabel Ellison was long dead, the first victim of the serial murderer we had stopped, but Haley Blake was alive.

Child Services tracked down Izzy's mother in Iowa. By all indications, Izzy's mother was overjoyed that her daughter was alive and well. She had cleaned up her act and was no longer seeing her abusive ex-boyfriend. She was living with her sister, in Iowa City, and was taking night classes at the University of Iowa. She was looking forward to her daughter's return.

Izzy was skeptical, but she was willing to give it another try. It wasn't like the authorities would allow her to stay in Maine, and she pretty much had nowhere left to go. "If it sucks," she told me once in my hospital room, "I can always just take off again, right?"

Since Izzy's injuries healed up long before mine, as soon as the hospital said she was good to go, a flight was arranged for her to return to her family in the Midwest.

Gone for good.

When that day finally came, I was dizzy with emotion. We spent the early morning in my room together not really saying much, just holding hands and watching the clock.

Just after eleven a.m., the Child Services people arrived: a woman with a tight line for a mouth and a tight bun for hair and a large man in a suit and aviator sunglasses. The woman did pretty much all the talking, so much so that I wondered if the man was just hired muscle in case Izzy decided to make a break for it.

I was annoyed at how the woman from Child Services kept calling her *Haley*. To me, she was Izzy. And Izzy seemed pretty ticked off too.

They let me walk out with her to the front of the hospital, where their car was waiting.

It had snowed intermittently through the previous night until the dawn, and even though it had warmed up in the later morning, a thin crust of white still outlined the ground and the treetops.

Both of my parents were there. So were Mr. Walker and Natasha and Terry. I was not surprised everybody had come to the hospital that day to see Izzy off. They were probably also worried I'd fall apart completely—just start shattering into pieces, and they'd all have to join in somehow to hold me together.

I couldn't blame them.

I was far from 100 percent healthy, but it was now almost three weeks after the farmhouse fire. I could stand and walk without too much trouble. Everyone backed away to give us a minute together.

Izzy took my hand and brushed the back of my fingers against her cheek.

"Well, Ceej," she said. "I guess this is it."

"I guess so," I said.

"Crazy, right?"

"Like, all of it?"

"Yeah," she said. She moved a lock of stray hair from my eyes and tucked it behind my ear. "All of it."

"Yeah," I said. "Crazy."

She leaned in and kissed me on the lips.

"The nightmares are gone, you know. Well, mostly."

"You told me."

She laughed. "I'm almost like an actual person again."

"Almost," I repeated.

"I'll write," she said.

"I'll write back," I said.

We stared at each other a minute. Izzy looked around. "This is so weird. It's like having a fucking audience. They couldn't give us a few hours alone?"

"I guess not," I said.

"If they had any decency, they'd have gotten us a motel room last night," she said.

I had to laugh.

"We really did it," she whispered.

"We really did," I said.

She took a deep breath. "OK," she said. "The world's waiting. Don't forget, though. Left eyeball of the Statue of Liberty."

"Left eyeball of the Statue of Liberty," I repeated. I could barely get the words out through tears. I couldn't help it.

She pressed up against me, kissing the tears off my cheek. Then my lips. Then she backed away. "Don't be late," she said.

She walked off toward the car. The man tapped the roof of the car while the woman opened the back door for Izzy. About to get in, she spun. She stepped toward me again.

"Haley," the woman said. "We're going to miss your flight."

"Fuck my flight!" She ran toward me.

The Child Services people made a move to grab her, but my parents held them back.

"Let them be," Mr. Walker said sternly.

Izzy ran across the snow and threw herself into my arms.

Now she was crying too.

"I love you, CJ. I love you. I'll always love you. After always. After always and anything and everything, I will love you."

We stood that way, in each other arms, for who knows how long. After all, time itself no longer mattered.

Only us.

ACKNOWLEDGMENTS

THE ORIGINAL DRAFT OF THIS novel was written in a maelstrom of emotion while marooned in my own head and small apartment during the initial months of the COVID pandemic. As CJ and Izzy came to life, they in turn kept me alive—giving me something to focus on and believe in as what I once thought was my world shrank further and further into a vague distance. So, I suppose the first people I need to thank are a pair of people who, according to literal definitions, are not even real. Yet, I assure you, they are real to me—and hopefully, once you read this novel, they will be real to you as well.

At some point in the story, Izzy tells CJ she only exists if you believe in her. In a wild sense, I suppose that is true not only for all characters of books and movies and plays, but also for the people who create them and the people who bear witness to their stories.

But there are also a huge number of people in the "actual" world to thank, and although I could never name them all, I will try my best to single out as many as possible. It's crucial to start with Anne Sanow, who is quite possibly the best editor in the galaxy. Anne taught me more about writing in a handful of months than everyone else combined had taught me in my entire life leading up to that point. I'd also like to thank the entire incredible staff at River Grove Books, specifically Morgan Robinson, Daniel Sandoval, Jen Glynn, Sheila Parr, and Hayden Seder.

In all likelihood, I would not even be here were it not for my closest lifelong confidants—the very best friends in the world: John Byrne,

Lou Tsai, Gary Pascal, Andy Berlin, Ernie Cuneo, Greg Sadowski, Jon Feinsilver, Vanessa Gluck, Chanda Calentine, every DiTolla sister imaginable, Jennifer Grochowski, Gabrielle LaTourette, and super-famous marine biologist/professional whale annoyer Dr. David Gruber.

Thank you to my second family at Lake Street, the coolest bar in Greenpoint—Lauren Gosch, Max Peebles, John Szalyga, Jeremy Wilson, Bobby Drake, Eric Oddness, Stevie Howlett, and legendary Ageist front man Frank Bevan.

Thank you to the good friends who kept me going all those crazy NYC days and nights: Roy and Liz Savelli, Zach Eichenhorn, Katrina Bee, Joon Taylor, Jennifer Whitelaw, David Schoichet, Eva Peterson, Liz Norment, Julie Brown, Jodi Ardito, Megan Teravainen, Annalisa Chamberlain, and muse of muses Heather Sprow.

Endless gratitude to all my extended family—all the Ives, Schlesinger, Dubiel, Thai/Lee, Godwin, and Canowitz families—every single one of you inspires me to be better, every single day, even Cousin Danielle when she complains about pickled strawberries.

Finally, thank you to the people who are most likely to recognize elements of themselves in this work: indomitable rock star Harley Hopkins and the irrepressibly Manitoban Allison Waters.

I apologize for not having the allotted space to thank everyone who has inspired and helped me throughout the years. To all the people mentioned and all the people not, to all the people who have believed in me and been believed in by me over the years—I love you all always, and even after.

ABOUT THE AUTHOR

STEVEN IVES WAS BORN IN the Bronx. After spending his early childhood in New York City, his family moved to Fair Lawn, New Jersey, where he spent his early adolescence.

After reading far too much beatnik literature in his teenage years, Steven took off at age twenty, armed with a mostly broken-down car, an already obsolete typewriter, and maybe the best cassette tape collection on earth, in the vague but idealistic hope of discovering the meaning of life and writing the Great American Novel. He spent the better part of the next decade driving around the continent, occasionally settling down in places as disparate as Colorado, Oregon, California, Iowa, Florida, and Montana. He got in a lot of trouble and somehow always managed to get out of it. He wrote tens of thousands of pages, which he hopes mattered at some point to someone.

In his thirties, Steven returned to New York City. Years later, he's still there. Currently, he lives and bartends in Greenpoint, Brooklyn, and still writes a ton. He's working on a new novel he'd love to talk your ear off about. Anyway, that's Steven's past and present. As for the future? Well, time is a curved line and, after all, anything can happen.

Made in United States
North Haven, CT
01 October 2024

58154136R00203